REVENGE & RAPTURE

A Snarky Urban Fantasy Detective Series

DEBORAH WILDE

Chapter 1

Vancouver was burning.

Glass broke outside my office window, followed by a wailing alarm and angry voices yelling ugly taunts. The simmering tension of the past couple months between Nefesh and Mundanes had exploded on this June night.

Police and ambulance sirens shrieked in the distance and the smell of smoke drifted in through my locked window. Every cop in the city must have been on patrol.

Inside, all was still, the air sharpened to a point. I rolled my chair back and forth in front of the wall that I'd turned into a link chart. At the top were photos of the four scrolls of the *Sefer Raziel HaMalakh* held by Team Jezebel. Small cards pinned underneath detailed the place of their capture and the nature of the encounters with Chariot in obtaining them, with pieces of string running between connected information. I'd rejigged the chart numerous times, but had yet to find either the one piece of the *Sefer* still held by Chariot or any more of the Ten's identities.

My phone buzzed and I distractedly stabbed the answer button. "Stop waiting up for me, Pri."

"They've closed the bridges in and out of downtown," my

best friend and roommate said in a tense voice. "And I don't know how much longer Hastings Street will be open. It's almost midnight, so if you don't come home now you might be stuck there."

"I'll sleep in my chair. I spoke with the company who bought the party warehouse where the golem was patrolling. Totally legit local developers are turning it into condos." I fired a dart into a photo of Isaac Montefiore's head, half-turned away from the camera. "Another dead end."

"Cut yourself some slack. Jezebels have been fighting this for four hundred years. You've barely been on it four months. And right now, you need to sleep."

"Saving the world comes first," I said.

"Is it about saving the world or is it more about beating your enemies?"

"Does it matter so long as they're stopped?" I said.

The noble cause of dispensing justice warred with my desire to destroy Isaac Montefiore so comprehensively that his life would be a smoking ruin, my signature writ large in the ashes like a painter signing their masterpiece. Work goals were important.

"It matters a lot," Priya said gently. "Your dad was murdered. Don't you think you should get help? This isn't healthy."

"I had enough of talking out my feelings when I was thirteen. Taking Isaac down is the only therapy I need," I snapped.

Mrs. Hudson, my pug, lifted her head from her doggie bed in the corner and whined softly. She hated when her mommies fought.

"That's exactly what I mean." Priya gave an aggrieved sigh. "This isn't about Chariot anymore for you. It's all about Isaac. He's cost you both men you loved and—"

I hung up on her and rubbed my eyes, nearly blinding myself when a boom rocked the building. After a second boom—someone ramming the front security door downstairs —came the joyous cries of emboldened rioters about to pilfer.

Not on my watch.

"Stay," I told Mrs. Hudson and crept down the two flights of stairs to the lobby.

The looters shattered one of the office doors.

I cornered a man carrying a stack of laptops out of the small game design company owned by two Nefesh women. They'd recently moved in after working out of their apartment for years and struggling to get a toehold in a male-dominated industry. I'd learned this while waiting in line with them at the café at the end of the block.

"Put them back," I said.

The looter's eyes narrowed. A short man in need of a haircut, he stank of stale beer and sour hatred. "You one of them fucking Nefesh?"

I crossed my arms. "If I was?"

His eyes darted left for a fraction of a second.

I spun, my spiky blood armor in place, and blocked the strike with my forearm. The baseball bat my attacker had used cracked down the center. My armor held up fine. Wrenching the bat away from him, I swung. It cut through the air with a whistle, embedding in the plaster inches shy of his head.

The stench of urine filled the air and he bolted.

"Now." I turned to the other man, my armor gone, and a cold smile on my face. "You're going to put the computers back, tidy up the office, and then you and your friends are going to stand guard here the rest of the night and ensure no one else tries the same thing."

With a scoff, he marched past me, still cradling the computers. I grabbed his arms and yanked sharply downward, dislocating both his shoulders.

His scream was a thin, high cry that sounded rather kitten-like. The laptops hit the ground, his arms dangling uselessly at his sides.

I made a note to check with the owners on how many computers would require replacing. "Do we have a deal?"

He whimpered, his gaze unfocused and his breaths coming in quick rasps.

"You big baby." I popped his joints back in one at a time, using a technique I'd learned from Miles during a training session, when he'd dislocated my shoulder during a sparring round. He showed no mercy when we trained. As a result, he'd taken my fighting abilities to a new level, but every time I staggered out of the gym looking like a piece of tenderized steak I hated Levi for abandoning me on that front.

"Deal or no deal?" I said to the looter.

He hugged his shoulders. "Crazy bitch."

Wrenching the baseball bat free with a shower of white dust, I tapped it against my palm. "I have magic and a baseball bat. You have about two hundred and six comically fragile bones. What's it to be? Insult me or conclude our business transaction?"

"We'll keep guard." His sneer was blown by his flinch as I hoisted the bat to rest it on my shoulder.

I raised an eyebrow. "Run along, then."

He fled back into the office, issuing instructions to his friends.

Satisfied that my building would be protected until these riots ran out of steam, I headed upstairs to retrieve Mrs. Hudson. With the fractured bat stowed next to my corner safe, I grabbed my leather jacket with a soft whistle.

The puppy knew the deal since we had the same routine several times a week. She stood still, allowing me to clip the leash to her collar, then we made our way down the stairs and into the night. The intruders, busy cleaning up the office, didn't notice our departure. I appreciated a man who followed orders.

Outside was pandemonium. Store windows had been smashed in, people using any excuse to ransack buildings.

Someone ran past me brandishing a box of tacky Canada T-shirts like it was the Olympic Torch. Hopefully their own stupidity would weed them out of the gene pool sooner rather than later.

I picked Mrs. Hudson up to spare her paws from the glass that made the cobblestones glitter like diamond dust. As we walked through the chaos, a distant part of me insisted I should give a damn. After all, my mother had written the proposed anti-Nefesh bill that had stirred this particular powder keg of hatred and fear.

We passed an old heritage building that was on fire. The roof had caved in and firefighters battled the flames furiously, using long jets of water to save the exterior art deco façade.

A couple of months ago, the Queen of Hedon had given House Pacifica intel that one of the original founders of the Untainted Party had laundered money through the magic black market. That was bad enough, but it was for a business venture that Jackson Wu, the current head of the provincial party, had a stake in.

I gave a chin nod to an enterprising youth with a duffle bag full of spray paint cans who was doing a brisk business—mostly to Mundanes with Untainted Party shared values, if the slogans freshly graffitied on nearby walls were any indication. Capitalism at its finest.

For reasons I couldn't fathom, Levi was sitting on that information about Jackson. The bill loomed large in news reports, and the daily coverage of Mundanes angry and Nefesh worried about its potential impact stoked public anxiety. Why did Levi put everyone through this emotional rollercoaster when he could just end it?

A cop on horseback trotted past me and blew his whistle at some people rocking a car. The industrious group whooped at the young man who stood on the hood stomping out the windshield.

As the days grew longer and warmer, tensions between the

two communities had grown, until a simple altercation between a Nefesh and a Mundane sports fan over Stanley Cup tickets earlier today had blown up into a city-wide riot that was now ten hours strong with no sign of abating.

I chuckled and stepped out of the path of a wildly veering pick-up truck with actual lightning crackling above it. Hockey tickets. How Canadian.

The young woman powering the electricity screamed, "Die, Mundanes!" as the truck careened past me.

Mrs. Hudson and I made it to my car, Moriarty, without incident. Even though my gray Toyota was the lone vehicle on this level of the parking garage, and as such should have been easy pickings, it was untouched.

At least this particular nemesis was never going to leave my life.

Once Mrs. Hudson had settled herself in the back, I eased the Toyota out onto Water Street. Between the packs of people roaming the city, police street closures, and general debris, making my way out of downtown was slow going.

The radio played messages from both the mayor and Levi calling for calm and for people to stay home. Levi was especially insistent that violence would not be tolerated. The chaos and hatred had to be killing him.

With the bridges out of commission and the streets a disaster, I was forced to zigzag my way through downtown until I cleared the on-ramp for the Cambie Street Bridge, and veered west once more.

In comparison to downtown, the rest of Vancouver was far too quiet. It was barely 1AM in early June and there should have been traffic from people heading to bars and spilling out of restaurants, but Moriarty was the only car on the road. We passed block after block of dim storefronts and boarded-up doors.

An empty bus passed by like a skeleton ship in the night, its neon destination sign eerily proclaiming "No Service" in urgent capitals. The billboard on its side depicted happy people partaking in an upcoming tournament to benefit Vancouver General Hospital. Golf. Ugh. The only reason to look that cheerful holding a five iron was because you'd just gotten away with murder.

My city's desolate atmosphere would have been disquieting had I not been gripped by the sense of predatory anticipation that always took hold when I headed down these roads to one particular destination.

I pulled up to the curb down the block from Isaac's mansion in Dunbar and cut the engine, staring into the darkness that enveloped his stately home. Wind whispered in the press of trees to my back at the edge of Pacific Spirit Regional Park, a vast forest with hiking trails that was larger than Golden Gate Park in San Francisco.

I drummed my fingers on the wheel, scanning for any movement through Isaac's windows.

He was the only one of the Chariot Ten whose identity we'd unearthed, but tailing him had yielded nothing. All his meetings were legitimately connected to his security company and his socializing included his wife, who hated her husband and certainly wasn't part of that group. That meant that anything Chariot-related was conducted via calls or texts.

If possible, we would have bugged every device he had in hopes of catching a break, but the man specialized in cybersecurity and data encryption. He knew how to hide his digital profile, including encrypting his internet history through a VPN, a virtual private network, and not syncing his phone to his car.

He seemed untouchable.

A familiar Tesla pulled up at the end of the block and my heart twisted. Sleep had eluded me most nights since I'd discovered Isaac's ties to Chariot back in April. I'd started these night-time hauntings figuring that I might as well put my insomnia to good use and case the Montefiore property.

Their alarm system protected the front and back doors and all the ground floor windows, though there were no cameras. As someone very publicly anti-magic, Isaac didn't use wards.

Once in a while, the Tesla showed up. It was the Chocolate Factory of electric vehicles: no one got in or out. It was always parked too far to away see into and I never approached it.

I didn't need to; Levi's features were burned into my brain. It was too easy to picture him, his long elegant fingers draped over the steering wheel. After the insanity of today, he'd have loosened his tie and unbuttoned his top button, allowing himself a modicum of unwinding, but he'd be on alert, attuned to the slightest thing out of place. Had he raked his hands through his midnight-black strands, tufting them up into cowlicks, the skin underneath his eyes the faintest purple with exhaustion?

He would never have left riot control central if he wasn't assured that police and firefighters had things in hand and his presence constituted a distraction. Even then, I'd bet my meagre savings that Miles had been instructed to call him if there was the slightest change in the situation.

He must be exhausted, but why come here? Did he know I was here? Had he realized what I was doing?

I white-knuckled the steering wheel.

During the day Levi and I took great pains to ignore each other. As House Head, he was still my boss, though I stayed away from HQ as much as possible, and on the rare occasion that our paths crossed, we kept up our pretense of being enemies.

Was it a pretense anymore? I no longer knew.

Mrs. Hudson's tail thumped against the seat, her sandy-colored paws resting on the dashboard. She'd only ridden in Levi's Tesla a few times, but somehow she always recognized her beloved's car.

I took a swig of the heavily sweetened coffee that I'd

bought at a drive-through, but no amount of sugar could clear the bitter taste from my mouth.

"No, girl. We don't—" For fifteen years, Levi and I had waged a war of taunts and one-upmanship that was almost as fun as our verbal sparring as friends. We'd shared our scars, he'd fed me biscotti, and then he'd gifted me with a perfect brief happiness. "Levi isn't for us anymore."

Usually the pug ignored me to continue straining at the window, but tonight, she gave up. She huffed a little doggie sigh and sank onto the passenger seat, her head on her paws in a gesture of defeat.

Blood pounded in my ears, a tightness surging up through my ribcage. He'd broken my puppy. And that was just too much; I put my hand on the car door and pushed it open. Maybe this was stupid or too rash. I didn't care.

I eased out of the car, tucked my dark wavy hair up under a black knit cap, and slid thin gloves on my hands. I left my familiar leather jacket in the car, shivering slightly against the cool breeze. Resolutely ignoring the Tesla and what its occupant might be thinking, I made my way into Isaac's backyard.

A couple weeks ago, I'd mapped out a route onto the garage roof and along a decorative ledge that ran right under a bathroom window. In my experience, the majority of people didn't lock bathroom windows on the upper floors. If Isaac did? No harm, no foul.

If not? One quick search of his study and then I'd go.

Thanks to my enhanced strength, I hoisted myself up with relatively little difficulty. My right thigh with the years-old injury throbbed in a token protest, but I compensated by relying more on my upper body. Flattening myself against the side of the house I inched along the ledge, impressed at the garden, which shimmered silver with night-blooming plants, and counted off windows until I'd reached the fourth one.

The sash was sticky and the angle from which I attempted

to ease it open was awkward, so I took it slow, careful not to make any noise or break the glass.

There was the faintest squeak of the gate hinge and a figure slipped silently into the backyard. Moonlight illuminated Levi's face as if it were broad daylight.

My chest grew tight. No amount of wishing turned Levi's eyes from this cold wintry blue, his expression schooled into an unreadable mask, to that mesmerizing deep navy right before he would kiss me, back when I was the center of his universe.

I swayed. My foot slipped and I crashed to the ledge on my knee, clinging to the windowsill by the tips of my fingers.

Levi took a step forward, then stopped. There had been a brief period of time when I could have fallen, secure that he'd catch me.

A muscle twitched in my jaw. I pulled myself up and adjusted my hold on the window frame, sliding it up to allow me entrance. Hauling myself into the bathroom, I admonished myself that I wouldn't look back. Again.

He was gone.

Chapter 2

Leaving my boots under the clawfoot bathtub, I snuck down the hallway to Isaac's study, knowing its location from a previous visit here. The night everything had gone to hell.

But I'd climbed out of hell before, hadn't I? I could do it again. And this time I had a war to win.

Slipping inside his office, I flicked on a penlight, half-covering the beam to mute the light. The room smelled faintly of a peppery spice. Search as I might, there were no architectural oddities concealing a hidden space. I shook out every one of the dozen or so books on the shelves and rummaged through the contents of the unlocked drawers, but failed to find a helpful villainous plan written in the blood of his enemies.

A pair of sharp red daggers had somehow appeared in my hands, despite me having no recollection of making them. I tucked them into my leather belt and sat down in Isaac's springy desk chair.

The chair didn't tower over the other seats, which would have created a subtle psychological power dynamic. No awards lauding Isaac's greatness crowded the walls. Behind his desk was a watercolor of a forest here in the Pacific Northwest that didn't signify much. Nothing in the space indicated aspirations of godhood.

According to all the digging we'd done on him in the past couple of months, Isaac was a respected member of the business community. Public personas were like curated spaces, and Isaac had perfected his. I admired the intelligence it took to maintain this flawless image, but one's home was another matter entirely. This study was his inner sanctum, so where were his tells?

A half-smoked cigar had been extinguished in a crystal ashtray on his desk next to an empty tumbler and a couple of newspapers in a neat stack. I sniffed the drink. Bourbon. A glass of expensive alcohol and a cigar before bed while perusing the day's headlines. Isaac was tech-savvy: he'd have been more than comfortable getting his news online. This smacked of ritual.

He liked his rituals; that much I knew from his habitual care of his wind-up clock engraved with a quote from the Old Testament that was tied to his code name. If he'd gotten it when he became one of the Ten, then he'd hidden his Chariot activities for years. That took an ironclad ruthlessness.

Isaac had played his games for a long time, using and discarding pieces as he saw fit. Outmaneuvering him would be delicious.

I ran the light over the top page of the half-folded international business section, curious about which of the fairly dry articles interested him, when a discolored patch caught my eye. I pulled off my gloves, and touched a finger to the sticky paper, sniffing it to verify that the stain was bourbon.

Why had Isaac spilled his drink? The story was a brief piece on the death of Deepa Anand, a Mundane woman in Bangalore, India, in her fifties, who owned a string of private finance companies, aka money lenders. It briefly discussed her role in the inflated interest rate scandal that had rocked the country a few years back, and that she'd died suffering complications from heart disease while on pilgrimage at a place called Char Dham.

Flicking off the penlight, I leaned back in Isaac's chair, twirling his cigar butt between my fingers and turning over the potential importance of this article. What if each of the Ten contributed something to Chariot, like how my teammates contributed to our mission? Isaac would be in charge of cybersecurity, just like Priya. Deepa would have been able to provide private funding and easily launder money.

Chariot may have had the power and reach of a global corporation, but it wasn't actually a single entity. It was more akin to a consortium of interests, some legal, most not, presided over by the Ten. Our side had unearthed only a handful of their ventures, mostly the illegal ones. The few legal companies we suspected were tied to Chariot were mired in confusing paperwork trails and shell companies within shell companies. Even Priya and all her hacking skills found them impossible to untangle.

I stiffened at a creak outside the door, straining to hear footfalls, but it was the house settling. If Deepa was a member of the Ten, my Attendant, Rafael Behar, would be ecstatic at learning her identity. It could prove a valuable new direction to find Chariot's one piece of the *Sefer Raziel HaMalakh*.

This mystic text written by the archangel Raziel had broken into five scrolls when it first fell to earth. Should Chariot get their hands on the rest of them and reassemble the book, they'd have the means to attain immortality, reshaping the world as living gods who cared only about themselves.

As I slipped into the darkened hallway, a figure stepped from the shadows. I palmed one of my blades. No one in this house knew I had magic, and I didn't have a reasonable explanation for being in this room. If this was my coming out party, only one of us was going to be alive at the end to celebrate.

A fragile-looking woman stood there clutching her bathrobe with her mouth hanging open.

Nicola Montefiore was trapped in a marriage with the brute, but I couldn't allow her to sound the alarm.

There was a loud snore from the bedroom, startling us both. Shaking her head vigorously, Nicola pressed a finger to her lips and motioned for me to go. Could I trust her not to rat me out? Did I have a choice?

I sighed. I wasn't going to hurt Levi's mom. Making the daggers vanish, I fled into the bathroom, grabbed my boots, and slipped back into the night, retracing my steps down to the backyard. My footsteps quickened when I came around the front of the house. I had a potential lead and best of all, the Tesla was gone.

I'd reached Moriarty and safety when someone grabbed me from behind.

My body reacted before my brain could, my fingers gripping Levi's biceps. His suit jacket was soft to the touch, but his muscles were corded steel. In my mind's eye they rippled, Levi's naked body poised above mine, and a devilish grin on his face as he thrust into me.

Swallowing, I jerked sideways. Levi had made me believe in a foolish, wonderful future, and then taken it away, leaving this gaping emptiness. Priya was wrong about rage. It wasn't unhealthy. It was what kept me buoyant when beneath me all was dark and deadly, threatening to pull me under.

"What the hell were you doing?" he hissed.

I stepped back against his oaky amber scotch and chocolate magic scent, but in our time together, he'd marked me, body and soul. There was no escaping him. "Take a wild guess."

Mrs. Hudson barreled out of the car, almost falling out in a somersault, her leash tangling between her feet in her haste to get to Levi.

"If you'd been caught? What then?" He bent down to

scratch her behind one ear and the puppy's leg thumped in doggie delight.

"Were you worried about me or the repercussions for the House?" I said.

"I'm always worried about my House."

While I wouldn't necessarily *enjoy* punching him in the throat, the idea held more appeal than, say, going home, putting on pj's, and flaking out in front of Netflix. "I'm aware of your priorities."

Levi motioned to his parents' house. "And I'm aware of yours."

His smile was sharp. I balanced on that same knife's edge, my every gesture ruthlessly cutting those who mattered most. His eyes glinted; he wanted me to slash back.

What good would it do for both of us to die by a thousand tiny cuts?

"So long as we're both clear." I grabbed Mrs. Hudson's leash to herd her back into the car.

"Crystal."

I didn't watch him leave.

After a quick walk around the block back home for the pug to do her business, I crashed hard, only to awake groggily at a shrill ringing. My bedroom was totally dark, which meant it was early afternoon. I fumbled for my phone, wiping phantom grit off my face. What day was it? Processing... right. Thursday.

Mrs. Hudson was nowhere to be seen, so Priya, the puppy hog, had her.

"Hello?" I mumbled.

"Ashira, I need to speak with you now."

I shook my head to clear the cobwebs because Talia sounded uncharacteristically agitated. "What's wrong?"

"Not on the phone."

"You want me to come to your office?" I said.

"No!"

15

Talia was scared I'd out myself in the middle of her work-place when I'd done nothing but show restraint and considera-tion for her position. My own mother didn't trust me. I kicked my covers onto the floor.

"My office," I said. "Half an hour." I jumped out of bed, already grabbing clothes, and got dressed in record time, spending five minutes looking for my car keys before finding them in my boot. Damn dog.

I hustled out the door, ignoring the other apartment belonging to Arkady Choi, the person formally known as my friend and neighbor. I wasn't speaking to Arkady, since I had yet to discover what he was lying to me about and he had yet to confess, but he was still a member of Team Jezebel.

Technically.

We'd decided to keep him on. Well, Rafael and Priya had decided, and I'd reluctantly agreed after they'd worn me down. However, there hadn't been much for him to do. Rafael and I did all the surveillance work on Isaac, so I hadn't seen much of Arkady, which was fine by me.

Shockingly, Moriarty cut me a break, given my haste, and started with only a minor complaint.

City crews had worked diligently to clear debris off the streets, but evidence of the riot was very much present in the boarded-up windows, bent and missing street signs, one burned-out husk of a car, and the workers installing a new front door on my office building.

I quickly checked in with the game design owners, confessing my role in the destruction of their laptops. They were happy to have the mystery solved of why they'd shown up this morning to find a man asleep across their doorway, who'd bolted awake, wide-eyed, threatening any who passed like a demented Gandalf. They also assured me that their insurance would take care of any damages.

None of the other offices on the ground level or the second floor had been disturbed, I was pleased to note.

Talia waited for me in the reception area of the shared workspace where Cohen Investigations was located. She twisted the hem of her raw silk blazer, her eyes wide and haunted.

My stomach lurched and I hurried to unlock my office. "What happened?"

She sank into the chair across from my desk and pushed her phone to me with trembling hands.

I hit play on the video and gasped. It was footage of me at the aquarium gala the night my magic manifested. The recording showed me pinning Levi down and holding a knife to him, but from the angle, you couldn't see that I'd also created that dagger from my blood.

I played it three more times, ruthlessly examining it for what it actually revealed. The video didn't even show that I had enhanced strength because I'd jumped off him so quickly. "It appears that I threatened Levi with a knife. There is no proof of my abilities and all the records state otherwise."

Levi had destroyed the House registration application when I started working for him, so there wasn't even that.

Talia half-laughed, half-sobbed. "They know. Look at the text that came with it."

It was from an unknown number. *If you don't step down from the party, I will reveal that your daughter is a Rogue. You have ten days to resign. Choose your futur wisely.*

They'd left the "e" off future. No one blackmailed my mother, especially not some illiterate douchebag. And why ten days? That seemed rather generous. Didn't blackmailers usually have a three-day rule? I checked the calendar. My deadline was June 14.

Someone out there was aware that I had magic but had sat on that fact until now. Who? And why? If this was Chariot's doing, why make Talia resign when Isaac was an ardent supporter?

What if it was someone much closer? I fast-forwarded

through the video one more time. What would Arkady have to gain in blackmailing Talia like this? If he intended to undermine me, there were far easier methods. Given all he knew about Jezebels, he could sell me out to Chariot no problem. I copied the text message down. Was this some misguided attempt to protect Levi? That didn't make sense either. Despite Levi's many issues with Talia, he'd never condone blackmail to take her down.

If this wasn't coming from someone with a vendetta against me...

"Do you have any enemies?" I said.

"The entire Nefesh community," she said flatly.

"Most Nefesh have no idea who you are or that you wrote that bill. Whoever sent this is attempting to use me against you. It feels personal."

"There's no one. My life isn't a television show of secrets and scandal." She stuffed the phone in her purse. "At least it wasn't until recently."

She was scared and upset. I made allowances for that and swallowed my sarcastic retort.

"What do I tell them?" she said.

"Nothing. Don't respond. They don't have proof, but if you reply it looks like you have something to hide. I'll take care of this. I promise."

"Your magic is going to cost me everything." Her naked pain undid me.

"Mom." I reached for her.

She shook her head, her hands up, and walked away, leaving nothing behind but the scent of her rose perfume.

We'd been doing so well. Sure, our relationship was built on a heavy helping of avoidance, but our weekly breakfasts were actually enjoyable. She'd even walked Mrs. Hudson with me along the seawall a couple of times. I rubbed my temples, feeling like a grenade had been lobbed into my day.

The only saving grace was that the pin had not been pulled. Yet.

I phoned Rafael to tell him about Deepa. He was pleased with my findings and agreed that this might be the break we needed. Happy that the day seemed to be turning around, I hung up, intending to contact Priya to get any dirt on the dead woman. Much of Pri's time had been taken up with House business lately, but she could never say no to some good old-fashioned fun unearthing dirty secrets.

That's when Nicola Montefiore walked into my office and said, "I want to hire you."

So much for catching a break. In the back of my head, a pin slipped out from a grenade.

Ka-boom.

Chapter 3

Instead of answering, I put a finger to my lips and shut down my phone, motioning for her to do the same. Who knew what tabs Mr. Cybersecurity kept on his wife?

For good measure, I locked up both of our cells in Eleanor's office, along with my laptop to really nail that paranoia. The graphic designer wasn't in, but we had each other's keys. Feeling that I'd secured our environment as best as I could, I returned to my office and indicated Nicola should speak.

"I want to leave Isaac."

I opened and closed my mouth several times in an excellent guppy impersonation. "Mrs. Montefiore—"

"Nicola, please." Levi's mother had always struck me as a quiet woman, slight of frame and backbone. Today her spine was ramrod straight, and there was a determined set to her chin and the tone of her Italian-accented words.

"Did something happen last night?" Had Isaac found out about my nocturnal visit and taken out his anger on his wife? "Are you in physical danger if you remain in your house?"

"No. Isaac has never laid a hand on me, but..." She fiddled with the artfully knotted scarf around her neck. "I don't know what that scroll was that I found when I was cleaning out Levi's old bedroom a couple of months ago, but I know it's important." She gave a very Italian shrug of her shoulders. "Why else would it be hidden?"

Why else, indeed?

"But it was not put there by Isaac. He didn't know about Levi's hiding spot, and even if he did, he would never have used it." Her coral-painted mouth twisted. "You know about Isaac and Levi."

Interesting that she hadn't phrased that as a question. "I do."

She nodded. "Levi didn't put it there either. How would he have gotten hold of something like that when he was a child? And now, he is a man with his own home."

"Yeah," I said, more wistfully than I intended.

"You know something about this. You can help." Oh shit. Nicola going down the path of this scroll and using it as some justification to finally escape Isaac's clutches was dangerous.

"I'm working exclusively for an insurance company and no longer take on domestic cases." I scribbled a phone number down on a sticky note. "I highly recommend this divorce lawyer. She can assist you in finding some way to leave—"

"It was..." Nicola pursed her lips, then sighed. "It was Adam, wasn't it?"

"Adam?" My voice was reedy, my smile more of a grimace.

"Sì. That's the only thing I can think of. He hid the scroll when he came to see Isaac that night. Many years ago. The last time I ever saw your father."

My mouth fell open. "H-how?"

She smiled, the amusement lighting her face making her look so much like her son that I had to briefly look away. "Everyone always underestimates the wives and mothers, but we know more than we let on, bella."

I tapped my pen against my thigh, my thoughts going a million miles an hour. She didn't understand the significance of the scroll. Did she know Isaac belonged to Chariot? It was true that it would never have occurred to me to talk to her about this, but she'd lived with the man for years. She wasn't oblivious, in the same way that Talia had known about the nurse's complaint about my magic after my car accident, and yet that had never occurred to me, either.

"Does the word 'Chariot' mean anything to you?" I said.

Nicola shook her head, her brown eyes unclouded and her expression guileless. "No. Is that connected?"

"Forget you ever heard it." It came out more harshly than I'd intended. I gentled my tone. "Please."

"Okay, ragazza. Will you help me? I can't live with him anymore. My son has already been so hurt and now he's heartbroken."

I snapped the pen in half. "That's not relevant."

"It is to me. *That man*"—her tone was laced with vitriol and her eyes darkened—"has done enough damage. To both of us. I'm done. Basta." She slashed a hand across the top of her head.

Nicola was the picture of resolve. With or without me, she was doing this. Isaac had killed my father for leaving him, so I'd have to be very careful history didn't repeat itself.

When it came to Chariot and betrayal, one strike and you were out. Permanently. That went double for Isaac and his abandonment issues.

Nicola was going to live a long and happy life.

Levi would hate me, but I was one of the few people who knew what Isaac was truly up to and could keep her from accidentally blundering into something that could put her life in peril. She stood a better chance of navigating this minefield with me than without me.

"I'll help," I said.

Her body went limp with relief and my heart ached.

"Where do you want me to start?" Generally, spouses

came to me about infidelity, sometimes fraud. I was very curious how she would answer.

"Find this thing he's so obsessed with so I can get half. I want him to know what I took from him."

I swallowed a hysterical laugh. The only thing Isaac wanted was the four scrolls in Team Jezebel's possession to achieve immortality, and you couldn't exactly go halvsies on them in divorce court. Except she knew Levi had a scroll, and she didn't mention it specifically, so what was she referring to?

She must have seen my hesitation because she leaned forward, her hands splayed on my desk. "You were looking for a clue to the same thing last night, yes? The bamah?"

"The what now?" I couldn't even look it up since my cell and laptop were in Eleanor's office.

"Bamah. A few days ago, I overheard a phone call. Isaac seemed to be learning about this for the first time. He got extremely agitated and has been going crazy trying to find it ever since."

If this bamah was important to Isaac, then it had become very important to me. Especially if it was also connected to this Deepa woman.

"Do you know anything else about it?" I grabbed another pen.

"He said it was chiuso... Come se dice?" She made expansive hand gestures with her words. "Closed."

I jotted that fact down. "It might not turn out to be anything you can use to leave Isaac," I said, "but one way or another, I'll get you out of that situation." She reached for her purse but I waved her off. "No. Please. I can't take your money."

I'll take your son's. I couldn't trust normal modes of communication to get hold of Nicola, in case Isaac had bugged her phone, so Levi would have to be the go-between. And wouldn't that conversation be the cherry on the shit sundae of our last encounter?

After retrieving our phones and my laptop, I gave Nicola instructions that I'd get hold of her via Levi, and pressed upon her the importance of going about her normal routine until she heard back from me.

"I've survived him this long. I'll be careful. And Ashira?" Nicola squeezed my hand. "I don't know what happened to Adam, but if Isaac had anything to do with it? Mi dispiace."

"Not your fault," I said, my throat thick.

"Please don't let the past dictate your future." She looked out the window, her gaze distant. "Don't wake up one day and realize you threw away your life, your happiness, because you were scared."

You're talking to the wrong person, lady. "Wouldn't want that," I said.

Once she'd left, I sank into my comfy desk chair, my head in my hands. Stupid fucking universe determined to shove me in Levi's path. This wasn't a romcom.

People always underestimated the wives and mothers. Had Nicola put this bamah, the scroll, and my father together, and come up with one private investigator with a vested interest? Even if she'd manipulated me into helping her, her relief at my agreement had been real. I couldn't go back on my word.

I exhaled slowly. Suck it up, Ash.

Levi's phone went to voicemail, so who did I want to call for his whereabouts? Evil or the lesser of evils? I wasn't up to sparring with Levi's pet dragon today, so lesser of evils it was.

I hit speed dial. "Hello, Miles. It's your friendly neighborhood Jezebel."

"And what had already been a stressful day has now devolved into an extremely shitty one. Wonderful," he said dryly.

"Sadly, I think that's less a function of how delightful I am and more an issue that you need to get a life. Where's His Lordship?"

Silence.

"Hello? Miles?" I switched over to speaker phone, put my cell on my desk and clicked on my mouse to bring my laptop to life. What was a bamah?

"You've gone out of your way to avoid him for two months," he said. "Why are you looking for him now?"

"We talked about your unhealthy interest in my life. Also, I haven't gone out of my way to do anything where he's concerned. That would imply a level of caring I no longer possess."

There was a rush of static and a sigh. When Miles finally spoke, his voice was far softer. "Are you going to hurt him again?"

I scoffed to cover the pain that caused me. "If I told you, that would take the fun unpredictability factor out of it. Also, fuck you. I have a case that he needs to be advised on stat."

According to Ye Wise Old Internet, a bamah was the Hebrew word for a place of worship. The angel feather had been buried at one of Asherah's sites near the archeological dig that Omar Tannous had worked on. Did Nicola mean buried and not closed? Could there be another important artifact that Chariot believed was hidden at a bamah, like our scrolls? And what, if anything, did Deepa's death have to do with it?

"Is this something I should know about?" Miles said.

"It is, but you'll have to get in line. Levi should be told first."

Miles chewed that over for a moment. "Come to HQ. And tell Rafael. There's another matter to discuss with everyone."

"You going to give me a heads-up on what?"

"Nope. Levi's office in half an hour." He hung up before I could protest the location.

It was just a room and I was a professional. Any memories I had of it were irrelevant, and nothing to do with the circuitous route I took to get to there.

House Pacifica was the same deep crimson color that it

had been for the past two months. I turned into the parking garage, shifting uncomfortably. There was no proof it was a mood ring tied to Levi and even if it was, it wasn't my problem.

Up on the seventh floor, I strode past the artwork hung on pale gold walls and leaned on the counter of Levi's Executive Assistant's reception desk.

"Verrrroooniiiiicaaaa," I sang, enjoying her grimace.

The blonde woman, impeccable as always in a hound-stooth skirt and cream blouse, stood up and crossed her arms. "You are not going to distract him. He has a very important meeting in ten minutes."

"I know. I'm part of it."

She groaned. "No. Go back to not speaking to him again. I liked that." She fiddled with one of her pearl earrings.

I smirked and pointed at her hand. "You have a terrible tell. Never play poker. Admit it, Levi's been a bastard without me around."

"Miles doesn't know when to shut up." She flipped through a pile of documents, adding "sign here" stickers to certain pages. "Well, Levi isn't here yet. Wait in the reception area."

"Can I...?" My voice wavered and I cleared my throat. "I think I need a minute to acclimatize before Levi arrives. Can I wait in there?" Confronted with the prospect of going inside, my blithe confidence wavered.

Veronica had been there the last time I'd visited the office, after I'd learned of my father's murder. She'd shown compassion then. I hoped she would now.

She peeled off another sticker, a muscle ticking in her jaw, and I braced myself for a "no." Something of my dismay must have shone through because her stern expression softened and she relented with a nod. "Touch anything and die."

"And give you the satisfaction? Hardly."

I hesitated for a moment in the doorway, because Levi's

unique magic scent permeated the air. The last time I'd visited, there'd been Sherlock Holmes books on the coffee table and that stupid lock he'd been so excited to have me teach him how to pick.

Every trace of me had been systematically removed. Even the sofa where Levi had comforted me after I learned of my dad's murder had been replaced with a model that was similar, but not quite up to the charm of the original.

I sat down on the memory-free furniture, my head bowed and my forearms braced on my thighs. Moving on was one thing, but Levi had erased me. Why was it so easy for him?

Irritating pinging sounds grew closer.

"Ark, enough," Miles said outside the office. "That sound is drilling into my brain."

"My unicorns don't stab the cherubs as effectively if I can't hear them impaled."

"For fuck's sake," Miles said.

"One more level, babe," Arkady replied.

"That's what you said last night."

His boyfriend gave him a lopsided grin as they entered. "As I recall, your patience was handsomely rewarded."

I cleared my throat and both men looked over.

Miles blushed and glowered in equal measure.

"Aw, you look like the love child of Grumpy and Bashful," I said.

"Shut it, Cohen," he said, and sat down in one of the extra chairs that had been set out for this meeting. Dayum, his glutes were so tight they didn't even sag over the chair like a normal person's.

Arkady, his black hair pulled back and in a T-shirt that said "Morally Flexible," backward straddled a chair and returned to the game on his phone, not bothering with eye contact.

Letting people into your life was a shell game, and trust was the little ball being shuffled around. It didn't matter how smart you were, how closely you kept your eye on the ball; at some point, you'd lift up the cup only to find empty air.

I'd known that, but I'd allowed Priya's optimistic beliefs to influence me otherwise.

My bestie arrived next with Mrs. Hudson. Priya picked non-existent lint off her polka-dotted wrap dress. "Are you finished being a little bitch?"

I reached for the dog but Priya pulled her out of repossession range. "Yeah. Sorry I hung up on you."

"Sorry I poked shit you didn't want poked." Priya unclipped Mrs. Hudson from her leash.

Mrs. Hudson barked joyously, immediately sniffing around.

A flurry of chimes went off and Arkady punched the air. "Nailed you, sucker."

Priya ruffled his hair. "Oh, you sad, sad junkie."

"Don't be jealous that you couldn't get past level two." He slung an arm around her waist. "We can't all be brilliant unicorn assassins."

Mock-affronted, Priya knuckled the top of his head.

I pressed my lips tight, not wondering at all about the dumb app they played together, and moved over so Pri could sit on the sofa.

Rafael hurried in, his cheeks pink with exertion, holding two mugs wafting Earl Grey–scented steam. He handed one to Pri. "I thought, perhaps, you could use this pick-me-up."

Her face lit up and she took the drink from him. "Thank you. That's so sweet."

"What about me?" I said.

He frowned. "Don't you usually drink coffee?"

"Lovely of you to notice. Did you bring me one?"

"I—uh—no?" Whose Attendant was he anyway?

Levi entered at that moment and shut the door. Rafael gave him a grateful glance and squished in between Priya and me.

"Everyone's here." Levi exuded haughtiness in his sharp black suit and slicked-back hair. "Good." He strode over to his desk, ribbing Arkady and Miles about their shit taste in some movie they'd dragged him to, teasing Priya about her caffeine consumption, and even asking Rafael if he'd enjoyed that restaurant Levi had suggested the other day.

New furniture, new friend group—my, His Lordship had been busy. I dug my boot heel against the couch to leave a black mark.

Levi could keep Miles. However, even if I was pissed at Arkady, he'd been my friend, not Levi's, so Montefiore had no business going to movies with him, regardless of Arkady's relationship with Miles. As for Priya and Rafael? They were right out as anything other than Levi's professional acquaintances.

I calmed down with my alphabetizing technique.

Asphyxiation, bludgeoning, choking, decapitation... my spirits were lifting already. "Is this or is this not a work meeting?" I said. "Because I have things to do."

"That's right. Your noble calling leaves little room for relationships." Levi tugged his cuffs straight.

"And yet, how nice to be a man of leisure and have all the time in the world for them."

Miles and Arkady shot me displeased looks at insulting Levi, but Priya and Rafael covered smiles, which cheered me up immeasurably.

Levi's lips quirked and my heart leapt. It was almost like the old days, trading barbs and smirking at each other. Or, like playing at a magician's booth, tracking the ball as it sped from cup to cup, and feeling certain of your choice. But I'd lifted the cup without the ball under it yet again, because he wiped his expression carefully blank, nodded, and said, "Let's begin."

Chapter 4

To add insult to injury, Mrs. Hudson scampered over to Levi, pawing at the hem of his trousers.

I crossed over to grab her, just as Levi bent down. Our hands brushed and a tingle went up my arm.

Without looking at me, he handed me the dog, who whined softly. "As most of you know," he said, "for the past two months, I've attempted to find proof tying Jackson Wu to the money laundering in Hedon."

He had? From the others' expressions, this was only news to Rafael and me.

"The contact there, Luca Bianchi, has been deemed off-limits by the Queen," Levi said, "and the team led by Priya and Miles haven't uncovered any irregularities in this company's accounting practices."

Priya made a frustrated noise. "They've hidden their tracks well."

She'd moved from overhauling House cybersecurity to this? Why hadn't she said anything?

This was supposed to be a meeting of Team Jezebel, but the lines had been redrawn. It was Team House Pacifica with Rafael and me the only ones left in the dark. I cut a sideways glance at my Attendant. Was he a shell game of an entirely different sort, only loyal because of what I represented as a Jezebel?

I shoved those doubts deep inside me. "Why am I only finding this out now?"

"I wasn't aware I was accountable to you," Levi said.

"I brokered the alliance with the Queen that got you the damn information in the first place and my mother's career is tied to the party. I should have been looped in."

Priya dropped her gaze to her half-empty cup.

Rafael shot her a troubled look. "Ash…"

"Why?" Arkady said. "The bulk of the work required computer skills you don't have and I handled the undercover operation." His loyalty had always been with Levi, but it still hurt.

And Levi? He watched the proceedings with a vaguely impatient expression.

I picked up Mrs. H's leash and wound it around my hands. "I didn't ask to be part of it, but it's rude to use me when it's convenient and then cut me out."

"I'm including you now," Levi said.

"Because you need me for something." I snapped the leash tight.

Rafael elbowed me and I set the leash down on the arm of the sofa.

Levi propped his hip against the desk. "Yes, Ashira. That's how it works. I'm House Head and I decide how and when people are brought in."

We were back to full name usage, were we? A muscle ticked in my jaw and I saluted him. "Aye aye, boss."

Mrs. Hudson trotted under Levi's desk, pushing a fallen paper clip with her nose.

"Arkady, fill them in," Levi said.

"Jackson Wu started his career as a business grad," Arkady said. "His first job out of university was working for the

Allegra Group, a property development company started by Richard Frieden."

"Frieden was one of the original founders of the Untainted Party," I said to Rafael, who was looking lost.

"Wu was the golden boy being groomed to eventually take over the company, until his abrupt switch to politics about seven years ago," Arkady said.

"Frieden was grooming him in other respects," Rafael said.

Arkady draped his elbows over the back of the chair. "Yeah, but even after Wu left Allegra, he remained the second-highest shareholder in the company after Frieden. Richard's shares were distributed amongst his family when he died."

"Even so," I said, "Jackson wasn't working directly for the company when the money laundering happened. If the extent of his involvement is as a shareholder, that gives him a lot of plausible deniability."

Levi's computer chimed with a notification. He glanced at it and shut the laptop. "All our fact gathering indicates that Jackson is still very hands-on with Allegra. There's no way he was in the dark. That said, we still need hard proof to bring him down and destroy his credibility so he can't move this legislation forward."

Arkady raised his hand. "Which is where I came in. For the past couple of months, I've been working at Allegra doing general office admin. It gave me a chance to get close to staff, especially the Head of Accounting Olivia Dawson. Very smart woman. Workaholic Mundane, divorced, no kids, not easy to get close to. But I wore her down."

Miles rolled his eyes.

"We went out after work a few times," Arkady said. "She was fond of unwinding with a drink or four and amenable to a sympathetic ear about how her entire life is bound up in the company. She also got very hostile whenever Jackson's name came up in the course of chatting about current events. Apparently, there was no love lost between them while they worked together. Last week, she made a throwaway comment about an 'insurance policy'"—Arkady did the air quotes—"and that certain people weren't as smart as they thought they were. Frieden is dead, so it's likely she was referring to Wu."

"If she collected evidence to protect her butt," Priya said, "she may well have named names."

"So lean on Olivia," I said.

"We intended to," Miles said. "But she died late last night in a car accident."

"Foul play?" Rafael asked.

Miles shook his head. "Drinking and driving. Not her first time."

"She didn't deserve that," Arkady said.

Miles spread his hands wide.

"You've searched her home and office, I take it," Rafael said.

Arkady nodded. "Thoroughly."

"There may be another way to find this proof, should it exist," Levi said. "A Bookworm, but they're so rare as to be an urban legend."

"What's a Bookworm?" I said.

"They have the ability to burrow into any printed material anywhere in existence," Levi said.

I raised my eyebrows at Rafael, who'd rolled his eyes. Hard. "If you're going to impersonate a fifteen-year-old girl, Attendant mine, you might want to wear less tweed."

Rafael glanced down at his brown blazer with the elbow patches. "Tweed is a perfectly adaptable fabric and Book-worms are barmy as hell."

"Do you know of one?" I said. "Why aren't we using them to get more intel on Chariot? We could gain access to Isaac's correspondence and find out where they're hiding the scrolls."

"Did you not hear the part about them being exceedingly rare? And we did use one. Or rather, attempt to," he said. "About thirty years ago when Vishranti was the Jezebel. This was the first Bookworm we'd found since we learned of their existence about three hundred years ago."

Priya tugged on his sleeve. "Thirty years isn't so far back. Could you find this person again?"

"Unfortunately, I can't. He was murdered by parties a little too interested in his skill set."

"Damn," I said.

"While it's true that Bookworms can find any information printed that is currently in existence," Rafael said, pushing his glasses up his nose, "the important caveat is that their skills don't apply to anything digital."

"Even printed information had to yield something on Chariot," I said.

"Certainly," Rafael said, "but it was about a hundred years out of date. Chariot knows about the existence of Bookworms as well, no matter how rare they are, and took appropriate measures to cover their tracks."

"And the barmy part?" Miles said.

"Data overload," Rafael said. "Their lucid moments are far and few between. Sad, really."

"All that notwithstanding," Levi said, "exceedingly rare doesn't mean nonexistent."

I shifted, stretching out my back. "If Olivia's insurance policy was stored on a laptop or something, you're shit out of luck."

"It's not," Priya said. "I searched every device she was connected to." If Priya couldn't find it with her badass hacking skills, then it didn't exist digitally.

"Based on things Elke's heard," Levi said, "she's of the opinion that a Bookworm currently exists. If one is alive, there's someone who'd be interested enough in their abilities to have their location."

"The Queen?" I said. "Ask her yourself."

"I tried. She denied knowing anything, but knowledge is power, right? You have a more personal relationship with her, and she might share information with you that she's reluctant to hand over to me," he said. "Pursue that avenue. Find me a Bookworm." He scrubbed a hand over his face, then caught himself, like he'd exposed some chink in his armor.

Levi was desperate. Provincial parliament was disbanded for the summer, but that hadn't stopped the Untainted Party from strengthening alliances for when the bill went to First Reading in the fall session. His best chance at derailing this ploy to remove Nefesh self-governance was to stop the legislation before parliament was recalled.

I worried my teeth against my bottom lip. If Levi wasn't after a Hail Mary, would he have brought me in at all? He hadn't requested assistance with any case since he'd dumped me, so how strong was our professional alliance?

"We'll do our best," Rafael said. "Right, Ashira?"

"Yup." This stupid new sofa hurt my ass.

"Thank you. Do you have any updates to share?" Levi said, without bothering to look to me for the information. Rafael had become the de facto liaison between Team Jezebel and Levi.

Rafael finished his tea. "Ash found a possible new member of the Ten." His synopsis on Deepa Anand didn't mention how I'd found out about her, but from Levi's assessing gaze, he suspected.

"Priya," Rafael said, "can you look into her?" He shared my theory about each of the Ten bringing something valuable to the table. "Deepa's death may expose more of them."

"Sure." Her shoulders slumped.

"Tell them, Priya," Arkady said.

I leaned over Rafael and tapped her knee. "Pri?"

She spun her empty mug in her hands. "There's only one of me, and I feel like I'm being pulled between the House and Team Jezebel. I can't do it all."

She'd confided in Arkady about this instead of coming to

me? My magic danced under my skin, but my emotions were tempered by how warily Priya watched me.

"You shouldn't have to," I said. Priya had every right to set boundaries. "We had a deal, Levi, and it wasn't that you monopolize all her time." Was this his plan? Undermine me by taking my team members out of the picture?

"I allocated my resources to the most pressing threat," he said. "The legislation."

"The digital trail is dead," Miles said. "And overloading Priya to the point of burnout doesn't do anyone any good. Least of all, House security."

I smirked and Levi's expression hardened. Bitten in the ass by his Security Chief's devotion to his duty.

"Priya is all yours. Are we done?" Levi arched an eyebrow.

Rafael glanced at Priya, who gave him a wan smile and nod. "I believe so," he said. He didn't know about Nicola and the bamah yet. I'd fill him in after I told Levi.

I raised a hand. "I need a word."

"Give me a moment with Miles," Levi said.

"Are we okay?" I said to Priya.

"You're my best friend, but navigating between you and Levi is exhausting, and I haven't been able to take on any outside clients because I've been pulling such long hours. This wasn't what I signed up for, Ash. I believe in your cause, but the House is where my professional opportunities lay right now."

"Next time, say something." Priya's normal usual vitality had dimmed to a lackluster waxy sheen, and looking back, she'd been coming home and crashing most nights.

"I've tried," she said gently.

Arkady strode over to us. "Are you going to keep ignoring me, pickle?"

I stood up so he'd tower over me slightly less. "Are you going to share whatever it is you're lying about?"

"We have this amazing process called innocent until

proven guilty," he said. "Do you have any proof that I've done something wrong, or are you so hyped up on your own self-importance that you've decided everyone is out to get you and I couldn't possibly have moved in next door because I needed a place to live?"

My eyes narrowed and I crossed my arms. "Excuse me?"

Priya jumped up between us. "That's it. I'm invoking forced socialization. Tomorrow night, the two of you are going to work this out."

Arkady and I gave similar sullen stares.

"Pout all you want, but I'm done with this. Rafael?"

He looked up from his phone.

"We're going out tomorrow," Priya said. "Come with us. You must be going crazy having basically only Ash for company."

"Serving his Jezebel is an Attendant's greatest joy," I said.

"Horrors." He shivered. "I'd be delighted."

Priya clipped the leash back on Mrs. Hudson with a nod. "I'll get started on Deepa's financials. See where that leads."

I reached for the leash. "Can I have my puppy back?"

"No." Priya batted her lashes at me to show we were good, but the dog was non-negotiable.

"Can I ask for one more favor?" I said.

"It depends."

"Talia is being blackmailed." I watched Arkady for his reaction, but he whistled softly under his breath. His shock seemed genuine.

Priya gasped. "What?"

"Bloody hell," Rafael said. "Who would do such a thing?"

"She wields power within a controversial political party," Arkady said. "Is it tied to the legislation?"

"Could be," I admitted.

After Priya heard the details, she said that she'd examine my mom's phone for any clues as to the sender from either the text, the unknown number, or the video file itself.

Miles came over and squeezed Arkady's shoulder. "Let's go."

The two of them, Priya, and my dog all left together, while Rafael said he'd meet me down in the House Library. He wanted to speak with Elke, the librarian, about resources pertaining to Bookworms.

Rafael shut the door, leaving me with Levi.

"Is this going to take long?" he said.

You insufferable bastard. "Your mom wants to leave your father." I brushed off my hands. "There. All looped in."

Levi's mouth fell open, then he frowned. "How would you know?"

"Nicola allocated the best resource to help her."

His expression grew more and more glacial as I recounted our conversation. He could rent himself out for parties, stuff beer down his shirt, and market it as a way to save on ice.

"Put a guard on her in case she isn't able to keep up the status quo charade or Isaac gets suspicious and she has to be pulled out immediately," I said. "Oh, you're our go-between."

Levi pulled out his phone. "Then I'll tell her you've changed your mind."

"I haven't."

"My mother isn't equipped to deal with you like I am. If you go scorched earth on her—"

"I went scorched earth on *you*?" Not only was that the furthest thing from the truth, but after our entire history, he'd reduced me to some destructive force? I clapped my hand over my mouth, pressing down to physically prevent a hateful response. Or a wounded noise.

I grabbed my purse to leave, needing distance.

He sighed and placed the phone on his desk. "I'm asking you not to do this."

I searched his face but there was no trace of the man I'd made love to and shared my secrets with. "Your 'ask' sounds more like a decree."

There was a knock on the door and Veronica entered with some file folders. "These require your signature."

"Thank you." Levi smiled at her as she left. It even reached his eyes. He flipped between emotions so quickly. Was this another mask? Did he ever take them off?

He used to with me...

"If you find this bamah," Levi said, leaning over his desk to sign the documents, "Isaac will suspect, if not know outright, that Nicola gave him up. You can't even be certain it concerns the *Sefer*."

I ruthlessly shoved my pang of sympathy away. "Of course this concerns the *Sefer*."

"What if my mom meets the same fate as Adam?"

"We're going to make sure she doesn't. And if I don't help her, she'll find someone who has no idea how carefully to tread. You didn't see her. She's going through with this and, as such, I'm her best and safest option. No harm will befall her on my watch."

"Can you swear that her trust in you will be sacrosanct?" There was a weight to his words and the way he watched me, his mouth in a grim line.

Were we talking about Nicola anymore?

Levi clicked the pen a couple of times, and the moment passed. "I'll talk Mom out of her plans and I'll make sure you have cases to occupy you besides finding the Bookworm."

"Thank you, O Great and Beneficent One, for throwing me a bone." I picked up a magazine, *Business Insider*, raised an eyebrow, and smacked it back on the coffee table. Since when did Levi care about Mundane business? What mask was this? My voice lowered. "Look, you know it doesn't work that way. I'm a Jezebel. You want me to ignore my purpose?"

"Three months ago, you didn't even know you had a purpose. How much of this is about some noble cause and how much is revenge for Adam?"

I froze, caught in his barbed sneer, and unable to stop the

flash of anger that speared through me at his contempt. "Two months ago, you had no problem with me wanting vengeance for my dad's murder. In fact, you promised to help me, so don't you dare throw that back in my face now."

"I didn't mean...fuck."

A curious calm settled over me. "Ah, but you did."

Levi held out a hand, his expression beseeching. "She's my mother. Would you charge blithely forward if Talia's life was on the line? If Adam's was?" He paused. "Would you have pursued this if stepping back meant keeping him safe?"

"There is no 'safe' anymore. Not for your family or mine. That ship sailed more than fifteen years ago and I have to do the best I can from day to day. So do you, and hiding your head in the sand isn't going to change that fact. What do you think will happen if the Ten bring about immortality?" I said. "How safe do you think your mom will be then? How safe is she living in fear of that monster every day?" I hitched my slipping purse back onto my shoulder. "You want Nicola to remain trapped with him? Isaac murdered my father for daring to leave. Nothing short of a complete and utter takedown of that man is going to allow her to be free."

Levi made a dismissive motion. "There are other ways I can help her leave."

"Are there? Why didn't you use them before?"

Levi dropped the pen and turned away. His mother had protected him as much as she could during his childhood, and he'd promised himself that he would help her once he felt powerful enough to take on his father once and for all. But Levi had never felt ready, and while he hesitated, Nicola remained with Isaac.

I reached out to touch him, comfort him, but I dropped my hand. I wasn't the one he wanted comfort from anymore, and I had no idea if he was still the version of himself who'd even be open to it. "I shouldn't have said that about her living in fear. Your mom is a survivor. She could have left once you were out of the house, but she wasn't ready. Now she is."

"Please don't look for this worship site. It's too dangerous for her to get involved. I'm asking you to put people ahead of this mission."

"This mission is precisely about putting people first. All people. Keeping them safe from a bunch of power-mad psychos."

He ran a hand through his hair. "You know what I mean."

"Yeah. I do. Where was your deep caring for all people when you walked away from *me*?"

Levi didn't answer. No matter. There was nothing I wanted to hear from him.

"Nicola wants this," I said. "She needs to reclaim her power where Isaac is concerned. You should take a page out of her book." I fired my words into him like darts, reveling in his flinch. "Keep your mother safe and don't get in my way."

Chapter 5

Friday morning, I woke up ridiculously early and spent a couple of restless hours going through a stack of books from the House library containing mentions of Bookworms and bamahs. Rafael had his own homework searching through the Attendant archives on the subjects.

Speaking of my teammate, I'd texted him with an offer to buy breakfast while we compared findings, but he'd asked to meet later, because he was visiting Gavriella's grave. Levi's people had taken away her body after she'd died in my arms and once he'd found out her name, he'd arranged for her to be buried in one of the Jewish cemeteries here under her alias of Gavriella Behar.

I'd only learned this fact from Rafael who visited the cemetery often, claiming it comforted him to sit with her. He'd asked me to come along but I felt uncomfortable intruding on his private time with the woman who had been like a sister to him. Nor was I ready to face the grave of my predecessor.

After reading the same page three times with still no memory of what was on there, I gave up, stretching my leg out on the sofa and shaking out the pins-and-needles feeling from having partially sat on it. Levi's words kept replaying in my head. How had the one person I'd banked on being in my corner ended up standing on the other side of a gaping chasm?

"Argh!" I ran my hands through my hair.

Mrs. Hudson squeezed her squeaky cow toy sympathetically. It was sweet that my dog cared about me.

The squeaks turned rhythmic.

I sighed. "It's nice one of us has an active sex life."

Priya wandered into the living room, wearing blue penguin pajamas and yawning.

"Reasonably fresh coffee on the stove," I said.

"You're a life saver." She patted the puppy, who looked up, tongue lolling out, but didn't stop humping the toy. We'd had her spayed, but that had no impact on this behavior. "Your turn to wash Pinky," she said.

Pushing aside some of Priya's shit that ran from cables to hair elastics to her latest book club novel, I dumped the library books on the coffee table. "Did you really have to name her?"

"Well, we certainly couldn't introduce them as Mrs. Hudson and her life partner Cow, could we?"

"I agree with you on the not introducing them part."

Priya winged an elastic at me. "I connected with Talia to get the phone. We'll see what that yields."

"There's something else I didn't tell you about." I dropped the Nicola fiasco.

"And so the story takes a sharp and unexpected turn." She blew a raspberry at my scowl. "The Cohens and Montefiores make the Capulets and the Montagues look positively mushy." She squeezed my shoulder. "Find your sense of humor, Holmes."

I stood up, grabbing the leash. "Yeah, yeah. Have a good day. I'm off to see Rafael."

She snagged the leash. "I'm taking Mrs. H."

"You hogged her all day yesterday."

"Give me my puppy time, Ashira, or I'll stick you on a No-Fly List."

"Why are you branching out from Password Hell? That was a perfectly good threat. No-Fly List is unnecessarily aggressive."

She tapped her head. "New challenges keep me sharp. Say bye-bye to mommy number two," Priya said in a cutesy voice to the dog.

I knelt down by the pug and kissed her goodbye. "Humor her," I stage-whispered. "We know who you love best."

～

"ON A SCALE of income tax audit to prison shower, how fun was our team meeting yesterday?" I braked sharply at a red light.

"It wasn't fun at all, Ashira, and I'm not sure why you insist on asking these inane questions." Rafael sat in Moriarty's passenger seat, his arms crossed. "Not to mention, Elke had nothing substantial to indicate that a Bookworm currently exists and I'm not happy about how much time this might take. The bamah is our priority."

"I'm with you on that." I slowed down to avoid hitting a jaywalker. "I appreciate you dealing with Levi."

"Yes, well, that task was rather awkward at first, what with his observation of the magic healing situation between us at his home."

"Come on, that was the perfect encore after the fuckery of that night." Once the pedestrian was clear of my car, I floored it, knocking Rafael back against his seat.

He grabbed the "oh shit" handle above the passenger seat. "You're an odd duck, Ashira."

"Laughter is cheaper than drinking. And therapy."

"Nevertheless, he never mentioned that incident again—"

"Yeah, well, it paled in comparison to learning his dad had murdered mine. Perspective, don'tcha know?"

"*And* as the larger strain is between the two of you—"

I snorted.

"I'm happy to do my part to keep the harmony on the team."

"Are you? Or do you feel like Priya, that you're pulled between the two of us?"

"You people are a hotbed of dysfunction," he said. "However, unlike Priya, I'm loyal to the House only so far as it remains an asset to our mission. As your Attendant, I'll handle whatever I can to focus your energy on the end goal."

Some asshole was riding my bumper so I crawled along to annoy him enough that he switched lanes with a sharp honk, at which point I sped up and passed him.

"Ashira, perhaps you could"—Rafael squeaked—"slow down?"

His wish was granted when I hit the streets around the Vancouver Art Gallery back plaza and came to a standstill, because a Nefesh rally against the proposed Untainted Party legislation had spilled into traffic.

A woman with a loudspeaker stood on the stairs discussing Nefesh human rights. Behind her stood a group, presumably other speakers. They were too far away to make out their faces, but even at this distance, I recognized Levi.

Part of me wanted to pull over and hear him empassion the crowd. He stood up for his beliefs, despite the many adversities he faced as leader of the Nefesh community. So very Watson of him. I smiled wistfully and made a sharp left, the rally growing smaller in my rearview mirror.

Several blocks later, we arrived at the Vancouver Public Library. Built in the early '90s, it resembled the Colosseum, topped by a green space dotted with trees that was a popular place to read or eat lunch on sunny days.

"See? I got us here in one piece." I backed Moriarty into a

metered spot on Homer Street and Rafael released his death grip on the handle.

The library glass doors led to an atrium with tiny coffee shops and a pizza joint, the tables provided for patrons already mostly occupied.

Once inside the library proper, I took a deep breath, drinking in the pyramid-shaped displays of staff picks laid out before me and the rows of stacks falling away to the depths of the building. Natural light flowed in from the floor-to-ceiling windows, and happy patrons basked in sunshine as they browsed.

Rafael opted to walk briskly upstairs but waited for me on the third floor when I hesitated getting on the next escalator.

"There's nothing to be nervous about," he said.

"Except for the fact that you never bothered to mention that there were still Asherah followers in existence. Are they like crazy sports fans but for goddesses? Do they have Asherah jerseys and wear face paint while sporting a rowdy cheer?" I widened my eyes theatrically. "Do we have team colors?"

Rafael bestowed an unimpressed stare upon me.

"Fandoms be crazy, man."

"They're not football hooligans."

"Here in the colonies we call it soccer." I stepped aside to let a mom with a sticky-faced toddler pass.

"Yes, well. We can get into the butchering of proper English in the New World some other day. I assure you," Rafael said, "these people are harmless. However, a site of worship, even with the assumption that it refers to Asherah, could be anywhere at all, and we will make little progress without pursing each lead."

"Bamahs are also known as high places. And this one is closed."

"Very good, Ashira. Your basic research skills are in top form. Is it a penthouse? How about a grove on a hill that's closed to the public because it's on private property? Your hypothesis about Chariot seeking the scrolls at the grove in the Sinai Peninsula has merit, but we are still dealing with far too many variables. Thus, this quick meeting with the Gigis. They may have insights as to whether any single place holds more importance these days."

"Gigis?"

"G.G. An acronym for Goddess Groupies."

"Riiiiight. But my sports fan analogy was totally out of line." I nudged him toward the next escalator. "Let's get this over with."

Our meeting spot was on the sixth floor at a set of metal stacks that were all pressed up against each other. In order to access any individual row of books, a patron had to press a button that allowed two stacks to separate.

Rafael double-checked call numbers on the sides of the stacks against his phone. "Here we go."

I hit the button and the rows parted. "As Moses with the Red Sea," I intoned in a deep voice, "so Ashira with the library shelf."

Rafael gave a long-suffering sigh and stepped between the bookcases.

I quickly followed, barely glimpsing some very dry titles before the library vanished. Were we transported?

Hot, sharp sunlight beat down on my head. Tier after tier of windowless stone arches soared high above me, the space rung with stone bleachers, but all was empty save for a small knot of people on the lowest level, all wearing some variation of Mad Max post-apocalyptic chic.

Dust covered my motorcycle boots with each step on the cracked, baked earth as I stalked over to the group.

Rafael hurried behind me.

"Hail and greetings, followers of Asherah." I snapped off a sassy salute. "Which of you is the Houdini?" Whoever it was hadn't bothered with the gritty taste of dirt at the back of my

47

throat to provide a full illusory experience. It was all sun and heat with no substance.

"Illusionist," a paunchy man said, with a haughty tilt of his chin. His bare belly hung over his leather pants.

"Kudos," I said. "This is a solid B."

He rose off his stone bench in a huff. If he didn't like the criticism, he shouldn't have pulled this stunt on us when we'd showed up to a meeting in good faith. "I beg your pardon?"

I pointed to the top of the stone amphitheater. "That upper level is kind of blurry, wouldn't you say? And those clouds look like they're about to break into a Disney song. Kills the whole gladiatorial menace you were so clearly trying to achieve." Levi had ruined me for perfectly adequate illusions, damn him.

"Like you could do better." He fingered one of the pale round plugs stretching out his ear lobes.

"Of course not. I'm not an Illoooosionist."

Rafael stepped forward. "What is the meaning of this?" he said with calculated menace.

A middle-aged woman in a studded bra sat on a stone throne with one leg thrown over the arm like a self-styled emperor. "You requested our help with information. We need help as well."

Some guy with a burnished gold tan, blonde locks that tumbled to his shoulders, and a six-pack that was more defined than armor rose like an Adonis and loped over to the low wall.

Now, that was how you wore leather pants with no shirt—strutting your lean frame like you were a rock god coming off stage to the deafening screams of a packed stadium. I swallowed.

He leaned over, beckoning me closer. Wow. Three more ab ridges had appeared. "Hi there. I'm Gabriel." His voice was rich wine spiked with cloves that warmed all sorts of interesting parts of me.

"Hi, yourself. I'm Ashira."

Gabriel quirked an eyebrow. "Like our goddess. Isn't that a wonderful coincidence? It's almost like this was fated."

Pretty *and* capable of three-syllable words. "Almost exactly."

He gestured at Rafael. "Your boyfriend says you have powerful magic capable of great destruction."

"Not my boyfriend." My brain caught up to the actual important part of that statement and my dreamy tone hardened. "He said that, did he?"

Rafael flushed. "They asked," he said in a low voice. "It sounded intimidating and is technically true."

"Call me Destructo," I said louder to Gabriel.

"Perfect." He unleashed a lopsided smile that made me think of rumpled sheets.

I fanned out my shirt. "Uh, why is that perfect?"

"Pull it together," Rafael hissed.

I stopped blinking dazedly at Gabriel and put on my best badass face.

Empress Studded Boobs made a sound that was halfway between a growl and a snort. "Get on with it, Gabriel."

He sent her a sweet smile that would have sent angels into a tizzy. "I'm doing it, Eileen."

"My name is Lux." She scraped her electric purple hair back, revealing shaved sides.

"What is it you require of us?" Rafael said.

"Despite our prayers, Asherah has not been seen for centuries," Gabriel said. "As our faith was insufficient, we hoped to bring her to us with an offering of our devotion." He swung his hands like he was opening a curtain and a thunderous roar rocked the stadium.

It punched into my solar plexus, hitting that deep primal part that urged me to simultaneously flee and curl into a ball, not drawing any attention to myself.

Most of the Gigis cowered, except for Lux, who merely winced, and Gabriel, who leaned forward, his eyes gleaming.

Every hair on my body standing on end, I spun slowly, and jumped. "Fuck balls! What's that?"

Ten feet tall, with curving horns and the face of a goat, the creature had red-flecked eyes that were vertically slitted. Were Miles standing next to its powerful human body, you'd tell the Head of House Security to stop embarrassing himself and hit up a gym.

The creature beat his meaty fists against a barrier that shimmered and rippled in the hot air, and the Houdini cowered.

My shoulders slumped. There went my hopes that this was an illusion.

"Meet Ba'al," Gabriel said. "God of fertility and storms, and coincidentally, also Asherah's true love." He placed a hand over his heart. "Know that in your death, you give him strength to call our goddess back." He flicked his fingers and the barrier disappeared.

Ba'al howled and charged us with the fury of a prisoner loosed upon his captors. Spittle flew from his mouth in his rage.

So much for mostly harmless.

Chapter 6

Ba'al's horns burst into flames, white-blue to orange-red and back again in an infinite undulation. His eyes glittered with malice and claws sprang from his fingers, the ground rumbling with each one of his steps.

Shoving Rafael sideways, I locked my blood armor into place and ran at the creature with a guttural cry. A blood red curved pike appeared in my hands, its satisfying weight bearing enough heft to do major damage. Sunlight glinted off its deadly sharp edge.

I stuck to a few tried and true weapons, low budget avenger that I was. Plus, my weapon deployment skills were pretty basic so no point getting fancy with some broadsword and losing my hand.

Raising the pike high, I swung downward into his neck, blood arcing out to spray me. Its hot tang failed to overpower the stench of wet clay that made me want to sneeze. None-too-gently, I ripped the pike out for my second swing, craving the sweet victory of this monstrosity's head at my feet. I'd have to neutralize its magic first in case it had regenerative powers. I wasn't taking anything off the table.

Ba'al lunged and grabbed me by the throat, but his claws

couldn't penetrate my armor. He ripped away the pike and slammed me onto the ground. Fire spat off his horns to crackle along my shield before dying out.

An eerie cackle burst out of me. He'd have to do better than that.

The shadow of Ba'al's enormous foot fell over my face, but I caught it an inch away from impact, flipping him up and onto his back.

Jumping to my feet, I called up two darts that I fired into his eyes. One hit its mark, the other he crushed in his fist, dropping the twisted weapon in the dust.

He snorted, his nostrils flaring, and his head hanging at an odd angle, courtesy of my earlier maneuver. That's right. Bring all that lovely blood closer for me to mainline into.

If this was a god, I'd eat my leather jacket. The scroll pieces of the *Sefer* that were merely made by an angel sent me into an uncontrollable longing. Put the actual angel feather in front of me and I'd slit my throat for a taste. I knew god magic. Or divine whatever-it-was. This upstart was nothing like that. Strong, sure, but barely a blip on the drive-me-into-terrible-longing radar. I could take it or leave it.

Rafael yelped, struggling against thick green vines that sprung from the ground to wind around his legs.

Paunchy dude sneered at me. Oh, I was so coming for him when this was over.

Ba'al sniffed the air. Extinguishing his flames, he bent his head, horns thrust forward, and changed course for the easy prey.

I raced after him, but he was faster than me.

The vines now waist-high, Rafael stared wide-eyed at the creature stampeding towards him.

Ba'al rammed into him, impaling my Attendant's shoulder on his horn.

Rafael screamed, bone spearing through his shoulder.

"Noooo!" My lungs couldn't inflate; my head spun. Rafael

fussed about silly things like British English being the only English, berated me for microwaving water for tea, and would need an exorcism to sever tweed's demonic hold on him. But I kept thinking about that time he'd listened to me talk about Adam, took my laptop away from me to help, and how he'd brought me a cup of tea, made the right way, when I couldn't find words to encapsulate my grief.

He'd probably been about to apologize for the mess his death would make, damn him.

Not today.

Ignoring the stitch in my side and the searing pain flaring through my injured thigh, I leapt onto Ba'al's back, my armor disappearing as I plunged one hand into the gaping wound on his neck. His flesh sucked my fist in deeper.

I gagged because yikes, that was new levels of disgusting, but still hooked my magic inside of him. Ba'al's magic didn't just feel wrong on a primal level, it was made up of so many different types that the overall taste was like swamp water that had been pissed in by a monster with a pus-spewing STI.

I spat several times to clear the taste, tightened my legs around his waist, and amped up my magic push, shaking with the strain. His magic was a mess, everything globbed together in a hardened gluey clump, underscored with a mindless pulsing hunger.

Ba'al jerked back, tearing his horn free from Rafael's body.

Rafael screamed again, his eyes unfocused as the vines disappeared and he fell to the dust.

The false god raked his claws against my right forearm, which was clamped onto his bicep for balance, managing to elbow me hard in the boob. I flinched. Note to self: upgrade bra from all-day hold to Defender of the Realms.

The flesh on my arm turned black, burning with an acidic fire, and a demented cry tore from my throat. I wrested magic out of Ba'al in a thick smudgy stream and slammed it into an explosion of red forked branches.

The abomination bellowed.

I rested my head against his sweaty neck and bloomed the shit out of the white clusters.

Ba'al shuddered. His body flickered once, twice, and he imploded, sending me sprawling onto my ass. All that was left of him was a foot-long crude clay sculpture in his image laying on its side in the dust.

Those fuckers had used some kind of golem base.

"Rafael." I cradled his head in my lap, one hand on the shallow rise and fall of his chest. Ba'al had ripped his shoulder open and Rafael's arm and shoulder muscles glistened, a broken shard of bone protruding. "Get help!"

The Goddess Groupies stood in the bleachers frozen, wearing identical expressions of stupefaction.

Lux fell to her knees. "O Great Jezebel. Forgive us for not recognizing you." She prostrated herself low. Like a row of dominoes, the rest of them followed suit, murmuring their apologies.

I lobbed the clay figure at them. Really? That was what they were sorry for? Not recognizing me? How about conjuring that thing up in first place? Or, I don't know, offering to have a lunch date with us and failing to mention that we were the main course?

"Good heavens." Rafael wheezed, his voice barely a whisper. "Now you'll be completely impossible."

"Save him!" I snarled in a loud voice, checking my friend for any invasive magic. "Or I will rain hell upon you all." There was a tiny spark of the weird magic deep in his shoulder which I snuffed out, but the remaining physical damage was serious enough.

The group broke into a panicked chatter. There wasn't a healer among the useless bunch, but there was a Transporter. Called it.

We landed at House HQ, where there was both an excellent medic and a healer on staff. I'd already cleared Ba'al's magic from my arm, and while no longer black, it throbbed like a bitch.

The Gigis stood in a ring, while I sat on the cold concrete on the sidewalk, refusing to let go of Rafael.

"Miles Berenbaum," I ordered. "Get him."

Two of them half-bobbed a bow and ran like the hounds of hell were on their trail inside the building. There might be some perks to this admiration shit. Had I finally found the house elves I'd been seeking? Did they do laundry?

Lux hovered anxiously over me until I barked at her to back the fuck up, while Gabriel mooned adoringly. He was hella pretty, but I preferred men who weren't total fucking idiots. Paunchy Guy had made himself scarce when we'd left the amphitheater.

Miles stormed out of the building with Arkady sauntering behind him. The Head of House Security glanced at Rafael and me and then raked a slower, more menacing gaze over the others, who did their best not to make eye contact. All except Gabriel, who I was beginning to think either had no self-preservation instincts or a very healthy ego that basically amounted to the same thing.

"Anything I should arrest them for?" Miles said.

"Reckless endangerment, attempted murder—give me time and I'll put together an impressive rap sheet," I said.

Rafael clutched my arm. "No. We can't draw attention to this. Just heal me."

Miles and I shared a rare look of perfect agreement that we disagreed, but neither of us would override Rafael's wishes.

"If anything happens to you, I am totally rescinding that kindness we're showing them. Miles, you need this." I snapped my fingers. "Golem."

A rangy black woman in a leather catsuit with holes strategically cut out of the sides clutched the clay figure tighter.

"Now," I growled.

Arkady took the sculpture away from her. "Golems," he

said in a breathy voice the way Marilyn Monroe said "diamonds." "Aww. You couldn't stay mad at me, pickle."

Looking very put out that he couldn't haul anyone in, Miles hoisted Rafael in a fireman's carry and walked away.

Arkady extended a hand to me.

Gabriel muscled in front of him. "Allow me," he said, pulling me to my feet. He yanked me up so hard, I practically tripped.

"First rule of Jezebel worship. Hands off the Jezebel."

Arkady's eyebrows shot into his hairline. "They know?"

"Asherah's followers. They know." He fell into step beside me, crowding out Gabriel, who clearly wanted that position of honor. "This doesn't make everything okay between us," I said.

"Yeah? Wanna fight?"

I tried to make a fist with my numb arm but nothing happened. "I shall spare you for now." I dropped my voice and turned to Arkady. "Is Rafael going to be okay?"

"He'll be in good hands." Arkady glanced over his shoulder at our entourage and shook his head. "This is going to be one hell of a debrief."

By the time we got upstairs, the doctor and the healer had whisked Rafael away into some other part of the infirmary.

Healer magic wasn't a shortcut to an MD. Nightingales stimulated the body's natural healing system in an accelerated way. Fracture a rib? Go see a healer. Same with an infection, unless you were anti-Nefesh, then it was a doctor's visit and regular antibiotics for you. With an injury requiring a lot of outside intervention and precision like my shattered femur, a medical specialist got involved. Technically a Nightingale could set a broken nose, but unless they were a level four or five (uncommon), chances were they'd set it improperly and you'd need a surgeon to rebreak it and patch you up anyway.

Levi kept both on staff and each of them examined Rafael now.

Meantime, a nurse pumped me full of antibiotics and stitched the gash closed.

My Attendant was still being worked on by the time I was done. I asked Miles and Arkady to leave after giving them the basics.

Miles grunted, still mourning his missed opportunity to menace the Gigis, and left without further comment.

"He's going to be a joy the rest of today," Arkady bitched, shaking the inert golem at me.

"You're welcome."

If the Gigis weren't going to face charges for what they'd done, they better prove useful.

Waiting to be updated on Rafael's condition was torture. I chose to pass the time tearing a strip off Lux and Gabriel, the lone two Gigis refusing to leave my side. The three of us sat in a small waiting area, furnished with much more comfortable chairs than I'd ever found in any hospital.

"What the fuck were you thinking?" I said.

"Lux—" Gabriel said.

"We wanted to see Asherah," Lux interrupted. "No amount of devotion over the years had been enough to summon her. We believed that if our faith wasn't enough, that gifting her with her lover's presence would be."

"Except that wasn't her lover. It was a golem that you infused with a fuckton of different magic. You think she wouldn't know the difference? Even I could tell that wasn't a god."

"It wasn't at full strength yet," Lux said. "The ritual wasn't completed. Our Ba'al would have achieved godhood."

I massaged my temples. Multiple magics in an animated artifact that could be fed to gain strength. These dipshits were almost as bad as Chariot and their immortality quest.

"It was extremely complex and all the various parts had to be timed to the second. It was very cleverly done." Gabriel turned bright eyes on me.

"Did you want a pat on the head and a cookie?" I said. "Had Ba'al achieved full power, you never could have contained him. The devastation would have been catastrophic."

"He couldn't have broken loose," Gabriel said. "I have level-four Lockdown Magic." Yeah, okay, Tupperware Boy. He tossed his hair. "But honestly, after this, I feel that I should be upgraded."

I folded my hands tightly in my lap so I didn't smack him. "Did you feed anyone else to him?"

Lux bit her lip. "You were our first."

"I leave you alone for one day." Levi stood in the doorway, his arms crossed.

"Who are you?" Gabriel said, rising.

I covered my mouth with my hand to hide my smirk at Levi's gobsmacked expression.

"Levi Montefiore," he said, managing to look down his nose at Gabriel, even though they were roughly the same height. "Head of House Pacifica."

Gabriel shrugged. "Oh. Him."

I coughed, choking on my laughter.

Levi pointed at the door. "Out or I'll have you arrested for attempted murder. And put on a shirt."

Gabriel slapped his six-pack that didn't jiggle one iota. "I'm good."

Lux grabbed his elbow. "We're going."

"One second." I held up a hand. "A closed bamah. Do you know where it might be?"

Lux and Gabriel shook their heads.

I ran a weary hand over my face. Rafael was badly hurt, I was exhausted, and it had all been for nothing.

"The Divine Rod might," Lux said.

I raised my head. "A divining rod?"

"Of sorts. Go to Just Dandy tonight at ten and see for yourself," Lux said.

The name sounded familiar. A gay club? Huh.

"Is there anything else we can assist you with, Jezebel?" she asked.

"Oh brother," Levi muttered.

"You may leave, but should you attempt anything like this again, you'll feel my wrath." I took Lux's phone number and Gabriel handed his over without any prompting or my wanting it in the first place. "If I have need of you in the future, I'll call. Pray that Rafael recovers."

Lux bobbed her head at me and fled. Gabriel took my hand and kissed it. "I look forward to seeing you again."

An untamed light flashed through Levi's blue eyes.

I beamed up at Gabriel and resisted the urge to wipe off my hand. "As do I."

He backed out of the infirmary like a thespian reluctantly exiting his encore.

"Delightful people," I said, once they were gone.

"Evidently," Levi said. "All my best friends create false gods that land me in the infirmary."

"Speaking of which." I stood up. "I should check on Rafael."

"Sit down, Ashira." Levi dropped into a chair and unfurled a cold smile. "We have a few items to discuss first."

I did as requested, crossing one leg over the other and swinging my foot like I didn't have a care in the world. "Sure. How was the rally? Did your speech go over well?"

"My speeches always go over well. What I wanted to discuss was your involving a bunch of radical wingnuts in this search my mother set you on."

"Technically, you have Rafael to thank for that. And to be fair, we did get a potential lead."

"It was bad enough when you were playing fast and loose with my mom's well-being," he said. "But to add this level of risk? For what? Your little fan club?"

I pressed my finger to my cheek, my head tilted. "I'm

confused. So revenge is now fine, it's my ego that's the problem?"

Levi hooked a foot around my chair and dragged it sharply toward him. "All of it is the problem."

"Explain to me in great detail how I've further endangered Nicola. Unless you've told anyone, no one knows she hired me except the two of us, Priya, and Rafael." I leaned forward, my elbows braced on my thighs, with a bone-deep sorrow that Levi was no longer the man I'd believed him to be. "Who are you really mad at? Me for pursuing every lead when it comes to Chariot, as I've always said I would, or you, because when push came to shove and you found out your father was involved, your renowned sense of responsibility failed you and you went back to being that scared little kid cowering before him?"

The walls broke into jagged shards, crashing and shattering on the ground. I curled into a ball, shrieking as chunks of the ceiling fell in on us. I tasted plaster, stray fragments grazing my legs like bullets. Lightbulbs exploded overhead like gunfire.

Levi sat immobile, carved from ice, his eyes flat. He closed his eyes and unclenched his fists.

Silence fell. The room was intact and undamaged.

I watched him warily, my heart racing, waiting for his self-control to fail and his magic to upend reality once more.

He glanced down at his hands, now faintly shaking, and jammed them in his pockets. "You've been many things, Ash, but you were never cruel."

"Cruel or honest?" I said, softly.

I'd gotten a lot of glimpses over the years into who Levi was. Smart, fiercely protective, kind, funny. This side of him was honestly disconcerting. I hadn't said what I did to hurt him. I longed for the man I knew Levi to be to come back and not be this shadow of himself so scared of every step that needed to be taken.

Levi stood up. "I don't know if I can be a part of this anymore."

An icy numbness stole through me. I'd accepted the loss of Levi as my romantic partner, but I'd never imagined he'd walk away from having my back. I opened my mouth to say that I couldn't do this without him, but looking at his face, he didn't care. He was so locked inside his own head and his own fear that nothing was going to get through to him.

"Are you taking House resources away? You'll cripple me in this fight." I stilled. "But you already know that, don't you?"

"I need time to think," he finally said, and left.

Two months ago, Levi had broken my heart, but I'd been the one to walk away. Being the one left behind was worse.

"Today has been bollocks and it's not even teatime." Rafael lounged in the doorway from the inner hallway of the infirmary. His shirt and tweed jacket had been replaced by a baggy House Pacifica sweatshirt. Rafael in gray jersey material—was the apocalypse nigh?

I jumped up and threw my arms around him, careful of his injury. "How do you feel?"

"Like a god shoulder-fucked me." His eyes grew wide. "Whoopsie daisy. That's the pain medication talking, I believe."

"It was only a wannabe god and more of a finger bang, but I'm glad you're on good drugs."

The Nightingale came out and assured me that Rafael would be fine. The wound had been cleaned and sealed, there was no trace of infection, and he could sleep off the lingering effects of the drugs.

I said I'd take him home with me. Miles had sent an operative to pick up Moriarty and it was parked in the underground garage here at the House. Apparently I owed the operative a bottle of wine for the stress of dealing with my devil of a car.

As we slowly made our way downstairs, Rafael demanded to know what Ba'al had been. My explanation about the golem and the ritual sent him into a paroxysm of giggles. "Gabriel is a wanker," he said.

"They're all a bunch of gits," I said.

Rafael beamed at me. "Why, Ashira, I'll make a proper Brit of you yet."

"Sure, dude."

He looped his arm through mine. "Is Levi really going to abandon us?"

I shrugged, helping him remain steady as we crossed the parking garage. "If he does, you'll get me all to yourself again, and won't that be a delight?"

He made a snarky face. "On a scale of income tax audit to prison shower?"

"Jerk," I said, fondly. "I'm sure Priya will stick with us at least part-time."

"That's good. I like her. Cracking girl." He poked my hair, a little woozy about the eyes still. "Too bad about the Montefiore chap, though."

Wasn't it just? There was a hot, restless buzz behind my ribcage. From the familiar rush of antagonism to the comforting purr from being the object of his desire, Levi had occupied a large part of my world for half of my life. Space was an airless vacuum that would kill you, but Levi's absence was worse, because I was still breathing.

Chapter 7

While Rafael rested in the car, I hurried back upstairs to the sixth-floor security hub and retrieved my dog, telling Priya not to be alarmed if she found a loopy man dozing in our living room.

She kept typing in her small cubicle as she fired questions at me. "Is he cute? Will the circumstances of his being there disturb me? Does this have anything to do with why you and Rafael ended up in the infirmary?"

"Yes, yes, and yes. I'm bringing Rafael to recuperate at our place."

She paused typing for a fraction of a second. "Okay."

Good save, cracking girl, but not good enough to fool me. Still, I decided to be merciful. Priya had been through a lot lately and the least I could do was not give her crap about this. "I have a quick errand and should be home before you are, but I wanted to give you a heads-up."

I installed Rafael on my sofa with tea, a cozy blanket, and the Wi-Fi password, then Mrs. Hudson and I went to see the Queen.

The gold token took us to a majestic lawn bearing tables strung with fairy lights and strewn with mostly-empty platters, save for a couple of lonely-looking wilted cucumber sandwiches. I inhaled the crisp night air, weaving around statues that rose up in purple shadows around me. Another scenic jaunt to the Garden of People.

Moran and Her Majesty stood between two large shrubs covered in a riot of purple and red flowers that smelled of honeysuckle and orange, inspecting a statue of an old man with a giant mole on his cheek, giving them the finger.

"Action pose," I said, coming up from behind them. "Nice. Is he a recent addition?"

"Yes," Moran said. "You missed the unveiling."

"I'm good, thanks." Having almost been an unveiling myself, I had no need to experience what I'd so narrowly avoided.

Mrs. Hudson flattened her ears and growled at Moran.

"Not now, Mrs. H," I said.

"Ashira," the Queen said. "To what do we owe the pleasure?"

"Updates."

The Queen gave the old man one last scathing look. "I could use a drink," she said. "Come."

Moran pointed at the pug. "Leave her."

Making a snarky face, I bent down and unclipped her leash. Mrs. H wouldn't run far, but I wasn't sure I trusted Mr. Insta-Blade to hold onto her. Plus, she still hadn't pooped today and could very well go down in history as the first dog to leave the Queen of Hearts a present.

The Queen led me up to her flagstone terrace where two glasses of sangria awaited us on a small bistro table. She lowered herself gracefully onto one of the rattan chairs, smoothing out any wrinkles in her red slacks with one hand.

The drink was perfectly chilled and not clogged up with too much fruit that would hit my nose every time I took a sip.

Below us on the lawn, the puppy growled again at Moran, ready to leap. He growled back and lunged at her with the sword. The dog went nuts, barking and jumping in rapturous delight, all while Moran taunted her that she'd never catch him. I knew it was a game and they were clearly having fun, but it still took some effort not to white-knuckle my chair.

The Queen sipped her drink as I filled her in on Deepa and the closed bamah, leaving out Nicola's role. "Anand was in the money lending business. Is it possible she had dealings here in Hedon even though she was Mundane?"

The Queen pushed her dark red hair off her shoulders and topped up my glass. "I've not heard of this woman, but my people will look into it."

"Thank you."

Mrs. Hudson ran back and forth at Moran. He swung a little too close above her head and I jumped out of my seat.

"Watch it!" I cried. "You almost decapitated her."

"I was nowhere near," he scoffed. "Stop being such a helicopter parent."

Mrs. Hudson barked, annoyed at me for interrupting their game.

The Queen swirled the liquid around in her glass. "I did not think it would be this difficult to unearth the Ten."

"Me neither."

"I'm going to get you," Moran threatened, brandishing his sword. Mrs. Hudson ran between his legs, her tail wagging.

I brought the dog to visit whenever I could in order to gentle Moran's disposition towards me, but if he shish-kebabbed my puppy, I'd flambé him. I sipped the very fine sangria and tried not to wince every time that damn sword got too close to her.

"Thank Levi for the heads-up," the Queen said.

Thank him yourself was probably not the correct response. And since when was she on a first-name basis with him? "For what?"

Moran shot a tiny lightning bolt into the ground and made Mrs. Hudson jump. I flinched, but she loved it, jumping to the spot where the spark had been. He shot another one and she tried to pounce on it as well. Great. My dog was part cat.

I jabbed two fingers from my eyes to Moran's.

"He always did like dogs," the Queen said with a fond look at her henchman. "But back to the matter at hand. Levi provided intel that allowed me to stop a planned assault on Hedon by the Mafia Romaneasca through the fixed door in Bucharest. It has been sealed up and the culprits dealt with."

"That man in the garden wasn't Romanian, by any chance, was he?"

She smiled at me as if I were a small but clever child. "I suspect Chariot was using this mafia group to stage a coup of Hedon. Whether or not they know that I am looking into them remains to be seen, but it is a reasonable assumption that I would not have stood idly by when they used my name in their kidnappings."

I fished an apple slice out of my drink and munched on it. "Levi's got a bee in his bonnet about finding a Bookworm."

Her Majesty regarded me over the rim of her glass. "I heard."

"My Attendant said they're pretty rare, but there's still a chance that one is around." I stirred my drink thoughtfully, debating what fruit to go for next. "The electronic trail isn't yielding answers for us anymore and we suspect the evidence we need is on paper. Do you know of a Nefesh like this or have any leads I could follow? The sooner I find this Bookworm, the sooner I can get back to the bamah problem."

The scent of her chili and cinnamon magic rose hot and fast, like I'd just chugged the sangria. I almost winced.

"Sorry, chica," the Queen said, her expression guileless. "But I know of nothing that would help."

I could have sworn she'd just lied to me.

"Ah well. No harm asking. It's a long shot anyway." Since I had the dog with me and a doped-up Rafael back at my house, I couldn't use the gold token to do any further digging in Hedon. I'd come back. For now, I kept my tone scrupulously polite, got my hyped-up puppy away from Moran, and blipped out.

Rafael was neatly wrapping one of Priya's connector cables when we got back. Priya had given me two tutorials and a test before I'd been allowed to handle them when tidying up, and for a moment I feared for Rafael's life, but his technique was perfect. He placed the cable next to the neat pile of power cords that he'd already wrapped.

Mrs. Hudson jumped onto the sofa next to him.

"Feeling better?" I said.

He rolled his shoulder out. "This is, but I've got a bloody awful headache."

I sank into a chair and eased off my boots, massaging my feet. "As much as I wish I could bring you tantalizing new information to prove your pain was worth it, that's still in the works. The Gigis didn't have a lot of ideas, but they're sending me to go find a divining rod tonight. Chariot doesn't worship Asherah, but they do worship the *Sefer* and its promise of immortality. What if the bamah Isaac is seeking is the original spot where the *Sefer* fell to earth?"

"Anything is possible." Rafael folded the blanket he'd been using. "These are good speculations but until we narrow down which site we're looking for, speculations they remain." He looked down at his House sweatshirt. "If I'm to accompany you on this social outing this evening, I should go home and change."

"Do I ever get to visit your place?"

He made a face. "Is that strictly necessary?"

"Yes. It's what friends do."

"When's the last time you invited a friend over to socialize?"

"I invited Arkady over," I said.

"Not in the past two months you haven't." Nice avoidance

67

of my friends comment. Rafael gave me a hangdog look. "I don't suppose I can get out of going?"

"You could, but the cracking girl would be so disappointed."

Rafael shoved the blanket at me. "What will it take for you to never mention that again?"

"I'll think on it." I was totally using it on every possible occasion.

~

WE MET at Just Dandy at 9PM. Priya had kept up a steady stream of chatter in our Uber to force Arkady and me to participate in the same conversation. Once we got inside the club, she declared herself in desperate need of a drink and abandoned us for the bar.

I didn't generally do nightclubs. With my leg, I'd never been able to dance, and there was something pathetic about sitting and watching everyone else have fun all night. It's part of why I'd gravitated toward dive bars.

"Why, pickle," Arkady said. "Look at you, all in the know."

"Because I brought us to a gay club?" Hmm. For a place that generally hosted theme nights like Bottoms Up and Head Hunters, there were a lot of women here tonight. It wasn't a huge club, but the dance floor was pretty spacious—and packed. The mostly female clientele grooved to an up-tempo song with a pulsing bass under swirling disco balls and twinkling lights. Others were crowded in at the bar that ran along one side or stood chatting in small groups by the stage framed with red velvet curtains. "Has this changed management or something? Is it no longer the purview of the penilely-inclined?"

A stunning redhead who was poured into a vintage dress with a sweetheart neckline raised her glass in cheers as she walked past. I blushed and fiddled with the deep V-neck of the black jumpsuit that Pri had made me borrow, once she'd stopped giving me shit for turning our social outing into a work night. Leather pants and rock-and-roll, those were my jam. I was out of my element in this cool, beautiful crowd, especially next to Arkady in black jeans and a button-up shirt showcasing the tattoos on his arms. His dark, chin-length hair floated free, and eyeliner rung his brown eyes.

No matter. Think of it as an undercover assignment.

"It is, indeed, usually dude friendly." Arkady waved at Rafael, who had secured a table by the dance floor. "But tonight is Paralypstick." He huffed a laugh. "Which you didn't know."

"And that means what?"

He smiled mysteriously. "Fabulousness." He strolled confidently through the crowd greeting some of the other clubgoers. "Rafael, my man. How's the shoulder?"

They knuckle bumped, Rafael looking adorably out of place.

I claimed a seat by tossing my blazer over the back.

Arkady eyed the fizzy gold drink on the table. "What's with the ginger ale? Are you a teetotaler?"

"I can't shake this headache," Rafael said. "They healed me quite thoroughly earlier, so I don't know why I'm affected like this."

"Oh no." Priya slid onto a high stool between me and Rafael, her beer sloshing over the top of the pint glass. She tugged down her gray leather mini skirt, one of the straps of her teal tank top that were tied in tiny bows coming undone.

Rafael's eyes darted to her shoulder.

"I hope you're not coming down with something," she said, tying the fabric tight.

"Me too," I said. "But what a *cracking* good sport of you to come out." I motioned over one of the servers, a very buff guy in gold lamé briefs and a turquoise feather boa, and ordered my usual Jack Daniels, while Rafael shot me the look of death.

The server checked Arkady out, but he didn't bite, politely ordering a gin and tonic.

"Should we have gotten one of those video baby monitors for Mrs. H?" I asked Priya. Tonight was the first time the puppy was being left alone.

"She'll be fine."

"You say that, but you're the one who leaves her shoes laying around. If she gets anxious and pees, I won't be the one in for a nasty surprise."

"We walked, fed, and massively cuddled her before we left. Relax." Priya proceeded to monopolize Rafael, asking to hear all about the Ba'al encounter, since I'd been too light on details for her satisfaction.

I didn't yet have a beverage to occupy myself with and Priya had already kicked me three times under the table, which meant speak to Arkady or face the No-Fly List. "So. How are things with Miles?"

"I don't kiss and tell. Unless you're my friend. Which you aren't."

"Buy you a drink?" A skinny guy with a Van Dyke beard and some hipster band shirt appeared at my shoulder. He wasn't speaking to Arkady.

I gave him a flat stare. "We're in a gay bar."

"It's Paralypstick. Lesbian theme night," he added.

Thanks. I'd figured that out. "Which helps you how?"

"Sampling Sapphic delights, pickle," Arkady said. "The Holy Grail of Het Boy Fantasies." He shooed the guy away. "Run along. She's straight."

The man waggled his head from side to side, like he was considering this consolation prize.

"Seriously? Fuck off," I said.

The server arrived with our drinks and the man departed.

Arkady insisted on paying for both our beverages, tipping generously.

He held out his glass. "To new unsuspicious starts?"

"To a truce for tonight."

He shrugged and we clinked drinks.

"So? You and Miles?" I said.

Arkady crossed his fingers. "Don't want to jinx it. And you? You weren't interested in that fine example of manhood?"

"Hardly."

"Your brush-off game is strong, pickle. What techniques do you employ for picking people up?"

I took a sip, enjoying the cool burst of alcohol down my throat. "I antagonize them for fifteen years and then kiss them."

"What a disappointingly small pool of candidates. Let's pretend you hooked up like normal people. You get a text asking for a booty call. Then what?"

I stoically sipped my JD.

Arkady pointed his swizzle stick at me. "Play along," he said. "I always thought it would be fun to be one of those sociologists who study sexual relations."

"Then nothing. It's never as simple as just sex. One way or another I'll have to work for my orgasm. My vibrator doesn't expect that level of effort."

"Foreplay is effort?"

"With some men? You have no idea."

"Trust me." He sighed. "I do." We clinked glasses again.

"Also, I'd have to get up and get dressed," I said.

"Easy. Tell him to come over."

I almost choked on my drink. "Don't do that. They might get ideas and want to stay the night."

"Would you stay the night at their place?"

"No. I have to feed my dog."

Arkady swirled the ice in his glass. "You only just got your dog."

"They don't know that. See? Now I have to keep track of lies, too. So much easier not to hook up. If I need a warm body in my bed, I'll cuddle the puppy." I pressed the cold glass against my forehead.

"You miss him, don't you?" Arkady tilted his head, understanding warming his eyes.

The lights dimmed and the dance remix of some annoying pop song cut out to wild cheers as a slender man of Indo-Canadian heritage in a royal purple suit swaggered out through the velvet curtains.

The top two buttons on the man's gold shirt were popped open, his rumpled bowtie slung around his neck like he was coming off a hell of a good night. A gleaming crown was perched atop his enormous pompadour.

Taking center stage, he planted one hand on his cocked hip, and slicked down his pencil mustache with a finger. "Welcome, my pretties, to Paralypstick!"

Divine Rod, I presume.

Chapter 8

Divine Rod had elevated flirting with the crowd to an art form. He winked, he preened, he threw out extremely sexually innuendo'd one-liners, all between singing pitch-perfect renditions of current pop songs and introducing the other drag kings on the bill tonight.

I'd been screaming as loud as everyone else in the joint when I caught sight of Rafael's pained wince. I leaned over. "Go home. I can talk to him myself."

Rafael shook his head. "I want to be there."

He grit his teeth, pain etched into every feature. Priya said something to him, probably telling him to leave from his small shake of his head. She bit her lip, staring hard at the table, before she said something else to him. He blinked at her, then slowly nodded, and turned his chair so that his back was to her.

Priya massaged his head in slow strokes.

Arkady raised his eyebrows at me and I shrugged. I'd had a couple months to become accustomed to Priya and Rafael's mutual interest. Also, the poor guy was suffering and Priya gave good head massages, having learned this technique with its Ayurvedic roots from her Indian grandmother.

Halfway through the show, I was on my feet cheering for Lucky Strike, a silver fox drag king who was performing the shit out of Tom Jones's "It's Not Unusual." Arkady nudged my hip and winked at me. I nudged him back with a grin, forgetting for a brief instant his suspected betrayal.

I wished I could roll back time to when Arkady and I were first friends and he'd won me over with his brash, no-filter teasing. That uncomplicated period when my relationship with Priya wasn't tested at every turn, Levi was just my nemesis, and I believed my father was alive.

I'd always thought of myself as kind of a lone wolf, but it had never weighed as heavily on me as it did tonight, surrounded by this crowd. How much more would being a Jezebel isolate me?

I reached for my drink, only to find it empty.

The show ended with two encores, the first one with all the drag kings together singing "Hanky Panky," which Arkady told me was from the old *Dick Tracy* movie, and then Divine Rod on stage alone closing out the night with "Save a Horse, Ride a Cowboy." He strutted and postured, reveling in a campy masculinity that put grins on everyone's faces and had us singing along for the chorus.

The hyped-up energy of the room after the show was redirected onto the dance floor. Arkady and Priya joined in with happy abandon, dirty dancing and laughing.

"Enjoy the massage?" I said.

Rafael shot me a suspicious look, his somewhat relaxed shoulders creeping back up along his ears.

"I'm not ragging on you. I'm just observing."

He weighed responses in his head. "It helped."

We gave Divine Rod twenty minutes to unwind, then approached the bouncer guarding the backstage door with our request to speak to the man himself. I flashed my private investigator license, adding this was about a case, not an autograph, and to say that Lux had sent us.

Five minutes later, we were escorted to a cramped room that smelled faintly of cologne and glue. There was a jumble of stage makeup on a rickety table, alongside a pitcher of ice water. Divine Rod sat slumped in a chair, still in costume, but minus the suit jacket, his legs extended carelessly in front of him, and his crown sitting askew on a styrofoam mannequin head.

"Thanks for seeing us," I said. "You're an incredible performer."

Rod inclined his head in thanks.

"I'm Ashira Cohen and this is Rafael Behar. Do you prefer Rod or Divine Rod?" I asked.

"Rod's good." His voice was scratchy. He cleared his throat a couple of times and then finished off his glass of water and set it on the table. "Lux told me to expect you. You have need of my magic?"

"Yeah." Even if we still weren't entirely sure what that entailed. "We're hoping you can help us find a closed place of worship, possibly connected to the goddess Asherah or the angel Raziel. Maybe somewhere high up like a hillside. We appreciate it could be anywhere, but can you narrow down the possibilities?"

Rod scratched his stubble. "If this was, say, a ring, I'd have you visualize the lost object and home in on it that way, but you don't know the item in question." He retrieved a slim black case from the bottom of a garment bag hanging on the back of the door. Inside was a forked branch, which resembled a large wishbone. A very familiar honey buttery scent rose off it. "Our chances of success are slim, but I'm game to try."

I leaned in and inhaled. "Is that almond wood?"

The drag king lifted up the dowsing rod. "Good nose. Yeah. Back in the Middle Ages, professional magicians preferred wands made from almond wood, and the Oracle of Delphi used almond wood dowsing rods to find hidden items of value."

"Fascinating," Rafael said with a pointed stare at me.

"Fix the idea of this closed bamah in your minds," Rod said. "Attach any relevant details, no matter how small. And make sure you don't touch me."

Rafael and I stepped back a safe distance. Eyes focused on the dowsing rod, I focused on Asherah, Jezebels, and the *Sefer Raziel HaMalakh*.

Rod gripped the tool by the forked ends, holding it arm's length away from his body, with the butt of the handles resting in the heels of his hands. He closed his eyes and the rod began to glow golden, quivering between Rafael and me.

A tingle ran up my spine and I concentrated even harder.

The device glowed brighter and brighter, Rod's arms shaking with the effort of holding it. He took a step toward me, then another. I held my breath, willing the answer out of him.

A spark cracked off the forked branch, making me jump.

Rod swore and dropped the wood, catching it before it hit the ground. He shook out his hands. "Sorry. Your criteria is too vague."

I swallowed my disappointment.

"You're sure you can't give me anything more? What exactly were you told?" Rod grabbed a cloth out of the case and polished the wood.

"Actually the person I got this from said 'chiuso,' not 'closed,' at first," I said. "But she translated it for me."

Rod looked up sharply. "Chiuso? That doesn't just mean closed."

"She's Italian," I said. "It should be correct."

He put the tool away and closed the case. "It is, but you can use in it other contexts, like 'enclosed.' Or how comunità chiusa means a 'gated community.'" He tapped his head. "Language major."

Rafael had gone pale and still.

"Problem?" I said.

"Thank you," he said to Rod, grabbing my elbow. "You've helped enormously."

"Happy to be of service." Rod waved off my offer of payment, which was good because Rafael already had me halfway out the door.

We stepped back into the club and I pulled free. "What's got you so freaked out?"

Rafael didn't stop moving so I had to jog after him. "I'm a fool. I was focused on the site. The place itself."

"You're not making any sense."

Some woman walked past, her hands full of drinks, and jostled Rafael.

"Can't talk here." Rafael motioned for me to follow him down a short hallway containing an old payphone missing its receiver and shouldered into the men's bathroom.

It was a triumph of 1980s decor with its floor of multicolored triangles and a red counter with a crackle pattern currently used by two men snorting coke.

"Out," Rafael said. He had that cold scary look he'd worn right before he'd shot Avi Chomsky, the assassin who'd murdered my father, in the foot.

The men turned, snapped their mouths shut, grabbed their drugs, and bolted.

I'd have run too, if I could. Rafael's eyes were haunted, and the air had swelled with an ominous weight.

"Bamahs were located everywhere," he said. "The worship sites weren't just high places, but valleys, buildings. What connected them was a platform. An altar, even as simple as a dirt mound, but devoted to religious worship. This 'gated bamah' is code for a powerful stone amulet, known as the Kiss of Death. It's reputed to have been created in the shadow of the Gate of Darkness, one of the Gates of the Temple Mount in Jerusalem, from the stone altar of the actual Old Testament Jezebel herself."

"Admittedly, names like the Gate of Darkness and Kiss of

77

Death don't conjure up kittens and rainbows, but how bad can it be?" I toyed with the wooden ring on my necklace.

"Our library is keyed to Asherah magic. Anyone who tries to transport in without it would instantly be fried. Same if they go through the front door or try to open the pillars."

"Okay."

"Previous Jezebels have been able to transport in and out without tripping any alarm alerting their Attendant to their presence, because our bond allowed us to know where they were. That Star of David tattoo compromised your magic. You can only get into the library with the assistance of my father's ring, so while you have safe passage thanks to the wards recognizing your Asherah-bestowed powers, I'm still alerted to your presence, as I would be with any intruder. I just don't find a corpse when I get there."

I dropped the wooden ring like I'd been burned. "You didn't think to mention the dead body potential before?"

Rafael straightened his bowtie. "Why panic you when you were settling into a new job?"

A woman opened the bathroom door.

"Use the ladies'," I said.

"There's a line-up," she said, with a moue of distaste.

I ripped the soap dispenser off the wall. "Well, this one is closed due to lack of sanitary facilities."

Her hand fluttered to her chest. "The line-up wasn't so bad." She backed out.

I propped the dispenser on the counter. It still worked fine. "Keep talking."

"The Kiss of Death was originally used to steal the very first scroll our side ever had." Rafael took off his glasses, rubbing the lenses on the hem of his shirt. He looked exhausted. "It gave the Chariot operative Asherah magic allowing them to safely bypass the wards."

"What?! They had this Kiss of Death in their possession?"

"Sadly, yes. The last time Chariot attempted to use it was a hundred years ago with Nikolia and her Attendant Vitalis. Our enemy closed in, there was a fight, and it was lost to both sides."

"If Chariot hasn't found the amulet in all this time, why the sudden hard-on for it now?" I said.

Rafael put his glasses back on and blinked against the harsh bathroom light. "This altar was where Jezebel communed with her goddess. Even a piece of it was a powerful relic infused with the goddess's presence. Using that as a base, a master Weaver created a binding that gave the user our magic when combined with a very specific catalyst. However, it needed to be replenished with each new wearer."

I waved the soap dispenser around. "Okay, while it's unnerving that a way into our library exists, I'm not sure why I should be more worried than usual. The catalyst's probably super rare, right?

"It is." Rafael leaned against the hand dryer.

"Out with it, buddy."

"It's the blood of a living Jezebel. If Isaac just renewed the search, it can only mean one thing." Rafael's face was haggard. "Chariot knows who you are."

The soap dispenser I was holding clattered to the floor.

Chapter 9

The revelation put a damper on our socializing. Rafael opted to go to the library to work on a way to block or locate the Kiss of Death, while I'd also put out feelers for the amulet.

Rafael's parting advice? Don't let Isaac catch me.

Solid battle strategy.

Our remaining trio rode home in silence, most of it spent behind a bus with another of those annoyingly upbeat golf tournament advertisements.

Arkady stopped me before we went into our respective apartments. "No matter what you believe, Ash, I have your back. You need a security detail or a personal bodyguard, I'm here."

"Thanks."

Priya slammed our front door and stomped into the kitchen, muttering loudly about all the bodily harm she'd inflict on Isaac if he so much as sneezed the wrong way at me. I leaned against the kitchen counter while she banged cupboard doors, accruing random items until she'd run out of steam. Amazingly, Mrs. Hudson slept through it all in my bedroom.

I picked up the peanut butter jar and package of ramen. "Starting a new food craze?"

Priya looked down at the jar of rainbow sprinkles she'd unearthed from a long-ago birthday cake-making spree and tossed her head. "Yes. Kawaii tan tan noodles."

"Mmmm. With chiba chicken bits?"

She shoved the sprinkles back in the cupboard. "Shut up. And don't die."

"Good plan. I'm also on board with keeping one hundred percent of my blood." I put the ramen away. "You should go stay with your parents. Get out of the disaster zone."

Isaac wouldn't go after Talia, because Chariot kept those of use and she helped him maintain his anti-Nefesh position.

"Do not even start with that nonsense again. We do not cut and run in this household." She grabbed the peanut butter and slammed it into the fridge.

"Okay, Adler."

"Quit comforting me. You're the one in Chariot's crosshairs."

"Is there a second draft of that pep talk?" I kissed her cheek. "I'd hoped to stay under the radar for longer, but it is what it is. I'm going to bed."

I changed into a sleep T-shirt and crawled under my covers, my body curled in on itself. It was one thing to operate in the shadows, but the safety of darkness had been eliminated. I pulled the covers tighter around me, wishing I had someone to hold me, just for tonight.

I grabbed my phone off the bedside table, tempted to hit speed dial, then ruthlessly shoved it under my pillow. This complication changed nothing. Isaac Montefiore may have painted a target on my back, but did he know I'd done the same?

Nothing would ever compensate for my dad's murder, but destroying all of Isaac's dreams would satisfy my revenge fantasies for a bit. I pounded my pillow into the precise fluffiness necessary for sleep. And it was even in my job description as justice.

With that thought, I fell asleep, a smile on my lips and visions of fiery vengeance dancing in my head.

~

PRIYA HAD good news for me when I woke up on Saturday morning, served with much-needed coffee. About ten years ago, Deepa Anand's company had expanded significantly, during which she'd upgraded all her cybersecurity. The company she'd used had proved to be a shell, but Priya had followed the trail all the way back to Lockdown Cybersecurity, belonging to one Isaac Montefiore.

It was more evidence that Deepa was part of Chariot, though not conclusive.

On the blackmail front, Talia's phone proved to be a bust. We'd have to try another angle, but it was nice to have something on Deepa, so I rewarded Pri with the dog's presence for the day.

That and this visit to Hedon might not be puppy-friendly. I fired off a quick text to Rafael before heading out.

Me: *Still alive. Aren't you proud?*

Dobby: *My delight has no bounds.*

Me: *Any updates?*

Dobby: *I'm diving into all the records. Staying positive about a fix.*

Me: *How are the headaches?*

Dobby: *Constant. Powering through.*

Me: *You got this.*

Bidding Pri and Mrs. H goodbye, I made a quick stop at Muffin Top, managing to arrive during a rare lull in customers.

Baby Miguel spied me first, gurgling and bouncing happily. His mom, Beatriz, the owner of the bakery, had him in a sling on her chest. She smiled indulgently as I played peekaboo with her son, making him laugh hysterically.

"He's going to demand that all day now, thanks so much." She wagged a finger in mock-sternness at me.

"My work here is done. As a reward, I'll have..." I checked out all the goods on offer in the gleaming cases.

The bell rang, announcing a new customer.

"I've got freshly-filled jelly donuts cooling on the rack," Beatriz said.

"That's a no brainer then. One, please."

Using tongs, she placed one in the bag and met me at the cash register.

"Add one more to that order and I'll get them both," the other customer said.

I glanced over my shoulder at Levi. "You have bakeries on your side of town, Montefiore."

"This is your fault," he said, pulling out his wallet. "You made me aware of this place. You can't expect me to stay away when I know how good it is."

Beatriz handed us our bags and gave Levi his change.

Cohen Investigations had been trashed by a murder suspect a few months ago and Levi had restored all my office furniture and framed a series of Sherlock Holmes book covers to personalize the space. In gratitude, I'd sent him into a sugar coma with three dozen jelly donuts from Muffin Top for his incredibly thoughtful gift.

Levi knew me so well, but the reverse was also true. Maybe that's why we excelled at hurting each other.

My goodbye to Beatriz and Miguel was as muted as my thanks to Levi for the pastry.

"About the other day." I squinted against the sunlight, tapping my donut against the inside of the bag to remove excess sugar.

Levi was doing the exact same thing. I was caught between an eye roll and a smile.

"Could we just exist right now with these crack donuts?" he said.

"More like cracking donuts." I laughed and he raised a quizzical eyebrow. "You don't get it."

"There are a lot of things I don't get, Ashira."

"Okay." I licked my lips. "Promise you won't tell Rafael I told you this."

He shifted the wax paper he was using to hold his donut with, so careful not to get any of the sugar on his expensive suit. He looked like a little kid, trying to prove that he was cool enough for you to let him in on the joke.

And yeah, sue me, I told him. For a moment, his eyes widened and crinkled like we were swapping stories of the ridiculous things we'd seen counselors do back at Camp Ruach during those moments when we weren't enemies. I swore him to absolute secrecy and for a moment, it was almost normal.

I wiped my sticky fingers on a napkin. "I feel like Sam and Ralph in the old Warner Bros. cartoon."

"The wolf and the sheepdog?"

"You know, how they were perfectly friendly until they punched in? Then it was war." I threw out my bag. "Guess it's time to punch in."

"Guess it is." He sounded resigned. "I'll see you around, Ralph."

"Why am I the stupid wolf in this scenario?"

"The sheepdog is like Watson," he said. "The moral center. Ergo…" Hands in pockets, he strolled off.

"That comparison is a fallacy," I called out after him.

I lived in the right now for a couple of moments longer, until I couldn't prolong the return of reality anymore. This interlude didn't change anything. I was Levi's scorched earth and he was mine.

A few blocks away from Muffin Top on a residential street, I took the Gold Token Express into Hedon. The ramen bowl sign floated magically over its stall in the business district, glowing jade-green against the ever-present night sky. There was something reassuring about it, an anchor of sorts to this world, and I waved at the jaunty owner.

The pickaxe business next door had been replaced by one selling scarecrows with sly smiles. They hung suspended on their frames, inert, save for one that sucked on a blood-drenched piece of straw, its eyes tracking me as I passed.

I scrunched my head into my neck and sped up, giving a wide berth to the steampunk cat who ran the store with its abundance of poisons because, been there done that, though I briefly considered a pair of leather gloves at a tiny kiosk that promised pickpocketing abilities to rival The Artful Dodger's. Then I saw that the previous owner's fingers were still inside them. Rest in peace, dead digits.

I beelined for a martini glass with a green olive that glowed in the sky a couple of blocks over. The Green Olive had been rebuilt in the two months since it had been burned down. Pulling open the heavy wood door, I did a double take. Instead of its faded grande dame décor, it looked like an old-fashioned pharmacy, where bartenders in white lab coats dispensed drinks from old-time medicinal bottles.

Presiding over it all was Alfie, a short, pudgy middle-aged man in his trademark pinstripe suit with red suspenders, having forgone his spats for black brogues polished to a high gleam. He circulated amongst the tables with a plump Asian woman with warm brown eyes, her face wreathed in smiles.

Alfie waved, hurrying over. "Get this lady a drink."

I motioned to the bartender to hold off. "It's still morning where I'm from, but thanks anyway. Can I talk to you?"

"Yes, yes, but first, come meet Mabel." Alfie waved the woman over and put his arm around her. "Mabel, this is Ash."

"Oh, you're as pretty as a peach." Her southern accent was as thick and slow as molasses. "You saved my big baloo. You dear thing."

"Just doing my job, ma'am." Jeez, where had that drawl sprung from?

"You come back now anytime, sugar. Drinks are always on the house for you."

Score! "I'll do that."

Alfie kissed the side of Mabel's head and led me to an empty table. "She's worth Gunter's revenge, right?"

A dead spirit with a vendetta who'd possessed Levi's ex-girlfriend had attempted to kill Alfie for stealing both Mabel and the Green Olive. So his statement was either the most deluded or the sweetest thing I'd ever heard. "She really is."

We took our seats and I looked around to make sure we wouldn't be overheard. "Know anyone specializing in powerful supernatural amulets?" I said.

He scratched his chin, doing his best to look mysterious. "I might." He bounced his leg. "Okay, I totally do. The best there is. Just sometimes she's prone to violent fits with strangers."

"How violent?"

"Weeellll." He shifted uncomfortably. "The police in her hometown in Portugal attributed her last incident to wolves." My eyebrows shot into my hairline. "It's fine now," he assured me. "They found all the pieces and none of the knives she'd used."

"That's a relief," I said faintly.

"If you're concerned at all, I could talk to her for you."

"I don't want to put you in any danger."

"Oh, Mamã won't hurt me." *Mamã*? With all my complaints about Talia, I'd never had to worry about Freddy Krueger tendencies. "What are you looking for?" he said.

Generally, I wouldn't risk a go-between on this, but Alfie was an open book and saving his life had bought me his loyalty. Sherlock had his Irregulars, and Alfie was definitely that, even if he wasn't a child. Plus, this was his mother and it's not like I was tight with dealers in supernatural antiquities.

"It's called the Kiss of Death." I described its altar origins and that it was powerful, omitting specifics about Jezebel blood giving it Asherah magic.

Alfie took my card, promising to call if he learned anything.

That left me free to pursue the main reason I'd come to Hedon. I clutched the gold token and thought of a Bookworm.

It brought me to an abandoned amusement park.

The wooden coaster glowed in the moonlight like the ribs of a beached leviathan. I picked my way through the ruins of the park, my breath unnaturally loud and my shoulder blades prickling.

A rusted scrambler ride cast distorted shadows, its cars listing sideways, while at the shuttered Floss Shack, a painted grinning clown munched on cotton candy the color and fibrous consistency of insulation. I jumped over broken cables, sidestepping a horse fallen off the carousel, whose smile was more of a grimace. I inched closer. Were those fangs?

Since I'd become allies with the Queen, or more accurately, bribed Moran with puppy time, he'd shared some of Hedon's history with me, though he refused to get into Her Majesty's rise to power.

The business district was the original part of Hedon, created about sixty years ago by Nefesh with Architect powers, including a young Abraham Dershowitz, purely as a black market for the magic criminal fringe. Over the years, more was added based on a combination of demand and whimsy. Some ideas worked out better than others, though I had yet to come across a section that was abandoned like this park.

Given the size, there couldn't have been more than a dozen rides here, tops. About half had been removed, with only black smudges on broken concrete marking where they'd once stood. On the face of it, this amusement park might have seemed like a dead end, but the Queen had been raised in a carny family and she'd lied when asked about a Bookworm. It had clues to yield.

I rounded the Pirate Ship, the wood now rotted through, and stopped abruptly at the mouth of a long tunnel, which was surrounded by large wooden pink hearts affixed to the frame. The entrance was locked tight with a solid metal corrugated gate. I stepped over patchy weeds that sprouted in clumps and into the dry riverbed made of concrete that ran under the gate, surrounding the tunnel like a moat.

A small placard announced that the Tunnel of Love was closed until further notice.

"Tunnel of Love?" a man said. "Who knew that existed outside of old cartoons?"

I spun around with a sigh. "Hello, Reasonable Facsimile Dad."

Adam grinned, the corners of his eyes crinkling. He wore jeans with scuffed-up runners and his favorite faded Beatles T-shirt, the exact outfit that had been captured on film in our last outing to the Pacific National Exhibition, Vancouver's amusement park.

I'd lost my dad twice: once when he'd left us, and the second time when I'd learned that Isaac Montefiore had murdered him. This empty illusion held little comfort for me, and still, I wrapped my arms around myself so I wouldn't hug him.

"You okay, little jewel?" The pet name grated.

"Shouldn't you be buried once and for all along with your real-world counterpart?" I kicked a piece of gravel at him. "You're dead. I am under no delusions that I'm going to find you again, so why are you still bothering me here?"

"That would be up to you, seeing as I'm in your head. Candy?" He proffered a round tin of lemon drops to me.

I helped myself, my mouth puckering at the sour burst of flavor. "Don't blame your appearances on me. You are a byproduct of Hedon. The knock-off purse of fathers."

He pocketed the tin. "I don't think that's been true for a while."

"I'm not the one conjuring you up. To what end? Our visits are cryptic at best and traumatizing at worst. I'm not that masochistic."

"You miss me."

"I miss my real father." Like a phantom limb that wouldn't stop throbbing, except in my heart. "You I can take or leave. Preferably leave."

"Then it beats me," Adam said. "Could be I'm some kind of coping mechanism?"

"Or I'm on the trail of something the Queen doesn't want me to find and she's sent another head trip. Since you're here, make yourself useful. Where would I find a Bookworm?"

He crunched his candy. "If I told you, you'd already know the answer."

Ass. I walked back into the middle of the park, but I'd already done the grand tour. There was no Bookworm visible on any of the rides, and the only locked structures to explore were the Floss Shack and the Tunnel of Love. I grimaced. Breaking into the abode of the candy-pimping psycho clown could be my second option.

The tunnel didn't have a ward on it. I jumped back into the dry cement riverbed, picked the lock on the gate, and hefted it up with a grunt.

Inside was pitch dark with a prominent aroma of mold.

"You go first," I said. If on the slightest off-chance I was sliding the slippery slope to crazy, might as well let the figment of my imagination be the one to bite it first.

Adam stepped into the mouth of the tunnel. "Remember when we went to that exhibit at Science World when you were six with the maze that we had to go through blindfolded?"

"Vaguely. Something about other heightened senses coming into play."

"You were so stubborn. Had to go first, even though it

meant you ended up mashing your nose on the maze walls a few times because you refused to hold my hand."

I crossed my arms. "Your point being?"

Adam held out his hand.

"I'm a twenty-eight-year-old woman with magic. I don't need to hold my fake dead dad's hand. Think of this as a coal mine and you're the canary. Get moving."

He shook his head, his eyes soft with an almost painful disappointment, standing his ground. "When did you get so hard, little jewel?"

"Diamonds are made under pressure," I retorted and pushed past Adam into the darkness.

I barely breathed. The tunnel swallowed all moonlight mere feet inside it, gloom pressing in like a heavy weight. My ears strained for the slightest whisper of danger, my steps slow and cautious. I kept my right hand on the wall, grimacing every time I hit a pocket of slime.

There was a pop of sulphur, a reddish-orange surge, and the left sleeve of my leather jacket was engulfed in flame. Cursing, I beat the fire out against the cement walls.

My spiky head-to-toe blood armor slammed into place in time with an explosion of motion from my left. A foot nailed me in the head, the blow knocking me back a few steps. Dazed, I shook my head, my fists up, but I couldn't see shit.

A ball of flame shot from the darkness and I threw myself sideways. It caught my right shoulder, danced briefly over the short stubby spikes, and died out.

Approximating my assailant's position, I lunged—and closed my fist on empty air. Two sharp daggers sprung into my hands.

"Come out, come out, whoever you are," I said in a singsong voice.

No one stirred, but the tunnel grew hot and tight. The sulphur stench worsened, making my eyes water. It was as if all oxygen was being sucked out. I spread my arms out to reassure myself the walls weren't closing in and dragged in a deep breath, but failed to get a good lungful of air, because my armor seemed to have shrunk and was now crushing my ribs. If I got rid of it, however, I'd be a sitting duck. The pressure grew and I crashed to my knees, bent over double with my head pressed to the concrete.

With a roar that echoed off the walls, a plume of water jetted into the riverbed, propelling me down a twisting channel, half-drowned, and all in virtual blindness. I battened down the terror that filled my lungs, scrabbling at the walls to gain purchase.

My fingers scraped over a wire and a peal of psychotic laughter ripped through the tunnel. Bursts of epilepsy-inducing pink lights lit up as the water slowed and I bumped to a stop against a wall, my hand pressed against my heaving chest.

"Tiptoe Through the Tulips" sung in falsetto and accompanied by electric organ streamed through the space, sending shivers up my spine. If you told me the singer was a serial killer who made clown suits of his victims' skins while fashioning balloon animals engaged in torture porn tableaux, I'd nod, because that sounded about right.

A figure leapt over me, spinning fireballs in both hands. Maybe they could dry off the rivulets of water running off my armor.

The person turned, revealing Isaac Montefiore's leering face. Unlike with fake Adam, I welcomed this illusion. Isaac wouldn't have been in Hedon, nor did he have any powers. This attacker wore his face, that was all. I jumped to my feet and rushed him.

The fight played out against a cacophony of pink spotlights, lending a disjointed, jerky quality to our movements: fire pitched in stuttering strokes, a punch with a time delay between landing on his chin and his head snapping back, all to that hyena-like crooning.

Spinning in under his guard, I manifested a pair of daggers, swinging upwards to slash his jugular and end this.

Light danced across Isaac's face, turning his blue eyes bright as a lazy summer day, while the play of shadows hid the silver at his temples and made him look younger. I jerked sideways, the blades whistling harmlessly past his face.

My heart hammered in my chest. If I couldn't deal the killing blow to an illusion because of the resemblance with Levi, the real fight was over before it had begun.

Another large ball of fire flew toward me, but I'd caught the bunching of his shoulder as he threw it. Willing myself to ignore any traces of Levi in his father, I dropped to a crouch and swung my foot wide in a sweeping kick the way that Miles had taught me. Fancy. It caught the attacker in the back of his knee. His leg buckled and he crashed to the ground. Making my armor vanish, I jumped him and sliced across his neck with my dagger with no hesitation.

Blood dribbled out in a Rorschach pattern along the concrete riverbed. Filled with savage satisfaction, I fired a red silky ribbon of magic inside him, ready to hook it to his magic and finish this Isaac doppelgänger off.

Isaac's face changed to Adam's and the song cut out into sudden and discordant silence.

I scrambled off him so fast that I crashed into the other side of the tunnel.

Adam dragged in a wet breath, his eyes cloudy. He held one hand to his bleeding neck and the other out to me. "Stay with me. Please?"

I'd done this. The least I could do was own my actions and bear witness. Except I couldn't watch someone I love die. Not when I'd already dreamed my father's death over and over again. Those nightmares were supposed to stay in the dark, not follow me into this rose-tinted light. So what if I wanted revenge? I'd been called on by the goddess Asherah to take

Chariot down. It was my calling. It was justice. It wasn't supposed to keep costing me over and over again.

"Ash?"

My vision grew blurry. "I'm sorry," I whispered and ran.

A stitch flared up my left side, but I didn't stop until I hit a heart-shaped door.

Was Adam still waiting for me to take his hand or had the light faded from his eyes, dead and alone? I glanced over my shoulder.

A single straight length of tunnel ran between me and the open mouth, where moonlight streamed in. While pink lights glowed softly in tiny bulbs about three-quarters of the way up the walls, there were no twists and no Adam. No body of any sort.

Had it all been an illusion? I checked my sleeve. A black scorch mark ran vertically along the leather and it smelled faintly of smoke.

Illusion plus tangible fire magic equaled one hell of a deterrent. Tenderize intruders with the mind-fucking, attack them, and then when they were injured and whimpering on the ground, bring out the big flambé finish. Had it not been for my armor, I'd have made an excellent tiki torch.

What was so valuable—or awful—on the other side of this door?

Making short work of the lock, I steeled myself and stepped through.

Chapter 10

Given a thousand guesses, I'd never have nailed what lay before me. My childhood bedroom hadn't been particularly fanciful, but had I run with the Disney princess crowd, I would have garroted someone with a skipping rope for this room. It was a space designed to play and dream in, painted all-pink with a bed featuring a massive ruffled canopy top. A girl could hide away with the giant smiling teddy bear sitting on the rocking chair or spend hours reading the dog-eared books like *Alice in Wonderland* and *The Chronicles of Narnia* with their worn spines that were stacked neatly on white shelves.

For the older lass harboring fantasies of being locked away and rescued, this room served that purpose, too, complete with its own prisoner princess. The beautiful woman in her early twenties with a spill of dark hair sat blank-faced and cross-legged in the middle of the canopy bed.

A milky film covered her eyes, her lids madly flickering and barely visible through the blue data stream that surrounded her like a cumulus cloud. Instead of binary numbers, it contained floating words and phrases in every language that grew brighter before dissipating into wisps that unfurled into new words in an endless bloom. Chemical equations morphed into Arabic phrases and then into IKEA assembly instructions and a snippet from *Winnie the Pooh*. It possessed a surreal beauty, but the sheer potency of magic in this room raised the hairs on my body.

I was very uncomfortable asking her for help when she was being held prisoner, but she was my only hope to learn more about Olivia's insurance policy. I inched closer to the woman, but she didn't register my presence. This must have been how supplicants to the Oracle of Delphi had felt.

"Hello. My name is Ash. May I ask you a question?" Should I have brought an offering? A rose? An apple? My Netflix password? "I'm trying to find written proof of some criminal activity."

Neither the Bookworm nor the word cloud gave any kind of response.

Rafael had warned me about the data overload and the rare lucid moments. If speaking didn't work, should I touch her to alert her to my presence?

I reached out and hesitated.

Did she always look this way, indefinitely hooked to this global knowledge stream like some IV drip? Or was this the Queen's doing? Any effort on my part to rescue her would terminate a very useful partnership in bringing down Chariot.

I massaged my temples, frantically working through plans. "Are you being held against your will?"

No response. Figured.

I toyed with the gold token. Would the Bookworm be better off in my care? What damage might moving her do and where could I even take her? House Pacifica was right out. Levi's hesitancy to stay on Team Jezebel aside, he couldn't strike out against the Queen.

Still, despite thwarting Her Majesty's use of this woman

and raining heaps of shit upon myself, I couldn't leave her here.

"I can help you get away."

She didn't react.

I sidled a bit closer and my knees hit the side of the mattress. It was then that I knew with a stone-cold certainty that this wasn't right. Whoever this girl was, she deserved a normal life, whatever that meant for her.

No one deserved to be locked in a weird fun house, especially not this one.

I pinched the bridge of my nose. What did a normal life mean to me? The only thing I was certain of was that this fight with Chariot had gone on for four hundred years and I had to be the one to end it, otherwise what was the point of all my suffering? I rubbed the scar on my right thigh. Everyone believed I was in it for revenge, when I was in it for meaning.

But truth be told, I was scared to have it end. Ending meant conclusion, no more. If I didn't have a concrete goal to take out Chariot, if I finished tying up these loose ends, what would I have left?

"Are you able to respond?" I leaned forward to place my hand on her shoulder, and as my fingers passed through the cloud, an earsplitting sound filled the room. Bright, buzzy, and a bit harsh, it was reflected in the data cloud jumping and pulsing wildly. I tried to pull away, but couldn't.

The woman swung her head in an unblinking stare, made *Children of the Corn*-creepy with that milky film that prevented me from seeing her eyes. She opened her mouth and a high-pitched scream joined the buzz.

My ears were ringing. I screwed my eyes tight and fumbled for the gold token with my free hand, but I couldn't move. I was trapped, this cacophony drilling into my brain.

The noise rose to a sharp crescendo and just when I thought my head would split in two, my hand disengaged from her shoulder and I vanished.

I was back in the amusement park—or some version of it.

Lit up in a cascade of colors, the dozens of rides were crowded with fairgoers, and cheerful carnival music played through loudspeakers. Food vendors hawked cotton candy in soothing pastels, fries, and giant hot dogs on sticks, the air spattered with hot grease.

I stood among them, a stone in a river of people, getting my bearings on uneven ground, while screams from delighted coaster riders swooped overhead.

Where was I?

"Visit the midway! A carnival of delights!" a voice called out from up ahead.

The crowd shifted, forcing me toward an archway cut into a huge Queen of Hearts card. The other side was empty save for a single tent and a young blond boy in his mid-teens, who beckoned me over.

"Let Serafina see into your heart," he said, with a Russian accent.

"Moran?"

He gave me a funny look, like I'd called him by the wrong name. "Two tickets for entry."

"I don't have—" The tickets lay in my palm. I clutched them tightly. No good ever came from the Queen seeing into my heart.

The gold token and wooden ring still were threaded on the chain around my neck. I might be able to use one of them to get out of here, but I was curious. My last thought before touching that data cloud had been about having a normal life. If Adam was the ghost of my past, was this to be the vision of my future?

I handed young Moran the tickets. Moving the beaded curtain to the tent aside, he motioned me in with a flourish.

A lone floor lamp cast a pale glow in the corner, but otherwise the tent was empty.

"Hello?"

Fabric rustled behind me. I spun around and—

I was in my office.

I ran a finger over the framed photo of Priya and me at our university graduation, frowning at the monitor with a highlighted passage of an insurance document on it. The Sherlock covers still hung on the wall but there was no dart board and no other desk, only the client chairs.

"Ash, my detective extraordinaire," Rafael said in a jovial tone, strolling in. He still had a British accent but it was far less posh.

I blinked at the electric blue golf shirt that he'd paired with khaki slacks. He didn't wear glasses and his hair was gelled to within an inch of its life.

"Nice shirt," I said.

"I told them the color was bollocks, but corporate said we had to wear them for the big tee-off this morning." He sat down, legs wide. "With you bowing out of the fundraiser because of work, I had a shot at the trophy."

I squinted at him, my mouth open. There was no illusion, alternate reality, or flat-out insanity where I played golf, let alone excelled at it. As entertainment it ranked somewhere between pointless and boring. "How'd you do?"

"Miller beat me, but it was close. Ah well. All for a good cause. Listen." He ran a finger along the neck of his collar. "I'm going to have to take over the Cooper file. They're fighting our decision on the life insurance policy and HQ wants it settled out of court. Sorry. I know the hours you put in."

Yeah, I sacrificed mightily for it. "It's yours with my blessings."

He fired double finger guns and I clamped my lips together to stifle my snort. "Thanks, sport," he said.

Did the Queen think my deepest fear was that my lie of working for an insurance firm would become the truth?

Hardly. I'd still have my Nefesh magic and many fascinating cases.

I glanced at my office door, a jolt spearing through me. "Where is it?"

"What?"

"The stencil reading Cohen Investigations."

"You shut that business down ages ago when you came to work exclusively for us," Rafael said. "Are you okay?"

"It still existed. I did work for House Pacifica."

Rafael scratched his head. "Why would they need you?"

"Because—" Of my Jezebel magic to find Meryem and the missing kids. Of my acquaintanceship with Mayan so I could tell if she was behaving strangely. Of my relationship with the Queen regarding the Bookworm.

Even the Queen had hired me on Omar's case because she'd needed someone who was Mundane on record.

None of those jobs had been given to me specifically because of my investigator abilities.

I had no clientele, no built-up word of mouth, and I couldn't exactly advertise the cases I'd already solved. Where did that leave me when all this was over?

Numb, I passed Rafael the requested file.

With another set of finger guns, he left, nodding politely at Priya on her way in.

The massive rock shining on her finger next to her wedding band was one thing, her huge pregnant belly quite another. "Look, smoochie, it's Auntie Ashira." She rubbed a hand over the bump. "Say hi to your niece."

I gently batted her belly out of my face. "It's not a directional mic, Pri. Um, hi, baby thing."

"Baby thing?" she grimaced. "What happened to 'Superstar Skittilitious Cutie Head?'"

Uh, I wasn't lobotomized and those words would never pass my lips?

Holding the arm of a chair, she did this weird backwards dip until her ass crashed down on it. "Do I still have ankles?"

I peered over the top of my desk. "You have feet attached to your legs. That's as much as I'm willing to commit to. So, how are you and Superstar Skittilitious Cutie Head"—I tried not to anally pucker as I said it—"doing?"

She rambled on about her weird food cravings, then she gripped my hand. "I need you there for the birth, asshole, so clear your schedule. You were the one who encouraged me to get pregnant, you giant baby hog. You're going to take smoochie to the park and teach her how to knit like you promised."

Wow, her grip was tight.

"I promise. How could I not when I have so much to look forward to?" I could always use those knitting needles to teach the kid basic stabbing techniques. Or gouge out my eyes.

"Yoo-hoo, darling girl," Talia said, breezing into the room. Was my mother wearing floral patterned yoga pants? Whoa. She kissed the top of Priya's head, bent down to say hi to the baby bump, and then enveloped me in a hug. "You look so good. I could eat you up. Nom. Nom. Nom."

I pinched myself but didn't wake up from this diabetic coma. "Okay, Talia."

"Talia? I'm your mother, annoying child. I earned that moniker with sixteen hours of labor, since your stubbornness started in the womb. Have some respect." She winked and dropped her enormous Coach purse onto my desk, where it hit with a thud.

A mother who loved me unconditionally.

A best friend about to make me an aunt.

I rubbed a hand over the pang in my chest. I hadn't ever dreamed of that future, but there was a sweetness to it. My relationship with real Talia was either fraught with secrets and lies or outright contentious and my friendship with Priya had been a series of minefields these last couple of months.

All because of my Jezebel magic. Would that all change once my mission ended? Was that the trade-off? My personal relationships would improve but my career would plummet?

Why would I ever take that deal?

"I brought your makeup kit," Talia said.

Priya clapped her hands together. "Makeovers!"

Fuck no. This wasn't about visions of what could be. This was a nightmare trip to the demon realm with complimentary torture thrown in.

The two women swooped in.

"I'm at work," I protested, batting away their hands. "This is extremely unprofessional."

"Putting effort into your appearance is always a smart professional move," Priya said. "A conservative insurance company will appreciate a more polished look from its subcontractors."

It was easier not to fight these two determined women than convince them of the truth of my situation.

"There's our pretty-pretty princess," Pri said, giving my lashes one final coat of mascara.

My mom rummaged into her bag. "Aha!" She brandished a small mirror in front of me.

I didn't look half bad. They'd made my eyes all smoky and huge and given me pouty red lips. Talia had even brushed my hair into a high ponytail that helped highlight my cheekbones. Only one problem. "This isn't polished. It's nightclubready. Unless part of catching fraudsters is getting them so hot and bothered that they confess?"

Priya and Talia exchanged knowing glances.

My eyes narrowed. "What?"

"Not everything is about work," Talia said.

"Hi."

My head snapped to Levi standing nervously in the doorway holding a small gift bag. I drank him in, from his jeans to the dark green sweater that hugged his shoulders and his jet-black locks loosely framing his face. His eyes were a deep blue that homed in on me like I was the only one in the world.

Oh. Those previous visits were the warm-up torture.

I dug my fingers into the armrests of my desk chair.

"We should go," my mother murmured.

Sure, doll me up, throw me in his path, and run away.

Priya tugged on my ponytail. "I'll call you tomorrow."

Talia kissed my cheek and then they both left, speaking softly to Levi on their way out.

He cautiously approached me. "Is it okay…?" He waved a hand at one of the chairs.

"Suit yourself."

He sat down and handed me the gift bag.

I pulled off the yellow tissue paper. Inside was a bakery box with a single jelly donut. "Twice in one day," I murmured.

"What?"

I shook my head. "You realize I'm not sharing."

He pointed at the tiny silver scar on his hand. "Yeah, no shit."

Was the Queen's magic reading my memories or…? "You remember that?"

"I remember everything. Especially how you'd been working yourself to the bone. And then how I…" He kissed my knuckles. "There's no excuse for how I treated you. I should have trusted in the two of us, and if you'll have me back, nothing and no one will ever stand between us again. I swear it."

I'd yearned to hear those words for two months, but they landed with a hollow thud now.

"I've missed you so much," he said.

Fool that I was, my heart swelled to have Levi back in my corner, in my life. Except, this wasn't my Levi. There was no "my Levi." But who would it hurt to have this illusion for a few moments?

I held out my arms. "Come here, Leviticus."

He grinned and that piratical look shot a bolt of lust straight through me. "I didn't think I'd ever hear that ridiculous nickname again."

"Meeting me. Best day ever."

He laughed and we positioned ourselves in my desk chair so that I sat in his lap. I buried my face in his chest and inhaled, craving the scent of his magic, but there was only a trace of cologne.

My head throbbed harder. Everything else about him felt absolutely real and right. "I missed you."

"I missed you too."

I turned my face up to his. "Yeah? Tell me why and don't stint on the reasons."

"You're smart, funny, and you have an enormous heart. It would take me too long to enumerate all of them, Ash. What I came here to say was that I want to try again. I know your parents didn't make it, but we will. I've had to face a lot of my own demons, and you have to face that your dad did a number on you. Neither of us can be scared little kids."

I flinched hearing the words that I'd thrown so callously at the real Levi.

"I'm not Adam," he said. "I'm not going to leave you. You're it for me, and I won't let you down."

I hugged him one last time, holding his words close to my heart before I let them go. This wasn't some vision of my future. It was a wake-up call. Levi and I could take a few moments and push reality away, but outside of that, we were over. This version of the man I'd loved existed only as a magic delusion.

As for the rest of my future? Once I'd stopped Chariot— stopped Isaac—for good, I wouldn't be the same person I was now. Speculating on that Ash's desires was pointless.

I tugged away and stood up. "It's too late for us."

His face twisted. "Fight for us, bella. I implore you."

Pain speared through me at this twisted parody of the words I'd said the night he walked away. Careful what you wished for, Ash. I'd longed for him to step up, but hearing it like this was killing me.

I lay my hand on Levi's cheek and clutched the gold token. "Goodbye."

Chapter 11

The token took me straight home to my living room.

Priya screamed and dropped her spoon into her granola, splashing milk onto her pajamas. "Where the hell have you been?"

I blinked stupidly at her candy cane-striped pajamas. "You weren't wearing those this morning."

"You monitor my pj's? Get a new hobby, Holmes. And I wasn't wearing them yesterday morning, but I did put them on last night. It's Sunday. I haven't seen you in twenty-four hours."

My brow furrowed. That wasn't possible.

"Why didn't you answer my texts?" Priya said, rubbing at the milk spot. "You can't tell me Chariot knows who you are and then ghost me." Her voice got high-pitched.

I checked my phone to find seven increasingly anxious messages from her. "I didn't get them."

Mrs. Hudson barreled into the room with Pinky in her mouth and leapt at my legs, knocking me onto the sofa. She jumped up beside me and pushed her head under my hand.

I scratched the puppy's ears while telling Priya all about

the Bookworm and the vision I'd had when I'd touched the data cloud.

Priya listened calmly to the entire story, though her hand fluttered to her belly for a moment at her being pregnant. When I was done, she set her empty cereal bowl on the coffee table. "I would never let you teach my child to knit."

I buried my face in a cushion. "Some part of me had stupidly been holding out hope, but it's really over with Levi."

Priya made a non-committal noise and rubbed my back. "Do what you do best. Work. That means getting answers out of this Bookworm. How are you going to deal with her?"

I dropped the pillow and exhaled slowly. "First things first. I have to find out if she's being held against her will. If that's the case then I can't leave her there. No matter what the Queen does in retaliation."

"Hopefully, Isaac will get caught in the crossfire of her wrath," Priya said cheerfully. "How are you going to get this woman lucid?"

"Blank." A designer drug, now manufactured exclusively for House Pacifica ever since Levi had learned its side effects included magic suppression. One dose only lasted for twenty-four hours, which was plenty of time to ask the Bookworm about any money laundering proof and help her escape, if desired, while she was alert. If she chose otherwise, she could return to her magic state with no long-term effects.

I tossed Pinky across the room for Mrs. H. to fetch and dialed a number on my phone, lowering my voice to a deep rasp. "Is this Kilo McSnorts's Drug Emporium? I'm in a bad way, man."

"It's Sunday, Cohen," Miles said on the other end of the phone. "My day of rest. From you."

"What kind of shitty Jew are you, Berenbaum? Your Sabbath was yesterday. Hope you enjoyed it. Now, how do I get my hands on some Blank for a case?"

"Which case?"

"Uh, the Bookworm."

"You talk to Levi," Miles said.

"Why would I do that when you're perfectly capable of procuring it from the Chemist?"

"Because in the past twenty-four hours his assholeness of the last two months has grown yet another asshole. Fix whatever you did."

"Oh my God, Miles. Quit blaming me every time His Lordship gets pissy." Our bakery encounter had affected Levi? Did it reflect poorly on my character to feel smug? Heh.

There was resounding silence from Miles.

"Fine," I said. "I'll get the Blank from Levi. Happy?"

"Put a smile back on his face and I'll name a fucking sandwich after you." He hung up on me.

If Levi got grouchier, Miles would kill me. On the upside, my impending demise gave me a deadline to solve all my cases and I worked well under pressure.

"Have I mentioned how much I hate Miles?" I said.

"Not in at least a week," Priya said.

I threw my phone on the sofa, sagging back wearily. *I should have trusted in the two of us. I've missed you so much.* "How am I supposed to face Levi with all those grand declarations of that other version's still in my head? It's over, I knew that, but he said everything I'd hoped for. I saw it, I heard it, and now I'm supposed to forget it because none of it was fucking real?" I divided the mess on our coffee table into neat piles. If only life was so easily sorted. "You know what the real kicker is? Even if the real Levi had said all those things to me, I wouldn't believe him."

"Believe him or trust him?"

I shrugged helplessly.

Priya gathered up her empty cereal bowl. "You want me to get the drug?"

I gave her a wry smile. "Thanks, but no. I pulled the

Jezebel card and I don't get to back away from that responsibility now."

Sherlock Holmes once said, "Education never ends, Watson. It is a series of lessons, with the greatest for last." So far this syllabus had been disorienting and heartbreaking, and this so-called greatest lesson might be my undoing. Then again, he'd also said "Work is the best antidote to sorrow, my dear Watson," so if anything could get me through my grief, it was a delicious mystery.

I armed myself with a host of nice neutral meeting-place suggestions that would allow for a quick turnover time and called Levi, who sounded subdued. He asked if we could go for a walk along Spanish Banks instead, to talk.

Had our bakery interlude clarified his position on removing House resources from my disposal? Shit. He was going to fire me. I transferred my phone to my other ear and wiped my sweaty hands off on my jeans. Might as well get the inevitable over with. I agreed to meet him at the westernmost beach parking lot in a couple hours.

With everything I'd been pursuing, I hadn't had time to look into Deepa Anand's personal life, so I grabbed my laptop. The information online was relatively superficial. She'd lost a daughter recently in a tragic car accident, and was survived by her husband and son. Photos before her loss showed a woman who smiled a lot and attended many social events, especially cricket matches. That changed after her daughter died. The sole function she'd been at since then was the Under-19 World Cricket Cup held in New Zealand, because her son played for the Indian national team.

None of that led me back to Chariot.

I checked my notes on the Mundane woman. Deepa had run a money lending company in India called D21 Personal Loan. According to Priya, that was the age Anand had been when she founded the company. She had professional ties to Isaac through his cybersecurity business, and had died on pilgrimage to a Hindu site. Not all of the Ten were necessarily Jewish these days, so her religion didn't preclude her being part of Chariot. What bothered me, though, was her making that journey at all. If Deepa was caught up in this, she was after immortality, same as the rest of them. How did that gel with going to a religious site to gain awareness or some higher spirituality?

I scanned a few more details. At the time of her death, she'd been in Northern India at Char Dham. Further research revealed that was actually a compound consisting of four temples, which Hindus visited to wash away their sins and help them attain moksha. I was unfamiliar with the term, but learned it was connected to their beliefs regarding reincarnation. They believed the soul passed through a cycle of successive lives, known as samsara. However, each incarnation was dependent on how the previous life was lived, aka karma.

Moksha was the release from the cycle of death and rebirth.

Had Deepa felt the need to achieve moksha in preparation for gaining immortality? There was no way of knowing how her Chariot goals intersected with her religious beliefs.

I danced a pen over my knuckles. I'd hit a wall investigating Deepa. For now, my best bet was to find the Kiss of Death.

If the amulet was a powerful Asherah artifact, then maybe the Gigis were a good place to start. Who were these people, anyway? Why had Lux been willing to let innocent people die to bring Asherah back? If she was power mad, then she wouldn't have become almost sycophantic upon learning who I was, but if she was desperate for the goddess's presence, what was driving her?

It didn't take long to find the answer in a photo from last year's Lung Cancer Foundation's Black and White Ball. The caption read: Breast cancer survivor Emma McIntyre with her wife, Eileen "Lux" Emmerson, feeling strong and looking dazzling in white.

There were no photos of them at the gala I'd attended a couple months ago.

I made a note to speak with Lux right after this meeting with Levi.

Hating myself that I cared enough to be petty, I took a shower, picked out a cute shirt and pants, and scrunched my hair into a riot of wavy curls. I even applied light makeup and lipstick, turning side to side to regard myself in the mirror.

Mrs. Hudson barked approvingly.

"Right?" I said. "Let them see what they're missing. Remember that if things go sideways with you and Pinky."

And now I was validating the toy cow as a life partner. Pull yourself together, Cohen.

I grabbed a jean jacket and the puppy's leash, and settled both of us in Moriarty. Driving through east Vancouver, I looped past Science World, a shining bright silver globe in the sunlight, with all the Dragon Boat racers slicing through the waters of False Creek beyond. I spared them the briefest glance, busy running through scenarios of this meeting and how I would keep my cool in each circumstance.

Shoppers bustled along West Fourth Avenue, darting into the many cafés and restaurants to rest their weary feet or socialize with friends. I passed Jericho Park, a huge green space that hosted the Vancouver Folk Festival every year, and took the turn-off down to Northwest Marine Drive, following the two-lane curving road along the waterfront.

Give Vancouverites a sunny day, no matter how brisk the weather, and they'd turn out in droves to jog and cycle or get out on the water, sailing and paddle boarding. Today was no exception, starting at Jericho, the first of the string of beaches that lay at the foot of the University of British Columbia.

I belonged to the other class of citizens in our fair city: the ones who enjoyed the après activities like patio sitting and drinking without all the mess and fuss of actual exercise.

There were only a handful of cars parked in the lot at Spanish Banks. Levi sat on the hood of his Tesla facing the water, his face obscured by a fedora pulled low and aviator shades preventing me from seeing his eyes.

This was not going to be an "exist in the moment" visit.

Mrs. Hudson practically dragged me along behind her.

"We're going for dignified here, dog," I said. "Conduct yourself appropriately."

She farted and waddled faster.

Levi looked up at our approach and slid off the car. "Want to walk?"

If having my still-beating heart ripped from my body wasn't an option, then sure. Oh wait, this visit might amount to the same thing. That other Levi was a delusion. It was over and I needed to move on because I'd been stuck in this limbo for two months.

"Walking is good," I said.

We headed away from the crowded area around the concession stand and beach volleyball courts.

"Miles said I had to speak to you about getting a dose of Blank for the Bookworm." Steady voice, not too much eye contact as I spoke, but not too little either, as if I was avoiding him. Gold star, Ash.

"You found the Bookworm?"

"Yes, but there are some lucidity issues." Also some Queen of Hearts imprisonment issues, but we were starting at the shallow end of the pool before moving into the deep.

"I'll get the Chemist to make more and deliver it to you. It might take a few days."

He didn't even want me coming to the House to retrieve it in person? Would he have me escorted out if I showed up on the premises? Or would I be allowed in the building, but enjoy an awkward handout from some random operative?

I should have trusted in the two of us. I've missed you so much.

"That concludes my business," I said a mite sharply, "so why don't you spit out whatever you wanted to say and we can both get on with our lives?"

"You mean our day."

"Do I?" I said sweetly.

His fingers twitched, then he jammed them in his pockets. "I made my mother cry."

I whistled and kicked a twig down the sidewalk ahead of us. "Wow, sounds like an asshole thing to do. What happened?"

His shoulder hitched in a careless shrug, but his expression was tight. "Does it matter?"

"I guess not."

We walked in silence for a bit. Had he called me for comfort? Absolution? I kept my eyes firmly on the ground and my lips clamped tight against the blackness rising inside me.

"I was needlessly cruel. Like *him*," Levi said. He slid off his glasses to glance at me, but my throat was choked with anger leaving no room for words. "I got mad and yelled at her about waiting until now to speak up." His mouth twisted in a sneer. "I demanded to know how bad it was and why she'd come to you and not me? Her own son. Pretty good, huh?" He stepped off the path and sat down on a bench.

I took a seat on the opposite end, gripping the armrest so tightly that I mangled the fancy wrought-iron.

Mrs. Hudson kept trying to go to him, but Levi was in no mood to play with her, so I gave her some bacon treats and attempted to fix the armrest. It went from a broken stick to more of an overall blob.

"Interesting design aesthetic," he said. "Very minimalist."

I fixed him with a cold stare. "I'm not your emotional therapy dog, Levi."

He gave me a placating smile. "No, we established you're the wolf."

"This isn't a joking matter. You can't use me when it suits you and then throw me away. Especially when you don't even want to keep up your end of our business arrangement anymore." Not ripping this bench out of the ground and braining him with it was the single greatest mitzvah I'd ever done.

He pinched the bridge of his nose. "You'd just accused me of being that little kid scared of my father and I was pissed at you. I'd spent years convincing myself I was invulnerable, and you forced me to see that my fortress was built on quicksand."

A little girl in a bright red helmet tore past on her bike, her father running after her and yelling to slow down.

Levi watched them with a small smile that faded as they got farther away. "Who taught you how to ride a bicycle?"

"My dad."

"Mine too." He wove a brief illusion of a very young version of himself wearing an ear-splitting grin, wobbling to a stop on a bike and receiving a high five from his father. "Isaac had his moments. Had his bad ones too, though I never suspected how bad. If my own father could hide being part of Chariot and worse, live with Adam's blood on his hands for all these years, does that same deceptive evil lurk inside me as well? Hell, the whole world thinks he's this great guy, even when he's publicly opposing his only son with heinous legal measures." His blue eyes turned dark and troubled. "Illusions are my stock and trade. What if it doesn't stop with my magic? What if I'm exactly like him? For fuck's sake, I made my mother cry."

"So apologize. My dad was a Charmer who could rip away a person's free will, like I can rip away magic. That doesn't mean you and I have some factory default set to bad. Stop thinking in terms of fortresses and start thinking in terms of choices." I wrapped my arms around myself. "Anyways, I'm not the person to talk to about this anymore."

His expression grew pensive, his focus once more out at sea. "Yeah."

My phone blew up with buzzes.

Dobby: *Chariot*

Dobby: *Library*

Dobby: *Help*

I shoved the leash at Levi. "Can you take Mrs. Hudson to Priya?"

The moment he took hold of it, the pug hopped about, her tail wagging so enthusiastically, orgasmic rapture wasn't far behind. He glanced at my phone quizzically, but all he said was, "Of course. Just… be safe."

Distracted, I nodded, slid the wooden ring on, and vanished, realizing that he'd never said if our business arrangement was still a go or not.

The library was in shambles, with books and manuscripts knocked off shelves and furniture overturned. A chair lay smashed into kindling by a wall.

My heart leapt into my throat. Had Chariot actually found us? The pillars were intact, with four still illuminated and one dark, so they hadn't gotten the scrolls. "Rafael?"

A low growl came from the shadows under the table. I crouched down, keeping out of lunging range, my magic dancing under my skin, and gasped.

Red-flecked eyes glowed back at me.

"Ba'al?"

"No." Raspiness had almost distorted the voice, but the British accent was unmistakable. "Chariot found the library. Tried to have a Weaver disable the wards, but he wasn't good enough. Couldn't get in."

They'd had a level-five Weaver in their employ but she'd been killed. I felt bad for being grateful about that.

"How many were there?"

"I don't know. I stayed inside shoring up the wards, but… the stress or adrenaline… I'm… oh God."

"Can you—come out, okay?" I backed up.

Two small horns nestled in short brown hair emerged first, followed by broad shoulders with tattered strips of argyle hanging off him like ribbons.

My hand flew to my mouth.

Rafael stood up. He'd gained height, but his face hadn't transformed into a goat's, nor were his eyes vertical slits. Yet.

My brain stuttered over a million questions but all I managed was, "What happened?"

He shot me a flat stare.

"Impossible. I checked you for residual magic from when Ba'al impaled you. There wasn't any."

He pulled his glasses with their bent and stretched-out frames off his face. "There was. There is. You, me, the Nightingale, we all missed it." He crushed them, the lenses dusting the ground in glittery powder.

"How? The Gigis created Fake Ba'al with one hundred percent Nefesh magic."

"Various types that were fused together, including Weaver magic." Pain flashed across his features. "It's knitting to my Asherah magic to become virtually undetectable." He gripped his head and bellowed, the sound punching into me.

I held my ground, refusing to call up my armor or any weapons until I absolutely had to. This was my friend. He was in pain, scared, and totally fucked. If the Nefesh magic had become indistinguishable from his Asherah powers, how was I going to help him?

He bent double, his body twisting as a shudder racked through him and gnashed his teeth together. "I can't hold on."

I forced myself to step closer. "Now that I know what the deal is, let me see what I can do."

I didn't think I'd be able to do shit, but the universe owed me a break, and I had to try. I gripped his biceps, which felt like two small boulders, and sent a ribbon of red silky magic inside him. On the face of it, only Rafael's Asherah-based powers appeared. They felt very similar to Nefesh magic, but if the two were siblings, the goddess-bestowed powers were the older, stronger ones who could easily sit on you and make you cry uncle. There was a profundity to ours, like a still-water pool of unfathomable depth. Only when I sank my magic deeper did I feel a faint disturbance in that calm, measured power. Fine muddy threads swam through it, impossible to fish out from the larger body.

I tried to snag one in a forked branch, but it drifted continually out of reach as if carried away by the tide.

Rafael roared and flipped me over, smashing me to the ground before my brain had time to process that I'd even moved and my magic snapped free of his. While I lay there, gasping and winded, Rafael dropped to one knee.

"You hurt me," he snarled. "Why didn't you prevent this?!"

A torrent of magic poured into me. Rafael's powers were based in serving and protecting me, but those same abilities used to heal could be perverted to cause maximum damage.

My right arm grew hotter and hotter, and an intense pressure squeezed my humerus, bearing down as if to snap it. I couldn't get my armor into place because Rafael's magic was holding it at bay. Useful if you had an injured Jezebel fighting your attempts to heal her, very much the opposite in this situation.

I kicked him off me, flinging him into the wall. Thankfully, my strength still worked fine.

He cracked the drywall, one of his stubby horns embedded there. After a brief struggle, he pulled free, sending down a cascade of fine dust.

Rafael stalked toward me, his face devoid of all recognition.

I danced between the pillars, weaving around and through

them to keep obstacles between us, while I got hold of my armor magic and locked it down nice and securely.

Rafael feigned left, then leapt over the dark pillar, tackling me.

I screamed, knocking into the ground. A satisfied flicker danced through his eyes, now solid red, and my armor disappeared once more.

His magic jumped to my lower right abdomen and my stomach began to swell.

"Rafael," I whimpered. "Stop." If he burst my appendix, I could die before it was treated.

Deranged laughter burst out of him and the pressure increased.

Reaching deep inside me, I fought past the pain enough to call up a dagger, which I plunged into his side.

He leapt off of me, blood streaming down his hip.

"What have I done?" Rafael looked at his hands, now tipped with claws. A look of horror crossed his face and he ran at the wall.

Where there had been none before, a door shimmered into existence. Rafael grabbed the knob, chest heaving, and fled into the night.

Chapter 12

I sat up, sweat-drenched. My appendix had been spared, but my entire right side felt like I'd been rammed by a bull. I took a moment to check myself for the complex magic that the Gigis had brought into being, but I was in the clear. Nor had I suffered from the headaches that had been a precursor to Rafael's change. Either I'd been lucky or my powers had withstood the effects. I forced myself upright, choosing not to question this stroke of good fortune, and hobbled outside, every step firing a wave of red-hot agony through me.

The evening was drizzly and cool and I shivered in my ripped jean jacket. Wherever this was, it was in a later time zone than Vancouver.

The library door slammed shut. It was located in a small warehouse with Broughton Manufacturing written on it, so we were in an English-speaking country. This perfectly ordinary rectangular building had loading bay doors and small, high-set windows studded with bars. Interesting, since the library was a much smaller, round, windowless room.

I hit the perimeter of the property and a tingle of magic tickled my skin. Glancing back, my eyes slid over the warehouse, and the strongest urge to busy myself elsewhere washed over me, immediately fading and then returning again a moment later. Rafael had built some kind of "don't look here" spell into whatever wards laced the grounds, but that specific protection must have been partially undone by Chariot, otherwise the spell wouldn't have wavered.

To my left down the road was a cluster of well-lit warehouses that made up the rest of this industrial park. I rejected that as the direction that Rafael had taken and headed the other way, to an undeveloped area.

I moved as quickly as I could, listening for any tell-tale sounds of his whereabouts. When the Gigis had infused the clay golem sculpture with all that magic, they'd treated it like any artifact and woven it into the inanimate object.

Then the Ba'al manifestation had stabbed Rafael, transferring his magic into my Attendant. Thanks to the Weaver magic at the base of the creature, that mix of powers was weaving itself to Rafael. Tragically, the situation was complicated by my Attendant possessing his own other magic type that wasn't even Nefesh.

I couldn't simply undo it as I had with the puppies since I couldn't even grab hold of the multifaceted Nefesh magic. It was part of that still pool now. I had to separate the two types of magic again in order to destroy the Nefesh ones, but how?

And how long could Rafael withstand this before he either lost himself entirely or it killed him?

The sound of smashed glass pierced the silence, coming from a single dilapidated building on a large plot of land bordered by a chain link fence. I squinted for a clear picture of what lay beyond. This wasn't another warehouse, but a former showroom for a development company. A weathered and partially rotted wooden development application was affixed to the fence, made out to the ward of St. Bonafice in the City of Winnipeg for a long-bygone date.

Our library was in Manitoba, one of Canada's prairie provinces. Not an obvious location, but that was the point.

Wiping away some loose dirt on the sign stating that the site was to be developed to house Laurier Mall, I grabbed an edge of torn chain link and pulled it aside, but before I ducked through, the French on the sign caught my eye. "Futur Emplacement des Galaries Laurier."

"Futur" without an e. Talia's blackmailer wasn't illiterate.

They were French.

I sucked in a breath, information suddenly tying itself into a beautiful, terrible web. Montreal. Arkady's lie.

You son of a bitch. I dug my heel into the ground. You might not be behind it, but I'd bet anything you knew who was.

More smashing glass rent the night, followed by a long, mournful bellow. I pursed my lips, let out a long shaky breath, and headed off onto the abandoned property. Arkady wasn't my priority right now, but that didn't mean he'd receive any less fury when I finally got to him. First, I had to stop Rafael from destroying whatever it was he was in the process of destroying.

I sighed. The men in my life left a lot to be desired.

Rafael had done a bang-up job shattering every window in the showroom. He had also left a trail of blood that was nice and easy to follow, at least until I got into the wooded area out back of the building.

That idiot better not get tetanus from this Hulk-rage episode. Or rabies, because when I found Rafael, he was bare-chested with blood streaming down his side from where I'd stabbed him. He pawed at the ground, attempting to catch a very confused but friendly deer—hopefully to eat—which darted in close to inspect him and then pranced away whenever Rafael moved. The game seemed to amuse the animal but aggravated an already-enraged Rafael further.

I slipped from shadow to shadow until I was right behind him.

His nostrils let out a smoky burst as he tensed to leap on

his prey, and I chose that moment to clock him with an armored-up fist. He went down like a ton of bricks, unconscious, but with a steady pulse.

Hoping that punch would tide him over for a bit with some cracking dreams, I tore off my jean jacket, pressed it to his side, and called Miles.

"What?" he snapped.

"Two to beam up, Scotty," I said.

"Pickle, you're disrupting our intimate and interactive time," Arkady called out over the phone.

There was an element of strain under his saucy tone. Perchance all was not well? I refused to feel any guilt in light of my recent epiphany about his lying ass. Words would be had and soon, but I didn't want to give up the element of surprise when I confronted him, so I focused on the irritating male from whom I required assistance.

"Miles, are you being naughty on a Sunday?" I gasped. "How provocative."

"You are my penance for whatever I did in a past life," he said.

"Oh, good. Since you're in a mood to atone, I've got a bit of a situation." I explained the problem, leaving out all mention of the library. Attendants hadn't trusted anyone with its location, not even Jezebels, and I wasn't going to reveal where it was.

"A bit?" Miles said when I was done.

"It could be worse," I said.

"How?"

"Rafael could have caught the deer."

"Fuck my life. Stay where you are," Miles said.

"You mean abort my plan to drag Rafael's large and heavy faux-god body through the woods for a good time?" I repositioned the bloodied jacket against the knife wound I'd inflicted on Rafael and pressed harder. "I never get to have any fun."

"Cohen," Miles growled at me.

"Geez. I'm not going anywhere."

Half an hour later, Rafael's knife wound had been treated and he was in the cell glowing with nulling magic in the basement of House Pacifica. This particular corridor had been commandeered by House operatives in the name of security, so not even the Nefesh police located at House HQ would know what was going on.

Rafael rattled the bars. "Let me out!"

"We can't." I stood behind the white line about ten feet from the cell, in the magic-safe zone. "It's the only way to keep you from getting worse."

"If you null my magic, I can't sense if Chariot gets into the library."

"You said the wards are strong."

"They are for now, but if I can't sense Chariot's return, they'll have all the time in the world to work on them without me there to fix any weak spots. What if they find the Kiss of Death and just waltz in?" Rafael pulled on his hair. "I have to get out. We can't leave the scrolls undefended." His voice ended in a half-sob.

"We won't. Look, I can hire someone to set up a motion detector security system outside the warehouse that will immediately alert me. No one has to know what's actually inside. If Chariot steps foot on the property to attack the wards, we'll know and I can get there immediately."

Rafael placed his hands against the bars. "What if they get the amulet?"

"They can't get in without my blood, remember?" I said gently.

"Right. I forgot." He sat down on the mattress in the corner of the cell and wrapped a blanket around himself, refusing to make further eye contact with me.

I wasn't infallible, but I hated that I'd let him down in any way. I scratched my arm. There was so much grief and anger soaked into my skin that I wished I could shed it like a snake. I'd sworn to fix this for Rafael, but he hadn't believed me since I'd previously assured him he didn't have any intrusive magic inside him. And honestly, I'd tossed that promise about so often lately, the words sounded a bit thin to my ears, too.

"Get out," Rafael roared.

It would have been crueler to stick around than to do as he wished, so I left.

I was in the hallway, arranging for a Winnipeg security company to set up the alarm system, when Arkady showed up.

"How's Rafael?" he said, once I'd finished my call.

"Awful."

"Miles ordered an operative be posted at all times outside the doors to secure the hallways and in case Rafael needs anything."

"That's good."

Arkady opened his mouth, then closed it. "Okay, well, if you're done here, Steven is on duty first—"

"Talia is being blackmailed," I said.

"You mentioned that at our meeting."

"By someone French." I watched him carefully for the tiniest sign of guilt.

He shook his head. "Well then, you should find someone else to interpret for you, because voulez-vous couchez avec moi is the extent of my linguistic abilities."

The flippant bastard. "Here's what's interesting about it. This blackmailer is threatening to expose Talia for hiding a Rogue kid unless she resigns from the party. They even have footage from the aquarium gala on the very night my magic first manifested. Isn't that quite the coincidence? I mean, who would have been watching me already, a documented Mundane, at that precise moment?"

Although Arkady didn't lose his expression of polite curiosity, he rocked back on his feet, creating more distance between us, and crossed one leg over the other—a non-verbal cue that he might feel threatened by my question. "I have no idea," he said.

"It seems rather personal. Not someone with an ideological bone to pick, but a specific grudge against my mother, wouldn't you say? In your professional opinion?"

"I guess."

"Then we have the fact that you slipped up, saying you'd been called home to Ottawa, while admitting under jet lag that you'd been in Montreal."

He spread his hands. "I told you that my grandmother lives there. She's old. I care. I visit her."

"And she does." I mimicked his hand gesture. "Of course, I verified that."

"Of course."

"But here's the thing, and correct me if I'm mistaken, but there's another reason to have gone to Montreal. One that fits this scenario perfectly. You're working for my grandparents. That's why you didn't want me to follow up with Dad's estranged family before I went to visit Uncle Paulie. Not because it would upset me, but because it would expose you." My voice hardened. "How am I doing?"

Arkady stiffened his hands, interlacing them with his fingers pointed out in a "V." He moved his fingers back and forth slowly. A classic cue that something was bothering the person. "You're wrong."

"I'm not." My smile had the cold satisfaction of a person who'd been lifting cups in this shell game over and over, only to find empty air under each, and now, finally, chose the one with the ball.

"Your grandmother died almost six months ago," he said. "I'm only working for your grandfather."

I did a double take and Arkady laughed bitterly. "Didn't expect me to admit it, did you?"

Blood rushed into my ears, along with a curious sense of relief that the secret was out. Arkady had betrayed me and put my mother in harm's way. He'd used Priya to get to me and insinuated himself into the lives of people I cared about. Now it was my play.

I shoved him up against the wall, my arm across his throat. "You fucking psycho, pretending to be my friend. Why did you do it?"

Arkady knocked my legs out from under me. I crashed backward onto the floor and he raised stone fists. "I don't want to hurt you," he said.

"Bit late for that." I locked down my blood armor and pushed to my feet.

The air grew heavy, the two of us circling like sharks.

"Do I get a chance to explain?" he said. "Or have you skipped judge and jury and gone straight to executioner?"

Part of my brain howled for payback first, answers later, but how would I face myself in the mirror if I did? Especially with someone I'd considered a friend, even if the opposite hadn't been true? I blinked through my red haze and shut down my magic.

Arkady watched me warily for another moment, before letting the stone turn back to skin. He slid down the wall to sit on the ground. "I never pretended that I cared."

"My mistake," I said frostily.

He scrubbed a hand over his face and swore softly. "That's not—whatever you think of me, the friendship was real."

Arkady thunked his head back against the wall lightly a couple of times. I'd never seen him agitated like this.

I sat down across the hall and threw him a lifeline. "Rebecca is dead?"

I'd only ever known Dad's parents as names, never even seen a photo. I didn't grieve at this news but there was a flutter inside my chest.

"Yeah. Heart trouble. She went peacefully, if that helps. I swear I tried to stop Nathan and he promised he wouldn't undertake this stupid plan."

"He broke his word," I said.

"No shit. As far as I'm concerned that absolves me of any professional loyalty. Anything you want to know, I'll tell you."

"If you were already spying on me the night of the gala, you'd have known I didn't have magic. What were you looking for? And why? Was he paying you well?"

"I wasn't paid at all. Nathan was a career civil servant who knew my dad through diplomatic circles." He scratched at a frayed patch on his jeans. Arkady's father had been the Canadian Ambassador to Russia, moving the family across continents when Arkady was young. "Nathan'd heard about my military training and that I'd moved out here, and he contacted me to do a quick job."

"Did he want you to find me?" Even if they hadn't spoken in years, there's no way Dad didn't send them a 'mazel tov, you have a grandkid' card when I was born. I drew my knees into my chest and hugged them.

"Do you know anything of Adam's upbringing?" Arkady said.

I shook my head. "Not really."

"What do you know about Hexers?"

It took me a minute to place the name. "Aren't they some lunatic-fringe magic supremacy group?"

"Very good, pickle." My heart twisted at the use of this nickname, when everything was so messy and hurtful between us. It was like seeing a glint of gold while standing in a shit heap. "Hexers are a lot less fringe and more organized than many realize," he said. "They have multi-faith temples, children's camps, and artists spreading the word. They're also very well funded. It's a deep and frightening rabbit hole, and your grandparents came from a long line of them, though they kept their affiliation quiet outside of like-minded circles. I'm not surprised Adam bolted as soon as he could."

"And you worked for them?" My voice was thick with disgust.

"I wasn't working for the Hexers, I was helping a family friend who'd asked me to find his son and daughter-in-law. I didn't even know about their connection with those people until I'd taken the job."

The reminder that *those people* were friends and community members, like Isaac, was one I wished I could ignore. It would be so much easier to paint people in broad strokes of good or bad, but that would be akin to underestimating them. That would be my downfall, just like Isaac underestimating Nicola would contribute to his.

"Nathan's request seemed harmless," Arkady said. "Then I learned that your dad had left your family, and Talia was Mundane, and I figured that his upbringing had rubbed off on him after all and he'd returned to his pure roots. Except I couldn't find any trace of Adam. I reported back to Nathan that your father had abandoned you both years ago without a trace. It wasn't enough to appease Nathan. Rebecca and he had cast Talia as the entire reason their son never came back. They despised her and wanted to cause her the same kind of pain she'd caused them. Rebecca made him swear it on her deathbed."

"Vengeance. Such a beautiful way to keep their love alive. Hang on. Do you know the date she died?"

"December fourteenth, why?"

"Nathan gave Talia ten days to resign. It seemed arbitrary and pretty generous." I shook my head. "June fourteenth is the six-month anniversary of Rebecca's death."

"That's one way to mark its passage."

"Why dig into me?" I said.

"Your mom didn't have any skeletons and to be fair, you're in an industry with its share of unscrupulous individuals. I figured I might find some shady professional behavior, but instead, I found magic." He tucked a strand of hair behind his ear. "I thought Nathan would be happy when he heard you were Nefesh, but he was too entrenched in his hatred of your mother to care."

"And the Montreal trip?"

"Nathan had been obsessing over the footage and he'd called me with this brilliant idea to use it against Talia to bring her down. I went to threaten him in person that I would bring in the cops and go very public with this. His reputation in government is important to him and that should have been the end of the matter."

"Did you tell him I'm a Jezebel?"

"No. I swear. Only about your enhanced magic. That's all I knew about at first. Once I learned the rest, I was already a part of all this."

I wrapped my arms around myself. "You mean you'd wormed your way into our lives. If this is all true, then how could you let our friendship go on, looking me in the face each time, knowing you were lying and passing on my secrets?" My voice cracked.

"You weren't supposed to matter," Arkady said softly. "But once you did, I tried to shut all this down. My loyalty was with you."

My lip curled. "Loyalty or fear of losing Miles?"

"Loyalty," Miles said, ridiculously ninja-good at walking up to private conversations unnoticed. "Arkady confessed all of this to me ages ago. He was ashamed and wanted to make it up to you by being a part of Team Jezebel."

Arkady winced. "Tell all my secrets, why don't you?"

Miles shrugged. "I told you it would only hurt more not to tell her."

There was a pause and a space where Arkady's shoulders rose, fell, and then he sighed.

"I'm sorry, Ash. It got harder and harder to confess the more time passed. I moved around too much to really have friends growing up, and I didn't want to lose you. I hoped that if I proved myself this way, my past actions could be swept under the carpet. I never thought it would go this far."

I wanted to believe him. I wanted my friend back, but I was too raw for forgiveness. I exhaled slowly, looking for items to alphabetize to calm down: Ash at the end of her rope, big fucking problem, complete shitshow, destroyed friendship...

I unclenched my jaw.

Miles held out his hand and pulled Arkady up. "Do we need arbitration? A time out? A clean-up crew?"

Arkady pointed at me. "Your call, pickle. Can we get past this?"

I honestly didn't know. "Set up a meeting with Nathan," I said. "Then we'll see."

Miles dragged Arkady away on other business. I allowed myself one lingering wistful glance before turning away.

My mother hated magic, my grandparents hated Mundanes, and I was caught with a foot in both worlds, being pulled apart by my own family. Magic delusion Ash was starting to have more appeal. Even with the golf.

Peeking in through the door for one last look at Rafael, I texted Lux about what had happened to him and that I'd like to speak to her about possible solutions. She was out of town for work but would contact me as soon as she got back.

Rafael sat huddled in the corner of the cell, his back to the door. He had given me his unconditional loyalty, just like I'd done with Arkady.

But unlike Arkady, I'd prove that I was worthy of it.

Chapter 13

I spent Monday morning putting the library to rights and jumping at every little sound, convinced that Chariot was back. I'd tested the alarm system and was satisfied that no one could enter the property without me knowing, but the fear was hard to shake. As I combed through the records for ways to block the Kiss of Death, I assured myself over and over again that even if they found the amulet, without my blood, it was useless.

That wasn't much of an assurance.

Much of the furniture was beyond repair and the records were disappointingly thin on useful intel. Plus, I was still waiting on Lux, Arkady, and getting some Blank, so Levi's text requesting assistance was an almost welcome distraction.

Until we met at my office and he filled me in.

"Golf," I said flatly. I doodled a putter in a circle with a line through it. "That's not in my job description."

"You don't actually have to play." He sat across from me, his leg jiggling, dressed in jeans and a short-sleeved business casual shirt. "My mother is at the tournament for Vancouver General Hospital and I need help getting her to meet with me."

I grimaced. "Nicola golfs?"

"It's not a communicable disease. She's involved in a lot of charities and this fundraiser is a favorite of hers."

"Why involve me? As I recall, I'm scorched earth." I added horns to the golf club.

"Not as much as I am, apparently," he muttered. "You were right about her going through with this, and… I panicked when you first told me."

Levi didn't admit vulnerability, but this confession didn't let him off the hook.

"Do you still think that about me?" I said.

He rubbed his hand over his mouth. "I think that you've always acted from your heart."

"So it's well-intentioned when I burn things to the ground."

"You weren't the only one hurt, nor were you some innocent bystander in our relationship. You made some pretty big fucking choices, Ash. And it matters—" His voice caught and he swore under his breath. "It matters that you act from your heart because sometimes it's the only goddamn thing that gets me through this." He waved a hand between us.

He'd acted from the heart, too. That's what was so damned unfair. If Levi had been slightly less heartless, he wouldn't have cared about Isaac, and I wouldn't have lost him.

But I wouldn't have wanted him, either.

None of which explained his current request. I didn't even like my family drama, so why on earth would I want to cannonball into the ocean that was the Montefiores'? There had to be a better way. "Why can't you contact Nicola directly?"

A muscle ticked in his jaw and he looked away. "She's not speaking to me."

I tried to add fangs to the horned golf club but my pen was dry. I shook it, trying to get some ink. "On account of you being an asshole."

He nodded somberly. "Yeah. But not just with her." He pulled a vial of clear liquid out of his pocket.

"Blank." I stashed the vial in my desk drawer. "You got it faster than I imagined you would. And personally delivered, even. Is it supposed to be a bribe?"

"It's an apology. I would never renege on our business agreement and I'm sorry for saying otherwise."

"Got no one else to turn to, huh?" I snickered.

But he just sat there, folded his hands on my desk, and waited. "Is that a comfortable fallback position for you?" he said.

My pen tore through the paper. Still dry. "I beg your pardon?"

His blue eyes were still distant, but it was more like looking at how dark and deep an ocean was instead of the coldness of a glacier. "You always accuse me of that. Of using you as a constant last resort, like I'm only here because I have no one left. It's getting old, Ash, and you know it. You're the person that even now, when you're annoying me so much I want to light my own hair on fire, I trust in ways I don't with anyone else."

My office was so quiet, the only sound was the air conditioner clunking on above us.

Levi pushed his chair back. "Look, if this is asking too much with my mom, just say so. I'm an adult. I'll figure something out."

Levi had come to me, not because he had to, but because he trusted me. I'd been furious when he'd confided in me at the beach because it presumed a level of intimacy between us that he himself had cut off. It was selfish and hurtful of him to put me in that position, especially when I needed an emotionally clean break.

Was it different with trust? What role did I see Levi playing in my fight against Chariot if I no longer trusted him? Was he simply the bank? I didn't know, and I didn't need to for this request. The smoother his relationship with Nicola, the better it was for my case. Levi could get to his mom faster than I could in the event of an emergency.

I shoved the dead pen in the *Baker Street Boys* mug with its fellow ink-impotent compatriots. "Unclench your testicles, Leviticus. I'll help."

He laid a protective hand over his groin, but at my laugh, slid a swanky silver pen out of his back pocket and wrote "thank you" on my pad. He left the pen on top of the paper. "Refills are available online," he said.

It was the same pen I'd used to sign the House registration papers when my powers had first manifested. I'd been so cocky, so certain of the path my life would take now that I had magic. That supposedly straight road to career success had turned into a twisty path through a dark forest, filled with personal pain and loss, but in taking it, I'd found new depths of resilience and courage. My scars were hard-won, but I was stronger for them.

"Do you bring your royal writing instruments with you everywhere in case you have to sign some edict?" I said, but I grabbed the pen and stored it in my desk drawer.

"No, I have my wax seal for that."

We took separate cars to the swanky golf club that hosted the annual charity event. As usual there was a lot of construction happening in the city. I passed one development on the west side where the tall plywood barriers that had been erected to keep the public off the site had been plastered over with giant flyers saying, "Nefesh rights are human rights."

Some guy was methodically scraping them off while his partner papered up the opposite Mundane viewpoint. Two pedestrians stopped and a shouting match ensued.

Even if we stopped the legislation, how would we stop the hate?

The only good thing about the tournament was the complimentary valet parking that came with the ticket that

Levi had purchased for me. Moriarty sputtered and belched smoke the second the snotty valet got behind the wheel.

I ignored the valet's calls for me to come back and headed into the clubhouse. It was the who's-who of Nefesh and Mundane business leaders, philanthropists, and generally loaded people. Unlike other galas I'd been to, there were no divvied-up spaces. The most they'd done was to safely stagger tee-off times between magic and non-magic parties. The pained fake smiles on people's faces when forced to make idle chit-chat at the water stations or waiting for canapes was a joy to behold.

I stole a volunteer badge off a table and pinned it to the black blazer that had been in my undercover outfit bag in Moriarty's trunk. It complimented my no-nonsense blonde bobbed wig, blue-colored contacts, and the stiletto sandals I carefully made my way around on.

One young socialite in a *darling* skort-and-visor ensemble immediately flagged me down and demanded I get her another drink.

I gave her the very special smile I saved for rich entitled assholes, but she was too tipsy to appreciate it. "I'll get right on that," I said.

In need of one further prop, I found the room where the volunteer coordinator was manning things. He was on the phone, with three other people waiting for him, so I snagged a clipboard with the entry registrations and a pen, throwing him a thumbs up.

He nodded and waved me off.

Props secured, I headed outside, positioning myself in the corner of the large terrace to scan the crowd. Beside me stood a stocky man in a green polo shirt and aviator sunglasses, who was nursing a beer and watching proceedings down on the lawn.

The most interesting activity, in my opinion, was journalist Leah Nichols interviewing Jackson Wu. A loose group of people stood off to the side watching the exchange. I recognized his assistant and a couple of other party flunkies, but even if we came face to face, none of them would see through my disguise and question my presence.

Levi believed that procuring proof of the money laundering would be enough to force Jackson to resign and not only undermine the party's credibility but kill the legislation entirely. I, however, had my doubts. Sure, a man whose entire platform was based on anti-Nefesh sentiment should go down in flames when his business dealings with a magic criminal community were revealed, but Jackson was a consummate politician. He'd find some way to wriggle out of it and come out squeaky clean.

From his body language, Jackson handled Nichols, a veteran reporter, with ease, and when their interview had wrapped up, displayed an easygoing charm with people wanting a moment of his time.

What would stop Jackson from simply denying the allegations? It'd be a case of he said/she said, where the she in question, Olivia, was dead. Jackson specialized in spinning issues.

What hard evidence would trump his denials? I didn't know yet, but there was one hypothesis I could verify.

Right after I found Nicola.

I finally tracked her down getting out of a golf cart with the rest of her party, stylish in capris and a structured tank top. The woman had crazy toned biceps.

I walked over to the group with a friendly-but-puzzled smile on my face. "Is one of you Nicola Montefiore?" I waved the clipboard. "There's an issue with your registration form."

Oh, the power of a clipboard. It was mightier than a sword. Her friends said they'd catch up to her after.

"What is the problem?" Nicola said, with a kind smile.

"It's me," I said, tapping a blank field on the top form and handing her the pen. "Ash."

"Has something happened?" Nicola filled out the form.

Nothing in her face or body language gave away the concern in her tone, she merely conveyed a vague impatience at having to redo paperwork. This woman was good.

"Levi asked if you would meet with him."

Nicola's hand stilled before she continued writing. "I don't see what that would accomplish."

"Thank you for your patience," I said brightly and took the clipboard back. As I did, I slid an old-fashioned key into her hand which Levi had given to me to pass on. He hadn't offered an explanation for it and I hadn't asked, but I was damn curious.

Nicola turned it over in her palm, her eyes wide, before closing her fingers tightly around it. "Where is he?"

"Meeting room B in the clubhouse basement."

She sighed. "This doesn't change anything. Tell him not to contact me, ragazza." She stuffed the key in her pocket and walked off across the lawn.

I pulled out my phone, but it seemed cruel to text Levi that his mother didn't want to speak to him.

Me: *Did your operatives obtain a photo of Luca? If so, now would be a good time to put your illusion skills to work and see if Jackson recognizes the Hedon contact.*

Imperious 1 responded that he had a photo and added a brief description of the man so I'd know what he looked like.

Sadly, my brilliant idea was a bust.

Jackson didn't give any indication that he recognized the swarthy man who accidentally knocked into him. Levi apologized and kept going while Jackson shrugged it off with a smile.

It was worth a try.

I tailed Levi, still disguised as Luca, back inside the clubhouse.

After the heat and crowd, the empty basement lined with golf clubs mounted on either side of the hallway was a cool relief. Did the male members come down here and compare putters?

"Excuse me," I said, pitching my voice higher than normal, "you're not supposed to be in this area."

Levi-as-the-swarthy-man turned around, smiling. "My mist—" He narrowed his eyes and approached me. "Not bad, but you look better as a brunette."

I smoothed a hand over my blazer. "Oh, come on. Different hair, clothing, eye color, body language, I should have fooled you for longer than two seconds."

"You've always been too real with me for a costume to hide who you are." He adjusted my wig slightly, his fingers brushing my cheek.

Goosebumps trailed in the wake of his touch. My lips parted and—

Levi shoved me to the ground.

A flurry of golf clubs flew over our heads to embed in the wall like knives.

The man in the green polo shirt stood there, four golf clubs now hovering around him. "You should have stayed in Hedon."

Ha! Jackson *had* recognized Levi's Luca illusion.

The clubs fired at us like missiles.

I rolled Levi under me and locked my magic armor into place.

"I don't need your protection," he said, attempting to shove me off him.

"Oh, shut uuuugh." I let out a series of stuttered groans as clubs slammed into my back. The armor protected me, but it was still a pummeling. Grabbing a putter, I jumped up, brandishing it.

The man gaped at my armor. "What's that?"

Had he never seen blood red spiky full-body armor before? I ran a hand over it like a show model. "Oh this? It's designer."

I whipped the club back at him, but he held up a hand and it dropped to the ground.

Heels tapped down the staircase. "Are you still here?" Nicola called out, reaching the bottom of the stairs.

Levi jerked his head in her direction. He tried to cover quickly and distract the man by tapping a club against the floor. "You want me? Come and get me."

Clubs tore free of their wall mounts and flew at an unsuspecting Nicola, who screamed and froze, protecting her body with her hands.

I manifested a long whip, hooked it around her ankle, and pulled.

Nicola toppled over with a yelp, while the clubs crashed into the wall and clattered in a heap.

I ran to her and crouched down. "Are you okay?"

"Sì." She rubbed her ankle. "Just startled."

Our attacker cried out. Levi had straddled him and was methodically and coldly punching him in the face. His Luca illusion remained perfectly intact and the combination of those factors was one of the most chilling things I'd ever seen.

I dragged Levi off of the man, who moaned and curled into himself, his face a bloody pulp.

Levi's blue eyes were scarily dead, like when he overtaxed himself with his magic, and there was blood on his fists and his shirt.

"Hey." I touched his face. "Come back to me."

He shook himself free. "I'm fine," he said brusquely.

Nicola hesitantly approached us. "Ragazzo."

He gave her a look that was so lost, it broke my heart. "Mi dispiace, mama."

She wrapped her arms around him, and he buried his head in her shoulder.

I hauled the man in the polo shirt into an empty meeting room to give the Montefiores their privacy, and phoned Miles.

A while later, Miles was interrogating me in his office

about what had happened for the tenth time. Our attacker had been "detained" by his people for questioning, since neither Levi nor I were in a position to come forward with our complaints and have him formally charged. We couldn't risk either of our true identities being attached to this.

Nicola had insisted at the clubhouse that she was fine and her friend would drive her home.

"Get this guy to turn on Jackson," I said, "and we can leverage that into a confession along with the proof of the money laundering." I removed the now-warm ice pack I'd been given for my back, and stood up.

The water feature in the corner of Miles's office burbled soothingly, and fresh patterns had been raked into one of the many sand gardens the Head of Security tended. Real plants populated the space as well, making it look like one big conservatory.

Miles moved from plant to plant, watering each with a small old-fashioned metal canister. "You going to see him?"

"I promised Nicola that I'd have Levi call her once he'd been examined, since she couldn't come to HQ with us." I braced myself for one of his trademark admonishments, but all he did was nod and continue his gardening.

I got to the infirmary to find Levi sitting on one of the beds in a clean shirt, with his arms crossed and a scowl on his face. "What's up, buttercup?" I said.

"They're making me rest when I have a House to run."

"So? Cower them into agreeing with you and go about your merry way."

"I can't."

"Why not?" I pulled up a chair and sat down.

"Patrice threatened to quit if I ignored his medical opinion one more time." He punched the pillow, resetting it behind his back. "Apparently there is a shortage of Nightingales willing to put up with me."

"Imagine that." He looked so petulant that I almost

laughed, but I was wrung out. "Call your mother and tell her you're okay."

"I did." He looked me over. "I'm glad you lost the wig and those contacts."

My mind flashed back to the last time he'd touched that wig. When I'd almost—that was my cue to leave. "Yup. Me too."

Levi and I weren't small-talk people anymore. We assisted each other when necessary; otherwise, we minded our own business. I'd almost made it to the door when I blurted out, "What was the key?"

Sherlock Holmes was my idol; I could be forgiven for my insatiable curiosity.

Levi gazed out the window.

So much for that. I took another couple of steps.

"It was for Mom's parents' apartment in Rome. The place was sold years ago."

"Uh, okay. Well, I've gotta go pick up my car. It's still at the golf course." Levi had been transported back to the House, and Miles had driven the Tesla—and me—to HQ, so he could question me along the way.

"When I was little," Levi said, "and things at home got… bad, I'd show Mom the key and say we should run away. She never would, but it made her smile." He waved his hand and an image of a young happy Levi with his equally happy mother appeared. "I wrapped myself in illusions until I no longer had to see the truth. But the thing about illusions?" He squeezed his fist and the image fell apart. "Yelling at her was a wake-up call." He shook his head. "No. That's not true. It took a lecture on choices that I wasn't able to ignore. I didn't help my mother leave. I was so focused on showing *him* up, proving him wrong about me, that I left her there, and provided myself with a thousand tiny illusions on why this was right."

He was confiding in me again. That asshole.

I manifested a blood red pin and poked him in the hand. "Snap out of it."

There was a very familiar stream of Italian cursing.

"You stabbed me? Again?" he roared.

I made the pin vanish. "It was a pinprick, you drama queen."

"Sane people don't go around stabbing others either over donuts or for *no reason at all.*"

"You really want to go down that rabbit hole of how sane people behave? Did they get the blood stains out of your other shirt today?"

Levi sullenly didn't answer my perfectly reasonable question, and instead rubbed the skin where I'd pricked it. It wasn't even red, the big baby.

"My question about the key did not require all that sharing, especially the part where you'd listened to me," I said. "What am I supposed to do with that? It doesn't change anything between us. I'll assist you in mutually beneficial situations, but that's it."

Levi looked at me like a shark assessing his prey, then he gave this quiet smile, like he'd come to some sort of decision. "Okay," he said simply.

Okay? Enough of him. I stood up. "I have to retrieve my car."

"I'll drive you," he said.

"You have to rest."

"Patrice," Levi called out, "I'm leaving to go rest at home. Ash will watch over me."

"Check in with me tomorrow," Patrice called back.

I opened my mouth.

Levi arched an eyebrow. "Contradict me and I'll have that shit heap you call a vehicle impounded before you can get to it."

"Insult Moriarty at your peril," I said.

Levi bared his teeth at me. "I'm terrified. Now move."

He walked out of there, expecting me to follow him. Which I did, because who was I kidding? The Tesla was a way better option than a cab or Uber.

The drive through the quiet streets was so restful that I reclined my seat and got comfortable.

"That was a good idea to test if Jackson recognized Luca Bianchi," Levi said.

"That's what you pay me the big bucks for. Here's another one." I yawned. "Isn't it interesting that Jackson hired a Nefesh in a secret security capacity?"

Levi made a smooth right turn, his biceps flexing. "Even if Jackson didn't recognize Luca, what else would he be so concerned about that he'd resort to a Nefesh bodyguard?"

"Right? Jackson had to have known about the money laundering. If Olivia's proof of Jackson's wrongdoing exists, that may be enough to force a confession out of him, but it's better to be safe than sorry. Jackson's willingness to use Nefesh despite his so-called political ideologies probably showed up before now. Find it and use it to your advantage."

Levi stopped at a red light, drumming his fingers on the steering wheel. "If anyone can get a confession out of our attacker that he was working for Jackson, it'll be Miles."

I dialed up the air conditioning. "Yeah, and taken together with any proof of Olivia's that we find, that's two instances of Jackson dealing with Nefesh. Make it three. Then it's a pattern. You'll need your case to be airtight given Jackson's position because you have to overcome years of people believing Jackson hates Nefesh and would never interact with them." Once I had the temperature adjusted to my satisfaction, I stretched out my legs. "A couple of years ago, this guy hired me to prove his ex had keyed his car. She claimed she hadn't done it, even had an alibi for when it happened, and it was hard to believe it of her since she was a doctor who volunteered with underprivileged kids. After a little digging, I found another occasion of her damaging physical property in retaliation. People act in patterns. We hope that someone won't be smart enough or persistent enough to spot our tells, but if the behavior is there, you can bet it'll show up multiple times. Dig into Jackson. Does he have the magic equivalent of an ex whose car he keyed?"

He nodded. "I'll get someone working on that. And thanks, you know, for talking through that with me. It almost makes me want to solve this other mystery from my past, one where someone used an innocent student's phone number as the contact in an online ad for a phone sex service."

"The car owner I worked for was a douche, so maybe the student wasn't so innocent."

"I had to change my number six times that summer," Levi said.

I hid a grin. "This is about Jackson."

Levi pulled into the parking lot at the golf course next to my car, the engine idling.

"Thanks for the ride." I got out.

"Sure."

He waited for me to get in Moriarty, but the damn car wouldn't start.

"Come on," I growled. There was a grinding noise and the acrid stench of smoke. I slammed my hand against the wheel. If I could put up with you freezing me to death, breaking down in the rain, and poisoning me with noxious fumes, you did not get to die on me, you fucking asshole. We were in this together.

Levi materialized at my window and rapped on the glass. I swear that man was half cat. "Problem?"

"Nothing I can't handle." I turned the ignition key again. The car shuddered and fell silent.

"Of course not. However, considering you also sustained some injuries from our attack, I'll stick around while you call a tow truck, then take you home."

"The driver can take me."

Levi held his key fob up and turned the Tesla's engine off with a pointed smile my way.

We sat in our respective cars until the tow truck showed up and took Moriarty away to the garage I frequented. I called ahead, telling them to do whatever it took to fix the bastard, then I returned to the Tesla, blurry with fatigue, my nerves raw from all the emotional intensity of the day. I yawned and must have fallen asleep, because suddenly we were only a few blocks from my apartment.

My stomach growled. Blushing, I rubbed it. "Sorry."

"Check the glove compartment," Levi said.

"Huh?"

He jerked his chin at it.

Nestled among the car insurance papers was a tin foil package.

"Lemon biscotti," I said. "And it's not even a support group meeting." Much as I salivated at the fragrant golden brown cookie, it was bound up with too many memories that I didn't have the energy for. I twisted the foil closed.

"It's just a damn cookie, Ash. Eat it."

Fuck it. "Needs more lemon." It didn't. The stupid thing was as perfect as all the others. I tsked him. "Pawning off sloppy goods, are we?"

Levi snorted. "Maybe don't lick the crumbs off your fingers to really sell it."

The jelly donut, the biscotti… Levi kept feeding me and I kept letting him, a gesture loaded with meaning—at least to me. No more food, no matter how delicious, or how cute he looked when he got that annoyed crease in his brows like he didn't secretly love me giving him shit.

He pulled up to the curb and put the car in park.

I unclipped my seat belt.

"Thanks again for your help." He placed his hand on the small of my back and leaned in like he was going to kiss my cheek. A perfectly natural gesture that he'd done with other female friends.

Was that where I'd been slotted?

I jerked back and Levi caught himself.

"God, sorry." His cheeks flushed.

"It's fine." I leaned forward to pat his arm and ratchet down the awkwardness, right as he switched tactics, stuck out his hand to shake, and jabbed me in the stomach.

He covered his face with his hand. "Fuck."

"That's okay." I waved at him with the fervor of one of those old-timey people seeing off a loved one on a transatlantic cruise. Kill me now. "Guess I'll see you around. Thanks for the ride."

"You're welcome. Try not to stab anyone else."

My indignant exit was foiled. Damn soft-closing doors to hell.

Chapter 14

I didn't return to the abandoned amusement park in Hedon until Monday night.

I'd chugged one cup of coffee too many, trying to untangle my feelings around everything Levi had confessed to me about illusions and choices.

Now at C-Game efficacy—low B-minus if I was being generous—I picked the lock on the metal gate to the Tunnel of Love, hoping I wasn't about to unleash Operation Off With Her Head.

"You're a glutton for punishment," Adam said.

No day at the fair was complete without the illusion of one's dead dad. "Hello, Fake Father. You could have at least brought cotton candy."

"Your sugar highs on that were nightmares."

I shoved the gate up hard enough that the resounding clang echoed through the park. "What do you want?"

"You should know the answer to that question."

"Well, I don't. If I'm conjuring you up, not Hedon, give me one reason why I'd do that, because I've got nothing."

Adam scratched his chin, looking skyward, exactly like he

always did when I'd thrown one of my million questions at him that he didn't immediately know the answer to. I wanted to both hug and punch him for it. "You loved your father," he said. "Maybe it's as simple as that. We live our lives in story form, and you need me to play a certain role. One day you won't."

"That day apparently isn't today," I said, and peered into the darkened tunnel.

Did Levi ever see Isaac in Hedon? What role did his father play for him here?

"I need to get going," I said, "and I'd rather you didn't come into the tunnel with me." Last time, I'd had to deal with him dying. My storytelling self had deeply masochistic tendencies.

"Be careful," Adam said, and vanished.

I eyed the tunnel, calculating the mental and physical dangers lurking inside. Could I bypass them entirely this time? Token in hand, I visualized the pink bedroom in great detail. There was a tug, like the gold coin had stuttered for an instant, then I was transported into the room.

Other than the fact that the Bookworm sat on the rocking chair instead of the bed, not much had changed. She was still in her trance, surrounded by that cumulus cloud with a milky film over her eyes.

Today's word flow included a Stephen King passage, followed by a long tract in Hindi, and then the phrase "Mind the Gap."

I pulled out the vial of Blank. "Hello. Do you remember me? I've come to help you. I have something to suppress your magic and make you lucid. It only lasts a day, but that's enough time to get you out of here if you're being held against your will."

"You think that will work?" The words were laced with disdain.

I spun around to face the Queen, feeling my racing heartbeat in my throat. I itched to put my armor on but that would escalate things too fast. "It should."

Her Majesty stalked toward me, a predator in red linen, and I held very still. "If you suppress her magic, she might not regain access to all the information," she said.

I waved a hand at the Bookworm. "She's a human being, Highness, not a tool for your ongoing lust for knowledge. She deserves a life, instead of being held hostage as your prisoner."

The Queen started. "Ah, blanquita." There was a lifetime of sorrow sunk into those words, and the skin on the back of my neck prickled. "Isabel isn't my prisoner." She paused. "She's my daughter."

My armor burst out in full force, with extra spikiness around my neck. I'd broken in and attempted to steal away this deadly woman's child by offering her drugs. I was so far up shit creek, I was heading over the fuck-my-life falls.

"How did you find her?" the Queen said.

In for a penny, in for a pound. I could only be beheaded once, right? "When I asked you about Bookworms, I smelled your magic. Why release it unless you felt threatened? Then I used the gold token and it brought me to the amusement park."

"Too clever by half, chica." She sat down on the bed, looking haggard for the first time in our acquaintance, and older than her fifty-something years.

"Why put her here? Wouldn't she be safer in your palace? She'd be protected by the Black Heart Rule."

"So was Vespa. How safe did that keep her?" She shook her head. "Isabel's magic is too rare. By the time she was five, there had already been three kidnapping attempts."

"In Hedon?" Who would be suicidal enough to go up against the Queen that way? The penny dropped. "That's why you took over this world, isn't it? This was never about ruling. It was about keeping your daughter safe."

The Queen laughed. "I'm no saint. I definitely wanted to rule, but yes, having somewhere under my control was essential. Despite the Black Heart Rule, the attempts continued, so I built her this place, woven from her memories of happy times."

"Hidden in the heart of the Tunnel of Love, kept safe by her mother. Along with the deadly illusions and that assassin dude."

"Animator magic on a mannequin," the Queen said. "My workforce isn't that dispensable." She straightened a teddy bear that lay slumped on its side amongst the pillows. "You shouldn't have survived breaching the tunnel." She hit me with her violet gaze. "None of the others did."

Abort! I dropped my armor and reached for the gold token on the chain around my neck.

"Can you really help her? Nothing else has." She watched me warily, but her words were laced with hope.

I stilled. "Yes. I've been on Blank. It suppresses magic. Levi has the only access to the supply and he would give you as much as Isabel required."

"You are asking me to trust you and Levi with my most precious possession." She crossed over to her daughter and murmured something in her ear.

A bloom of words around Isabel's head grew larger and brighter than the others. "'I had a mother who read to me / Sagas of pirates who scoured the sea.'"

The Queen stroked her daughter's hair. "It would be easier to kill you."

"My body disposal would be very messy. Lots of gristle." I held out the vial. "You know where I live if I ever betray you. Not that I would. I was willing to risk your wrath and save Isabel when I thought she was here against her will and I would never cause her harm when you just want to protect your kid."

"Not willingly, but you are engaged in your own

dangerous mission, and I don't know how long you would last under torture."

Well, this was a really depressing conversation. I shrugged, too tired to engage. "You'll do as you will, Highness."

The Queen braced a hand on the back of Isabel's chair, looking between her daughter and me. "Imagine my surprise when after years of failed attempts to help her, I met a young woman whose magic had been suppressed by a powerful ward."

I wanted to crow that I knew she'd been surprised by that fact, but now was not the time to gloat. "Did you try to find a Van Gogh for Isabel?"

"Yes, but despite my careful inquiries, I was unable to locate anyone with that ability."

"Thank Chariot for that. They're the ones who murdered Yitzak," I said.

"It's just as well. Desperate as I was to help her, I was loath to do anything of permanence without her consent. You could have taken her magic," she said, too casually.

"Not ever," I said in a hard voice.

She nodded like I'd confirmed something for her. "Give her the Blank."

I opened the vial and almost spilled half of it as Moran appeared next to me out of nowhere, sword glinting. "I'm putting one drop under her tongue," I said. "It takes about half an hour to kick in and will last for roughly a day."

The Queen nodded at me to proceed. Moran didn't give his assent, but he didn't decapitate me, either. Close enough.

I gave Isabel the drug and then handed the Queen the vial with the rest of the liquid.

"And the gold token, por favor."

I handed that over as well, keeping quiet about the wooden ring.

"Now we wait," she said.

I sat down on the ground against the bookcase and prepared for the longest half hour of my life.

"You didn't bring the puppy," Moran said petulantly. Yes, this was all a plot to deprive you of your playdate.

"Prison breaks rile her up too much. Next time." Twenty-nine minutes and thirty seconds to go.

The Queen hovered over her daughter, and every time Isabel twitched or breathed funny, I flinched.

The silence stretched on.

"It's growing lighter." Moran pointed to the data cloud.

I sighed. There went my best shot at learning whether or not Olivia's insurance policy could take down Jackson. I wanted the Blank to work for Isabel's sake, but I had an obligation to Levi and that legislation had to be stopped.

"You had a question for Isabel, didn't you?" the Queen said.

"Yes."

The Queen motioned me over. "Before her magic is suppressed entirely, put your hand on her shoulders and think of what you want to ask her. Bookworms can either pull the information for you, if they are lucid enough, or direct you to where you need to go via a psychic bond. Ask your question. Just don't touch the magic cloud surrounding her. Its effects can be dangerous and unpredictable."

I snorted. That carnival vision of my alternate life definitely qualified as both.

There was a moment, one that I'm not proud of, where I almost asked for Rafael's cure instead of helping Levi. I'd have asked about Chariot's scroll in a heartbeat if Rafael hadn't made it clear that Chariot had taken pains to conceal that knowledge from these Nefesh. Here was a chance to help my friend and I yearned to selfishly take it.

I placed my hands on Isabel's shoulders, and did the right thing. *Did Olivia Dawson create physical documentation implicating Jackson Wu in illegal activities?*

That bright, buzzy, and harsh sound from my previous visit drilled into me. I tried to clap my hands over my ears, but they were stuck fast to Isabel's shoulders.

The Queen watched me, frowning in concern, but with no sign of the same distress.

Blood trickled out of one nostril and I swayed, the world spinning and lurching. A battery of words rushed in to swarm me, serifs pricking me and round B's and P's whapping the side of my head, those treacherous little bastards nowhere near as soft and bouncy as they appeared.

I was going to die via the alphabet. How basic.

The horrible noise cut out and the pink bedroom disappeared. I stood in a softly glowing blue space. Backwards words with a silver tinge streamed around me against a soft pink glow.

I spun in wonder. "I'm inside the cumulus cloud."

"Yes. My apologies. I understand the transition can be a bit discombobulating." Isabel's hands were clasped in front of her and she wore a serene expression.

"You're very…"

"Sane?"

"I was going to say composed, but yours is better."

She twirled her finger around the space. "I've had years to create a mind palace of different spaces to make order of the chaos and keep from drowning. In here, that is. Out there?" She shrugged. "It's another matter entirely. I try to come out of the stream because I can't always be plugged in, but that's when I'm most likely to be overwhelmed with the amount of information I've ingested."

"Am I really here?" I poked a series of mathematical symbols flowing past. Cool to the touch, they rippled and shimmered gold before settling back to their normal flow.

"Your body is out there." She gestured to the pink glow. "But whatever you experience is reflected outside. Cut yourself and you will bleed. Die and, well, you get the picture."

"No dying. Got it. And you? Are you all right?"

Her smile lit up her violet eyes. I'd never seen their color before, because the data cloud and milky film had prevented me from seeing the likeness.

"Yes."

"I see the resemblance to your mother now."

"Gracias. How is Mama? You are with her now, aren't you? You're her friend?"

"Friend might be generous. It's complicated."

"Everything about my mother is."

"No kidding. She's fine. Listen, I've given you a drug called Blank that will suppress your magic. Sorry I couldn't get your consent first."

"You tried. I heard you. It will help me become lucid enough to decide what I want for my life." She paced the perimeter of the space, dragging her fingers through a series of German and Italian words which lit up in light colors and a soft melodic chiming. "What if I don't know?"

"Then this will give you time to figure it out."

"It would be nice to spend time with Mama again." She smiled again, and my heart clenched. Years of her life had been stolen from her by her magic and a well-meaning parent. Any path she now chose would be fraught with challenges.

"Do you know anything about my question?" I said.

She closed her eyes briefly. "If it exists, it's a personal belonging and not something shelved in a library or for public display. That makes it Reference Only. Restricted area." Her voice had dropped, taking on a slightly robotic quality and I shivered.

"Can you access it?"

"Now that you're here?" She shook her head. "Not if I want to hold that section of the mind palace intact. Which I must, otherwise your brain will be crushed by the staggering amount of information. The drug is muting my ability and

153

my time is running out. I do have enough magic to get you inside."

The data cloud turned a stormy gray and the temperature dropped. A thin sheen of ice coated the insides of the words and my breath misted the air.

I hugged myself, trying to keep warm. "But?"

Her violet eyes were large and sorrow-filled. "I won't be able to extricate you."

The ground rumbled and pitched, words plummeting around me. I yelped, my armor settling into place and my arms held out for balance while I surfed the tremors.

Isabel stood calmly in the center of the chaos, unruffled and untouched.

"Is there an exit?" I said.

"Yes." She motioned at my blood armor, sweeping an assessing glance over me. "If you are what I believe you to be, you can free yourself, but you may not survive the onslaught of knowledge."

The phrase "Carpe Diem" crashed onto my head from the cloud and hit the ground, still intact.

I rolled my eyes. "Do it."

"Good luck and… best you don't mention me." Isabel flicked her fingers.

"Excuse me," a woman said from behind me in a sharp voice. "You do not have library privileges."

I turned around and jumped back. "Fuck me."

The giantess, easily twelve feet high, with red horn-rimmed glasses and blond hair pulled into a tight bun, placed her gnarled hands on her massive hips. Her heels could double as vampire stakes. Because more height was required in this scenario. "You are exceedingly rude."

"My deepest apologies. I didn't expect anyone else here." I offered a hand to shake, sending a near-invisible red ribbon into her when she reluctantly clasped mine. Whoa. Magic was all that held her together. She must have been a construct created by Isabel.

That didn't make her any less dangerous.

"Where is 'here,' exactly?" I said.

She gave a flat-eyed stare at the rows of neatly-stacked bookshelves that blurred into the very far distance. "Guess."

"We're in a library. Yeah, I got that much."

"The bare minimum," the giantess said. "As your mental faculties meet the requirements for seeing yourself out, I suggest you do precisely that." She pointed at the exit sign, blinking an insistent red.

"Wait. Please." I jogged to catch up to her, because one step of hers was two and a half of mine. The enormous ring of keys hanging from her waist jangled as she moved. "Is this the Reference Only section?"

"Obviously not. One doesn't simply waltz in to—wait." She stopped so abruptly that I had to backtrack. A massive mace appeared in one hand. "Did *she* send you?"

I widened my eyes. "She who?"

If she was Isabel's creation, they were really embracing that Dr. Frankenstein/monster dysfunction.

The giantess tapped the mace against her meaty palm. "Then how do you know about the Reference Only section?" She grimaced. "You're not one of those, are you?"

"It depends. I might be." This library was way better stocked than Rafael's. He was going to cream himself when I told him about this place. I wonder if Isabel would consider giving tours of her mind palace?

"A supplicant," the giantess said.

I mean, I didn't particularly want to beg, but I wasn't entirely averse to it either. "Yes. I am Ashira the Supplicant."

She pursed her lips. "We've never had a Jezebel supplicant before. Your kind tends to keep to themselves."

"You know about me?" I shook my head. Of course she

did if Isabel did. "I am a new kind of Jezebel for a new day and age."

"How lucky for us all," she said dryly. She slid behind a massive counter shaped like a U, each side easily fifty feet long and all of it covered in towering piles of books, and stashed the mace underneath. Half-filled library carts were lined up in a row next to one side.

"Let's jump ahead six or seven sarcastic bits. I have a question, this library might have the answer. How do we connect the two?"

The giantess took a book off the nearest pile, though technically it was several pieces of papyrus bound with a frayed rope. Bet it was a bestseller in its day. She scanned it and set it on a library cart. "First you tell me what you're looking for and I determine whether or not you meet the criteria."

I explained about hoping to find proof of Olivia's money laundering.

The giantess sighed, sounding like a deflating bagpipe, and scanned the last book on the pile. "You would appear to fit."

"Excellent. For the record, what criteria was that? My insatiable curiosity? My drive and determination?"

"A challenge. Your request is a long shot, but knowledge enjoys a good challenge." That was a rather fortune cookie pronouncement.

"Then let's challenge that bitch up." I clapped my hands together.

Failing to hide her distaste, the giantess opened a drawer and handed me a laminated card with "temporary visitor" stamped on it, along with a barcode. She pointed to a blue door. "Scan this. It will give you access to the Reference Only section where you should find your answer." She placed a book on the cart. "You won't survive the onslaught of knowledge."

Isabel and her creation were really lacking in the faith department. Or they thought I was a half-wit.

"I'll be fine."

The scanner turned a friendly green when I used the pass and the door swung open, allowing me to cross into a forest made up of towering redwoods awash in gauzy sunshine. I tilted my face up to the warm light, fighting the urge to take a nap.

I strolled through the clumps of ferns, inhaling the rich scents of earth and rotting moss. The smallest tree was at least one hundred feet high and every single one had an arched opening at its base large enough to drive a car into. I placed a hand on the thick fibrous bark and peered into the arch with a soft gasp.

Inside was rung with books, spiraling up to the very tops. I ran over to examine some other tree interiors—each one was identical. This was wild.

And impossible. There were dozens of trees with thousands of books. How would I ever find the answer?

An owl hooted. Wise old owl. Got it. I followed the sound through the woods, peering up at the branches until I spied the bird perched in one, waiting patiently for me to approach. I entered the archway of this particular redwood. On a podium made of thick twisted vines with a broad leaf fashioned into a platform, was a nondescript black hardcover accounts ledger.

The first few pages were columns of numbers that seemed fairly innocuous, but several pages in, the numbers became some kind of lettered code written in a tiny neat block print. On the final page of code, the lower part of the sheet blurred away. The pages in the rest of the book were filled with more accounting entries.

My phone was with my physical body out in Hedon, so photographing the pages was out. I didn't want to piss off that librarian by taking something marked Reference Only, but maybe if I showed it to her, she'd know its real-world whereabouts, so we could find it and decipher the code.

Exiting the tree, I held up the ledger for the bird who waited on the ground nearby. "Thanks, Wise Old Owl. You wouldn't know where this is hidden, would you?"

"Reference Only!" The owl screeched, swiveled its head like the *Exorcist* baby, and puffed up to twice my size, its shadow blanketing the forest.

I looked way up past the owl's very sharp beak and into its beady eyes. "Knowledge?"

The owl stabbed down at me. I narrowly rolled out of the way, the book flying to land in a pile of leaves. The bird's beak cracked my armor and the patch protecting my left calf crumbled away. Mind palace, different rules on how my magic behaved.

The owl thwacked me into a redwood with a backhand—backwing?—that Serena Williams would have envied, followed by a swipe of its talons that shredded my remaining protective wear.

Pro tip: a little knowledge is a dangerous thing; a massive fucking Knowledge is fatal.

I clubbed the symbol of wisdom with a magically created mace until it was a bloody mess, allowing me to then destroy the library's foundational magic and wake up in the bedroom, once more in my physical body. I was covered in owl guts and feathers.

I bolted upright, having been left rather unceremoniously on the carpet. I didn't have the ledger, but this was still a win; seeing it was proof it existed.

"That is not a good look for you," the Queen said.

There was no sign of Moran.

I flung off a sticky glob that dangled from my elbow. "I dunno. It might have a certain caché with the baby seal clubbing crowd."

Isabel lay curled up groggily on the canopy bed with her head in her mother's lap. The faintest hint of the data cloud swirled around her. "I see you found Knowledge."

"Capital K. Hilarious. You are so her daughter. Who might your other parent be? Any Russian in your family tree?"

Isabel smiled sleepily and closed her eyes, while the Queen stared at me impassively.

I had to ask.

"No problems with the drug?" I whispered.

"No." The Queen stroked her hand over Isabel's hair and the final wisp of data cloud blew away. The drug had fully kicked in. "You got your answer, blanquita?"

"Yup." I spat a downy feather out of my mouth.

"Then go home. And Ashira?"

"Yes?"

"There is nothing I won't do to protect my daughter. Remember that."

I wasn't likely to forget.

Chapter 15

After the world's most-deserved shower and a good night's sleep, Mrs. Hudson and I paid a visit to Lux. Her texted directions took us to a pharmaceutical company downtown.

On the way, I put Miles on speaker to discuss the results of my Bookworm expedition, such as they were. He agreed with me that if Isabel's magic produced a coded ledger in answer to my question, chances were, this was Olivia's insurance policy. Since the Allegra Group did all their accounting digitally and Arkady hadn't come across any archived paper records in his search of the premises, I suggested Miles look for a storage facility where they housed their old documents.

Wrapping up the call, I gave my name to reception at Lux's work and settled into the bright corporate lobby to wait.

The goddess groupie exited the elevators clad in a white lab coat, with a lanyard slung around her neck. Her head was still partially shaved, but she'd dyed the electric purple a deep blue.

I crossed the floor to meet her, the pug's claws clicking against the tiles. Lux suggested a coffee place around the corner, so I waited until we were settled on the patio with our drinks and a bowl of water for the dog to dive into the matter at hand.

"Your daytime look is surprising," I said.

She toyed with her lanyard. "Did you imagine me doing crystal readings in my time off or fashioning post-apocalyptic jewelry?"

"Either would have beat this. You're a medical researcher?" I stirred milk into my coffee.

"Ph.D. in Chemistry. Lots of student debt and Big Pharma pays well. Even if my soul shrivels a little more each day." She pulled the lid off her caffè latte and blew on it. "I'm really sorry about your friend." Lux shifted in her seat, the epitome of contrite.

Too contrite.

"That's why you transported us, wasn't it? I'll bet the actual location that was illusioned up to look like the Colosseum was somewhere nice and secluded. You're not sorry my friend was hurt, you're sorry you didn't get away with it." The brew was too bitter so I dumped in a liberal amount of sugar.

Her eyes flashed, her spine tempered steel. "We spent months planning to bring our goddess back and you ruined everything."

You kids and your meddling pug. Her actions were foolish, but her motivation hadn't been.

"I'm sorry about your wife's cancer," I said. "How is she?"

Lux coughed on the sip she'd taken. "You know?"

I nodded.

She sighed, her eyes bleak. "Not good. It's metastasized to her liver."

Shit. That made it terminal. "Can Nightingales do anything? There's a talented one on staff with House Pacifica. I could speak to Levi."

"Even Nightingales don't have good odds when it comes to curing cancer."

"That's why you wanted Asherah to appear, isn't it?" With

enough sugar, my drink was hot and delicious. I considered getting a second one.

"I'd prayed and prayed. I thought if I could summon her with a gift, she'd be inclined to help Emma." Lux unraveled the rim of the cup.

"There wasn't a less extreme way of going about it?" I said gently.

Lux shot me a look of disdain. "You think I didn't try? When we learned that the cancer had spread to Emma's liver, I asked Gavriella to help."

"You did?" Mrs. Hudson had gotten herself tangled up in the table leg, so I redirected the puppy and loosened the leash. "What did she say?"

"That there was no way to summon Asherah and not to do anything stupid that would call attention to myself or else I'd have her to deal with." Lux sneered. "You Jezebels are all the same, thinking you're better than those of us who actually believe in the goddess, and threatening to keep us in line."

"I didn't even know you people existed until about ten minutes before I met you. I had no opinion of you one way or the other."

"No? You don't call us Goddess Groupies?"

Damn it, Rafael. You were supposed to be subtle. My mind evaded my attempts at a good reply. "I, uh…"

"Where do you think the first Jezebel came from? She was a Gigi, as you so charmingly put it." Lux shredded her napkin into smaller and smaller pieces. "Did you really think you were the only one out there serving Asherah? Our faith keeps her alive. Do you even believe in her? Most of your kind don't anymore. Not really. Not the way we do. You just lucked into being her Chosen One."

"'Lucked into' is debatable, but I get your point, and you're right. I was short-sighted and narrow-minded, and while Gavriella handled her interaction with you poorly, she didn't lie about not being able to call the goddess. If I could get her to show up and help, I would."

"To destroy the *Sefer Raziel HaMalakh*."

"How much do you know?" I said.

"Jezebels' origin story has been passed down orally amongst the goddess's believers. I don't know where things stand between you and Chariot at this moment, but I understand that Gavriella wanted to keep us off their radar. She just shouldn't have assumed I was ignorant of the situation and threatened me like a little kid so I wouldn't act stupid."

I pulled Mrs. Hudson away from a cigarette butt. "No, she shouldn't have. I wish there was something I could do for Emma, and I hate asking after all this, but do you know anything about the Kiss of Death?"

Lux tapped the rim of her destroyed cup, pensive. "I mean, we've all heard rumors. Nothing concrete."

That was too bad, but it wasn't the real reason I'd come today. "What can you tell me about the magic you used on the golem?"

Lux had no insights on why the combo magic hadn't affected me the same way, but she did have a suggestion on how to help Rafael. "You have to filter the Nefesh magic out," she said.

"How? It's almost indistinguishable and I can't catch hold of it."

"Same principle as basic filtration of a homogeneous solution."

"And the explanation for someone who didn't take Chem?"

"Like salt in water. You can filter the mineral back out. These two types of magic can't be untangled on their own, but when you put them through the correct filter, one will go through and the other won't."

"How do I find that filter?"

"I don't know. I've been researching but haven't come up with anything viable."

"Please keep looking. Meantime, I hope Asherah hears you and Emma goes into remission."

"Uh-huh." Lux looked away. "Will do."

Just like with the Queen, something was off. My eyes narrowed. "Don't you dare tell me you're intending to try again. You're damn lucky that Rafael and I were the ones who faced Ba'al. If anyone else had been in that ring with him, they'd have died. Would Emma want that?"

Lux leaned across the table, her eyes hard. "Fuck you."

Something whipped across my leg, burning through my jeans. It was a vine, which now bound my ankle. Great, that hadn't been the illusionist who had imprisoned Rafael during the Ba'al showdown.

I gathered all my fury and let it show in my eyes. The blood red dagger that casually appeared in my hand didn't hurt either. "Asherah isn't coming back. Should I get even the faintest hint that you're pulling this shit again, I'll—"

"What? Rip our magic away?"

The vine burned hotter against my leg and I hissed, sorely tempted.

I made the dagger disappear. We may have gotten off to a bad start, but we were on the same side. Asherah good, Chariot bad. "I wouldn't do that to you, but if your faith is as strong as you claim, then respect that Asherah wanted to protect people, not hurt them. I don't see how feeding people to Ba'al falls into the protection category, let alone would be something she'd be proud of."

Lux didn't back down at first, which I gave her props for. I also wanted to smack her, but I didn't fault her wanting her wife to recover.

"If I can't get that magic out of Rafael and he has to live out his life in a cell," I said, "I'm honestly not sure he'll survive much longer. No one deserves cancer, but you did that to

Rafael. Deliberately. Even if Asherah suddenly shows up and cures Emma, can you live with Rafael's death? Or the next person you use to power Ba'al up?"

Lux dropped her gaze to the table. "No," she said in a small voice. "I won't try again."

The vine disappeared.

"Call me if you find a filter." I tugged gently on Mrs. Hudson's leash and the two of us departed.

I'd be first in line to help Lux take revenge on cancer, but that wasn't possible. It was unfair Emma was ill and unfair that Rafael was caged and injured. I liked my villains to be clear-cut, but I couldn't slot Lux into that label. I wished otherwise, because letting her off the hook for her actions bothered me. She'd hurt one of my people and everything in me cried out for payback, or at the very least, justice. I cursed Gavriella for how she'd treated Lux. If she'd shown more compassion, maybe Lux wouldn't have felt compelled to go this route. Now it had fallen on me to show mercy.

Probational mercy. If Rafael got worse or…

He couldn't. End of story.

After a quick trip to the Nightingale at HQ to heal the welts on my leg, if not the ragged tear in the leg of my jeans, I contacted my mother.

Talia still refused to have me come by her office, so we met on my home turf at Cohen Investigations.

Mrs. Hudson had gotten a quick walk to do her business and was now spending couple-time with Pinky on the doggie bed in the corner.

My mother dropped into the chair across from me, clutching the straps of her purse.

"I found the blackmailer," I said. "It's your father-in-law."

Talia's grip relaxed, her brow furrowed. "Why? I've never even met Adam's parents."

"You kept their son from them." I shared what Arkady had

told me, leaving out his role in things. As far as I was concerned, that was between the two of us.

My mother didn't answer, just shook her head with a dazed expression on her face, because she hadn't known about her husband's upbringing. She stood up, then seemed to forget why she'd done that, and sat back down, rubbing her eyes. "How can I be certain this doesn't happen again?"

"I'm going to meet with Nathan and put an end to this," I said.

"He's a fanatic. Why would he listen to logic?"

"I can be very persuasive."

Talia's laugh was half-sob. "Violence? No. This is just going to keep happening, if not with Nathan, then with someone else." She leaned forward, her eyes blazing. "Ward up your magic again."

While Talia didn't know about me being a Jezebel or my blood powers, she did know about the ward, if not Adam's role in it. I'd told her that much and about my low-level strength.

My magic churned, stinging my skin with the force of suppressing it. I stuffed my hands under my butt so I didn't accidentally produce a weapon and do something rash. "It's not that simple," I said through gritted teeth.

Talia smacked her hand down on the desk and Mrs. Hudson whined softly. "Yes. It is. If you don't have magic, it can't be used against me. You're a documented Mundane. That video will appear to be garbage."

"I won't do it."

"And if Nathan doesn't agree? I'll be forced to step down. When we win the next election, Jackson has asked me to serve as Minister of Finance. You'd rather I throw my entire life's work away because you can't bear to part with some half-assed low-level ability?"

She was climbing the party ladder now? Committing herself even further to this dangerous and deluded ideology?

My head pounded. If she insisted on putting her party before her child, then she could damn well know the truth. No lies. No games.

When I was a kid, my family had a favorite picnic spot at a lake a couple of hours' drive from Vancouver. One summer, we were anchored at the far shore, horsing around in the water when the sky turned black and a line of storm clouds rolled in.

We jumped back in the boat, watching the rain hitting the lake grow closer. Lifejackets on, my parents rowed us back to the rental place all the way across the lake. Thunder and lightning split the sky, but Dad cracked jokes and Mom sang songs off-key, and every time the wind whipped up the waves, we all whooped loudly. I clasped the wooden bench, swaying from side to side, strung out on adrenaline and exhilaration.

By the time we pulled up, banging into the wooden pier, we were soaked. The owner of the rental place met us with towels and much relief that we'd made it in safely.

I hadn't been scared because I'd had a safe harbor: my parents.

There was already scar tissue on my heart from the two of us, and I was so tired of hiding. I'd had to navigate all the skeletons in our family closet by myself with no comfort from my mother to help me process and grieve, and if any of that safe harbor still remained, I could hand her my deepest secret and trust that she'd guard it and stand by me.

I summoned my magic, coursing through my body as vital to me as my own blood, and coated it over my skin until it hardened into place as my armor.

This was the real me. This was the unavoidable truth.

Talia screamed, one hand over her mouth, and jumped back so fast that she knocked the chair over.

I pushed to my feet. "I am a Jezebel, my magic bestowed upon me by the goddess Asherah for the express purpose of stopping the men and women of the Kabbalistic organization Chariot from achieving immortality."

My mother shook her head in jerky movements. "This is crazy."

"No. It's the truth that I've attempted to shield you from. The original ten who released magic into our world were trying to pull the ultimate con. Achieve that divine spark of Yechida, not through study and faith, but magic, and become immortal. Your precious Isaac is one of them and I'm the only one capable of thwarting them. If it comes to you or me stepping aside? I'll do what I have to in order to protect my magic, my secret, and my cause."

"You sound like your father's people. You're not some holy crusader on a made-up quest."

"Nothing about this is made-up, Mother." Mrs. Hudson pressed up against my leg and I picked her up, the armor vanishing. "I'm still Ash. Still your daughter. I just have a destiny that I never bargained for." Petty though it was, I couldn't help adding, "Jezebel magic is passed down through the mother's bloodline, same as being Jewish."

She looked ill. "Your father. Was he part of this?"

"Yes." I waited for her to ask for further clarification.

Leaching of all color, she grabbed her purse. "I—I can't."

She ran out of the office, the outer door slamming behind her.

I buried my face in Mrs. Hudson's fur, and gave a shuddery sigh. Had I been too cruel? What would have been the right way to show her? I watched through the window as Talia hurried to her car. She hit the fob to unlock the door three times, finally swearing loud enough for me to hear it up here in my office.

A million admonishments swam through my head. I could still go after her to make sure she calmed down before she got behind the wheel of her car. I flashed on the image of the Queen stroking a hand over Isabel's hair and, quietly but firmly, shut my office door.

Rafael, Isaac, my mother... a storm was gathering again. There were no clouds to presage its arrival, no subtle static charge that lifted the hairs on my skin, but it bore down on me just the same. It was going to break—and soon.

Where was my safe harbor now?

Chapter 16

"Why are his horns back?" I said quietly to Miles.

Rafael's eyes flashed red and a low growl rumbled up from deep inside him. He punched the bars several times until the fight went out of him and his eyes returned to being black and clear. His nose had widened into a vague snout, and he'd brushed his hair forward to hide the horns, which made him look like the nerd demon who got picked on by all the cooler demons, especially combined with the baggy House sweats he wore.

Miles shook his head. "It shouldn't be possible. All his magic should be suppressed, including whatever he was hit with."

I pointed at the flecks of blood on the bars from Rafael hurling himself at them. "I'm going to call a guy I know with Lockdown magic."

"How will that help?" he said.

"I identify as part of the Nefesh community, but technically, I'm not and neither is Rafael. Our magic comes from a different source."

Miles frowned at a text that had come in and fired off a quick reply. "Yeah, I know that. And?"

"While nulling should work on us, the combination of many layers of Nefesh powers with Rafael's innate Asherah ones is complicating shit. If the magic suppression on the cell is failing, do you want to chance the physical structure itself being enough to contain him? Put an extra layer of protection on it and buy me time to find a solution."

Miles rubbed the back of his neck. "Why is this guy better than anyone I could produce?"

"He's one of the people who originally got us into this mess and he contained the fake god-manifestation before."

Miles lifted his phone like he was going to call one of his own people, then he put it away. "Do it."

I stepped out into the hallway and found the contact info. "Hello, Gabriel," I said. "It's Ashira."

"The woman with the goddess name." His voice slid into a purr. "It's so good to hear your voice."

"I need a favor."

"It would be my pleasure."

"Actually, scratch that," I said sternly. I wasn't about to owe this guy. "This isn't a favor. You need to come and help fix the very bad mess you helped to create. If you don't, you'll feel my wrath."

"That might not be so bad," he said, laughing.

I shuddered. He was a sexual harassment case in pretty tissue paper. "It will be. Trust me. Get here, stat." I gave him the details and hung up.

Arkady had arrived in time to hear the last part of my call. "Tell me you didn't call Fabio."

"Fab—I mean, *Gabriel* is a useful asset. Find Gramps yet?"

"No. He's disappeared without a trace."

"June fourteenth—"

"Is less than a week away. I know."

I patted Arkady on the shoulder and he smiled gratefully at me. His confession of working for my grandfather to undermine Talia and me had hurt, but with it, the festering wound of his betrayal was draining.

We sat down to wait, killing time on our phones, both of us trying not to sneak glances at Rafael every few seconds.

"Oh fair Jezebel, I have arrived." Gabriel breezed into the corridor, wearing a silver shirt so metallic it could pick up signals from space.

"Lucky us," Miles muttered, escorting Gabriel in.

I stood up and pointed at the room with the jail cell. "Rafael's in there. Get to work. I'll be in in a sec."

Gabriel inclined his head and left us.

Miles jabbed a finger at me. "Are you planning on getting buddy-buddy with my boyfriend again?"

"Yeah. What of it?"

He made a "ugh" noise and walked away.

"You good to deal with this on your own, pickle?" Arkady tilted his head at the jail cell room. "I can stick around if you want."

"Thanks, but there's no need. I can handle Gabriel."

"That's what he's hoping."

I elbowed Arkady, who winked and sauntered off. I smiled at his retreating figure and entered the room.

Rafael reached through the bars, flames dancing over his horns, trying to grab Gabriel. "You did this to me!"

Gabriel scuffed his ankle boot along the ground. "Sorry, bro. No hard feelings?"

Rafael bashed his horns against the bars, shoving his arm out as far as it would go.

Gabriel jumped farther away.

"Stop it!" I cried. "We need Gabriel to keep you safe."

Rafael growled at me, but he pulled his arm in, calming himself with harsh breaths.

"Thank you," I said, and moved over to the far wall to be out of the way. "Get on with it, Gabriel."

Levi strode in as Gabriel was marking out the perimeter of

the cell with his footsteps, explaining to Rafael what he was about to do.

His Lordship stood beside me, his back against the wall. "I hear you're worried about the cell's nulling abilities. Did you bring your groupie here to test it out on his shirt?" He smirked.

"Actually," I said, matching my volume to his so Gabriel didn't hear us, "I'm checking his powers." I batted my lashes at Levi. "You never know when someone might do yet another one-eighty and there's a sudden opening on Team Jezebel."

Levi straightened his cufflinks and my gaze snagged on the shift of his biceps. "Ash, I cannot express how misguided you are to think that he could ever replace me. Those words about me walking away were said in the heat of the moment, and while as your ex, I can appreciate you wanting to dally with Boy Band Lite as a fuck you, as House Head, I guarantee that if you try and bring him on board, he'll find out the meaning of the word 'expendable.'"

His voice slid through me in a silky caress. He sure as hell didn't use that tone with Miles.

My nipples hardened and I crossed my arms over my chest, crossing my legs for good measure. Just because we'd had fun working together at the golf charity did not make us the kind of exes who could flirt with each other.

"I'm not eating more of your cookies," I said.

Levi gave a strangled laugh. "What?"

"You heard me."

"I'm ready to begin," Gabriel announced and pulled his hair into a man bun.

"Helps him focus," Levi said.

I refused to smile.

It took Gabriel only a few minutes to work his containment magic on the cell, but Levi hummed NSYNC's "Bye Bye Bye" the entire time.

"You're not as funny as you think you are," I said.

"Beg to differ," Levi said with an imperious toss of his head. "You think he has choreography?"

I pushed off the wall, my lips clamped firmly together. It would be horrifically unprofessional to laugh at that, which was also why it was so difficult not to.

Rafael could still pace the length of the cell, but when he tried to put his hands through the bars, they caught on an invisible barrier that sparked.

"I'm trapped well and good," Rafael said.

"No more horns, either." Gabriel cracked his knuckles. "Told you I should be a level five."

My Attendant eye-rolled like a teen influencer, while Levi gave a you're-welcome-to-try smirk.

"We'll get you out of here as soon as possible," Levi said.

Rafael sighed. "Chin up and all that. Thank you, Levi."

"Anything else I can do for you, most wonderful Ashira?" Gabriel took out his elastic band with a flourish, shaking out his locks.

Levi snorted and mouthed "choreo."

I stepped on his foot. "Nope. That's it."

"I like to eat something after expanding all that energy, know what I mean?" Gabriel said.

If you meant 'expending' all that energy, then sure.

"There's a sandwich place around the corner," Levi said. "Try the corned beef. Alas, Ash must return to work now." He waved at Gabriel. "Bye bye bye."

Rafael "coughed," and I glared at him.

"Another time," Gabriel said with a sultry look at me and left.

Rafael lay down on his mattress, staring up at the ceiling. There was no point trying to talk to him until I had some hope for a fix.

"Ash—" Levi said.

My phone buzzed. "Hang on."

Alfie had sent a text. According to his mother, the Kiss of Death surfaced briefly sixty years ago, when it was owned by a rich French philanthropist, Avril de Leon. Its location died with its owner.

Did it, though? Death wasn't the final frontier I'd once believed it to be.

Alfie texted again to say that there was a lot of renewed interest in the amulet lately. My heart stuttered. I had to get the jump on Chariot and find it first.

Levi and I said our goodbyes to Rafael and left the room. I waited for some sign we were done but Levi leaned a hand against the wall.

"I said you had my trust," he said. "Give me the chance to win back yours. Let me fight alongside you."

"Why the change of heart?"

He gave me a wry smile. "The trouble with having your head up your ass is the shit view. You told me to take a page out of my mother's book and reclaim my power from Isaac. One of many wise things you've said to me lately."

He really had listened and internalized the things I'd said. That was huge. Nicola had come to me for assistance, so I'd leverage this into helping her and accept his offer as an olive branch from a team member.

"Get me to Jonah Samuels," I said.

He blinked. "I was prepared for you to ask me to do several things, but that really wasn't one of them. He's—"

"An older guy. Kind of a dick." I ducked out from under his arm. "But most importantly, tight with the dead."

"And also, inconveniently, in prison." Levi dropped his arm, a muscle ticking in his jaw. "What do you need him for?"

"I'd like to ask him about the Kiss of Death." I filled Levi in on the amulet and my tentative plan. "Isaac is looking for it. And, uh, well, he knows about me. Being a Jezebel and all."

The world didn't blow up or crack into shards. Levi held

himself so stiffly that if I knocked him into something hard, he might shatter, and his hands were clenched into fists, but he stayed in control. A knot in my chest eased.

"Jonah is awaiting trial," Levi said. "Necromancy is illegal, and as Mayan is a key witness, I have to be careful not to find myself in a conflict of interest." His lips flattened. "I'd rather we'd have gotten him on attempted murder."

We'd decided it was best to leave my surprise visit to Sheol out of the charges laid against him because my escape was too dangerous a can of worms to put on public record. Jonah was still under the impression that he'd gotten away with my death.

"So that's a no?" I said.

Levi slowly walked the length of the corridor and back. "You'll give me a chance?"

"To win my trust?"

He hit me with a blazing blue gaze. "Yes."

I ran a finger under my collar. Back in the carnival vision encounter with Levi, he'd been the one wanting to fight for us, whereas this Levi had experienced some profound realizations in a very short time.

Was I one of them?

Could I trust him again? I sucked my bottom lip into my mouth. I gave my trust as freely as I gave my love—slightly less often than a blizzard in hell—and Levi had already broken and discarded both.

Was that another comfortable fallback position? Giving people one chance and then never forgiving them when they made a mistake, no matter their reason or how good I knew them to be?

"I will," I said.

Levi's nod was almost startled. "Okay, then. Let me pull some strings."

Please don't let me regret this.

"I'd better go." I hurried out of HQ without a look back, wondering if a reset was even possible between us.

When I got outside, I looked up at the House, bathed in moonlight. There was a faint smear of pinkish orange across the crimson exterior, almost like a smile.

I touched a hand to it. Okay, then.

Chapter 17

Wednesday was spent in a frustrating limbo. Levi texted that he was really sorry, but the prison had refused our request, despite calling in a favor from a very high-placed government official in the area. He was working on it, but it didn't look good.

Priya found nothing on the dark web about the Kiss of Death and Lux didn't come up with any possible filter solutions to separate the Nefesh and Asherah magic and return Rafael to normal. Miles's people hadn't figured out where the ledger might be, while Arkady still couldn't locate my grandfather.

If all that wasn't enough, my mother had yet to contact me after our last meeting, and to add insult to injury, my car repairs cost me the equivalent of a small nation's GDP.

I'd just brought Moriarty home when the alarm went off for the library. I'd opted for a silent alarm so intruders wouldn't know they'd set it off. Upon inspection, nothing inside the library had been disturbed. I reached for the doorknob, which had been visible to me ever since Rafael had run out the front door, and hesitated.

If Chariot was on the premises, it was likely I'd be

outnumbered. On the other hand, this might be a rare opportunity to identify more of the Ten. It was a risk worth taking.

I cracked the door open. All was clear, so I eased outside, and crept around the building, checking the perimeter. Nothing. Had it been a raccoon or a dog?

"Not much to look at, duckie, are you?" A blonde woman in her forties stood near the closed loading bay door. She held a man in a mechanic's coverall captive, a gun to his head.

"Please," he said. "Don't kill me. I have a family."

"That's up to Ashira," she said. "Will she save you and take your place or save herself? Does the famous Jezebel sense of responsibility live up to its reputation?"

I couldn't let an innocent man be harmed. It was anathema to everything I stood for as a Jezebel, but I wasn't stupid enough to hand myself over to Chariot, either.

"The oil smear on the front was a good start," I said, "but you should have rubbed some grease under the nails to really sell it. It's always the little details..." I shrugged. "Go ahead. Shoot him."

The man yanked away. "Told you she wouldn't buy it."

The blonde vanished, but before I could go after her accomplice, I heard her say from behind me, "I hate smart-asses."

She struck me on the back of the head and the world went dark.

I came to with my arms chained above my head. Struggle as I might, there were magic suppressers built into the cuffs, and I couldn't wrench free. The back of my head throbbed and when I moved my neck, my hair was matted to it.

With each breath, I gusted out white puffs of freezing air, goosebumps covering every inch of skin. I was rapidly losing feeling in my extremities, and every blink was slow and sticky, frozen tears coating my lashes.

A hard blue light bathed the slabs of beef hung on hooks

to either side and the empty metal shelving stacked against the wall.

I was in a walk-in freezer.

"Help!" I screamed myself hoarse, my cries swallowed by the cold, and my heart knocking against my ribs. Terror gnawed at my thoughts, first with needle-sharp precision, then like a muffled blanket, smothering all rational thought.

The blonde woman came and yelled at me but her words were fuzzy. There was a sharp sting, and my blood flowed sluggishly into a vial. Such a pretty color.

"I need that," I slurred, though I couldn't remember why it was important.

I lost track of the woman, but it wasn't so bad because my friends came to visit me. Priya brought Mrs. Hudson, and even His Lordship deigned to share some jelly donuts with me.

He fed me one and the jelly glooped out onto the concrete floor.

"Whoops." I laughed.

A hot copper tang assaulted me and my stomach lurched. That was a lot of jelly for one donut and something lay next to the puddle.

I screwed my eyes shut.

"Ashira," a male voice said. "Wake up."

Another friend had come to visit. I opened my eyes.

Moran leaned on his sword, breathing like he'd just run a 5k. Maybe it was one of those weird food ones, where you have to stop at different stations, eat a donut every kilometer, and then finish without throwing up. His normally pristine white disco suit certainly looked worse for wear.

"Dude, you got jelly all over your stomach," I said, and blacked out again.

I came to screaming, my limbs burning with a pins-and-needles tingling, and a heavy warm weight surrounding my body. My mind caught up with me. I'd been captured—the blood—what was this around me?

Blind with panic, I lashed out with everything I had. It wasn't much, but I was pleased when someone grunted. Yeah, take that, asshole.

Two arms tightened around me. I spasmed in their grip, continuing to fight. Get free or die. I was not about to be another slab of meat in this freezer, but damn it, I'd take that over giving Chariot any edge.

"Ashira," Moran said, wincing as my elbow caught him in the stomach. "You're safe. Breathe."

Warm. I was wrapped in heated blankets. Although I couldn't control the hitch in my ragged breathing, I stopped struggling and took stock of my environment: a study lined with warmly stained bookcases that were packed with titles in Russian and English. The spines I could read were all non-fiction history and politics. A small fireplace tiled in white blazed cheerfully, with an arresting red abstract painting hung over the mantel. It was the perfect ambiance for the busy henchman to unwind.

Moran stepped back, his hands up.

"You were stabbed." I wiggled my fingers and toes, my eyes watering at the pain. I'd almost have taken the hypothermia and loss of blood flow back.

"I was, yes. It's been quite a little while since that occurred." He was clad in a white button-down with—what else—sharp pleated white pants, but looked more relaxed—and totally healed. "Although in my defense, they were, as you would so eloquently put it, stabbed worse."

Blood on the floor... the library... Chariot...

I fumbled for my gold chain. "I need to get out of here."

"Your library is safe." Moran resettled the blanket around my shoulders.

"What library?" I said in a mostly even voice.

He moved to a small free-standing bar cart and poured

himself a whiskey, holding the decanter out in question. I shook my head. "Your quaint little book nook with the scrolls of the *Sefer Raziel HaMalakh*," he said. "Chariot was very forthcoming on the details. With a little encouragement, of course."

Of course. Moran was always very good at getting the details out of people. I sat back in the birch white chair and contemplated the vase of white orchids on his windowsill. The Queen knew about the scrolls, what they were, and the power they possessed, and now the literal most other dangerous person I knew besides Isaac knew where to find them.

I took a deep breath. What had I learned from Arkady? Trust was a two-way street. Her Majesty knew about the library, true, but she also trusted me with the knowledge of her daughter being a Bookworm. If we were truly allies, then this had to go both ways. I had to trust her with this.

"Were you tracking them?" I opened an app on my phone. The silent alarm had been reset. Moran must have used my finger to gain access.

Moran smiled, like I'd passed a test, and smoothed out the edge of his white fluffy area rug with his boot. "After that unpleasantness with the Mafia Romaneasca, Her Majesty requested that I find out who in Chariot gave the orders to attack Hedon. The Ten are now Nine. Theresa Magnon now only exists in the past tense."

Theresa's head on the freezer floor, her blonde hair fanned out, the tips dipped in blood. Her skin was waxy and her eyes wide with surprise. I hadn't wanted to face it back there, but I couldn't get it out of my head now.

Moran had killed her.

Moran had saved me.

Two stories, both true. But my father had been right back in Hedon: the way you told a story mattered. A woman had lost her life, but she had tried to take mine. I'd been saved by a friend and had one less enemy to worry about.

I dropped my head to my hands, shaking. I was still alive.

My relief was buried under a curious numbness. I wrapped the blankets tighter around me. "Thank you. What about her accomplice?"

Moran swirled the amber liquid in the glass, the ice tinkling. "An unfortunate soul who chose the wrong person to ally himself with for the sake of a paycheck. He has, as you might imagine, also bid farewell to this mortal coil."

"Oh." I allowed myself a moment to process that before the rest of the night's events rushed back to me. The blood. They'd taken my blood. "Did you find a vial?"

Moran's keen eyes glittered over his whiskey glass as he set it down next to a decanter. "I took the liberty of annihilating that as well. Do be careful, Ashira. The Kiss of Death is quite the valuable bauble, I doubt much beyond the *Sefer* would make Chariot happier to possess."

I hugged a white decorative cushion to my chest. "Sounds like you and Theresa had quite the chat."

His sword flashed briefly in his hand. "I bring out the… conversationalist in people."

One of the Queen's Nightingales thoroughly checked me out, while I stared at the sconces with white frosted glass, each etched with the Queen's heart and crown logo, that were mounted on either side of the painting. Only when he pronounced me physically fine did Moran agree to let me go. I didn't see Her Majesty, as she was with Isabel, but Moran said that she'd checked on me when we'd arrived in Hedon.

When I got home, I sent Priya a quick text asking her to look into Theresa, then grabbed every extra blanket and buried myself under them in my bedroom. Even sweating, there was a cold knot inside me that I couldn't melt. I'd been so focused on Isaac that I'd dismissed the danger that the rest of the Ten posed, and nearly died.

Restless, I tossed the covers off, grabbed my car keys, and drove mindlessly around the city, constantly changing radio stations to surround myself with voices, and telling myself that I was here. I was alive.

I ended up in the one place I'd known I would. In front of Levi's house. I rested my head against the steering wheel. What a fucking hypocrite I was, bitching at him for seeking comfort in me, when I yearned to do the same.

Luckily he was at work, so I couldn't make a fool of myself. I sat there, imagining the sound of the waves through his open living room window, sunlight bathing it all in a hazy gold. Eyes closed, I hugged myself, pretending I was safe in his arms.

Someone rapped on the window and I screamed and jumped, only to be strangled backward by the seat belt.

Levi stared at me through the glass. "You've been sitting outside my place for an hour."

His house was monitored. Of course it was.

I gripped the car key, but couldn't make myself turn on the ignition.

"Were you casing the joint?" His voice was light but there was a tightness at the corner of his eyes. "Or do you suspect members of Chariot using this as a hideout, too?"

"Could we punch out for a few minutes and you ignore everything I said about emotional therapy dogs?"

He bit his lip, rocking back on his heels. "Do you want to come inside?"

I was already halfway out the car door, so that was a yes. I followed him through the gate and up his drive, rubbing my hands over my arms, convinced my breath was puffing out in cold white bursts.

Levi motioned to his living room with a questioning glance but I shook my head and went into his office, filled with functional furniture and the massive aquarium with multi-colored fish darting quick-silver that dominated the space. He didn't have jellyfish, but the tropical fish were soothing enough.

I sat down in his ergonomically aligned desk chair, while Levi leaned against the desk, both of us bathed in the muted blue light of the tank. A fat orange fish with a black stripe head-butted his way through a school of neon tetras, scattering them.

"That's Nacho," Levi said. "He's an asshole."

"Would it be all right if I sat closer?"

He frowned, but nodded. "Sure."

I rolled the chair over to him, and lay my head against his side, drawing my knees up to my chest.

Levi sank his fingers into my hair. I tensed for a second, then relaxed under the slow pressure of his massage.

"How close did you come to dying?" he said conversationally. He chuckled when I started. "You wouldn't be here otherwise."

"Chariot got me."

He stilled. "Isaac?"

"No, a woman." I told him about it as succinctly as possible, by which time I was in such a tight ball with my head pressed against my knees, that my words were muffled.

Levi tried to tug me up, but I shook my head, not wanting to see pity on his face at how easily I'd been captured.

"We're punched out, you infuriatingly stubborn dork. You almost died, so let me give you a freaking hug."

I glanced up. His annoyed brow crease was in full force.

We sat down on his area rug and Levi wrapped me in his arms. I leaned back against him, my hands over his, wishing we could keep existing in the right now.

Levi propped his head on my shoulder, his cheek resting against mine.

Secure and lulled by the fish swimming in the tank and Levi's arms around me, I felt safe enough to acknowledge how vulnerable I was going up against that behemoth. I'd intellectualized how bad it could get, but never felt it on this primal level. I hadn't anticipated Theresa being a Transporter and it had cost me. Being a Jezebel meant I couldn't hide away, but how could I anticipate every possibility?

I'd been hung on a hook and left to die. If Moran hadn't arrived…

I shivered.

Levi's hold on me tightened.

Almost dying had given me a clarity about how much I wanted to live. I took the fear and adrenaline and anxiety of my near-death encounter and honed it into a weapon. Whatever Chariot threw at me, I'd overcome it. I would win.

But I wasn't sure if I'd ever be warm again. And not just warm like the way Moran's blanket had felt, like an emergency ebbing back to survival, but warm, like cozy. Like feeling truly at home and happy again.

"I should go," I said, twisting around to face Levi. "Thank you."

He caressed my jaw with his knuckles and met my gaze, the silence between us as sweet as cotton candy. It didn't take away our hurt or resolve anything, but knowing we could exist outside everything and act from our hearts, mattered.

The moment shifted and spun away. I mimed punching back in but Levi gently caught my fist.

"We're fighting together now," he said. "If you sense Chariot is close, call me."

It was one thing to discuss Chariot in the broad sense, but how Levi would cope if I needed help with Isaac remained to be seen.

"I won't forget," I said.

∽

GIVEN the physical and emotional fuckery I'd been through, I was stress-eating chocolate chips out of the bag for breakfast on Thursday when I got a text from Levi.

Imperious 1: *We're in.*

I punched the air. One obstacle down and one necromancer to shock the hell out of with my death-defying reappearance, coming up. This would also be the first test of trust between Levi and me. I tossed the bag down, slightly queasy, but damn, I missed working with him on a regular basis. I pressed the phone to my chest for a moment, then fired off my reply.

Me: *Let's rock and roll.*

Located on an Area 51–type tract of land that showed up as a giant blank on Google Earth, Jonah was currently incarcerated in a maximum security prison designed to contain powerful Nefesh. We'd used the House operative with Transporter magic to take us to the front gates, since Levi didn't have the time to spare for a regular flight.

Were I him, I'd have foregone air travel entirely for Star Trek Beam and Go, but frequent use severely depleted the woman, so he generally only used her powers for short jaunts in emergency situations.

Two guards, one male, one female, both with machine guns, met us at the electric fence to verify our paperwork. They had Australian accents, fitting the red dusty landscape dotted with scrubby brush. We were in the Outback.

They were exceedingly thorough, verifying details, checking the papers themselves under some kind of anti-forgery light, and subjecting us to eyeball scans. I thanked my luck that was my only body part subjected. Once we were clear, they provided us with a jeep to drive the mile or so up to the prison proper.

A buzz of magic that I'd held at bay under my skin flattened out to an emptiness the second we passed through the gates, because the entire massive property was nulled. I couldn't begin to imagine the constant magic power it took to sustain it on that scale.

The only radio station that I could tune in played scratchy hits of the '60s and '70s, which was fine by me, especially when Elvis's "Jailhouse Rock" came on. I cranked the volume, head bobbing as I sang, but had barely gotten through the first verse when Levi snapped the music off.

I held my blowing hair out of my face. "Methinks you don't find a festive air appropriate for this occasion."

He took one hand off the wheel to wave dismissively. "Nah, I just can't stand Elvis." He glanced at me briefly before turning his eyes back to the road. "How are—"

"I'm dealing. Let's focus on today."

His Lordship had foregone a suit to dress in all black, jeans and a T-shirt that hugged his biceps. He even wore motorcycle boots. With his hair slicked back from his face and his dark shades, he exuded this ruthless vibe that had me pressing my legs together and covertly checking him out from under half-slitted lashes.

His thigh muscle tensed as he shifted gears in much the same way as when he thrust inside me and—

"So, what music do you like?" I said, too chirpily.

He shrugged. "Whatever."

I lowered my sunglasses to give him the full effect of my raised eyebrows. "Oh, Leviticus, had I known this about you, I'd have insisted on some clauses in this probationary trust period."

"Yeah, your negotiation skills were pretty thin." He broke out a tiny grin.

"A mistake I won't make twice."

The prison was a delightful structure made of turrets, barbed wire, and misery. The building glowed a dull silver, evidence of the nulling magic on it, and should that fail, armed guards with "fuck off and die" weapons manned checkpoints on both the ground and roof.

"Subtle. I like it." I waved at them.

Levi pulled into one of the stalls marked for visitor parking outside yet another fence that surrounded the prison building itself.

I tapped my foot as the gates slowly swung open.

"Nervous?" Levi said.

"Excited to see that asshole's face when he realizes I survived." That was true, but even I had to admit that what I was proposing was somewhat insane. Ever since Rafael had told me about the Kiss of Death and his conviction that Chariot knew my identity, I'd felt like I had a target on my back. How right I'd been. They hadn't waited until they had the amulet to attack, and that strike had left me with a low-grade stomachache that wouldn't go away.

"We can still walk away," Levi said.

"No, we can't. The other interested parties have a lot more resources at their disposal. This is the one thing they don't have. I survived Jonah's magic before and there's no reason to believe otherwise. This avenue is worth pursuing." I scuffed my toe against the dirt, kicking up a tiny cloud of dust.

"But you're nervous."

"I... yeah."

Levi fist-bumped me. "You're not alone. We got this."

"Totally." I crossed my fingers behind my back that my idea didn't backfire horribly, then steeled my shoulders and marched inside.

Chapter 18

A very solid metal door was all that stood between us and the rest of the prison. The soundproofing in this grim reception area was amazing because I heard nothing beyond the hum of the air-conditioning.

There was another delay while our identities were once more verified, but finally we were led through a maze of indistinguishable corridors and into a windowless room. Levi and I sat down at a metal table that was bolted to the concrete floor.

A door buzzed open and Jonah was led in by more armed guards. He stumbled, his face draining of all color. "You're alive? Impossible." He jabbed a manacled hand at Levi. "You're using illusion magic."

Levi arched an eyebrow. "In a prison that nulls all magic? Come on, Jonah. You know better than that. Ash is just hard to kill."

"Much like a cockroach," I said. "You know why we're here?"

Jonah pushed a hand into his red hair, tufting it up messily. "I thought I'd be doing this with him."

"Never assume." I leaned forward and spoke in a low voice so the guards couldn't hear us. "I escaped your death trap once so understand that anything you try and pull, I'll survive that, too. Then I'll come back. Mr. Montefiore," I said, patting Levi's arm, "is extremely powerful to have secured the prison's consent. Fuck me over, and next time it will be you and me with no guards and no nulling. Then it'll be my turn for magic show and tell. Got it?"

Jonah attempted to scoot back, but as his chair was bolted to the ground, didn't get as much distance from me as he'd hoped. "Yeah."

I actually had no clue how Levi had pulled this off. I'd asked him why Jonah had agreed, been told it was in exchange for a better lawyer on his case, and then the Transporter had shown up.

A small militia accompanied Levi, Jonah, and me back outside the prison grounds to where the necromancer's magic once more functioned. The sun beat down unmercifully on us, heat waves rippling off the parched earth.

Even with my sunglasses on I was squinting, and sweat plastered the back of my T-shirt to my skin. It was glorious and almost enough to thaw me out.

Jonah was sweating way too much for it to be temperature-related. He looked nervously over his shoulder at the small arsenal of guns trained on him. Plus, now all the guards' magic worked as well. One wrong flinch and he'd be a smear on the earth.

Jonah crackled his knuckles. "Avril de Leon?"

"Yes," I said.

The largest and most menacing prison guard, with a semi-automatic slung across his chest and his skin glistening from the poison magic coating it, stepped forward. "You have three minutes."

He clicked a button on his watch.

Jonah closed his eyes, murmuring under his breath. I caught Avril's name, but most of it was too quiet for me to hear.

The wind stirred in this desolate land, ruffling my hair, followed by an awful stillness. I held my breath and even the tiny spiky lizard crawling past paused.

A black smudgy shadow materialized and slammed into me with much the same sensation as I imagine being whapped across the face with a wet fish would feel. The Repha'im got comfortable inside me, expanding to take up space like an entitled white man. My Ash consciousness or soul, or whatever you wanted to call it, was effectively stuffed in the corner of my meat sack.

"Bon sang, qu'est-ce qui m'est arrivée?" said a delighted and saucy French-accented voice from my mouth.

I tried to speak but Avril, the Repha'im, bid me "tais-toi" in my head and did the mental equivalent of kicking me to the curb and skipping over my prone body to step into the limelight.

"Oh là là." Avril ran a hand over my body, all manner of French and probably filthy thoughts whispering in my head as she thrust out my chest in Levi's direction and flicked my hair back. "Are you my welcome-back present?"

Levi clamped his lips together, his shoulders shaking.

I was going to kill him. We'd agreed he should ask the questions in case I was in no condition to once Jonah had bonded Avril to me or in case she responded better to a man. Seems I'd made the right call. Still.

I squashed the dagger starting to manifest in my palm.

"Two minutes, forty seconds," the head guard said.

"Avril, ma chère." Levi kissed her hand. "Je suis enchanté à vous rencontrer."

Fine. Avril and I both swooned at how a simple statement turned into word porn in Levi's low gravelly voice, but we were on the clock here. I muscled my way back into control and stepped on his foot.

Levi smirked, not quite ducking his head in time for me

to miss it. "I have some questions about the Kiss of Death. Did it really work as advertised?" he said.

Avril covered my mouth with my hand. "You know about that? Ah well. I certainly hoped so. Unfortunately, life got rather dangerous for me and I was unable to use it before my demise."

"Do you know what happened to the amulet after you died?" Levi said. "Did it go to another member of your... religious organization?" We had no proof that Avril had been part of Chariot, though it was a reasonable assumption. "Can you give us any names of the Ten?"

"You've unearthed all my secrets, haven't you?" She trailed her fingers down Levi's arm. "Smart and handsome."

"Fucking hell," I snapped in my voice. "Answer the damn question already. Where is it?"

"Hmph." She sniffed and fell silent. In fact, I felt walls slam up, dividing the two of us.

"Hello?" I pointed at Jonah. "Make her do something."

He scuttled back a couple of steps. "You pissed off a French woman. This is beyond my control."

"If we may have a moment of privacy?" Levi said. He pointed to a spot several feet away but still in sight and firing range.

"Two minutes," the guard said.

Levi took my elbow and led me away. Speaking in flawless French, he cajoled and flirted. I didn't actually understand what he was saying, but I could read tone of voice and body language, and Levi was pulling out all his famed charm.

The performance may have been for Avril, but I was literally standing right there. It was my body he caressed with casual touches, and how come he'd never bothered using the charm offensive on me?

Scowling, I stepped back, which amused him.

"One minute."

Avril finally deigned to reply.

Levi said something in response and then switched to English. "Ash? How bad do you want this answer?"

"Oh, I'm cool with whatever," I said sarcastically. "The joy of having this French Mata Hari inside me is reward enough."

"Yeah, but she—"

"Thirty seconds," the guard called out.

"Levi," I snapped. "Get the damn location."

He nodded and, cradling my face in his, kissed me.

I froze in surprise, but Avril launched into action, kissing him back like a woman starved for affection. I guess if I'd been dead a while, I'd have done the same.

The rational part of my brain insisted that this kiss was fairly chaste by Levi's standards and to let Avril have it for the sake of the mission. That resolve lasted .025 seconds before my libido mentally elbowed Avril in the head. I grabbed Levi by the belt loops, and pulled him flush against me. He met my eyes and the tiniest grin quirked up his lips before he dipped me into a hot reckless kiss, our tongues tangling, that made my toes curl.

The floodgates didn't simply open, they crumbled under the tidal wave of desire, sorrow, and pent-up emotion that exploded between us.

I bit down on his lip and Levi's eyes darkened. He growled against my mouth, turning the kiss punishing.

"Time!"

Levi broke the kiss with a dazed expression. I clung to him, his shirt bunched up in my fists.

Jonah slow-clapped. "Good show."

My cheeks blazed and I pried my fingers off Levi, resisting the urge to run them over my swollen lips. This was bad. I mean, it had been good. Very good. Except, it clouded my judgment on how to proceed where Levi was concerned. Which was bad.

The guards looked unimpressed by the entire episode. Bless them.

"Fair is fair." Avril told us the name of a French town where her family had an estate. While she didn't know if the property still belonged to them, she gave directions to the exact spot where the amulet was buried. She'd hidden it before her death, refusing to give any of the Ten the satisfaction of having it. What a team player. Then she rattled off something else in French that was too fast for me to understand.

I walked over to Jonah and jabbed him in the chest. "Send her away now."

"I like it here," Avril pouted.

"Not up for debate," I said.

Jonah did more muttering under his breath, along with some complicated and hopefully necromantic hand movements.

Avril laughed.

"I can't get her out." Jonah looked flummoxed.

"Excuse me?" Levi's voice had a dangerous edge.

Jonah's gestures grew more and more flustered as he tried again. And again. Eyes wide, he looked at me, and then crowded up against the head guard. "This sometimes happens with a very strong-willed soul."

"This body is not optimal, but it's better than being dead." Avril gave a very Gallic shrug with my shoulder. "I can work with it."

"You've had your allotted time. The prisoner must return to his cell," the head guard ordered.

"No!" I lunged for Jonah. Approximately seventy-two thousand red dots appeared on my body. I froze and put my hands up.

Two of the guards seized Jonah and the entire militia escorted him back inside the prison fence.

Jonah glanced back over his shoulder with a contrite expression. "Sorry."

And then there were three.

Avril was moving my various body parts around like she

was taking them for a test drive while I suffered a crisis of conscience. I'd expected Jonah to send Avril back to Sheol. I could get her out of me—Jezebel, after all—but I destroyed Repha'im. It hadn't been a moral quandary when I'd done it to Gunter inside of Levi's ex, Mayan, because he'd already committed arson and attempted murder and he was doing his damnedest to add me to his body count.

It was different with this woman. She'd probably done unspeakable things when she'd been alive and part of Chariot, but I was only familiar with the woman sharing my body who was guilty of nothing more than being a flirt. Souls in Sheol still existed on some level. The finality of this act made it cold-blooded murder.

Levi had been on his phone arranging for his Transporter to come back, no doubt certain I could handle this. Of course I could, what choice did I have? My body was prime real estate and this squatter had to be turfed, but my magic didn't rise as fast as usual.

I snagged Avril's smudgy self in my red forked branches with a curious sense of detachment, almost outside my own awareness. Imagined or real, I'd swear her shock echoed through my bones, and in my head I heard her pleading for her life.

The worst thing about this was the absolute clarity. I wasn't lost to a magic high, and when those white clusters bloomed, so too did an icy certainty that I had somehow irrevocably stepped onto a path from which there was no redemption.

The operative with transport magic brought us to Levi's office. After we'd thanked her for her assistance and she left, I asked Levi the most pressing question.

"What did Avril say to you in French after we got the location?"

"She gave me the name of a member of the Ten back in her day who may still be alive. Misha Ivanov."

"Misha is a short form of Mikhail." I did a quick calculation. "Avril died sixty years ago so even if Misha had been only twenty, he'd be in his mid-eighties today. A good wind could have him shuffling off this mortal coil. Time is of the essence in following this up." I got all of four steps closer to the door, before turning around. "How'd you secure the prison's permission to take Jonah into magic range?"

How badly did he owe someone for this? I gnawed on my thumbnail. Would paying up land Levi in trouble?

"That was all you." Levi grabbed two bottles of water from his small fridge.

I caught the one that he tossed me. "I didn't do shit."

"The Queen called me about a supply of Blank right after another frustrating conversation where my request had been shut down. She said she'd take care of our entry for you in thanks for helping her daughter." He uncapped the bottle and chugged half of it back. "You left out a few details about the Bookworm when you asked me for the drug."

"Selective fact-telling is kind of my jam." I rubbed a hand over the back of my neck. "You and I weren't in a great place at the time. I shouldn't have withheld that from you, though."

Levi leaned against his desk and regarded me. "You got really quiet back there. Do you want to talk about it?"

"Nope."

"Ash."

He was going to harp on me until I shared all my feelings about Avril's death. Sighing, I pressed the heels of my palms into my eyes. "It was monumentally horrible."

He cleared his throat. "I did ask if you were okay with it."

I blinked up at his flat tone. "Not the kiss, dummy. That was…" I traced a line of condensation down the outside of the water bottle. "I meant Avril. I killed her. Snuffed her out of existence. I'm not some deity playing with the lives of mere mortals, and yet, look at me." I scrubbed at my skin, but the stain was on the inside. "I've taken a lot of shitty steps on this journey and I keep swearing that this time that line isn't going to move another inch, but it always does."

At what point would I cross so many lines that I no longer recognized myself? Would I even like who I was at the end of all this?

"I'm going to see Rafael," I said. "Could you send Arkady to retrieve the amulet? I don't have the emotional bandwidth right now to focus on anything other than curing Rafael."

"Sure, but Ash, you didn't have a choice."

"I told myself the same thing, but the hell of it is, Levi, that I did. Life is a series of choices and in the end we hope we come out ahead. I backslid hard today."

"Are we still talking about Avril?" To all outward appearances, Levi was the picture of casual and relaxed—if you ignored his fingers tightening on the edge of his desk on either side of him.

If I had a time travel machine, how far back would I send myself? Two months ago? The revelation about Isaac would have happened regardless, leaving me re-living the heartbreak all over again. Hard pass. The night of the auction in Tofino before I kissed Levi for the first time? I rubbed a hand over the pang in my chest. Or the day back when I was thirteen that I picked Camp Ruach of the two options that my grandmother had presented me with?

His unscrupulous gaze didn't waver, waiting for an answer I didn't have.

"Your old couch was better." I flicked a hand at the offensive furniture and left.

Chapter 19

When I got to Rafael's cell twenty minutes later, I was a carton of mint chocolate chip ice cream and two plastic spoons richer. The regular nulling magic worked on me, but Gabriel's Lockdown magic was specific to Rafael, preventing him from reaching through his bars.

I sat down on the cement floor next to the bars, and thrust a spoon into the cell. "Unless you'd prefer some healthy granola?"

Rafael sighed, looking miserable, folded himself cross-legged on the other side of the bars, and took the utensil. "Priya came to see me," he said. "She offered to visit Gavriella's grave while I'm in here."

"That was nice of her." I unlocked the cell with the key that Miles had given me and slid the carton in to him before resettling myself on the other side of the bars. The memory of Gavriella, tortured, broken, and dying in my arms, overwhelmed me. I had an eerie premonition that if I went to her grave, I might not ever leave. Reaching through the bars for some ice cream, I sucked on the cool mint, focusing on the chocolate chip melting on my tongue and not my premature demise. "How are you holding up?"

"Depends. How close are you to finding a way for me to get out of here?"

I told him about Lux's hypothesis about a filter. "I just haven't found the right one yet."

"Then I am slowly going mad." He dug out a giant scoop and crammed it in his mouth.

"Do you have any ideas?"

"No."

I scraped at a solid section of the dessert. When Rafael had been upset about the effects of me using his magic as a healing boost, he'd soldiered on. He'd attempted to find another solution for my cravings, had worked on the code name, and accompanied me in hunting for the fourth scroll piece so that he could be the one to physically handle it and mitigate my symptoms.

This version of Rafael, the one who'd given up, unnerved me. First Levi, now him. Two strong, confident men of action had retreated in defeat. Levi might have turned the corner, but what was getting in Rafael's way from bouncing back?

"Enough of the pity party," I said. "Get your head in the game. You're a fighter and a Seeker of answers just as much as I am, and you know the most about your magic. What could I use to separate them out?"

He rallied, but in the end, we remained as stumped as ever. Rafael dropped the spoon in the carton, his shoulders slumped.

"It's not all bleak," I said. "I may have found the Kiss of Death. It did belong to a Chariot member, and I got the name of another man who might be one of the Ten. Misha Ivanov."

I quickly searched on my phone through some P.I. databases I had access to. There were a number of Mikhail Ivanovs, but the only one in the correct age range was recently deceased. No cause of death was given. I smacked the floor. "Damn it. If this is him, it's a dead end. Literally." If I had the correct Misha, had he been replaced yet? Had Deepa or Theresa?

Whatever Chariot's number, I was too used to calling them the Ten to switch now.

"Have you checked on the library?" Rafael said.

"All is well. You think Chariot knows you're my Attendant?"

"Of course. They knew my father was Gavriella's and how the power is passed down."

"Why didn't they ever go after you for the library's location?"

"To what end? Torture it out of me? It didn't work with my father." He stabbed his spoon into the carton. "We Attendants are very hard to break."

Shit. That's the reason Franco had been killed? I reached through the bars and squeezed his leg. "I'm so—"

"Worry about yourself," Rafael said. "It's your blood that's required to gain entry to the library once they've found it."

"About that…"

Rafael turned one shade short of apoplectic at my capture.

I waved a hand around his face. "Is your distinctive coloring about Theresa, the freezer, or the Queen knowing about the library?"

"You could have died, Ashira. I should have been there watching your back. The situation has become deadlier than ever and I'm nothing but a burden."

"Is that what you think?"

"Do you see any evidence to the contrary? I underestimated the Gigis, and now I'm stuck here in a cage when you need me." He slammed his hand against the bars.

I winged my spoon at him, hitting him on the cheek. The spoon bounced off and landed in the carton. Ten points.

Rafael wiped off the splat of ice cream with a scowl.

"First off all," I said, "lose the offensive nickname. They're Asherah's Followers."

201

"Getting rather chummy with the people that did this to me, are you?" he said bitterly.

"Yeah. We're weaving friendship bracelets. I'm not condoning their actions, but Lux masterminded the whole Ba'al thing because her wife has terminal cancer and Gavriella was a dick when Lux asked for help in summoning the goddess."

"No one knows how to summon Asherah," Rafael said.

"Don't be obtuse. Now, I said this before when you were all weirded out about your hard-ons from those magic boosts, but you obviously are too bone-headed to believe it. No one expects you to be infallible. If you're setting up some standard of perfection, do you have any idea how much stress that puts on me to live up to it? Geez."

Rafael smiled wryly. "That's what Priya said."

He'd discussed actual feelings with her? Interesting. "That you don't have to be Mr. Responsibility at all times and can let others have your back?"

"That you being some paragon of perfection was impossible."

"Ha. Ha."

"But it's not about perfection." He stood up and smoothed out the blanket on his cot because apparently its hospital corners weren't sharp enough. "It's about choice. Our journey together hasn't been as I envisioned, but with every step, I've made my choices and I stand by them. Being locked up has given me a lot of time to think, and I've been unable to envision any choice now that changes my situation. I feel powerless."

"You're angry."

"Wouldn't you be?" He snorted. "Isn't that your basic setting these days?"

"It was." I wrapped my arms around my bent knees. "Too much has happened in the past few days."

Rafael re-tucked a corner of the blanket under the mattress. "What did you replace it with?"

"Uncertainty? Fear?" I thought about Levi. "Misguided hope? I'll tell you when I know for sure. I chose anger for a long time, but I'm on the other side of these bars and I dunno, in some ways, I feel as powerless as you do when it comes to what to choose next. Perhaps our only choice is as simple as keep going."

His bed made to exacting standards once more, he sat down and handed me back my spoon. "Did I really attempt to eat a deer?"

"Yeah. It was pretty, um…"

"Badass?" he said hopefully.

"Psychologically damaging."

Rafael rubbed a hand over his jaw. "I suppose while we're baring our hearts to each other, I also have a confession to make. The rage associated with this otherworldly interloper is getting rather hard to control. Almost impossible, in fact. Even with the cell and its warding, I fear with time I'll be lost entirely to it." He gave me a sad smile. "That won't bode well for you regaining consciousness after destroying the *Sefer*."

I snapped the spoon in half. "That's it!"

"What's it?"

"The threat the *Sefer* poses." I jumped to my feet. "Rafael, my brilliant Attendant, you may have given me the cure. I'll be back soon. I promise."

"Wait." He banged on the bars to get my attention before I ran out of the room. "Get me a laptop. Let me investigate Theresa." He sounded excited for the first time in ages.

"You got it."

Miles flagged me down in the corridor. "Walk with me."

I shivered, and handed him back the cell key. "Oooh, so commanding. Could you use your dominatrix voice for good and rustle up a laptop for Rafael?"

Miles shot me his "you are such a pain in my ass" look

that I'd almost become fond of, but he also stopped to speak with the posted operative about doing as I'd asked.

The section of the basement we crossed into was also used by the Nefesh police force and Miles nodded to a number of cops. "Jackson didn't hire your attacker, one Billy Chesterman. Olivia Dawson did."

"Say what now? Was she buddy-buddy with a myriad of shady Nefesh?"

Miles cracked a grin. "Billy and Olivia met because she mentored him in prison. She worked with convicts teaching them basic accounting and bookkeeping skills."

"Nefesh prisoners?" I said.

"Some. We looked into this mentorship program. It's legit."

"Was Billy hired for Jackson's protection or Olivia's?"

"Both?" Miles shrugged. "All Chesterman knew was that Olivia was scared that Luca Bianchi would come after Jackson for screwing up some business deal. If the police started investigating, it wouldn't look good for her. Wu didn't even know Billy was shadowing him."

"Then Jackson really didn't recognize Levi's illusion of Luca. Fuck." I pushed the call button for the elevator. "Screwed up a business deal, huh?" I scratched my head. "That means the money laundering wasn't Jackson's idea. Damn it. I had it all wrong."

"Yup." Miles smirked and I shot him the finger. "My guess," he said, "is that Jackson learned about it after Frieden's death and made Dawson shut it down. He's on the level about hating Nefesh."

Dealing with Chariot made me suspect that everyone had a hidden agenda, but Jackson was exactly who he purported to be. Unfortunately.

"There's still Olivia's insurance policy," I said. "She documented something in that ledger."

"Chesterman didn't know anything about that either." Miles motioned for me to step into the elevator car first.

I pressed the button for the parking lot. "Hang on. When I asked Isabel, I didn't specifically mention money laundering, only if Olivia had documented any illegal activities of Jackson's. If it wasn't about the money laundering, then whatever I was shown relates to something else."

"That something else was bad enough that Olivia wrote it in code," Miles said.

I rubbed my hands together. This case was getting fun. "Where's Billy now?"

"We let him go. He didn't know much and we had nothing to keep him."

"Have you located the ledger yet?"

"Possibly. We found the company that the Allegra Group hired to store old records, but the place is like Fort Knox. It's also warded so we can't transport in. We're working on it."

"Send me everything you have on them. A fresh pair of eyes might catch something you missed."

The elevator bumped to a gentle stop and the door slid open.

Miles braced a hand on it to keep it from closing. "You got it."

"In return, I need the angel feather. Stat."

To Miles's credit, he didn't explode with a hell, no. "Why?"

"I need it to cure Rafael." We didn't need a filter, we needed a catalyst. I couldn't destroy Rafael's magic, but I could drain him nearly dry. If I managed that without killing him, then once his magic replenished, it should be free of the Ba'al interloper's powers.

The only problem was that I couldn't simply take his magic at a drop of the hat. We'd tested that about a month ago. Rafael had hoped that when it came time for me to destroy the *Sefer Raziel HaMalakh*, that we could do it under controlled conditions where I was calm and relaxed. The idea was for me to introduce Rafael's magic healing into my system *before* tackling the *Sefer* to build a base that would stave off any cravings rather than starting from a point of panic and danger.

Rafael had run through some meditation techniques with me in the library and when I was good and relaxed, he'd cut his arm for me to partake of his magic. He'd intended to then lower the pillars and release the scent of the four scrolls in our possession and see how well I fared.

We never got to the final part of the plan. I couldn't grab hold of his magic. It simply held mine at bay.

Rafael had concluded that the threat to the Jezebel was precisely what allowed this particular healing process to work. Thus, I required the angel feather for my plan now.

Miles dismissed a call on his phone. "Are you positive this will work?"

I stepped out of the elevator. "Given the solid scientific evidence and massive precedents for this procedure? Sure."

"I can't get the feather before Saturday," Miles said. "Security protocols."

"I'll take what I can get."

Chapter 20

Miles delivered a couple of banker's boxes full of information about the Allegra Group to my office, bright and early Friday morning. He also released Priya from House duties to go through it all with me, since she already had a working knowledge of the company.

Priya lifted out a stack of folders. "Adding to your collection?"

"Hmm?" I lifted the lid off a box, glancing over at the wall of framed Sherlock Holmes covers. Under the grid of the original framed covers hung a new addition: "The Final Problem."

The story where Sherlock Holmes dies. I dropped the lid. Chariot had been in the office and sent me this message.

Priya raised an eyebrow. "Was this a surprise?" she teased.

"No," I lied. I pulled the print off the wall and shoved it in a drawer. "I thought it would work with the others, but I don't like it."

Mrs. Hudson was hanging out with Bryan, who'd bought her affection with a steady stream of expensive doggie treats. He didn't mind playing Fetch Pinky and generally returned Mrs. Hudson all tired out, so I let him have her. Besides, his office was ten feet from mine in case my puppy needed me.

Tedious didn't begin to cover this work. I mainlined so much coffee trying to stay awake while we waded through everything that my leg was stuck in a permanent jitter. I was putting drops into my poor dry eyeballs when Priya said we'd covered all the business interests, but could move on to the charitable donations if I wanted.

I shrugged and said sure. Big shock, Allegra supported causes that served the Mundane community and only the Mundane community.

"Then there's the Sunshine Youth Shelter," Priya said.

The bottle of eyedrops hit my desk and I grabbed them before they rolled off.

"Are you sure?"

"I'm positive. What's the big deal?" She handed me the paper with the information.

I tapped the sheet. "This is the shelter that Meryem used."

Meryem Orfali had been my first case after my magic manifested. She'd gone missing, abducted by Chariot as a marginalized teen who they'd hoped to steal magic from.

Priya frowned. "The Allegra Group doesn't support organizations benefitting Nefesh."

"They supported this one." I was already dialing a number in my contacts. "Hello, Meryem, this is your favorite P.I. calling."

"I wouldn't say favorite," the teen said, "but for ten bucks you can be in the top three."

I smiled, thrilled to hear that she was well enough to give me attitude. "How's life, kid? Still living with Charlotte Rose and Victoria?"

"Yup. It's all good. I've got class in five minutes, so get to the point."

"The Sunshine Youth Shelter. Why'd you choose it over others? Did they know you were Nefesh?"

"Like I could hide it. Yeah. I went there because it was nicer than the other places. They'd upped their game, kept it really clean, decent food. Church people running it, doing their good deeds and shit. Why do you care?"

"One of their donors doesn't like Nefesh so I'm wondering why they'd fund them."

"Could be they didn't know about the change. Hang on." She spoke to someone with her for a moment.

"What change?" I clenched the phone like I could reach through the line and hurry up her explanation.

"They only started taking Nefesh a few months before I showed up."

Chariot initially had been abducting Mundane kids as well, to test out giving them magic abilities. When that didn't work, they gave up that pursuit, and by the time Yevgeny Petrov used all-ages parties to lure kids in, Chariot was only kidnapping Nefesh.

"Do you remember the name of the Church behind it?"

Meryem laughed. "Nah. We called it His Divine Spit. Something like that." A bell rang on her side of the phone. "Gotta go."

"Thanks." I tossed the cell on my desk. "Get this. The shelter used to be Mundane only, but it had a policy change a few months ago."

Priya slammed the file folder onto the desk. "Right around the time these Nefesh kids started going missing?"

"It wasn't a bad plan. Those kids are pretty transient. Get this one youth shelter that stands out from the rest, funnel Nefesh kids through there who no one is going to be looking for, and give Yevgeny the heads-up on which ones to target. The million-dollar question is whether Jackson knew this was happening. If he did, he was an accessory to Chariot ripping away their magic. That's heinous."

"It's also in line with Jackson's ideology," Priya said.

His Divine Spit—or as it was actually called, His Divine Spirit—had no website or other common social media profiles, but it did have a Yelp presence with a handful of reviews. People had to give their opinion on everything: annoying as fuck as a cultural tendency, but handy in my line of work. There were a few positive ones, but I jumped to the negative assessments. The most generous one called them "a lunatic Doomsday cult," followed closely by "an evangelical pimple on the backside of God's beautiful earth." My favorite was the most succinct: "hardcore."

I called their number, only to reach a voice mail listing the time of the Sunday service. True believers were welcome. I was Jewish, with magic bestowed upon me by the much-despised Bride of Yahweh. It would be a miracle if I didn't burst into flames when I crossed the church's threshold. I marked the service time down in my calendar, but there was no harm in casing the joint beforehand.

The church was located about ninety minutes outside Vancouver in the Fraser Valley, an area known as "the Bible belt." I pulled into the lot next to a roofing truck and found ladders resting up against the modest clapboard building. Workers lay a blue plastic membrane over the front half of the roof, while others nailed down new tiles in neat rows along the back section.

The foreman didn't know much about the congregation and neither the Pastor nor his secretary were around. That made it ideal to break in and snoop, but I couldn't risk getting caught by one of the roofers. Any answers would have to wait until the Sunday service.

Priya guilted me hard when I arrived home to visit Gavriella's grave with her. "Come on, Ash. This is important to Rafael and would show support when he's really hurting. The cemetery isn't open much longer because it's Shabbat tonight, so it will be a quick visit."

I'd built this visit up as some kind of harbinger of my own mortality, but I could put away this childish superstition and pay my respects. "Fine. I'll go."

Priya and I had just put Mrs. Hudson on Moriarty's back seat when my phone rang with an unfamiliar number.

"Hello?"

"Ash?" The woman on the other end was whispering. "It's Nicola."

I held up a hand for Priya to wait a moment. "What's wrong?"

"Did you find the bamah?" Her anxiety spiked down the line. "I think Isaac knows where it is."

Fuck. "Yes. Didn't Levi tell you?"

"I am not speaking to my son any longer." Her voice was firmer, louder.

Yes, she was. I'd been there for the reconciliation, so Isaac must have been in earshot.

"When can we meet?" she whispered.

Extracting Nicola was a top priority, but it couldn't be done in haste. If all went well, Arkady was retrieving the amulet as we spoke. Fingers crossed that he wouldn't be too late. Meantime, Levi and I could meet and formulate a plan for Nicola's safety, including how to make sure she wasn't fleeing with the clothes on her back and an angry and dangerous husband on her heels.

"This weekend, I promise. Meantime, are you safe? Cough if you're not."

There was silence. Okay.

"It's better if Levi contacts you," I said, "so answer his calls."

"Yes. Grazie."

"Don't mention it." I frowned at the phone when she disconnected.

Priya leaned against the hood of the car. "You think her situation has escalated?"

"Hers or mine." I sent Levi a quick text about the call and how retrieving the Kiss of Death had gone to code red urgent.

He responded when we were on the road, so Priya read the

text for me. Since the Transporter had been severely depleted by our Australia mission, Levi had sent Arkady on the jet, along with three other operatives as back-up.

"He what?" I slammed on the brakes at a red light.

Priya chuckled. "Levi said that they only know it's a retrieval mission, not what the item in question is, so calm down."

"I'm always calm."

"Uh-huh. Apparently the team went dark once they landed and the earliest they'll be back is tomorrow."

My fingers tightened on the steering wheel. "I should have gone with them."

"You were following up on Olivia's insurance policy and there's still the pressing matter of Rafael." Priya switched the radio station from hard rock to top forty, tapping her foot along with the fast beat.

"Not to mention stopping dear old Granddad from black-mailing my mother."

"See? A full calendar."

We hit the turn-off for the Jewish cemetery. There was little traffic on the winding road up to the gates and plenty of parking next to the small funeral chapel. Low gravestones dotted the large property and neat hedges were interspersed along the rows of graves, none of which had flowers.

Flowers weren't part of the Jewish tradition, though a number of them had small rocks on the headstones. I'd heard a lot of different explanations for why we did this, but I liked the one that my Zaide—Talia's dad—had shared with me. We placed a modest stone on our loved one's grave to tell them that even though they were gone, the impact that they had on us was everlasting. It was certainly true of me and Gavriella.

Mrs. Hudson cocked her head at us, sitting obediently on the ground and waiting for direction.

"Do you mind if we go see my grandparents first?" I said.

"Not at all." Priya followed me to a back corner where

Talia's parents were buried, hanging back with the puppy to give me some privacy.

I hadn't been here in years, but I didn't feel guilty about it. I had my memories of them, and these graves held no emotional connection. Still, I knelt down and kissed my fingertips, pressing them to the headstones that were flush with the lawn, before laying a small rock on each. "Hi, Bubbe. Hi, Zaide."

What would they have made of me being a Jezebel? Horrified? Happy that I found some link to my Jewish heritage, even if it was this?

"Guess what? I actually dated a Jewish guy." For all of five minutes, but why disturb their peace? "You remember Levi, right? It's over now, but you always despaired that I'd never date inside the tribe, so there's that."

I glanced over at one of the few other visitors here tonight: an old woman seated on a bench, chatting away happily to whomever she'd come to visit. Funny, I felt like a fool standing here talking to empty air. "Anyway, Mom's... Mom."

I could hear my Bubbe laughing at the answer that I'd given her so many times. "Hey. Priya's here." I motioned her over to say hello.

"Hi Chava, Saul." She ruffled my hair. "Your grandkid remains a pain in the ass, but she mostly grew up okay, so don't worry about her."

I turned away to dab at the moisture in my eyes. Stupid pollen. "We have to visit someone else before the place closes, so I'm going to say bye now. I love you both."

We headed across the cement roads that crisscrossed the cemetery, Priya marking off under her breath whatever landmarks Rafael had given her as guides. "Crooked tree, directly east of the hand washing fountain..." She slowed down, peering at each headstone. "Chaikin, Abelman, Zlotnik... here it is."

Priya stopped next to an unmarked grave close to the

parking lot. Gavriella wouldn't get a headstone until Yahrzeit, the one year anniversary of her passing.

A cloud passed in front of the sun and the temperature dipped. I rolled down the sleeves of my hoodie, looking around for anyone suspicious. All was normal; I forced my paranoia down.

Priya and I placed rocks on the grass, avoiding stepping on Gavriella's neighbor's head, since the graves were really close together in this section. Priya conveyed a short message from Rafael about how sorry he was that he couldn't be here himself and that Gavriella shouldn't worry, Ash and he had things in hand.

I snorted at that whopper, watching Mrs. Hudson chase a butterfly in circles.

Priya elbowed me. "Say something."

"I..." A torrent of words rushed up to clog my throat and my grip on the leash slackened. Mrs. Hudson bolted, running away as fast as her chubby legs would take her, the leash trailing on the ground.

I dashed after her, passing an old man sitting on a bench by the hand washing station.

Dressed casually in slacks and a blazer, he wore a dark hat on his white hair, while his hands rested on top of a wooden cane. He stepped on the leash, effectively trapping my dog, who landed on her rump with a startled yip.

"You should keep better hold on your animal." His voice had a trace of an Eastern European accent, sending me straight back to my teen years and the sound of my Zaide and his friends arguing in a mix of English, Russian, and Yiddish over card games. "This is a sacred ground, not a park."

Mrs. Hudson hadn't been hurt, but what an asshole. I bent down and tugged on the leash until he lifted his foot.

I curled the leather around my fist and picked up my puppy, cradling her close. "No harm done."

"No?" His eyes spat hate before he wrestled it down under a bland expression. "Keep a better eye on him next time."

Unsettled by his reaction, I didn't bother to correct his gendered assumption.

Priya caught up to us, throwing a wide smile at the stranger. "We're sorry. Still training her."

That smile had gotten us out of parking tickets, being grounded, and on one very memorable Vegas trip, resulted in an upgrade to first class. It radiated out towards the old man.

He rose stiffly, shot me one last penetrating look, and knocked Priya aside with his cane to push past us.

Unhurt but upset, my friend gaped, her brows creased at his behavior.

Thrusting Mrs. Hudson into Pri's arms, I followed him to a car parked near mine. "The puppy didn't know any better. You do. You didn't need to treat my friend like that."

"T'as du front de me parler comme ça." He shut the door and drove off.

I didn't need to speak French to recognize an insult. My eyes widened and I scrambled for my phone to snap a photo of the license plate.

"What a grump," Priya said. "Are we going back to Gavriella?"

I zoomed in on the picture and swore faintly at the sticker on the back bumper. "It was a rental."

"So?"

I swallowed, trying to find my voice. How did I know this with such clarity? I didn't, but some things just made too much sense not to see. "I think that was my grandfather."

Chapter 21

On the Go car rentals had three branches in Metro Vancouver and a handy central database with lax security. Priya had a name for the man from the cemetery before we'd finished breakfast on Saturday morning, along with the hotel he'd written down as his residence while in town.

The message to Talia had been delivered last Thursday with a deadline of tomorrow, June fourteenth. I'd faced worse. If Nathan was here, it implied that he'd come seeking a front row seat to her resignation.

The video wasn't conclusive proof of my magic. However, proof or not, it would be ammunition for Talia's enemies. The Nefesh police might decide to take an interest as well. Should that dickhead Staff Sergeant Novak push his way into every aspect of my life, he could complicate my Jezebel duties immensely. Or worse, find himself in Chariot's crosshairs.

"David Wise." I snorted at my grandfather's potential alias. "You've got to be kidding. A king, he's not." I stifled a yawn, having spent the night stewing over all the things I wanted to say to him. But, hey, insomnia kept the nightmares away.

If this David was actually Nathan, he'd used me to blackmail my mother, and then snuck into my city and spied on me. Trying to see this from his point of view didn't summon up any sympathy, because he and my grandmother could have had us in their lives if they hadn't been so fanatical. They had no one to blame for driving Dad away but themselves.

If Adam hadn't been estranged from them, would he have gotten lured into Isaac's schemes? I'd never know. One thing I was sure of: if this was Nathan, there'd be no reasoning with him. His venom toward me yesterday had made that abundantly clear. Eh. Freaking him out was more fun anyway.

Priya had to get to work at House Pacifica, so I drove her, parting ways in the elevator when she got off on the sixth floor. Mrs. Hudson and I continued up to the seventh, strolling through the mostly empty Executive area.

"It's Saturday. You are allowed to have a life," I said.

Veronica didn't even pause her typing. "He has a meeting."

I smiled sunnily at her. "The only good thing about meetings is how reschedulable they are."

"You're not pulling him away to play spy or whatever it is you do."

I went around the back of her desk.

"You can't threaten me," she said, her hands up.

"If I wanted to hurt you, you'd never see it coming. I need Levi for half an hour and look who would require babysitting in the meantime." I nudged the puppy with my foot and she looked up with an adorable openness.

Veronica stared down at the pug, her expression going from soft to stony and… soft. Heh. Got her. "Half an hour or I swear I'll have you arrested for disturbing the peace."

I shoved the doggy bag of supplies at her, pulling Pinky out and tossing it onto the ground where Mrs. Hudson immediately began humping it. Veronica's face went squelchy in disgust.

Today was shaping up to be a beautiful day.

I knocked on Levi's door. "Guess who's here to light up your life?"

"Caitlin?" He spun his desk chair around from its normal placement facing the window and blinked at me. "Oh. Hi."

"Was that your ten o'clock, Leviticus? A booty call?" I'd run into Dr. Caitlin Ryan, a brilliant and beautiful woman, once when she'd been on a date with Levi. I leaned against his doorframe, unable to keep from staring at his desk, imagining him bending her over it late at night. He'd grip her waist, his skin hot on hers, and his body bowed to press his lips to the back of her neck. Then he'd thrust inside her roughly, pausing for a second for them to savor this connection, before slowly rolling his hips, sending shivers tumbling down to her toes.

I bit my lip.

A wicked grin slid across his face. "My ten o'clock was with my Head of Security and I'm not his type." He was doing a very poor job of holding back his laughter.

"Asshole. You knew it was me."

"Of course I did. You can put away the daggers now."

I scowled down at the weapons I seemed to be white-knuckling. "The day is young and I like to keep my options open."

His piratical smirk widened as he craned his neck to peer out to the reception area. "How did you get in here? Did you kill Veronica?"

"No." I made the blades vanish and shut his office door. "I'm saving that for a special occasion. Thank me. I got you out of a very boring meeting to do fun illusion things."

Levi tapped his pen against his thigh. "That's quite the assumption."

"That your meeting with Miles would be a yawn-fest? Nope. I'm speaking from experience."

"That I'd be doing fun illusion things."

"You get to Houdini me up as my dad to intimidate my grandfather to quit blackmailing my mom. He's forcing her to resign from the party under the allegation that she's been harboring a Rogue kid." I threw jazz hands.

Levi stroked his chin. "Hmmm. Illusion you to look like your murdered father to browbeat and probably traumatize an old man into not striking a blow at an enemy of mine. I'm going along with this plan that holds absolutely no appeal for me, why?"

"Did you miss the Rogue part? He has video."

"Yes, and from what I've heard, it doesn't really show anything other than you assaulting me. Which, if we're being honest, is par for the course for you."

"Must you know everything?" When that earned me another grin, I flipped him off. "I'll buy you a donut." I tried not to gag at the thought, remembering Theresa's head and how I'd thought her blood was jelly. I was never eating another one, but I wouldn't ruin them for him.

Levi stalked toward me. "No deal."

"No deal on the jelly? Do I even know you anymore?" I backed up all of one inch since I hadn't moved and hit the door. Talk about poor space management on my part. "Name your price."

In a feat of incredible control, I did not look at his full lips even once. The oaky amber scotch and chocolate scent of his magic shivered inside me and I pressed my hands flat behind me on the wood.

He was going to ban me from the angel feather and then I'd have to argue with him into getting my way. Because I would get my way on this; Rafael's life was at stake.

Levi leaned an elbow against the doorframe, his bicep flexing. Arguing might not be so bad. "Destroy the amulet," he said.

"Huh?"

"The Kiss of Death. As soon as Arkady gets back with it, promise me that you'll neutralize its magic. The amulet is powerful, dangerous, and what my father wants."

Either Miles was going behind Levi's back with the angel feather, or His Lordship was on board. Either way, I was smart enough not to bring it up.

Was there any reason I shouldn't do as he asked? I didn't need the amulet to access the library and neither Rafael nor Avril had mentioned it having any other use.

I ducked out from under him, moving into the center of the room. Levi followed me.

"Okay," I said. "I promise. We also have to come up with a viable strategy around your mom so she can't be harmed and so Isaac doesn't freeze her out of a single cent that she's entitled to."

"I'm working on it." He truly had put aside his fears and accepted Nicola's decision. Good man. Levi held out his hand. "Show me a photo of Adam."

Fun as it would be to greet Nathan as the Ghost of Children Past, we opted to go with what Adam would look like today. I stared at my reflection in the mirror of the executive washroom, tracing the shape of my father's face. Dad's left eye that crinkled wonkily when he smiled, the three freckles along his right jaw, the slight bump in his nose: Levi had nailed it.

I gripped the sink, a lock of salt and pepper hair falling into my eyes. At least those were the same brown as mine. My breathing sped up and my hold grew tighter.

Levi pressed a hand to the small of my back. "Want me to undo it?"

I leaned back into his touch, but he'd moved away. "No," I croaked and turned abruptly from the reflection. So long as I didn't have to see myself, I'd be fine. "We better go."

There were a lot of mirrors in the lobby of the Hotel Vancouver where this David Wise was registered, and my pulse jumped every time I saw my dad. As I'd suspected, Levi was well aware of the existence of Hexers, including the few players in his territory. He called David's room on the hotel phone, pretending to be someone with common interests who'd heard he was in town.

David took the bait and agreed to meet him in the restaurant.

Levi and I sat separately at the bar, with my partner in crime watching the door as he nursed a beer. He'd changed his appearance—now middle-aged and South Asian, he was one of many businessmen dining here. He gave me the signal that David had arrived, and I approached his table. If I picked up the folded napkin, that would be Levi's sign to illusion up some distraction to get me out of there.

David sat ramrod straight, his white hair carefully combed, and his cane leaning up against the table. He wore a dark suit with cufflinks, giving off an overall air of quiet authority.

There was no connection, no sense of emotional familiarity. If this was my grandfather, shouldn't I have felt something?

I wiped my hands on my pants, and stepped up to the table from behind the man, unsure of whether I hoped I was right about his identity. "Shalom, Abba," I said.

David looked up and turned ashen. "Adam."

I sat down across from him, glad that one of the few facts I knew about my father's relationship with his parents was that he used the Hebrew terms for mother and father with them.

David, or rather, Nathan, broke into rapid French.

"English, please," I said in my best approximation of my dad's voice. Reasonable Facsimile Dad had actually come in handy for once.

A server approached us, but I sent him away politely, saying we needed a moment.

"I haven't seen you in years and you bring me here under false pretenses?" he said.

I made myself comfortable. "I haven't seen *you* in years

221

and you sneak into town under an assumed name to blackmail my ex and my daughter?"

A muscle in his jaw ticked. "Your mother died. You disgraced her memory by not being there."

I didn't rise to the bait, sitting quietly to see how he'd fill the silence.

Nathan had saved up years of vitriol, which all came spewing out now. Everything from what a disappointment Adam was as a son, to his betrayal of everything he'd been raised to believe in by marrying that harlot, and how the only good thing Adam had done was leaving her.

All that sustained this man was hate. Was this how Dad was raised? Or had my grandfather only become twisted in the wake of his son cutting him off? Dad's absence left a pretty big hole.

I tried to find something of my father in him but I couldn't. Adam had been charm and a ready smile; this man was spite etched into every wrinkle.

"Enough." I kept my voice low, cutting him off mid-sentence. "This blackmail campaign of yours ends now. You know exactly why I stayed away all those years. You and Eema. Force Talia to resign or expose my daughter and you'll be sorry. All your colleagues will know every dirty little secret about Hexers and how entrenched you are in that movement. Where will your precious status be then when they find out you're nothing more than a garden-variety fanatic?"

Nathan turned a splotchy purple. "Are you threatening me? Your father?" He rattled off something in French, then slammed a hand down on the table, making his water glass jump.

There was a crash and I did a double take, thinking he'd knocked it over, but the glass breaking had come from the bar.

The bartender mopped up a spilled drink on the bar top, carefully picking out the shards of glass, while the customer who'd knocked it over apologized.

Levi, still in disguise, had frozen on his stool gripping his pint glass, his attention on the entrance.

I followed his gaze and my heart stuttered.

Isaac Montefiore stood stock-still, staring at me—well, Adam—like he'd seen a ghost. A businessman at a table waved him over, but Isaac only had eyes for me.

How flattering.

Nathan glanced around with a curious expression.

I pushed my chair back and stood up, keeping Isaac locked in my gaze. A knife's edge of anticipation and vicious glee uncoiled inside me.

"Adam," my grandfather snapped. "Where are you going? We're not done."

I leaned forward so my face was close to his. "Yes, we are, but if you want to test me, then be my guest. You'll lose everything."

Uncertainty flickered through his eyes. "I'm your father," he said plaintively.

"If you cared about that, you would have reached out when you learned of Ashira's birth. But she didn't have magic then and so she didn't matter, did she?" My Adam voice shook. "She's your blood. Your only granddaughter. How could you put your beliefs over her?"

Why should Nathan be any different from the rest of my family? Dad had initially left us because of his love of the con, and Talia had prioritized the party over me. I bit the inside of my cheek, welcoming the sharp bloom of pain to keep me steady.

"Do we understand each other?" I said.

He nodded shakily. "I'll leave Talia alone, but my son is dead to me."

More than he could imagine. However, those words freed me from grief's hold. Blood didn't make a person family. "Goodbye, Nathan."

I strode toward Isaac. An earthquake couldn't have thrown

me off course. I stopped in front of him and clapped his shoulder. "Long time no see."

Isaac flinched.

"Impossible," he whispered. His hands bunched the hem of his fine cashmere sweater and a bead of sweat glistened at his temple.

I just smiled.

Isaac stumbled backward out of the restaurant.

Levi stood less than five feet away, but I couldn't read the expression on his illusion's face.

I clenched my fists. Levi had come to *me*, wanting to win my trust, knowing full well what it meant. He'd stated his intention and now it was time to walk the walk.

"You wanted me to trust you," I said. "It's me or him." Pivoting sharply, I stalked out after Isaac. I'd know where Levi and I stood depending on whether or not he followed and maintained my Adam disguise.

I caught up to my enemy in a quiet alcove with a sofa next to a large potted palm and sat down next to him. The illusion remained intact.

Something golden raced through my veins, heady and triumphant. I'd trusted Levi and he'd come through.

He'd chosen me.

I cocked Adam's head up and gave Isaac my most charming smirk as I used my father's voice. "Guess some horses are harder to put down than you thought. You didn't even have the guts to shoot me yourself. That was sloppy." I tsked him. "When you want the past to stay buried, don't farm out the kill shot."

Isaac rubbed his chest, shaking his head like he could physically ward me off.

All I had to do was sit here, wearing my dad's face, and let Isaac panic himself into a heart attack. As a revenge fantasy, there was a beautiful symmetry to it.

It would also solve all of Nicola's problems. And Levi would be free.

Isaac bent over, his breathing labored.

I could wipe out an evil power right here, right now, without lifting a finger, but I'd promised Rafael a while ago that I wouldn't hurt Isaac until we had the scrolls.

And I'd promised myself that when I took him down, my face would be the last thing he saw.

I patted Isaac's arm, the sour odor of sweat undercutting his sandalwood cologne. "See you around."

Levi was doing a poor job of skulking nearby. He'd passed this test, but could I trust him again on a Jezebel mission or would our trust crumble once more? What stories had Levi written about Isaac? That his father could be redeemed? That Levi could find closure for the scars of his past?

Whatever they were, he'd been willing to write me in as something other than the villain. And that, in my book, counted for a hell of a lot.

I gave him a buddy punch to the shoulder. "Welcome back to the Zone of Trust."

Chapter 22

Miles and I met back at Rafael's cell, and he handed over the familiar metal pouch with the strange symbols etched on it that held the angel feather. "Do not make me regret getting this for you, Cohen."

The Head of House Security wore the doctored lead apron and a ridiculous tin foil hat guaranteed to protect him from the feather's compulsion abilities.

My mouth watered at the thought of the magic inside, but I didn't fall on it like a starving wolf. My pride was good for that much.

"You worry too much," I said. "Unlock the cell."

Miles opened the cage, which glowed with nulling magic, and Rafael stepped out, holding one of the bars like this might all be a trick. He towered over me and Miles, a solid wall of muscle.

Miles craned his neck up at Rafael and burst into flames.

"What if the tangled-up Nefesh magic interferes with mine and I can't bring you back?" Rafael said.

"Then be gentle with my prone body when you go on your murderous rampage," I said. "My health insurance is pretty good, but it's not unbeatable."

"This is no time for jokes," Rafael said.

"On the contrary, dude." I ran my finger over the symbols. "It's exactly the time. Count of three, step over the white line and back into magic range."

Miles double-checked that the door to the room was locked, his magic on full display.

"No pressure," Rafael muttered, and made a small cut on his forearm with the dagger I'd given him, before dropping the weapon to the ground. The blood made a mocking smile against his skin.

I glanced at the door, unable to believe a certain other person wasn't about to crash through it. "You didn't tell Levi, did you?"

Miles took a deep, calming breath, like he was about to trim a particularly difficult bonsai. "I felt this would proceed more smoothly on a need-to-know basis."

Smoothly? Miles was on fire, Rafael was about to go full Ba'al, and all of that paled next to the giant fluffy bomb I was about to release.

"I believe in you," Rafael said.

"Back at you. Okay. One..." If he couldn't hold it together to save me from the feather, or if his magic held mine at bay, I'd spend the rest of my shortened life in that void, offering myself up to be hollowed out one atom at a time. I forced myself to unscrew the cap on the metal pouch.

Rafael edged closer to the white line.

"Two." I lifted the cap off. The scent of a hot sandstorm and dread swirled around me and a soft sigh escaped my lips. My entire body relaxed, yearning to accept it like a lover's touch.

"Steady, Cohen," Miles said, his flames crackling higher.

"Three," I said in a breathy voice.

Rafael stepped over the line and staggered sideways, his body curving over as if he'd been punched in the gut. Large curved horns burst out of his skull, his face lost its humanity to become Ba'al's doppelgänger, and his eyes morphed into vertical slits of hellish red.

I plunged my hand into the pouch and pulled out the feather, hooking a red silky ribbon of magic into it. The feather magic was mine for the taking. A sliver of my brain recognized it for the lie it was, but I didn't care. It was cotton candy and the best summer day I'd ever had. All my anger and my hurt faded away, and the weight of the world was no longer on my shoulders. There was only me and this epic bliss.

I exhaled, crashing to my knees.

Rafael roared so hard he blew my hair back, his next few footsteps cracking the cement floor.

The room swirled around me, Miles's and Rafael's faces blurring out of focus, like Dorothy's tornado had touched down, rendering this room ground zero of chaos. Still, all I wanted was to grab hold and ride it to my own personal Oz. Maybe I'd find the wizard.

I cackled, colors sharpening with a vicious edge that cut deep inside me.

Rafael grabbed me none-too-gently and plunged my fingers into his bloody gash. His eyes were wide with a wild desperation, a savage light flickering in and out of them.

With shaking fingers, I dropped the feather, plunging into all the refreshing magic my Attendant had to offer. Its cool rich flow was enough to keep me on task.

Barely.

Rafael fell to the floor, rolling me half on top of him, and gazed up dreamily. His phallus was the size and hardness of a crowbar, tenting his sweats.

Miles swore.

Magic danced out of my Attendant. It was a delicious appetizer but—I glanced at the feather—there was a banquet that was mine for the taking.

I could have both. Drain Rafael, heal him, and partake of

the feather to my heart's content. Wasn't this exactly what we'd wanted to test? How far I could go?

I reached for the fluffy temptation and a ball of fire engulfed it. I snatched my hand back.

"Touch it again. I dare you," Miles said.

Miles's magic sizzled out on the feather with no damage done. He eased around me and slapped the feather back into the pouch, sealing it up.

I snarled at him and a wall of flame sprung up between us.

"Focus," Miles said.

Rafael pressed my fingers deeper into the gash on his arm.

There was still so much magic inside of Rafael that I was starting to feel sick. Could I get magic poisoning? It was like being back at my first and only horrific frat party, chugging away and knowing I'd regret it.

I stuffed my nausea down and pulled harder, Rafael's magic rushing into me in a smudgy blur.

His eyes rolled back and white foam flecked the corners of his mouth.

"Ash!" Miles extinguished his magic and pointed at Rafael. "His horns." They were receding. It was working.

I amped up my efforts, gagging against the sheer amount of power I was ingesting. My intestines twisted like a pretzel, and I doubled over from the pain, sweat dripping off me.

Rafael convulsed. His body snapped up off the ground and slammed back down, sending concrete chips flying. One grazed my jaw, blood welling up hot and fast.

There was banging on the door to the room and muffled voices outside.

I blinked, seeing double. Did I continue? Would it be worse to stop? We were so close, I could feel it.

Rafael's body rippled, gaining and losing size and muscle mass almost too fast to track. His features were warping between human and goat.

Panicked, I tried to stop, but there was some kind of vacuum effect happening and I couldn't disengage.

He convulsed again, his fist clipping me in the eye. Stars danced in my vision, pain rolling through the side of my head.

I sucked the last of his magic out and felt his heart stop. "Miles!"

Miles started mouth-to-mouth.

Rolling onto my back, I swallowed hard against the metallic taste of bile, shaky and nauseous.

The door banged open so hard that it cracked into a spiderweb pattern. An operative holding a battering ram raced into the room, took one look at Miles and Rafael, and called for an ambulance.

Levi stormed in, taking in the entire scene with one cold glance. He stopped in front of me. "What. The. Fuck—"

I vomited all over his Italian loafers, cutting his tirade mercifully short.

THEY'D MOVED Rafael to the infirmary to be monitored because he wasn't waking up. No one could explain it. Physically, he once more looked like his librarian self, his vitals were stable, and the Nefesh magic was out of his system. I'd checked and double checked until I was dizzy. His Asherah magic was down to a tiny flicker.

One of Miles's operatives had been posted to stand guard.

I slumped in a chair by Rafael's bed, watching him for the slightest change in his breathing, the tiniest flicker of a finger. Nothing.

Levi hadn't come by.

I fiddled with the bandage on my jaw, debating whether or not to ask for another ice pack for my eye. His Lordship was probably chewing Miles out. He'd be by to yell at me soon.

Wouldn't he?

How had Levi intended to finish his *what the fuck* question? What the fuck happened? What the fuck is wrong with Rafael? What the fuck did you ingest to turn your puke Pepto Bismol–pink?

What the fuck were you thinking, Ash?

Well, I had a very good answer to that, thank you very much. I couldn't leave Rafael all messed up. My regular method of destroying magic hadn't worked, healers and doctors hadn't cured him, and the situation called for more extreme measures. And yes, while tangoing with the angel feather certainly counted as extreme, it had also been effective. The Nefesh magic was gone. Sure, it had been a little sketchy for a bit, but as soon as Rafael woke up, we could all put this incident behind us.

I grasped his hand, but my friend didn't stir and the infirmary door remained closed with a depressing finality.

Until it slammed open, and I jumped.

Miles stormed in, his eyes wild, grabbed me by the shirtfront and dragged me into the waiting room, where he released me with such force that I staggered back. "You have no idea how lucky you are. If he'd been seriously hurt…"

Confused, I just gaped at him.

He leaned down and spoke in a low, dangerous voice. "What is it about you that people are so willing to throw themselves in danger?"

There were only two people whose well-being mattered to Miles this much.

My pulse fluttered in my throat. Swallowing, I forced myself to meet his eyes, my magic at the ready, and dread churning in my gut. "What happened to Arkady?"

"Chariot happened," Miles spat.

I gasped. "How is he?"

Flames rippled over Miles's body. "He's got three broken ribs."

"Where is he now?" I said.

"Why?" Miles sneered. "Because you want the amulet? That is all you care about, right? Stopping Chariot?"

"Fuck you."

"Like it's not true," he snarled.

There was a sharp clap from the doorway. "Let's put the dramatic focus back where it belongs." Arkady stood in the doorway, pale, his arm across his torso. "Me."

I marched over to Arkady and jabbed my finger in his face. "You were not supposed to go up against Chariot and get hurt. That totally undermines my moral righteousness and ability to be mad at you."

He gave me a wan smile. "But it was fun."

Arkady gave me the rundown, brief as it was. Chariot was already on the property when his team arrived. Six of them against four of our people. The fight was short, brutal, and bloody. Team Jezebel Strike Force had gotten the Kiss of Death, but one of the operatives ended up with third degree burns from a fire elemental. The operative was okay, but it had been dicey.

Chariot was a hydra. No matter how many heads we lopped off, another one took its place. How many more fronts would we find ourselves attacked on? The library was compromised—hell, I'd been compromised. Now Moran, Arkady, and even some operatives had been hurt. The damage was spiraling out of control like a bicycle chain gone wild. Even with more people taking up the fight, how could we possibly counter them?

How could we possibly win?

"Did you apprehend Chariot?" I said.

"No." Arkady's expression darkened. "They got away."

Priya flew into the room with Mrs. Hudson. "I got your

text! How badly are you hurt?" She went to hug Arkady but Miles gently tugged her aside.

"His ribs," he said.

Her face fell. "Do you need anything?"

Arkady pulled her into a one-armed hug. "I'll be fine. Miles is going to wait on me hand and foot."

Miles shot me a look of death.

"Where's the amulet?" I said.

"Levi has it. I'm taking you home," Miles said to Arkady.

Arkady mock swooned, pressing a hand to his forehead. "I do feel rather weak." His expression turned serious. "Am I forgiven?" he asked me.

Our lives are lived in stories. I'd written one about Arkady and me, casting him as the villain, instead of a guy helping out who regretted his actions, but, caught in his own shame spiral, was trying to make up for it in his own way.

Almost dying had put certain things into perspective, as did people being hurt on my behalf. Did I really want to lose more of our time as friends because I couldn't move on?

"I'm still mad," I said to Arkady.

"Are you fucking kidding me?" Miles lunged for me, but was body-checked by Arkady, his eyes on mine.

"But I forgive you and I'm working on the rest," I said. "It's hard rewriting a story."

Arkady frowned. "What?"

"Nothing. Just take care of yourself and don't do anything stupid."

Arkady nodded. "I will."

Priya said her goodbyes and once the men had left, escorted the puppy and me back into the room where Rafael remained unconscious. She dragged another chair up to his bed and sat down.

"Suzy Jones wanted to be my best friend in grade ten," Priya said. "She was a nice girl." She flung a fresh ice pack at me, hitting me square in the chest.

I eased myself into the other seat. "Suzy Jones became a hedge fund manager and anti-vaxxer. Her conservative bullshit would have gotten on your last nerve and you'd be in the big house taking prison showers. You hate public bathing."

"I'd have been Queen Bitch of that prison yard. See? You routinely take years off my life and cost me my life goals."

I snorted, unclipped the leash, and lifted the puppy onto the bed. She sniffed Rafael's arm and then snuggled in against him. I held my breath, but he didn't miraculously wake up.

"I want to kill those fucking Followers in the most painful way possible for getting Rafael injured in the first place," I said, at the sight of him laying there helpless. I pressed the ice pack to my eye. It numbed my skin—numbed me—enough to blurt out the fear that had been crawling up my throat. "But I did this to him. I'm just as culpable, even if I meant well. Lux and her friends meant well too. They wanted to save Emma." I placed my hand on Rafael's chest, checking that his breathing was steady. "Did I take too much of his powers for him to recover? What if he never wakes up?"

"It's only been a few hours," Priya said. "And this is still better than being stuck in a cage for the rest of his life. Which, by the way, might have been greatly shortened because of that Nefesh magic."

"I'm making a wins and losses column. Wins: Arkady successfully got the amulet and Isaac didn't." I ticked items off on my fingers. "Nathan isn't going to force Talia's resignation."

I'd texted her that her career aspirations with the Untainted Party were secure. She'd replied with a terse "thank you."

No word on whether or not mother-daughter brunches were back on the table.

"We can connect a charity that Jackson supported to the missing kids." I looked at my hands. Huh. There were still a lot of available fingers.

"Losses?" Priya looked at Rafael. "Other than the obvious?"

"Talia saw my magic. Not the enhanced strength." I made a face. "I told her all about Jezebels. She took it pretty much as expected."

"Yikes."

"To put it mildly. Then there's Nicola, who is still stuck in her marriage." I pulled my hair into a high ponytail, using the elastic that had been on my wrist to secure it. "Not to mention, there's this dangerous amulet that Levi was all on fire to have destroyed and now crickets. I mean, get a sense of responsibility."

Priya rummaged around in her giant purse. "Hang on. Let me say something reassuring and noncommittal. Uh-huh, totally."

"You suck. How goes the digging into Theresa Magnon?"

"Not great. She's a rich socialite from old family money made during Prohibition. I'm not sure what she has to offer Chariot, but I'll keep looking." Priya pulled out a copy of *Dune* with an "aha!"

"Are you staying a while?" I said. "What a kind, platonic gesture with no ulterior motives such as the sound of your voice penetrating Brit Boy's haze so that when he wakes up, your emerald green eyes are the first things that he gazes into."

She opened the book to the first page. "I'm going to read to him."

"Yeah, I can see how sandworms are very soothing and not at all phallic."

Pri blew her hair out of her face. "Oh my God, there is so much more to this story and that's all you ever go on about. I am totally calling Suzy Jones later."

"Suzy Jones hated sci-fi. I, however, made it through two and half books in the series."

"Uh-huh, totally."

"Just for that, I'm taking the dog. Oh, and if you could try kissing Rafael to wake him?"

Priya paused, glanced at Rafael, then quickly away. "Not funny."

"I'm not entirely kidding?"

Grimacing, she tucked her black bobbed hair behind her ears, her chin dipping down. She gave a soft explosive argh and kissed Rafael. A perfectly sweet brush of the lips that lasted two seconds too long to be completely chaste.

We both leaned in…

… and were severely disappointed.

"This never happened," Priya said.

"Didn't see a thing." I clipped Mrs. Hudson's leash back on her, set her on the floor, and off we went to see a man about an amulet.

Chapter 23

The walk across the seventh floor had never felt so long. It was late and only a couple of employees were around.

"How is it even possible?" a man said. "There's no color. It's totally flat."

"Creeped me right out," his co-worker replied, nodding hello as she passed me.

"What did?" I said.

"The exterior of the House," the woman said. "A few hours ago it went kind of dead-looking."

"How weird." I hustled Mrs. Hudson out of there, beelining straight for the elevators. Shit. I'd broken Levi.

My sense of responsibility caught up with me somewhere between my fifth and sixth stab of the call button. "We should check on him in case he's stroked out or something. That would be bad."

Mrs. Hudson barked, up for anything.

I dragged my feet towards His Lordship's office with a level of enthusiasm generally reserved for French aristocracy hooking up with Madame Guillotine. Sadly, Veronica had left for the night. Damn. I'd kind of hoped the dragon would have actually barred my way. There was a first time for everything after all.

I rapped twice on his office door. No one answered. Duty fulfilled. I could go home.

Mrs. Hudson sat down in front of the door.

"You're impossible. Fine." I opened the door. "Knock. Knock." Shoot me now. I'd become one of those people who made the damn sound effect with a pleasant middle management smile on their face.

Levi sat on his repellent sofa, his legs extended along the cushions. He'd taken off his suit jacket and tie, undone the first two buttons on his pinstriped shirt, and was turning an obsidian black stone circle over and over, his expression distant. Its thin gold chain hung between his fingers.

The metal pouch containing the feather was on the coffee table. Levi's Emporium of Wonders.

"Is that the amulet?" I said.

Levi glanced at me, briefly, but didn't say anything. His eyes were bleary and dark stubble dusted his jawline.

Mrs. Hudson strained against her leash, so I freed her. She ran over to him and raised her paws, scrabbling against the sofa. Levi picked her up and placed her in his lap. She licked his hand and, content, closed her eyes.

I scratched my head. "Is your dad all right?" That might have been the correct question to lead with.

"He's fine." Levi traced a finger around the smooth edge of the amulet. "Chariot is going to double down on their attacks on you." His jaw clenched. "The Jezebel with the blood catalyst and the amulet all in a handy one-stop shopping package."

"I'm going to destroy the Kiss of Death now so that won't get them very far."

I set his desktop pendulum in motion and sat down on the table, surreptitiously sniffing my pits to make sure I wasn't too vile smelling. At least I hadn't puked on myself.

Levi's loafers, however, were nowhere in sight and he'd changed his black dress socks to ones with tiny white squares.

The pendulum balls clacked rhythmically for some time with still no reply from Levi.

"I never specifically told Miles to keep our angel feather plan from you," I said. "Though I didn't exactly tell you myself, but you would have tried to stop me." I glanced sideways at him. "Maybe you wouldn't have. It wasn't an issue of trust, though I could see how it would appear that way from your perspective." I sighed. "Could you just get mad at me already because I think you broke your House and you need to get this out of your system, and then I'll apologize." I bit my lip. "I'm doing that a lot, aren't I? Apologizing after the fact."

"What does game over look like to you?" Levi said, quietly.

Should I be relieved he didn't want to revisit what had happened—or worried?

"The *Sefer* no longer exists. Chariot is…" I pushed on one end of the pendulum to speed it up again. "I don't know. I'm not sure it'll be possible to dismantle it and have the Ten ever see the inside of a courtroom. The world can't learn what was really at play when magic came into existence."

"No. It would unite Mundanes against Nefesh." His fist closed over the amulet.

"Nor have we spent centuries acquiring proof of their shadowy power plays," I said. "Our directive was extremely specific. Asherah made Jezebels to stop Chariot from becoming immortal, so that's my focus."

"Other than my father."

"Other than your father." It was pointless to deny it. "You didn't drop the Adam illusion."

"I wasn't going to let you down." He gave me a wry smile, idly scratching the sleeping puppy's ears. "This time."

Ever since Levi had dumped me, I'd been so angry with

239

him for not putting the two of us above our family histories, above our fathers, but had I? Hadn't I expected Levi to be part of my mission without reservation? I'd made ruining his father a condition of the two of us.

All these stories that I'd written in permanent marker, certain of their indelibility, were now filled with glaring errors in bright red ink.

"I'll trust you even if you walk away from helping me," I said. "There's a difference between refusing to let Isaac have any power over you and actively taking him down. My quest isn't yours."

"But it ends in the same place." He curled his fingers and an image of Isaac clutching at his heart appeared in miniature in mid-air. Levi let the illusion play out for a moment, before waving a hand through it, blowing it away. "I would have stopped things from going too far today, so you see, I haven't returned to the Zone of anything."

Was that why the House had gone dark? Not because Levi was mad, but that he was disgusted with himself because he'd failed me? It wasn't even true. Levi had pushed past his line in the sand and provided the fuel for my petty act of revenge because he refused to let me down.

He was so close. I could cross the room, sink my teeth into his lower lip, and unleash the storm charging the air. I could also run like a bat out of hell because I'd learned the hard way how much power Levi had over my heart, and that was when we'd barely been together at all. I couldn't go through that again. I was crazy to imagine otherwise.

Wasn't I?

Was there hope for us, now that we'd both had time to think things out?

I imagined myself as some wizened old woman, rocking on her front porch. Looking back over my life, what would be the bigger regret—that I tried again with Levi and got my heart stomped on for a second time when he decided that he couldn't handle this, or that I ran away? My heart and my brain had two very different opinions on the matter. I took a deep lungful of air and slowly exhaled.

I sat down on the sofa and dug my palms into my thighs, the denim rasping against my skin. "*If* our Zone of Trust was extended beyond work at some point..." My voice came out hoarse and I cleared my throat.

Levi had never actually indicated he was interested in a reconciliation.

"At some point what?" Carefully placing Mrs. H on a cushion so she didn't wake, Levi swung his feet onto the floor, his head cocked to the side.

"I have to meet you halfway." I shook my head. "No. I have to—I'd want to—give you something important in return. I'm just not sure I can."

"Maybe any expansion of trust has to wait until we're both sure of what we can live with."

My shoulders slumped.

Levi slid closer and took my hands. "But..." He looked down before saying quietly, "With the acknowledgement that we want to try and find that common ground?"

My heart thundered so fast, I tasted the beats in my throat. Due to the "S" shape of the building, other parts of the exterior were visible from Levi's office. House Pacifica was lit up behind Levi in a pale yellow like a sunrise, the dawning of a fragile hope that I wanted to turn deep gold. Except even the thought of being in that freezer again didn't scare me as much as letting him back in.

"Yeah. With that acknowledgement," I said.

Levi's answering smile was dancing fireflies on a perfect summer night. He tossed me the amulet.

The second it touched my hand a deep sense of security settled over my shoulders. I held it up to the light. The stone circle wasn't solid black. An X made of a dark burnished wood was inlaid on one side. I inhaled the familiar buttery honey scent: almond wood.

"I'm going to open the metal pouch."

"You think that, do you?"

"I know that. I won't remove the feather, I want to test a hypothesis." I held my hand out. "You can't say no to science, Leviticus."

Levi placed his hand over the container. "This isn't science. It's magic."

"It's the scientific exploration of magic."

"What's the hypothesis, Ash?"

I held up the amulet. "This comes from Jezebel's altar, right? Where she communed with Asherah. Chariot perverted its use for their own gain, but to me, Asherah's chosen? It makes me feel safe."

"Your point?"

"If this protects me against the cravings from the angel magic, I won't have to…" I searched for the right words. "Use Rafael when I destroy the *Sefer Raziel HaMalakh*. Which we can both agree would be a good thing."

Levi shook his head, but he handed me the pouch.

I crossed over to the window so that he'd be out of range of any compulsion and slipped the chain over my head.

Levi picked up one of the fire irons from a stand next to the wood fireplace, propping it on his shoulder like a player at bat.

"What are you going to do with that?"

"Knock the damn pouch out of your hand if you lose control." He motioned for me to open it.

I can withstand the craving. I opened the pouch.

The scent of a hot sandstorm enveloped me…

… and I didn't care.

"Holy shit." I held the container aloft, breaking into a wriggly happy dance.

Levi lowered the fire iron. "You want to keep the amulet, don't you?"

"Pretty please, can I? I'll totally walk it and feed it."

"You're not cute," he said.

I opened my finger and thumb a couple inches. "Little bit. Yeah, I am."

Was suppressing my cravings really this simple?

The faintest tang of a sandstorm hit me. Uncertain if the scent was real or imagined, I sealed the pouch up.

"This amulet would make my life a lot easier," I said. Except for Chariot coming after me again. "However, it's not essential. I get how dangerous it would be if Isaac got hold of it and I'm willing to keep my promise. Your call."

"Great. I get to be the bad guy if I say no."

I dropped the pouch on Levi's desk and crouched down in front of him. "You're not the bad guy, Watson."

Levi rolled his eyes. "We've talked about that."

I'd missed him so much. My hands tightened on his thighs, my gaze dropping to his lips. I could close the gap between us and be laid bare to him, but it was too soon. Any type of intimacy would cloud things between us.

Being a grownup fucking sucked.

I pried my hands off, finding the same mix of longing and resignation in his expression. "What do you want me to do?"

"Meet me halfway. You're the Jezebel. Make the call."

I spun away, barely refraining from stomping my feet, but he was right. I had to decide.

The little devil called Selfish raised its hand, jumping up and down on my shoulder yelling "pick me!" The Noble angel on the other side shook its head slowly, sighing heavily. It was barely making any effort to win me to its side. At least Selfish showed an appreciable level of enthusiasm.

I ran the Kiss of Death back and forth across the chain, my hand clamped around it so tightly we might as well have been surgically fused. Isaac didn't need to know we had the amulet and I could tell Nicola I'd destroyed the bamah.

The Ash of four months ago wouldn't even have hesitated. Or indulged in this half-hearted charade of convincing herself there was any other course of action, save one.

I pulled the amulet off in a swift motion. "I'll nuke this puppy, but let me show it to Rafael first. Maybe the good news will get through to him. Want to come?"

Approval warmed Levi's eyes. "Sure."

We made our way back to the infirmary with the pug, like a family. I sped up, forcing Levi to match his strides to mine.

Priya was reading animatedly to Rafael, who was still unconscious. She didn't mind the interruption, though, when I produced the amulet.

"Rafael, we got it. Behold the Kiss of Death." I placed it in his hands, telling him how the operation had gone down and about the amulet protecting me from the feather's magic.

His eyes popped open.

"Fuck!" In my shock, I jostled him and the amulet slid off the bed.

Rafael went right back into his coma.

"Whoa." Priya picked up the amulet, wiping it off on the hem of her blue sweater.

I met Levi's gaze. The seconds spun out between us. I grimaced. "I can't…"

In a millisecond, I assembled a treatise-worth of arguments.

Levi placed his hand on my arm. "I know," he said in a kind voice. "Promise me that you'll stay alert."

"Don't worry. Either of you. Chariot isn't going to get the jump on me." Again.

"That's just dumb," Priya said. "Obviously we're going to worry."

Levi smiled. "She's not wrong."

Pri held the artifact out. "He's your Attendant. Do the honors."

I put it over Rafael's head. "Wakey wakey, buddy."

His eyes snapped open once more. He felt for his horns, and upon failing to find them, sagged against the pillow. "Bloody hell, Ashira, what kind of bollocks plan was —oomph!"

I'd crushed him in a hug. He tried to squirm out of it, but I tightened my hold, and eventually he patted my back in a "there, there" manner.

We hadn't won the war, hadn't even won a battle really, merely recovered from this side skirmish. Isaac knew about me and if he got his hands on the amulet, it could tip the balance of power in his favor. There were so many ways for me to be defeated and right now, they all fell away, because this awkward embrace was the sweetest victory prize I'd ever claimed.

Chapter 24

Other than his ongoing depleted magic, my Attendant was back in fine health and very excited to learn everything about his shiny new possession. He also majorly scored with the discovery that Theresa Magnon had inherited her position on the Ten from her grandfather, Misha Ivanov.

Levi planned to talk to his mother alone about coming to stay with him. He'd enlisted Priya to build a picture of all his father's financials, declared and otherwise, to determine what Nicola would be entitled to, and was lining up divorce lawyers. We'd agreed it was best to withhold the knowledge of what exactly the bamah was so that she couldn't accidentally implicate herself. It would be up to Levi to convince her that this wasn't something she could get half of. Nor was she to gloat about thwarting Isaac's plans for it.

Let him believe that was all on me.

Lux called me about Rafael's condition, very relieved that he was free of their magic. That made two of us. I warned her to tell the other Followers about Chariot's attack. I didn't think they'd go after Lux and her friends, but if they knew we'd been in contact and thought to use them against me somehow…

"Desperate people do desperate things," Lux said wryly. "I'll let them know. And Ash? If you need us, we're here. We all serve the goddess together."

After that unexpected but appreciated gesture, I was free to turn my attention to the Sunday service at His Divine Spirit to find proof that the shelter handed Nefesh kids over to Chariot. I created a demure persona, selecting a sedate floral dress with long sleeves and a hem that hit mid-calf, left over from some past event of Talia's. I even put on a small strand of pearls and pulled my hair into a bun, secured by about ten bobby pins. Freaky jabby torture devices.

Thanks to traffic delays on the highway, I didn't arrive until right as the service was starting. I slipped into a back pew, the heavy smell of incense tickling my nose.

Oddly, there were no families among the roughly thirty congregants, only adults, presided over by a whip-thin pastor in his fifties with a pronounced Adam's apple and a surprisingly melodic voice.

Whatever ostentation the building lacked, it made up for with the fire-and-brimstone sermon that sent its worshippers into a frenzy. There was nothing metaphoric about their belief. To them, the Rapture was a matter of when, not if.

Among the non-believers who wouldn't make it to the pearly gates in the preacher's version? All Nefesh, whom he deemed "abominations." There was no mercy or compassion in his worldview.

I white-knuckled a prayer book, the words on the page blurring. The hypocrisy between their so-called Christian values and the hate necessary to run that shelter as a front to destroy magic and torture those innocent kids disgusted me.

After the sermon, the pastor invited everyone to stick around for coffee and baked goods in a small room off the chapel.

I grabbed a styrofoam cup, perusing the framed photos on

the walls of bland beaches and sunsets overlaid with biblical quotes.

One of the larger prints featured a longer passage about a stubborn and rebellious son. It was advised to bring him to the gates of his city and stone him to death to purge out the evil. Seemed a little extreme to me, but in keeping with the rest of their dogma. At the bottom of the print was the source of the quote: Deuteronomy 21.

I spilled my coffee. Setting the styrofoam cup down, I grabbed a napkin to wipe off my hand. D21. Deepa's company. Deuteronomy was from the Old Testament. Was there an Asherah quote that fit D21 and would confirm Anand as one of the Ten?

I yanked out my phone and quickly googled it. Holy... *Do not set up any wooden Asherah pole next to the altar you will build for the LORD your God.* Deuteronomy 16:21.

There was a light touch on my sleeve and I started, hastily shoving my phone away.

"Be welcome here," a woman said.

"Thank you." I shook off the bombshell of my discovery and smiled politely.

I could dismiss the rhetoric in this church, but not the people. Among the ones who introduced themselves were a married couple who were teachers, a nurse, a mechanic, and a civil servant at the local City Hall. It was the very gap between this "normalness" and the extremity of their beliefs that unnerved me. For them, the impending Rapture was as much a fact as the cars they'd driven here or the weather.

After accepting a second serving of delicious homemade apple pie that had been pressed upon me, I complimented the baker, Susan, an athletic woman who baked to destress from working as a parking enforcement officer, adding that they must be proud of the good work they did with the youth shelter.

Susan cut up the rest of the pie. "Oh yes. Those children are part of our flock."

"But you let Nefesh in. How come?" I said.

"God spoke to Pastor Nephus. It was not for us to question His desires." She lay the knife down on a paper plate. "Sadly, our invitation didn't work out. The Nefesh children were troublesome and we had to restrict it back to Mundanes only."

I bet you did. Right after that operation was shut down and Chariot no longer needed you.

By now, the gathering was breaking up, so I took my leave with the other congregants, filing past the pastor to shake hands.

He clasped my hand in a firm grip. "Pastor Nephus."

"Jennifer," I said. "Thank you for the service."

"We don't get a lot of new faces, but I hope you'll come back again." There was no crazed glint in his eyes, he didn't hold my hand overly long, and nothing about him raised any suspicions. My work would be so much easier if all guilty people acted shifty.

"I'm sure I will. I enjoyed your sermon a great deal," I said.

After a few more pleasantries, I took my leave, driving away in full sight of the remaining congregants. I made sure I wasn't followed for a couple of kilometers, then pulled off to wait for the church to clear out. I gave it an hour. When I returned to the tiny parking lot, there were no cars. Still, I parked farther down the road at the foot of their neighbor's driveway and walked back to the church, slipping on gloves and a knit cap.

The front doors were locked. I climbed onto the railing, using the wall for balance and peered in one of the windows. Inside was empty, so I went around back, where there was another door, also locked. I manifested a pick and was inside in moments.

A cool hush enveloped me. One lone light provided the illumination in this back hallway, revealing a set of double doors to the main part of the church, with another door to the pastor's office. A bleeding Christ on a cross was nailed up across from his desk, while off to the side hung a rather lurid painting of the Rapture. There was no laptop, merely a lot of religious texts and some notes for next week's sermon. The only evidence of the church's connection to the Sunshine Youth Shelter were some brochures.

Other than the restrooms, there was one more door, leading to a narrow staircase into the basement. I sighed. The last basement I'd found myself in had contained a sentient yarn monster.

I clicked on the pen light stashed in my small purse and carefully made my way along the rickety stairs. The most suspicious thing in the main area was a washing machine, but there was another door to investigate.

Someone lightly touched my back as a bulb snapped on overhead.

"Nefesh!" the pastor cried.

"I'm not—"

"You drew from your blood."

Ah, crap. The lock pick. I went on alert, ready to bust out my magic, but he didn't try to hurt me or burn me with holy water or anything.

He pressed his palms together in supplication. "God sent you."

"Say what?"

Pastor Nephus opened the door at the far end of the room.

A coltish young woman about Isabel's age, with hair the color of bleached-out wheat, knelt, praying silently, her lips moving.

What the fuck?

The pastor lay his hand on her head. "God has not forsaken us. Our prayers have been answered."

They had no weapons and I had my magic. Since I was in no danger, I stuck around to satisfy my curiosity. "Answered how?"

"Show her, Eve," the pastor said.

Eve looked up at him with terrified eyes. "But, Dad—"

"It's okay," he said in a more gentle voice. "Show her."

Fire burst into a halo above Eve's head. Neat trick. Too bad her father didn't appreciate the control it took to do that.

"You drew your blood out and manipulated the magic within it," he said. "Do the same for my daughter. Remove the evil from within."

Eve's flames died out. She wrapped her arms around herself, and I caught a glimpse of scars along her wrist under her long sleeves.

That poor girl. She wasn't the evil one here.

I punched Pastor Nephus. His eyes rolled back into his sockets and he collapsed on the ground.

Eve gasped, backing up, until she hit the wall.

I put up my hands. "I'm not going to hurt you, I swear. Your magic isn't bad. It's a beautiful thing."

"No!" Fire exploded into life all over her body. "I'm evil."

"You're really not. Listen, I can give you something to take away the magic."

The crackling died down to a bare pop, and then sputtered out altogether. "You can?"

The hope in her eyes broke my heart.

"Yes. It'll only last twenty-four hours but that will give you time to decide what you want to do about it."

"Get it out of me! I'm going to hell." She fell to her knees, sobbing. "God sent you. Help me."

Eve was so committed to this single detrimental way of thinking that she couldn't even show mercy to herself. The absoluteness of her beliefs left no room to entertain any other path. I rocked back on my heels, these insights hitting uncomfortably close, then shook my head. It was different with Isaac.

Eve continued her crying pleas.

Was she beyond assistance? Had a lifetime of being told she was evil twisted her beyond any hope of understanding how amazing her power was? She was of legal age, but was she of sound mind? I glanced at her scars. Would it be crueler to try and rehabilitate her than to take her magic away? Could I even do that without... the image of Mr. Sharp, the man who'd led the auction for Chariot and whose magic I'd destroyed, rose up, his cries echoing in my ears.

Her flames extinguished, Eve threw her arms around my legs, her nails digging painfully into me through the fabric of my thin dress. Her gaze was frighteningly clear. "Please."

"Please," Pastor Nephus slurred, sitting up with his hand pressed to his head.

My magic had never weighed so heavily on me.

I paced in a tight circle. The last time I'd prayed to a deity, I'd been twelve years old. My prayers hadn't been answered and my father never came home. I wished that I had the pure faith of the others who came to this church. That I'd received a sign instead of being the damn sign.

Eve whimpered, her pain naked and raw in the twist of her shoulders, her grimace, and the stiffness in every muscle. I couldn't leave her like this. May the universe forgive me, but I was going to take her magic.

I sat down on the floor next to her. "You need to relax for this to work."

Tears glistened in her eyes. "Yes. Thank you."

"Move a muscle, Pastor, and I'll make you regret it."

He nodded, pale.

Working as carefully as I could, I pulled all the magic out of Eve. It smelled like charcoal and tasted like cream. I forced myself to stay grounded through the rush that heightened my senses; not to divest her of it too quickly, and carefully snagged it in the forked branches.

Her whimpers turned to wheezing breaths and her eyes clouded with fear, but it was too late to stop. The clusters had already begun to bloom. The magic was eaten up, leaving a milky taste on my lips, and a shocked silence in the room.

Eve slumped over, not broken like Sharp, but not moving either. Her pulse was faint.

"Will she…" Her father swallowed. "Wake up?"

"I don't know." Nothing like this had ever happened.

He pushed me out of the way, cradling her head and murmuring for her to say something.

Then a miracle occurred. Her lids blinked open and she took my hand. "It's gone."

"Yes," I said.

She hugged me tightly, but I didn't feel her joy. I'd granted her wish, but the scars of this trauma would live on.

My only satisfaction was that I hadn't harmed her. I'd taken someone's magic and they'd recovered, proving I was more than a destructive force. I wasn't a monster. My heart swelled with an enormous lightness.

"Promise me, you'll live well," I said.

"Oh, she will," Pastor Nephus said, an odd darkness to his voice.

I was about to turn back and ask him what his deal was, since I'd just done some major magical heavy lifting for his kid totally pro bono, but electric current knocked the breath from my lungs.

Tasered. So much for gratitude.

My body stiffened like a board and I fell over, though I was completely cognizant. The smack of concrete against my cheek felt far away next to the sharp agony rolling through me. I cried out as every muscle simultaneously seized up in a giant charley horse.

Black shiny shoes stepped into my blurred field of vision.

Pastor Nephus snapped a pair of magic nulling cuffs on

me. Through my haze of pain came a terrifying flatness. I was powerless. I shook my wrists, my brows drawn together in confusion.

"You asked about the youth shelter," he said. "These came in handy for dealing with some of our more temperamental flock."

He dragged me upright, propped me in a wooden chair, and tied me up with several thick ropes.

By the time I had control of my body again, all I could do was tug uselessly on the bindings. "I helped you with Eve."

"Praise be to God. He sent you to cleanse my daughter, and now you shall offer your blood as the catalyst to make the Rapture a reality and reunite us with our Lord."

I thrashed against the ropes. "You think you'll be one of the Chosen after you murder me? Basic commandment, Pastor." Plus, how about some non-homicidal gratitude for the person who'd saved your daughter, asshole?

I jumped to my feet, the chair stuck to me like a turtle's shell, and knocked him to the ground. Thanks to the cuffs, my magic was still suppressed, but my legs worked. I ran towards the stairs as fast as I could, hit the first step and gasped.

The entire congregation stood at the top of the stairs.

They carried me into the church, still tied to the chair, like a Jewish bride at her wedding dance. I resisted the urge to hum Hava Nagila.

"Killing me won't get you to heaven," I said, hoping to appeal to some vestige of goodness in the congregants. "Just to prison."

Doubt flashed over some of their faces. I'd swayed a solid sixty percent of them to my side. Fifty percent. High thirties for sure.

"You're wrong," Susan the pie lady said, conviction in her voice. "God brought you here because you are not one of His Chosen. You belong to the Devil. We shall wipe you from the earth, ushering in the End of Days to destroy your kind for good. Our reward shall be the Rapture." She swayed, madness bright in her eyes.

Hysterical laughter stuck in my throat. The biggest irony here was that God hadn't sent me, I'd brought myself in the name of one of those fascinating cases I was so gung ho about.

"You sent those Nefesh kids at the shelter to be tortured," I said. "Some died."

"We saved them," Pastor Nephus said.

"Yeah? How come you didn't send Eve to them?"

"It wasn't God's will," he said.

Hypocrite. You knew what those people were doing and even you couldn't put your child through that.

My heart stuttered. "Those people" were Chariot.

Reality fractured, connection upon connection folding over my life. My father working for Isaac when my magic appeared, Adam using a Van Gogh to ward me who was loyal to Chariot, Isaac being Levi's dad, my first case with magic happening to involve Meryem and Chariot, Omar and the angel feather at the archeological site, and now Jackson Wu's involvement on a seemingly unrelated case of money laundering tied to Isaac's support of the Untainted Party.

My existence was a dot trapped in the center of outward-spiraling concentric circles. Was there any end to them? Was everything in my life destined to be connected to all of this? I fought to breathe.

"God tested me with Eve," the Pastor said, his voice rising to the rafters.

Fucking narcissist. Eve hunched into herself and didn't make eye contact.

"But we proved that our desire was pure and now we will do His work and be rewarded."

"I'm not your ticket to eternal paradise." I looked at each of the worshippers in turn. "You're about to make a terrible mistake, but you can stop this before it's too late."

255

Pastor Nephus walked behind the island near the pulpit and opened a set of doors. He returned with a silver watering can contraption, and poured the contents over my head, praying about anointments.

I screwed my eyes shut against the sting of oil.

"Let this holy fire cleanse us," he intoned.

My eyes snapped open. Susan was handing him one of those boxes of long matches. They were going to burn everything down, using me as a Presto log.

I thrashed against my bindings.

The worshippers formed a circle around me, singing about trumpets and God and life after the Rapture, their faces upturned like the Whos down in Whoville.

Pastor Nephus lit the match.

"If this is God's will," I said, "then release my magic. Prove that He truly desires this."

"He does. We have faith and I'm not afraid to prove to you that in this we do His will." The pastor nodded at Susan, who unlocked the cuffs.

Three things happened at once: the cuffs hit the ground with a clink, the lit match was flicked toward oil-slicked skin, and I popped the ropes holding me.

Oh wait, there was a fourth thing. My blood armor locked into place. The match bounced off it and fell to the ground where I stamped it out.

The parishioners' voices grew louder, and at their crescendo, the pastor anointed me with more oil.

I grabbed his arm, forcing him to fling the canister away, but Susan, that eager beaver, was on it.

She hit me with another lit match and this one took. I lit up like Fezzik imitating the Dread Pirate Roberts.

It stung, but that was about it. I slapped at the flames to douse them.

My body spasmed as someone hit me with the Taser again. The armor sputtered and I screamed as fire burned my

256

exposed skin. I crashed to my knees, desperately batting at the flames. Gritting my teeth, I used that sage kindergarten advice to stop, drop, and roll, smothering the fire.

I fell into a dark void where there was no pain. Dimly, I remembered that third degree burns cauterized the nerve endings and the pain would come. My heartbeat was skipping and charred patches bloomed across my skin where the armor no longer held.

I smothered the flames as one of the parishioners reloaded the Taser. Still on my back, I fired a blood dagger at him, nailing him in the arm.

He dropped the weapon.

Miraculously, nothing other than me had burned.

Sweat and soot stung my eyes. I pushed to my feet, knives in both hands.

Everyone stared at me in horrified silence.

"It didn't happen," one man whispered.

There were murmurs and worried glances, some shuffling back to distance themselves from the fallout.

The pastor smacked Susan's arm. "Again! The Rapture must—"

With a guttural cry, Eve barreled into her father, knocking him to the ground. "Leave her alone!"

I stood over her father and shot the daggers into the carpet on either side of his head.

He whimpered and flinched.

"Get your daughter some help, you son of a bitch."

No one stopped me when I made my way to the exit on rubbery legs, lurching from pew to pew for support.

I shouldered out the front door, squinting against the sunlight that momentarily blinded me. Ripping off the cap, gloves, and those damn bobby pins, I lurched down the road toward Moriarty, taking deep breaths and focused on the mountains in the distance as a solid touchstone.

How many more times would I brush up against death

because of a fanatical belief? How close had I come today? Would they have found my body? I fended off the memory of Gavriella dying in my arms. Would Levi have buried me up on that hill next to her?

If there was karma, it was a joke, because I'd tried to live my life honorably. All Jezebels did, and what did it get us?

Oh... I stumbled. Deepa's pilgrimage involved cleansing her karma. What if she'd meant to atone for her role in Gavriella's death? To fix things in her life before moving on and mend the bridge between Jezebels and Chariot perhaps?

Rafael was wrong. The bamah wasn't code for some amulet. It was exactly what it purported to be: a high place. Specifically, the Jewish cemetery, located up a hill. Very specifically, the one where Gavriella was buried.

Connection upon connection. My gut had never steered me wrong: Gavriella's grave was key to something. But what?

Chapter 25

The pain of my burns rushed in. My hands were slick on the wheel, the world fuzzy at the edges, and I barely made it to a local clinic where I was rushed to the Nightingale to be healed.

I was capable of the drive back, but it was a long way from the church to the Jewish cemetery, and I did my best not to brood. Or shiver, even with the heat cranked to high and my leather jacket on.

One lone bobby pin poked my scalp. I tore it out, wincing as a couple strands of hair came with it, and shoved it in my pocket.

HOOONNNK!

I wrenched the wheel to the right, back into my lane, keeping a careful distance between me and the logging truck ahead. There was a silhouette of a woman on its mud flaps with a breezy tilt of her head and the wind ruffling her hair. Oh, to be that carefree.

A zippy blue convertible shot past in the left lane, honking at both me and the silver SUV with a dented bumper behind me keeping a sedate speed.

I rolled down my window, the breeze blowing my

cobwebs away, and called Miles on Bluetooth to update him on the events at the church.

"Almost getting caught up in a fanatical attempt to bring on the Rapture," he said, when I was done. "Only you."

"We can get the congregation on varying degrees of attempted murder, right?"

"I'll send a team, but you'll need to make a statement, and it'll depend if they close ranks on their testimony. You think Eve will side with you?"

"We could pressure her and..." My hands tightened on the wheel. Did she deserve being forced to testify against her father and fellow congregants after all she'd suffered?

This would ruin their lives. I had the law on my side, but I also had the power of choice. Instead of an absolute insistence on punishment, could I show mercy? What would help more? Anger or forgiveness?

"I don't want them arrested," I said. "Is there some way to get medical professionals involved for rehabilitation purposes? Let's get Eve the help she needs and work with the other congregants."

"This might be an uphill battle," Miles said. "But yeah, I'll reach out and put people into place. I'll also go out there and impress upon them that it's in their best interests to go with the program."

"Thanks, Miles."

By the time I reached the iron gates of the cemetery, it was early evening and they were locked tight. A curl of anticipation knifed through me as I put the car into park, made short work of the lock on the gates, then closed them behind me so that someone driving by wouldn't notice anything amiss.

I walked over to where Gavriella was buried and knelt down, placing my hand on the grass, my fingertips tingling. This was the bamah in question, I was certain of it. I half-expected that Gavriella's body wouldn't be here, having been stolen by Chariot for some nefarious purpose.

There was one way to find out if I was right.

Jews had a lot of prohibitions and grave digging was probably one of them, so how far was I willing to go to determine if my instincts were correct?

I smiled. Pretty far. Except I hadn't brought a shovel. Eh. What were another couple of sins at this point? I broke into the groundskeeper's shack and stole one, along with a ladder.

Now I was in business.

The shovel made a "che" sound as it bit into the grass, the dirt flying to one side with a soft "ffffp." Good thing Asherah had given me enhanced strength, because digging up a grave was freaking hard. Even so, by the time the shovel struck the lid of the plain coffin with a dull thud, I was deep in the pit and soaked in sweat, my skin streaked with dirt, and my pony tail half-fallen out.

I cracked the lid open, recoiling from the stench inside. It was rotten broccoli, unwashed feet, and a sewer. The body was mercifully buried in a linen burial shroud, which had been stained with its decomposing fluids.

One hypothesis disproven: there *was* a body. Was it Gavriella's? It felt pretty skeletal, so identifying features were out.

The faint hum of traffic floated on the breeze and birds twittered in the branches of a leafy tree. I made the mistake of taking a deep breath, then gagged as body rot went up my nostrils. I flinched, accidentally jostling the body with the shovel.

A glint of metal caught my eye. I reached under the deceased and pulled out a short tube, shaking it. Nothing rattled.

I tapped my finger against the metal cap, an icy prickliness dotting my skin. The smart thing to do was get this back to Rafael and let him open it, but I couldn't. Fifteen years ago, my magic and my father's actions had set something in motion and if I was correct—my hand tightened on the tube—tonight it came full circle.

I had to be the one to open it.

I ripped the cap off. Inside were two scrolls. One gave off nothing. It was the fake created by my Uncle Paulie. The other assaulted me with the smell of a hot sandstorm.

I slammed the cap back into place, sealing the scrolls up, and took shallow breaths through the adrenaline flooding my body.

"Isaac wanted the bamah because somehow, someone in Chariot buried their two scrolls here." The real one and Dad's fake. Connections. I bumped the tube against my forehead. "Deepa Anand."

"Very good, Ashira," Isaac said, rolling the "R" in his Italian accent. He stood at the top of the grave, looking down at me with an approving smile.

"Lookie lookie," I said. "It's one of the Ten. Nine? Poor Theresa."

His smile faltered for a second, replaced by a shrewd look. "You knew about me." Wow. Such compassion for his dead co-villain. "Then I was even more correct to set you the task of finding these scrolls."

There are two types of people in this world, Ash, my girl. Those who are marks and those who aren't.

I'd hallucinated an entire alternate version of my life, and yet not for a second had I imagined a reality where Isaac Montefiore had played me.

I still couldn't.

The shovel's wooden handle that I held broke into splinters. "You didn't hire me. Nicola did."

"We always underestimate the wives and mothers, don't we? You'd never have believed she could be that duplicitous, but she's a fine little actress. When it matters to her." He casually called back over his shoulder. "Your precious son's life mattered a great deal, didn't it, my love?"

Nicola cried out.

I cracked the metal shovel in half. "I am not a mark," I snarled.

"I'd have to disagree," Isaac said. "Rather delicious, fooling the daughter of the man who tried to con me by hiding your magic. Adam always did think he was smarter than everyone else, even when it was painfully obvious that he was not. It seems you share that trait. How sad that your family is now zero for two on attempts to put one over on me. Sorry, zero for three. Isn't that right, Talia?"

"Leave my daughter alone," Talia said, her words practically a growl.

My heart skipped a beat. Had Isaac turned that charming smile on her, convincing her to come with him under the pretense of a donation to the party? Had she fallen for his honeyed lies, not seeing the blood in the water? Was my mother so used to being the predator in the room that she failed to see she'd become prey?

A pair of daggers flew from my hands but I was down in a grave, my arms already throbbed from digging, and I missed my target.

Isaac tossed down a pair of magic nulling cuffs. "Put these on and come up or I'll shoot your precious mother."

I clicked them onto my wrists, filling with that dull flatness. I didn't bother hiding the hate in my eyes as I climbed out of there. It was almost a relief. There was no more pretense, no more hiding, no more pretending that I could let him live after this.

And Levi?

He didn't matter. He couldn't. Isaac had killed my father and then he'd conned me. One might have been forgivable, for Levi's sake. For our future. Not both. And especially not when Isaac had brought my mother into this. There wasn't a corner of the world far enough he could go to escape me.

I hissed, a splinter from the ladder lodging under my skin,

but I pressed my hand harder against the rung, relishing the pain, and climbed out of the pit.

Isaac stood next to a familiar slender man, who trained a gun on Nicola and my mother. Nicola was clearly terrified, barely holding it together. Talia, however, was pale but defiant, her chin up, despite the purple and black bruise around her right eye.

A red wave rose up hot and sharp inside me, before it was swept away by my core fusing, cold and hard like a diamond. My father's voice whispered in my ear. *If you want to spend the extra money, spend it on clarity.*

The tableau froze for the briefest second, and realization slammed into me. Fifteen years of secrets and cons, of loss and rage, all driving me towards this night, this moment. The journey that my father had embarked on with Isaac that had upended my life ended tonight. This wasn't coincidence, it was inevitability.

It was closure.

I sketched a mock bow. "I'm *delighted* to make your acquaintance."

"And I yours," the German assassin said in a heavy accent.

"Confirm something for me, Isaac," I said. "Deepa's pilgrimage. Was she atoning for everything she'd done in Chariot's name, including having Gavriella's death on her conscience?"

Isaac jammed his hands in the pockets of his light trench coat. "None of that would have caused Deepa a moment's loss of sleep had her daughter not been killed. That's when her childhood beliefs in karma got the better of her and she decided that none of us should attain immortality."

"So, she stole both scrolls. But why hide them... oh. Gavriella's grave was the last place she expected you to ever look, wasn't it?"

"She was right."

Nicola was shaking so hard, I was scared that she'd crack her skull against the gun. "Mi dispiace," she kept saying.

My mother squeezed Nicola's hand.

As angry as I was at being betrayed, I couldn't blame Nicola. She'd been afraid, and Isaac had spent a lifetime proving to her that he considered Levi expendable. Faced with that decision, how could she have acted differently? I wasn't a mother, but I was loyal to my friends. If there had been a way to keep them from being hurt, these people who I cared so much about, I would have taken that too. No wonder she was so relieved when I'd agreed to help her at first.

I could understand, but I still couldn't forgive her. Not yet.

I planted my hands on my hips. "Is it time for the big villain speech now?"

Montefiore laughed, looking so heart-stoppingly like his son for a second that my breath caught. "Funny girl. Why not? I've always enjoyed a good villain monologue."

My mother snorted. I bit the inside of my cheek while shooting her a "behave, there is a gun" look.

Isaac held out his hand. "But first, the scrolls please."

I clutched the tube to my chest, the cuffs jangling, and Isaac sighed.

"Fail to hand it over and Hans will shoot the women. Even twitch wrong and, well…" He shrugged, a monster in luxury brands.

Nicola pressed her fist into her mouth.

Talia clamped her lips in a thin line. She'd shifted to keep both Hans and Isaac in her view. If Mom tried something heroically stupid, I'd kill her.

I held out the tube, but he had to tug it out of my hold. For one precious moment, Team Jezebel had possessed all the scrolls. There went my chance to destroy them all.

"Seriously?" I said. "Hans? Because Viktor or Jafar weren't

available? Where do you hire your henchmen? Bad Guys 'R' Us?"

"Yes," Isaac said, grinning. "We handpick them from around the world, giving them names sourced from only the finest of Hollywood clichés."

Hans exhaled through his nose like this was not the first time he'd encountered people being idiots about his name.

"Now," Isaac said. "Where to start?"

"How about when you murdered my dad?"

Say it out loud, you bastard.

Talia let out a strangled sob. Fuck. I briefly closed my eyes. I'd never told her the circumstances of Adam's death.

Isaac was all paternal concern. "How tragic. Was Adam murdered? I had no idea. And here I thought I saw him the other day. Speaking of your father, he is to be commended on how he hid you all this time. In plain sight." Isaac tucked the metal tube with the scrolls into his deep front pocket. "I didn't realize you were a Jezebel until the other night when you were outside my house with Levi."

The night before Nicola had hired me. I winced.

"To be fair, I didn't immediately realize it then either," he said, "but then I remembered how Yitzak, a level-five Van Gogh and very loyal to my people, ended up in isolation in a Nefesh cell because of an assault complaint against him. By you. That got me thinking."

"I'm sure that was a full-time job," I said, keeping a careful eye on the gun.

"I stayed up all night putting the pieces together. Why did Adam decide to cut and run after Gracie Green supposedly died?" he said. "Why did you suddenly pack in your business after that Jezebel died for good?"

"Let's not mince words, Isaac. Gavriella didn't die of old age. You tortured her until her body was so battered that it gave up the fight."

Gavriella's body falling into my arms, so light. Bruises

covering her body, her arm broken at an odd angle and one single clot of blood caking her left nostril.

I blinked away the vision. "So, you put all of that together, and believing I was the next Jezebel, decided to use me to find the two scrolls that Deepa had hidden." I paused, but Isaac still didn't correct me that one of them was fake. Dad's con held. "Backstabbed by one of your own. That had to hurt."

"She paid, in the end. Though it wasn't supposed to go that far." Isaac frowned at the German. Ah. He'd killed her and made it look like heart failure, despite Isaac wanting her alive.

"Did you kill Misha Ivanov, too?" I asked Hans.

He wrinkled his nose. "Old people. They are so flammable."

That was just… wow.

Talia's brow was furrowed, her mouth agape, and she kept rubbing her temple like that could restore order and turn the world back into something that once again made sense. I should have tried harder to press the truth on her in tiny drips, instead of drowning her in a torrent.

I kept my expression neutral, refusing to give my enemy more ammunition. "Your Ten is down to how many now?"

The silver SUV with the dented bumper that I'd seen on the highway was parked next to Moriarty. Isaac had been following me. Did he have more people hidden out there or was this a bare-bones intimidation?

Isaac wagged a finger at me. "You don't get to know everything."

"Come on, share. I do so love facts. If Deepa stole the scrolls sometime in the past couple of months, how come you only tried to torture the location out of her last week?"

Isaac paused for a long moment, then shrugged. "She was careful. The pilgrimage was our first opportunity to confront her."

"Even then she didn't talk."

"She talked enough," Hans said. "She gave up the bamah."

"Big deal. You still needed me to find it for you." I raised an imaginary glass in cheers. "Quite the stroke of genius for her to bury the scrolls in the one place you'd never think to look. Now that's good use of Gavriella's murder. You could say Deepa killed two birds with one stone."

"Do you harass my son this constantly?" Isaac said.

My smirk fell from my face. "Keep him out of this."

"Oh, but he's so very much a part of it, don't you think?"

"He was," I said. "Then he chose you."

Isaac did a double take.

I laughed. Bitterly. "Your mole didn't report that back to you? My payback plans were too much for the poor boy to stomach."

"Is this true?" he said to Nicola.

"Yes," she spat out. "All you've ever done is hurt him and deny him any chance at happiness."

Isaac frowned, tapping his finger against his lips like he was rearranging things in his head.

If he'd done anything to Levi… I flexed my fingers, but no dagger pressed into my palm, only the cold press of metal. I edged closer to my jacket, tossed by the top of the grave. If I could just get to the bobby pin in the jacket pocket…

Hans tutted me, motioning with the gun to stay where I was.

"Have I covered everything to your satisfaction?" Isaac said. "Because now it's my turn to request something from you."

"If I'm being honest, there wasn't a lot there that I didn't figure out for myself." I snapped my fingers. "Hey, did you really convince Jackson to accept Nefesh into that youth shelter he supported? You know, to kidnap those teens and tear their magic from them to sell to the highest bidder?"

My mother lunged at Isaac with a snarl I'd never heard come out of her. Even Isaac flinched.

Hans jerked her back.

"You bastard," she said. "You used our party leader for that?"

I felt far less guilty about dumping that particular truth in her lap than I had about Adam's murder. I also intended to lie like a motherfucker when I recounted that conversation for Jackson's benefit. In my version, Isaac gave him up.

Isaac ignored Talia. "My request, Ashira."

"Go nuts."

"Bring me the scrolls from the library."

I cupped a hand to my ears. "I didn't hear a please in there."

"Hans, shoot the women."

"No!" I threw my hands up placatingly. "Talia may not mean anything to you, but Nicola is your wife."

"She represents my old life," Isaac said. "There is no place for her once I have the *Sefer Raziel HaMalakh*."

"You mean, once whoever is left of the Ten partakes of it equally."

Isaac smiled.

"None of you were ever going to share it with the others, were you?"

"With great power," he said.

"Comes great responsibility, Spidey?"

"Comes great desires."

I flicked a glance at Talia's black eye. "Nicola and my mom in exchange for my scrolls. You have no way into the library and no way of ever achieving your dream of immortality without me, so this is not up for negotiation."

"You have your deal." Damn. That was too easy. He'd intended that trade. For how long? Since Nicola had called and asked if I'd found the bamah? "The handover will happen when you give me the rest of the *Sefer*," he said. "One hour from now at Lockdown Cybersecurity."

"You've got me in cuffs way the hell out from anyone who

can help me. Tone the evil bullshit down a notch and make it two."

"Two then, but not a second later." Isaac looped his arm through his wife's as if he was escorting her out for the night and not dragging her, begging and pleading, to the SUV.

Hans grabbed Talia.

"Ash." She reached back for me.

Don't be scared. I'll come for you. I love you. "Mom," I croaked out.

"That was a really expensive dress, Ashira." She shook her head. "It's ruined now."

Hans jammed the gun into her back, forcing her to the car.

Laughter burbled out of me. Oh, Mom. Her Talia-ness calmed me. Maybe that had been her intention all along. She knew which buttons of mine she pushed.

I didn't follow since I couldn't risk anyone being shot. Also, Hans had Transporter magic so I literally couldn't get the jump on him. I dove for the bobby pin in my leather jacket, desperate to get the cuffs off, watching my mom get farther and farther away.

I bent the metal into shape with my teeth and shoved it into the cuff's lock, but it wouldn't click. Yes, I was rushing it, but how could I slow down when I had seconds before Talia would be put inside the vehicle?

Isaac opened the driver's side door and got into the SUV. "Don't be late," he called out.

The bobby pin bent double.

Jaw clenched, eyes narrowed, I pulled the pin out, straightened it, and reinserted it once more, forcing myself to find the rhythm of the lock.

This time the bobby pin caught and the cuffs fell off me. I was sprinting toward the SUV before they hit the ground. Magic rushed up under my skin, my blood armor locking into place.

Gunfire cracked and a bullet bounced off me.

"Hans," Isaac snapped through the open window.

His minion kept the gun pointed at me a moment longer, before lowering it slowly and climbing into the car. They roared off, the taillights fading away as they turned left out of the gates and were lost to view.

Two hours. That was all the time I had to come up with a plan and tell Levi that his worst fear had come to pass about his mother.

I dropped my armor and reached for the wooden ring. We were down, but we weren't out. Nicola was not going to die. My mom was not going to die. Isaac was not going to win.

I was not a mark.

Did that still mean killing Isaac? I'd absolved the congregation after they'd tried to bonfire me. Even Lux had been forgiven for what she'd done. Isaac *had* murdered my father though, and he'd never face justice for that. He didn't deserve mercy. Except... wasn't that precisely the time to show it? Who, in the end, was mercy for?

In the case of the Church, it was for Eve. Isaac wasn't an innocent.

I slid on my ring. My time in the shadows may have been short, but it had indelibly marked me. Isaac would learn that the hard way.

Chapter 26

"You—no—" Rafael threw himself between me and the stone pillars in the library.

"You want Nicola or my mom to die?"

He hesitated. "It wouldn't be the first time that we've made sacrifices…"

"Rafael!"

"Of course not, but you cannot simply hand the scrolls over. It would be one thing if you had your magic, but there's every chance they'll bring a null. You could be a sitting duck."

"Put the scrolls in the tube. The team is waiting for us at my house. We need a strategy meeting."

He didn't move.

I sighed. "Look, if there is a null, this team meeting is even more important to solve that problem. All the scrolls in one place, Attendant. We end this tonight."

"Or we watch Isaac become a god on earth. Unstoppable."

"That was always the risk." I tossed him the tube. "Be a good sport."

"Oh, I'll be a *cracking* good sport." Rafael slammed his hand down on the first illuminated pillar and I used the dark wooden ring to get out of there before the magic affected me.

Arkady, Levi, and Priya sat in my living room, unsure of why Miles had told them all to assemble here. I'd phoned the Head of Security on my way back from the cemetery to put the grave back to rights and I'd had to tell him what happened, but I didn't want to repeat myself on multiple phone calls. Once Miles had stopped cursing me out, he'd agreed to call the others.

"What did you say to Mimi, pickle?" Arkady said, changing track mid-sentence from telling Priya about one of the House operatives being pregnant. "I could hear his teeth gnashing through the phone. That's not good for him. He already has to wear a mouthguard at night so he doesn't grind his molars into little stubs."

"What?!" I swiveled my head to look directly at him. "Miles does what?"

Arkady grinned. "Oh, he is so stressed and it is adorable."

Rafael popped into the room and nodded at me. Ashen-faced and somber, he leaned on the wall by the window, checking the street below.

Levi leaned back in his chair, his fingers steepled and his expression unreadable.

"What's going on?" Priya said, glancing from Rafael to me. "And why do you look like Laura Ingalls Wilder crawled out of her grave?" She fanned the air in front of her face. "You sort of smell that way as well."

"Sorry. You're not that wrong." I sat down, snapping my fingers to call Mrs. Hudson over. Picking her up, I stroked her fur for fortification.

She sniffed me, sneezed, then butted me in the stomach with her damp nose.

"The bamah didn't refer to the amulet," I said. "It *was* a high place. Closed, too. Gavriella's grave. Inside her coffin were two scrolls: the fake one Adam had made and Chariot's real one. Deepa Anand, who was one of the Ten, suffered a crisis of conscience after the death of her daughter and decided no one in Chariot deserved immortality. So she hid both their real scroll and the fake, believing them to both be authentic, in the one place that the rest of the Ten would never look."

"That's kind of brilliant," Priya said.

That was the easy part to share.

"And?" Levi said, in a deceptively calm voice.

I dragged my fingers through the puppy's fur, seeking comfort in her warmth. "Nicola didn't hire me to find them. Isaac did. He played me and now he's got their two scrolls, and both our moms. The German assassin is with him and I have approximately ninety minutes to trade our pieces of the *Sefer* for Talia and Nicola."

Blood seeped out of our walls in long gashes. Rafael jumped away.

"Fuck!" Priya pressed back against the sofa cushions, one hand thrown up over her face.

Levi reacted to bad news with illusions. I'd made a note to that effect on my palm in pen, but it didn't stop me from pulling my feet off the floor and away from the blood oozing out from the planks like a ghosthunter's wet dream.

"Levi," I said with a calm I didn't feel. "Stop."

A muscle ticked in his jaw. The air turned fetid and a low growl rumbled from wall to wall.

Mrs. Hudson raised her head and growled back at each wall in turn.

The room shook, everyone except Levi clutching furniture, terrified. Levi. Right. I checked my note, hoping it was correct.

"Please shut this down," I said.

Levi's nostrils flared, his chest rising and falling in harsh rasps, but the illusion vanished.

Arkady glanced around once as if to assure himself he was safe. "Where's the tradeoff happening?"

"Lockdown Cybersecurity," I said.

"Oh." Priya cracked her knuckles and opened her laptop. "There's got to be some weak spot we can exploit there. Professional cybersecurity, my ass."

"Right." Arkady flashed her a thumbs up. "And Levi could illusion us to—"

"Assume Isaac will bring a null." Rafael's voice cut across Priya and Arkady's brainstorming, silencing them.

Pri's hands stilled on her laptop, mid-type. "You can't go up against them without magic."

Levi prowled the perimeter of the room. "Two women at gunpoint, an assassin, a null, my father's possible immortality, and fifteen years finally coming to a head." Stormy blue eyes met my brown ones. "Did I miss anything?"

Time spun out between us, a million variations of Levi's reactions happening in an instant. He left, he stayed, he comforted me, he cursed me. What story was this about to be?

"That about covers it," I said.

He nodded. "So how do you want to tackle this?"

I blinked rapidly at the moisture in my eyes, lowering my head, until I was back to my kickass in-control self. "The main problem is how to take out the null. I'll be frisked before I get anywhere close to Isaac, so I can't bring in anything suspicious. Once magic is back in play, our chances of success shoot up." I injected a light-hearted note into my voice. "Until I throw my Attendant back into a coma because someone has torn the Kiss of Death from his inert body to use on me."

Mrs. Hudson yelped. I released my hold and she jumped down.

Rafael waved his hands excitedly. "Oh, that's right! I was hoping to get the chance to tell you about my research developments."

We all stared at him with varying degrees of incredulity that he was talking about dusty old facts that didn't matter when we were all maybe going to bite it.

"I mean," Rafael said, composing himself, "that our assumptions about the amulet in the first place were off. It isn't the Kiss of Death, but rather Asherah's Kiss. It took a while to translate, but thanks to the notes of the first Attendant, I learned that when the original Seeker was given magic, Asherah also gave her this amulet as extra protection. The kiss of the goddess. That's why it took your cravings away, Ash, and why it woke me up when my own magic was too low to allow me to do so."

"Then the name got changed when Chariot got hold of it?" Arkady said. "Because if they had the blood of a Jezebel, it meant the Jezebel's time had run out?"

"Partially, probably," Rafael said. "But it's also a play on words. In Hebrew the root word of kiss is the same as the root for weapon. Neshek."

"That's so cool," Priya said.

"That's what I thought," he said.

"Or it opens the door to a lot of awkward misunderstandings," I said. "Imagine a cop pulling someone over and saying, 'Excuse me sir, are you carrying kisses?'"

Levi half-grinned, but Priya and Rafael shot me identical looks of pity.

"Your lack of a sense of humor aside," I said, "the amulet will keep me safe because of the goddess's protection on it. I figured that out already."

"It's not a passive protection," Rafael said. "It involves choice. The records document this and my experience confirms it. I had a choice of whether to wake up or not."

"Not much of a choice," I said.

"It was when I had no idea whether your plan had worked and if I'd wake up as myself or as that Ba'al freakshow. I chose to believe in Ashira." Rafael paused to smile at me. "Once the choice was made, the Kiss's magic made it so."

Arkady quirked an eyebrow. "The power of decision making? That's not much of a weapon."

"Isn't it?" Levi said. "If you're holding a gun, you can choose to end someone's life or show mercy. You can choose to keep going in the face of adversity. Choose to face hard truths and make more empowered decisions."

Rafael pushed his glasses up his nose. "Exactly. Choice is the most powerful weapon there is. Nor was the decision easy. When faced with the *Sefer's* magic, Ash, you'll need to do the same. You've already done it with the feather."

Had I?

I thought I'd smelled the feather's magic faintly again when I wore the amulet in Levi's office. Was that my doubt creeping in or a failure on the amulet's part?

"That was different," I said. "The feather remained in the pouch, and I didn't mainline into the heart of its magic like I'll have to with the *Sefer* to destroy it. We have no idea how powerful the combined scrolls will be. I could drown in that magic and do it with a smile on my face, no matter how much I choose otherwise. Forget the amulet."

"You're second-guessing yourself," Rafael said.

"Regardless, if you're not at full strength to pull me back from the brink yourself, Rafael, this isn't going to work."

We were so close. I had to be realistic about my limitations because we couldn't afford any mistakes, least of all from me. The fate of the world depended on me.

My mother depended on me—for the first time ever.

Rafael sighed. "I can do it." He removed the amulet from around his neck and handed it to me. "Will you at least consider what I've said?"

You face a choice, a voice whispered in my head as I took the necklace. *But it is not what you think.*

I dropped the amulet.

"Ash?" Levi frowned and bent down to retrieve it.

"It's nothing." I shook off the weirdness. "If it makes you feel better, Rafael, I'll factor the Kiss into the plan as a secondary source. The essential protective power on it will still do something against the *Sefer's* magic."

Crunching noises came from the kitchen as the puppy chowed down.

Levi handed me the amulet, then perched on the arm of my chair. He was close enough to feel the heat of his body, but he didn't actually close the gap between us.

I shifted away from him.

"We'll keep both of you safe," he said. "I hate to bring it up, but there's another major obstacle to overcome. The rest of Chariot."

"That might work in our favor," I said. "The Ten's numbers have thinned out due to in-fighting, and it seems to be every person for themselves where the *Sefer* is concerned. Any of the others who show up will cause as many problems for Isaac's people as they do for us."

"They'll still be gunning for you," Levi said. "I'm going to put operatives in place outside the perimeter."

I patted his thigh. "Good plan. I'll call Lux and her people. They offered to help."

"You can't be serious," Arkady scoffed.

"Ash, I get that you're trying to give us the best shot you can, but I don't think these people will stand much of a chance. It would be cruel to ask them," Levi said.

"Enough," I said. "The only other opinion I'll consider here is Rafael's. We're the ones with Asherah magic. They are the followers of Asherah. This is the will of their goddess in action on earth. If I were them, I'd like the choice of being involved. We owe them that respect. Rafael?"

We all looked at him.

"It's possible we made tactical errors by not including them in the past," he said, carefully. "I'm no longer willing to take on all the risks myself. If they are truly followers of Asherah, then we are better working together. Call them."

By the time we'd come up with a workable plan, predicated on every single thing going right, there was barely over half an hour left. I took the world's fastest shower, chucking the floral dress in the trash. Once I was fortified in all-black with my hair in a high ponytail, I felt stabilized enough to dash out to pick up a very important piece of the plan.

Priya slipped into my room. "Arkady and Rafael left. They'll meet us at Lockdown."

"Good. Once you've done your part, stay the hell away. I mean it, Pri."

Her eyes flashed. "I heard you the first six times."

I spread my hands wide. "I can't afford this palace on my own."

She snorted, her donkey braying laugh bursting free. "You're an idiot, Holmes."

"Yeah, well. Karaoke tomorrow?"

"First round is on me." Priya pressed her lips together and spun around to leave, but I grabbed her hand and pulled her into a tight hug.

"Love you, Adler."

Priya swiped at her eyes. "I'm not saying it back until you're home safe. So there."

I smiled. "I can live with that."

"I have to get ready," she muttered and stomped into her bedroom.

Mrs. Hudson came trotting into the foyer with Pinky as I was slipping into my motorcycle boots and dropped her girlfriend at my feet.

"You want to help too, don't you, baby? I'll be back soon, okay?" It would have been so much easier striding into this battle without worrying about all the people—and puppy—I might never return to. Who might not return with me. The old Ash would have preferred it that way.

I'd been a happy kid, but when Dad left, my life was overtaken by a fiery rage. Fire can be beautiful, but it needs to be stoked, and I'd fallen into a trap of constantly feeding it and

279

calling that motivation. When my team had come into my life and my relationship with Levi had changed, I'd been in danger of that fire consuming me, but I'd made a choice.

For a brief shining moment, I'd chosen happiness.

When it was snatched from my grasp, instead of finding another path to that same emotion, I'd thrown myself back into the familiar and comforting arms of anger like any good addict. How would I right all those many wrongs without it?

What motivated me didn't always have to be sadness and destruction or a twisted revenge. I could do things just because I wanted to.

For no other reason besides the fact that they made me happy.

I pressed a kiss between Mrs. Hudson's ears, and threw the toy into the living room. Tail wagging, she waddled away.

"How was my mother?" Levi sounded subdued. He hadn't been that gangly boy I'd first met in many years, but his eyes were still the bluest that I'd ever seen, even clouded and troubled.

"Scared, but unharmed." We both ignored the implied "for now" that hung heavy in the air.

"Levi, I..." I didn't know what I wanted to say. There should have been something profound, but I kept seeing that thirteen-year-old in the Camp Ruach T-shirt the day I'd first met him. Before things had gotten so twisted up and muddled between us, back when he was one more conceited rich kid with a perfect life and I swam through a cloud of anger.

We weren't in that story anymore. I didn't know the ending to whatever this new one was.

I didn't even know what the next page, or line, or words were. All I had was a sense that this mattered.

It was now or never. I swallowed and raised my eyes to his—

Only to have him press a kiss to my forehead. "Kick ass, Ashira Cohen."

It was just like when he'd illusioned me to look like him when I was fighting smudges and just as disappointingly platonic. I mean, wow. Avril de Leon had been dead and evil, and somehow she got a better sendoff kiss than I did. Didn't final showdowns count for anything these days?

He slipped out the front door without another word.

I picked up a metal briefcase containing the tube with the scrolls, and pressed my finger against the lock to secure it. With the wooden ring now in Rafael's possession, I clutched the gold token on its chain, standing a heartbeat later in Hedon, in the business district under that yellow crescent moon.

Vanilla-scented night air kissed my skin. Following the ramen bowl to my destination, I found the store owned by the steampunk cat and made a purchase: a small black rose hair ornament that I used to pin my ponytail down.

My next stop landed me on Her Majesty's flagstone terrace. The Queen, Isabel, and Moran were eating BBQ salmon and pasta, drinking wine, and laughing. While Her Majesty hadn't deviated from her usual color signature, the tablecloth was bright yellow and the dishes were cheerful multicolored ceramics. Isabel had brought color back to her mother's world.

I would do no less for mine.

Moran saw me first and pushed his chair back. "Ashira?"

Isabel waved at me and I gave her a wan smile.

Moran frowned. "Is there a problem?"

I hugged the briefcase to my chest. "I'm going to trade Isaac the scrolls for my mom and Levi's mom. So, it's not in the top ten greatest days." I gave them a quick rundown.

"How can we help, blanquita?" The Queen walked over to my side.

I did a double take, caught off guard by this unexpected offer. "Uh, well, keep the token for me? I can't risk it falling into the wrong hands and this is the safest place I could think of. But I'm coming back for it."

She took the gold coin from me. "Of course you are." I appreciated her saying it without a trace of sarcasm. "Is there anything else we can do?"

"Take me to Lockdown Cybersecurity?"

"Absolutely," Moran said.

"When you're done with all this, maybe we could go out sometime," Isabel said.

"Priya and I are going to karaoke tomorrow." I crossed my fingers that I wasn't jinxing myself. "You should come."

She smiled shyly. "I've never had a girls' night out before."

I had to survive. We all did. Isabel had been through so much. She deserved a girls' night in a dive bar with sticky floors, crispy fries, great music, and laughter.

All the laughter in the world.

And sure, this might not last forever. If the last few months had taught me anything, it was that relationships didn't come with guarantees, no matter how badly you wanted them. Maybe we would be friends, maybe we wouldn't, and that would hurt, but I'd be okay and find new people. I just had to keep going and letting people in, despite, sometimes, my better judgment.

Being a P.I. wasn't enough anymore.

"It'll be the first of many girls' nights," I promised.

The Queen hugged me. Her shoulder under my cheek was softer than I expected and she smelled like roses. "Hasta la próxima, chica."

Moran took my arm. "Ready?"

I allowed myself one last moment to drink Hedon in. Magic signs lit up the sky in the distance, the Garden of People was shrouded in shadow, and, hidden by the fluttering white curtain leading through the open sliding doors into the palace, stood my father.

But he didn't offer me a pithy quip or call me pet names.

He just nodded at me and then tapped his fist against his palm twice. That had been his sign for whenever I'd been about to do something scary—like ride a bike on my own for the first time or jump off the high diving board—that he was about to give me the countdown to go for it.

As humans, one of our greatest talents was our ability to tell ourselves stories. And it didn't matter if they were real or not, because sometimes all you needed was a story to tell you who you needed to be. A detective chasing a shadowy mastermind. A girl who, against all odds, lived.

But eventually all stories end.

Maybe it's as simple as that. You need me to play a certain role, and one day, you won't.

"I'm ready," I said.

Adam held up one finger, a second, then a third.

Go.

I smiled, my eyes damp, and then nodded.

He winked, and then Moran and I were gone, appearing about a block away from the building that housed Isaac's company.

"Well." Moran bowed low. "Until we meet again, Jezebel."

"Until we meet again, Bunny Boy."

He gave an exaggerated sigh and vanished.

Five minutes to get to the building. My boots thudded against the ground, echoing up off the empty buildings around us. Night had fallen and the street was empty.

Or so it seemed.

The House operatives and Lux's people were in place. Miles was in charge of all of them, commanding the operation to keep any other Chariot members from getting inside. He'd assessed the Followers' magic and teamed each one up with an operative.

I'd barely stepped onto the property before my magic flattened out. Isaac had brought a null to the party, just as anticipated.

I looked up at the stars. It was a perfectly ordinary night with no sign that four hundred years of struggle was about to end. I whispered the names of my predecessors under my breath like a prayer: Serach, Tehilla, Liya, Catriona, Atef, Vasilisa, Thea, Rachel, Nikolia, Freyja, Vishranti, and Gracie Gavriella. I won't let you down. Your deaths will not have been in vain.

This long game of chess had put me in check, but I could still be crowned queen. Chin up, I went to make my final move.

Hans waited for me outside the front door to the four-story building with his gun, a hulking man, and Avi Chomsky.

The null who'd executed my father. I betrayed no emotion beyond a muscle ticking in my jaw. Isaac wanted me unnerved? He'd have to do better than that. Adam was dead. I couldn't save him, but my mom was in peril. All this bitch move had done was given me absolute clarity on how much I'd enjoy destroying Montefiore once and for all. My focus was laser sharp.

"You cunt," Avi hissed. "I almost died because of you. I hope I can return the favor tonight."

I didn't bother answering, spreading my arms and legs when the guard stepped forward to frisk me.

"What's this?" he grunted, his fingers pressing against the right side of my boob.

"Well, Jimmy," I said, "those are called breasts. You probably don't recognize them without nipple tassels and—shit. Watch it."

He dug his cold meat sticks into the side of my bra, pulling out a pink mini Taser that was about the size of a USB drive. He laughed and clicked on the flashlight part before stuffing it in his pocket. "Cute."

"Anything else on her?" Hans asked coldly.

The man finished patting me down. "Clean."

284

"Open the case," Hans said.

I shook my head. "When we do the trade."

"Cut her finger off," Avi said. "Open the case yourself."

"Do you know which way to lay my print on the lock?" I said. "Do it wrong and the case will flood with ink, ruining the scrolls." I shrugged. "Your call, since I have no magic to stop you." I kept my gaze steady and my body relaxed, despite not wanting to part with any digits today.

Hans examined the lock, taking so long that I was convinced he was going to take Avi's advice, and my pulse spiked. "Isaac will take great pleasure in personally unlocking your case," he said.

"I know English is your second language, but way to make it weird, dude."

Hans jerked his chin at the minion, who grabbed my arm and hauled me inside. Levi had assured me there were no wards, but I still braced myself when I crossed the threshold because my intents were definitely hostile.

The walls in the large reception area were steel gray and the furniture was all hard lines and unyielding fabrics, everything projecting an image of strength.

Using a keycard and a thumbprint scan, Hans led us through a metal door and into a large room with rows of white tables, each of which had two workstations with sleek monitors. Moonlight streamed in through the many windows and the inset overhead lights cast soft pools. We crossed to the other end and through another door.

This space was almost as large as the other one, but it was dotted with beanbag chairs, couches, and ugh, a foosball table. How hipster of Isaac. There was a small kitchen along one wall.

Furniture had been pushed out of the way. Nicola and Talia stood close together, looking haunted under the watch of another goon, this one bald and also armed. Nicola's betrayal still stung, though I'd forgiven Talia for asking me to ward up my magic. However, even if I'd been furious at both of them, I'd do everything in my power to extricate them safely. I clenched my fists and kept myself in check.

Two guns, two goons, one assassin, and a null. The odds could be worse. Not by much, mind you, but still.

Isaac sat on a swiveling chair, the tube with Chariot's two scrolls in his lap. "Right on time."

I barely suppressed my smirk. It had been a gamble that Isaac would bring the scrolls with him, but I figured that he wouldn't want to wait another second to put the *Sefer Raziel HaMalakh* together and became immortal. Bonus points for rubbing my nose in it.

The hulking goon who'd accompanied me fell back to block the door. Hans and Avi stayed to my left, out of arm's reach, while Baldy remained where he was with his gun trained on the women.

There were shouts from outside. Everyone glanced at the windows except me and Isaac.

"Theresa's faction came," Hans said. "So predictable."

"Our people will deal with them and any of my former associates who wish to oppose me," Isaac said.

Ironically, in taking out the newcomers, my people would be helping him, though the reverse was also true. I forced my shoulders down. Isaac couldn't know that I, too, had team-mates in place.

Isaac motioned impatiently at the metal briefcase. "Let's get this over with."

"Hold your horses," I said. "First, Mom and Nicola come over here and your men stand down so I have a clear path out. Then I'll unlock the case and slide it over to you."

Isaac frowned, swiveling the chair from side to side. "I don't trust you."

"I don't trust you either, but I'm magicless, I've been frisked, and I'm out-numbered. You killed my father and you're not getting my mother, so I'm not going to do anything stupid."

Talia watched me intently, biting her lip.

I chose to interpret it as faith in me.

"Fine." Isaac lined all his people up across from me, sending Nicola and Talia to stand by my side. It was the world's deadliest game of Red Rover.

Both guns were trained on the three of us.

Ignoring the sounds of the ongoing battle outside, I carefully set the case on the ground and bent over to press my thumb against the lock, bringing my other hand up to hit the button on the tiny box stashed under my left boob.

I'd intended for the minion to find the mini Taser, and most men didn't check *under* the breast. Women were much more thorough, but Isaac was an old-fashioned kind of villain. He wouldn't employ women to do a man's job.

My sonic weapon discharged and a high-pitched frequency sound barely within hearing range caused pained cries.

I reached for the rose in my hair to fire it into Avi's arm and kill the nulling magic, but before I could get to it, a gun went off, deafening in the space.

Talia screamed and collapsed on the floor, clutching her arm.

I gasped, my hands flexing on empty air, because I still had no magic. I jerked my head to the door, but it hadn't been breached by the outside factions. Talia had been shot by Hans.

"You bastard. I'm coming for you." I pulled off my sweater, leaving me in a tank top, and wrapped it around my mom's wound.

Hans smiled cruelly and lowered the gun. He was the only person other than me not recovering from the noise. "With what? Your little trick didn't work. You think you are the first to try this? You are nothing."

Talia clutched my hand, silently crying, interspersed with tiny hiccuped whimpers. I squeezed hers back.

Nicola fell to her knees and pushed me out of the way to take over applying pressure.

Leaving his position at Isaac's side, Hans pressed the barrel to my mom's head. "Now, let's try that again."

Chapter 27

I opened the case, removed the metal tube from the spongey interior, and slid it over. Icy hooks dug into my chest, but I batted the fear away. My powers were suppressed. I wouldn't be able to sense the angel magic until Avi was neutralized. I had time.

Isaac's face lit up with reverential awe. He removed the scrolls and pressed them together.

Nothing happened.

For Isaac.

In the world's most unfair twist, the *Sefer's* magic—and my ability to sense it—defied Avi's nulling.

I fell to my knees, my body clenching in yearning, trying not to belly crawl towards the hot gritty scent of a sandstorm that filled every inch of me. This wasn't just a craving, the magic owned me.

Isaac whirled on me. "Make it do something!"

"Like what?" I scraped my fingernails against the cold tiles, my mouth salivating since I had neither the amulet nor Rafael to help me. "I've never had all the scrolls."

Isaac shook the *Sefer* pieces. "Tell me or I'll kill your mother."

End this. Come to us.

Yes. Take me.

I was already crawling towards the *Sefer* and it took a second for Isaac's threat to register because anything other than the angel magic failed to matter. Even then, I'll never be sure if I stopped because of the desperate gleam in his eyes or because Nicola grabbed on to my foot and dragged me back.

"The pieces," I said, unable to explain to her beyond that.

"Stay strong," Nicola hissed.

"Tell me what to do," Isaac demanded.

"Please, no." I wasn't sure if the plea was for Isaac or the *Sefer*. I rubbed my hands over my face. My stomach twisted, that angel magic reaching deep inside me to re-arrange my organs and bite into my soul. "All right. You need to put them together in the correct sequence. But I don't know what that is, I swear."

Isaac studied me, trembling on the ground, then nodded, believing my bullshit. Adam wasn't the only con artist in our family. Isaac examined the first scroll intently, seeking some clue to the sequence.

The fight outside fell ominously silent.

Talia reached for me with a bloodied hand. Her eyes were cloudy with pain. "I love you, Ash. I always have and I always will."

"Can we get on with this?" Avi said. "I had a long flight."

The callous boredom from the man who'd murdered my father snapped me back into taking a tendril of control back from the *Sefer*.

I whipped the rose out of my hair and stabbed Hans in the leg with it. He screamed, and I fell on top of Talia, pulling the metal briefcase over my head. That move saved my life as a bullet discharged from Hans's gun and lodged in it.

Black poisonous lines spiderwebbed across the German's skin. Gun still in hand, he smacked himself like he was putting out a fire, but the poison spread.

"Holy fuck!" Hulking minion jumped back. "Is that contagious?"

I ripped the dart out of Hans's leg and winged it at Avi, catching him in the shoulder.

Fainter black lines snaked up his neck, the poison a fraction of what it had been in Hans.

Baldy shot me, but Avi was injured enough to have dropped the nulling and my armor snapped into place. The bullet bounced harmlessly off.

I was unable to help myself from stealing a glance at my mother.

She flinched and looked away. Whether or not she ever came to terms with my magic, I'd stand by her, regardless of her feelings.

Assshhhhhiiiirrraaa. Coooome.

I jerked towards the *Sefer*. Nicola's fingers dug into me again, but I tore free.

The door behind me was bashed off its hinges and the *Sefer's* hold dimmed, clouded by some kind of staticky interference.

Baldy swung his gun to the doorway, and I fired a couple of sharp red daggers at him. One blinded the armed assailant in his left eye and the other stabbed into his gun hand. Baldy shrieked, and fumbled the weapon, but managed to keep hold of it.

No one had entered... yet.

"Isaac... help..." Hans staggered towards his boss, his gun held loosely, but Isaac gave him the barest dismissive glance before returning his attention to the scrolls.

Red eyes appeared and disappeared as a growl punched us deep in the guts, the most primal part of my brain screaming at me to flee. Huge hairy spiders dropped from the ceiling, landing on Isaac's people.

Baldy freaked out and shot at them, while Hulking tried

to stomp them dead. Isaac held the scrolls over his head, jumping sideways to avoid them.

Talia and Nicola cowered and I shuddered, inching away from the wriggling monstrosities, but unable to change course for the *Sefer*.

"Fuck this," Baldy said.

The two goons abandoned ship, running for the door, while a wounded and terrified Avi limped behind them, beating spiders off his body.

The ground thudded and I glanced back.

Arkady, a stone warrior, blocked the three fleeing men. If he'd made it here, then Miles had secured the outside perimeter.

The spiders vanished, the illusion gone, and the Sefer's call grew louder, free of other magic interference. It wrapped around me, stroking me in its embrace, crooning that all would be well if I came and tasted it.

Let me go. I begged for release, but there was no choice. With every inch that I crawled closer to Isaac—who was still trying to make the pieces into a single entity—I hated myself a bit more.

Baldy emptied the rest of his clip into Arkady and I cried out, wishing he'd shot me instead, preventing me from help-lessly drawing towards my doom.

"Did you chip me, asshole?" Arkady swung his stone fist and the gun went flying. "That's gonna leave a bruise." His second punch cracked the man's jaw. The goon went down like a ton of bricks, Arkady making quick work of taking out the other minion and Avi.

Priya ran inside and slapped magic nulling cuffs on them all.

"Leave," I begged her.

She scowled at me and said something I couldn't catch, the siren song taking up all the room in my brain. All I knew was I couldn't lose her. I couldn't lose any of them.

The crooning in my head cut out, replaced by a feeling of having disappointed someone that was so profound, tears streamed down my cheeks.

"I'm sorry," I whispered.

"Ash?" Arkady said.

I stared blankly at him. There was something important I had to tell him.

Hans collapsed, the poison spiraling in black circles along his skin.

"Stone," I gasped, wiping my eyes.

Arkady looked between me and Hans, swore, and grabbed my briefcase. He lifted the sponge lining and withdrew a blue heart-shaped stone pendant that he crushed into powder over top of Hans. The poison began to fade.

Arkady jerked his chin at Avi, holding up his powder-dusted hands. "Do I do him, too?"

The scrolls were almost in reach.

"Not 'til his magic is far from here," I said, absently.

Priya helped Talia up and led the women to safety, while Arkady placed Hans in cuffs as well and herded all the men out to where Miles waited.

I reached Isaac, pushed myself to my feet, and ripped the scrolls away. There was no sandstorm, no disappointment. Nothing but a gaping hollowness in my chest. A bead of sweat formed on my forehead and trickled down into one eye. I flicked it away and rubbed my hands over the scrolls faster, as if that could spark them back into responding to me.

What was I doing? I stilled.

Isaac grabbed Hans's discarded gun and pointed it at me. "You can't do anything to them unless you drop your armor," he said. "How long will it take to put the *Sefer* together and destroy the magic? Is it faster than I can shoot you?" He glanced at the door. "Don't hover, Levi. Join us."

Levi stood on the threshold, his expression unreadable. "Isaac."

"Spiders," Isaac said. "I never did care for them."

Levi smiled. "I know."

"Here to save your girlfriend after all?" Isaac said.

"Ash doesn't need me for much," Levi said, joining his father and me. "I came for Mom. You shouldn't have dragged her into this."

"Sì, your sainted mother," Isaac sneered. "Don't you see that she is weak? But you, my son, are powerful. I feared it, but now I understand that I should have embraced it. My boy. A leader. A visionary."

Levi's expression softened, a wistfulness making him appear younger.

Assssshhhhhh. Come.

Not now! Desolation filled my lungs like brackish water. I was losing Levi to the validation he had so desperately sought his entire life. I tried to speak up, but my armor was already slipping, the tips on my boots flickering in and out. There was nothing left in my reserves to create any weapons or draw upon my enhanced strength, never mind put together a convincing argument of how Levi should stay strong.

"Give me the scrolls." Isaac aimed the gun at my head.

My armor would protect me. Shaking, I clutched the scrolls to my chest, blood tears streaming from my eyes. I had to hold on… a little longer…

When our standoff didn't resolve itself, Isaac turned to Levi. "You want to make a real difference for your people? Stand by my side. Become immortal like me and shape a meaningful future." He held out his free hand.

Levi rubbed the heel of his palm against his chest.

My heart stuttered four times before he came to his decision.

"Here's the thing, Dad…" A tarantula appeared in Levi's hand and he flicked it into his father's face.

Isaac jumped sideways and I laughed. That scared little boy was gone and I'd never been so proud of Levi.

"Cracking good illusion," I said.

Levi winked at me, before facing his father with an icy expression. "There's nothing you could offer me to be like you."

He twitched his fingers and Rafael appeared, standing right next to Isaac. Levi's illusion hadn't just been the spiders —it had been making Rafael appear completely invisible while he positioned himself behind Isaac, in a perfect position to take the man out.

Rafael quickly disarmed my enemy, training the gun on Isaac, and tossed me the amulet, which I dropped around my neck. I knew I'd be searched and I hadn't wanted it found, so Rafael had kept it.

The cravings dimmed to a tolerable level. Mostly.

I made my armor vanish and hastily unrolled the five scroll pieces.

Even having lost, Isaac leaned forward, eager to see the *Sefer Raziel HaMalakh* made whole. When still nothing happened, his face fell. "Is it all a lie?"

"No," I said. "It was a con. A beautiful con." I dropped one of the pieces on the ground. "The reason none of this worked? Adam gave you a fake scroll. Dad might not have been smarter than everyone, but he was smarter than you."

Rafael whipped out a metal tube he'd hidden against the small of his back and opening it, tossed the real fifth piece to me.

I pressed the scrolls together and braced myself for a craving beyond anything I'd experienced.

It never came.

The pieces took flight weaving and soaring, reaching out for each other. Those brittle yellow parchments combined into a single solid gold scroll with pearl inlaid handles, its body etched with gems and symbols that were dizzying and beautiful to behold.

A sigh escaped Isaac, and even Levi and Rafael gazed wondrously upon it.

The scroll floated into my arms, light as a feather.

Understanding flashed through me. All the *Sefer* had wanted was to be whole once more and now that it was, it infused me with a sense of peace. How could I destroy something so magnificent?

Isaac reached for it, and Levi elbowed him in the nose. Blood spurted, Isaac swearing in Italian and cupping a hand to his face.

"Ashira," Rafael said in a flinty voice. "Don't make me shoot you."

He didn't understand. The *Sefer* merely wanted to survive and love us. Poverty, hunger, illness, all that could be cured.

The world could be perfect, it whispered.

I could be perfect.

I rubbed the rods in my femur, throbbing in a dull ache. "You went too far," I told the book. "I earned my scars."

I sent my magic into the *Sefer Raziel HaMalakh* and pulled out a smudgy shadow.

It flowed faster and faster, expanding and changing shape, until a single form remained: the life-sized silhouette of an angel, attached to the gold scroll like a genie to a bottle.

Isaac jumped into it. Without thinking, I did the same.

We came out in the grove with the almond tree. The scroll lay in the dirt at the base of the tree, lifeless and sucked dry. I touched a hand to it.

No magic. It was all inside Isaac.

Isaac spun, laughing manically, a white dazzling light snapping off his skin. He glowed from inside, his blue eyes burning with a cobalt fire.

My head ached trying to grasp the amount of power pouring off him. Most would fall down before him and proclaim him a miracle, but there was darkness behind the dazzle.

The monster had won and it was all my fault.

The pink blossoms on the tree withered and fell off the branches.

He caught one, crushing it in his fist. "Is magic always like this? So alive? I feel my heart. The blood moving through my veins." He closed his eyes, tiny starbursts exploding off him.

I grabbed his arm, quickly slashing it with a dagger and firing a red ribbon of my power inside. His magic burned to the touch, but Isaac wasn't an angel. His immortality tasted of clouds, but it was still Nefesh.

There was only one question: did I rip it from him as painfully as possible or show mercy, delicately removing it like I had with Eve?

Isaac tore free. "You lose, Ashira. Just as Adam did."

He shouldn't have mentioned my dad. Thank you for making this choice easy.

The grove rumbled. The pomegranate tree cracked and hit the ground, its fruit smashing to stain the earth like blood.

I braced a hand against the almond tree, riding out the aftershocks.

The next rumble brought down the date palms—and opened a portal.

Isaac ran for it. I wouldn't be fast enough to catch him so I fired a dagger into the back of his knees. He howled, his leg buckling.

Ripping the blade out, I dove on top of him, throwing him to the dirt and punching him in the mouth. I didn't need more blood to access his magic; knocking his tooth out simply gave me a vicious satisfaction.

Isaac clapped his hands against my ears, following it up with an elbow strike to my throat. I gasped for air, then punched him again. Unfortunately, to destroy the magic, I couldn't manifest my armor.

Our fight was dirty and brutal, but besides his longevity, he didn't have any other powers. Considering his injuries, his determination to get to the portal was impressive. Twice we skirted dangerously close to the swirling mass of blue and purple light.

"I'll take everyone you care about away from you." He laughed. "I have all the time in the world."

The amulet warmed against the base of my throat. *You face the choice that Asherah gives all Jezebels. The choice to live as one wishes, which was denied to her as the Bride of Yahweh. Destroy the Sefer's magic inside Isaac and lose your Jezebel magic for good.*

Isaac tussled with me, his magic smoking against my skin.

I'd been created to destroy the magic on the *Sefer Raziel HaMalakh*, but it had never occurred to me that when I'd completed that task, the magic would end.

Had Rafael known? No, he would have told me.

The amulet tingled. *Or keep that magic and the fight rages on. Immortal doesn't mean unkillable. Once the host is dead, the magic returns to the Sefer.*

I pinned Isaac under me. I'd wanted free will to pursue a fascinating private investigator career, which being Nefesh had made possible, and here it was, within my grasp. To keep my magic, all I had to do was the one thing I'd sworn to since I'd learned of Isaac's role in this.

Kill him.

A red ribbon of magic woven around one hand, a dagger held in the other.

Choices.

It was easy to make them in a moment of calm. End Isaac, and we could hide the unified *Sefer* in the library, safe from all.

I clutched the dagger tighter, Isaac's fear a delicious elixir.

Revenge wouldn't fill the hole left by my dad's murder and the best revenge was living well. There was only one way to honor my father's memory.

I gently sent my magic inside Isaac and hooked it to his.

Isaac cried out, begging me to stop.

Delicately, I gathered his magic up, threading it in my red forked branches.

The wizened blossoms on the tree turned pink and healthy, gently swirling around us.

My body felt lighter than it had in ages, and I swear Asherah herself beamed down upon me.

"No!" Isaac cried.

An initial white cluster bloomed and it was as if the first of many fuses was turned off deep inside me. I made another bloom and felt the same sensation.

I stilled. I'd chosen this, but there was a deep ache inside me as my magic shut down.

Isaac somehow sensed what was happening, because he started laughing. "You're going to lose it all, aren't you? All that precious magic? Am I worth it?"

Yes, because I still had to face myself in the mirror every day.

I let the rest of the clusters eat up the magic as I hollowed out one white bloom at a time. Was this a reset to who I'd been as a Mundane or was some essential part of me disappearing, and all I'd be left with was a shadow of my former self? Would I recognize myself when this was over? Would I even care?

No matter how difficult, I'd find my way back and be the best version of myself imaginable. The version I could live with, knowing I'd done the right thing.

I wiped sweat off my brow and gave one final push.

Isaac screeched, his magic sparking out, and his skin turning ashen and gray.

The *Sefer* was no more.

Isaac was mortal.

And I was Mundane.

The almond tree discharged all its blossoms in a snowfall of pink and the grove quaked, pitching us through the portal into darkness.

We crashed landed back in Lockdown Cybersecurity.

Isaac tore the gun from Rafael's hand and aimed it at me.

"This isn't like my father," I said. "You have to look me in the eye if you want to kill me. Hasn't there been enough death?"

Rafael and Levi tensed, ready to spring into action.

Isaac didn't shoot me and when I met his eyes, he broke the stare first. He sagged. "You're right."

Then he shot me in the leg.

"Son of a bitch!" Pain, true unadulterated pain railed through my body. For months, I'd had my Jezebel magic to ease my discomfort in daily life with my repaired leg. Now, sore and aching already, I pressed my hands to my ruined thigh, seething, knowing there would be no power to help me heal this. Rods and canes and a lifetime of rehab and pain spun out before me.

This was the cost of mercy.

Levi dropped down beside me, calling 911, while hastily pressing his sweater onto the wound. "Why didn't you use your armor?"

My bottom lip trembled. "I couldn't."

Rafael, slapping regular cuffs on Isaac, whipped his head toward me. "Whyever not?"

"It's over. All of this is over." I scrubbed a hand over my face. "The *Sefer* is gone. My magic is gone."

"Impossible," Rafael said.

Levi put his arms around me and I clutched his shirt, my jaw clenched, biting back the pain.

I'd made my choice and I stood by it. But, universe? Cut me a break, and don't let Dr. Zhang be my operating physician.

Chapter 28

Lights blurred overhead as I was wheeled through to the trauma bay. I gripped the metal rails of the gurney, fighting my panic. Once in the OR, I was tethered to an IV and hooked to all manner of monitors, but the final insult?

"You've got to be kidding me." Dr. Zhang's normally warm brown eyes glared at me above his mask. "And the same leg? I did beautiful work on that leg." He boffed me lightly across the top of my head.

I sighed. Thanks for nothing, universe. He'd probably amputate.

"Gotta keep you on your toes, doc." I grimaced through a wave of pain. Then I was being told to count backwards and any further scoldings melted away.

I woke up in a hospital bed, my head filled with cotton.

My mother sat in a chair, reading. She was wearing yoga pants.

"Which one are you?" I mumbled.

She arched an eyebrow, placing the book back in her purse. "Which mother am I? Do you have a secret family stashed somewhere?"

"You're wearing yoga pants," I said.

"Yes. They're soft and easy to put on with my arm wound." She reached for a cup of water and brought the straw to my lips. For a moment, I was thirteen years old, groggy and scared, my mother sitting by my side promising everything would be all right. "Dr. Zhang said you were lucky," she said. "None of the rods were broken and it was a clean wound. You'll be back to normal in no time."

Isaac, the *Sefer*, my magic loss, it all came rushing back to me. "Normal. Right."

"Sorry," my mom said quietly.

I gently squeezed her arm. "No, I'm sorry. I dropped a lot of painful facts on you. I wasn't kind and I knew that even as I was doing it. You didn't deserve it."

She took the cup I handed her and placed it on the bedside table. "You didn't deserve all the behavior I dished out to you, either. There's blame on both sides."

We sat with our respective thoughts for a bit, then she rolled up the sleeve of her sweater. Her upper arm was bandaged, the same as my thigh.

"We match," she said.

"Yeah. Both of us have scars and no magic."

"I wish that wasn't the case."

I fiddled with my hospital bracelet. "It's okay. You get to feel about magic however you want."

She pursed her lips together, looking down at her lap. "When I was pregnant, I used to talk to you about how excited we were to meet you and all the fun things we'd do together. And I'd tell you that even if you didn't get magic like your father, you'd always be magic to me. I'm sorry that I forgot that, because when I saw what you could do, it was…"

"Magic?" I said, dryly.

"Yes, you little wise ass. You were fierce." She folded her hands primly in her lap, a steely set to her jaw. "That's why I not only declined the opportunity to be Minister of Finance, I've left the party."

"What? You can't? I didn't go through all that with Nathan so he'd win."

"He didn't win. I let go of the anger that had been blinding me all this time. Besides, I'm not leaving politics altogether. I'm joining the Federal Liberal Party. I told them they needed my policy experience to make Nefesh rights inherent to the constitution."

"Whoa. You're pretty fierce yourself, Mom."

"Where do you think you get it from? I am a descendent of Jezebel, after all."

I turned my head to the sunshine streaming in through my window and smiled. No lies. No games. Mom and I were going to be fine.

Nurse Sarah came by a while later to take my vitals. She had bunions, was allergic to dogs, and could quote episodes of *Breaking Bad* verbatim. All things being equal, she was a pretty scary nurse, but I always felt better when she told me my numbers were good. Nurse Sarah was not the kind of person who sugarcoated things, and I appreciated that.

She wrapped a blood pressure cuff around me.

I sniffed the air. "I smell peppermint."

"Gum. I'm cutting down on my coffee consumption."

"*What?*"

"Hey." She frowned, pumping the bulb to inflate the cuff. "Calm down. Your pressure is spiking. Don't you like mint? It was your idea."

"You said you'd rather, and I quote, take it up the ass with a donkey's dick than go without caffeine. Unquote."

The cuff slowly deflated. "And you told me that I knew what was best for myself and I should follow that."

"Then keep drinking the stuff," I said.

Sarah ripped the cuff off and jotted down my blood pressure. "What are you, some kind of lobbyist for Big Coffee?"

No, I was a pissed-off girl with a sneaking suspicion that

sounded crazy. Isaac hadn't killed me and a self-professed caffeine junkie had given up her fix, both on my say-so?

By the time Dr. Zhang announced I could be discharged, I was ready to go home and get my life back. Pri was coming to pick me up, so I was surprised when Lux arrived in my hospital room with a wheelchair.

"Heard you took a bullet." She shook head. "Jezebels. I follow Asherah all my adult life and I never ended up in the hospital eating ice cream and getting wheeled around like a princess."

"Ladies and gentlemen, Lux. She's here all week." I gingerly moved from the bed to the wheelchair. "How's Jean-Pierre?" The illusionist had been badly beaten by Theresa's people, but he'd rallied to help turn the tide.

"Mending. The House took good care of us."

"You deserved it. We couldn't have done it without you."

"True." She grabbed my bag and slung it over her shoulder, then pushed me into the hallway. "In lighter news, Gabriel is bugging Miles to let him become an operative."

I laughed. "Miles must loooove that."

"Gabriel is convinced he can win him over."

"I'm sure he is."

Lux shared how terrified she'd been during the battle, but how it felt good to have something concrete she could influence. She lapsed into silence, no doubt thinking of Emma.

"Finally, she's leaving," Dr. Zhang said, cornering us in the lobby.

"That anxious to get rid of me?" I said.

"Not quite." He produced two mustaches. A droopy handlebar one for himself and a pencil one for me.

I crossed my arms. "Where's my Luigi 'stache?"

"You're a grown-up now, Ash. Have a little dignity." Dr. Zhang pulled out his phone and fiddled with the camera.

"This is… weird," Lux said. "I'm going to leave you to it." She placed my bag in my lap.

"Don't be a stranger," I said. "I mean it."

"Wouldn't dream of it. We Gigis have to stick together." She squeezed my shoulder and made for the door.

"I think you mean Followers," I called out. "Asherah's Followers. AF. As in, you know, Goddess AF. We're rebranding."

"Goddess AF. I like it." Lux hitched her purse higher on her shoulder. "We could get T-shirts." With a wave, she left.

Dr. Zhang leaned down to be in the frame with me. "Say cheesy!"

"Cheesy!"

He snapped the photo, gave me some forms for a physical therapist I was to follow up with, and wheeled me outside to where Priya waited with Moriarty. Dr. Zhang patted my head. "Okay, kid. This time, I really mean it. I don't want to see you again."

"Hold up there, mister," I said crossly.

He turned back, the picture of innocence. "Yes?"

I held out my hand.

Grinning, he pulled a candy from the pocket of his scrubs and tossed it to me. Orange lollipops were the bomb.

PRIYA and I hit up Blondie's early to snag enough space for all of us. Our karaoke date had been delayed, but we made it happen the same day I got home.

Jodie, our ancient server, grunted as we pushed tables together. "You people better not cheap out on tips," she said.

I pressed my hand to my heart and staggered back. "Are those your eyes I see looking into mine and not down at your phone? I hardly recognize you without your beauteous visage bathed in the glow of your cell. Is it the apocalypse?"

"Nah, that was last week," Pri said. "You botched it."

"Oh yeah."

"Taunt a woman when her screen is broken. See if you get your fries tonight," Jodie grumbled, and wandered away.

Rafael was the first to show up, nattily attired in his black-and-red argyle vest with his matching red bowtie.

Priya and I both patted the chairs next to us and Rafael froze for a second, before sitting down beside me.

"It's cracking to have you back," he said to me in way too hearty a voice.

"You really want to sit next to Pri, don't you?"

He blushed. "No."

I prodded his shoulder. "Did something happen while I was convalescing in hospital that you have not seen fit to share with me?"

"As if." Priya picked at the hem of her T-shirt that she'd paired with dark jeans.

Priya in pink. It wasn't a monochromatic freneticism willing herself to be happy, it was just her being happy. I rubbed my right thigh, back on track with my P.I. mojo, but before I could tell Rafael to change seats, he pushed his glasses up his nose.

"No, Priya. I shan't deny it and neither shall you. We have begun a romantic relationship. I'd like your blessing, Ashira, because you are important to us, but even if you disapprove, we will be together."

Priya melted in her chair, smiling dopily at him.

"Okay, gross," I said. "Don't emote all over me, dude. Aren't you supposed to be all British and into concealing your true feelings or something? Jeez. Go sit with your girlfriend. I approve." I made a religious-looking gesture. "Consider your union blessed."

Priya leaned across the table and kissed my cheek.

I'd texted Levi to let him know about our plans, but he'd begged off with no explanation. I cut him some slack, having heard from Miles after my shooting that Levi had been run ragged in the aftermath of everything. Isaac had exercised his right to remain silent, but after he so summarily dismissed Hans in his moment of need, the German had rolled over on whomever was left of the Ten. No mention was made of the *Sefer*, but Hans had plenty to say about a number of illegal activities that the cabal had been involved in.

Meantime, Miles's operatives had gotten hold of the ledgers in storage and were poring through them for the one I'd seen. The chances of killing the legislation had shot up significantly.

Levi was swamped. It was totally normal that we hadn't spoken yet.

I checked my phone, just in case.

Arkady and Miles showed up next, holding hands. I was trying to flag down a passing server, willing to pay top-dollar tips for an unending supply of booze to get me through being bookended by couples, when Priya said, "Yaaas, Queen."

Wearing red jeans, a red scoop-neck top, and red stilettos, Her Majesty sailed through this drinking establishment like she walked a red carpet strewn with rose petals.

All conversation died until she arched a perfect brow and people hurriedly looked away. If their chatter had a nervous edge to it, well, she had that effect.

Isabel bounced beside her mother, grinning and craning her neck all around. In shorts, a cute top with ruffled sleeves, and blue nail polish, she radiated a carefree joy. Good for her.

Moran brought up the rear.

"Damn," Arkady said, eyeing his white suit, "that's a man comfortable with his style choices."

Miles knocked over his water glass. "That—that's..." He made a noise like he'd swallowed his tongue, grabbed a handful of napkins, and blotted at the spill so frenetically, that Arkady pushed his hand away and took over the clean-up.

I poked Miles's shoulder. "Breathe. She comes in peace. I invited her daughter."

A text buzzed on my phone.

Imperious 1: *Come over tonight?*

To talk? To have sex? To go our separate ways once and for all?

Arkady hit my bouncing leg with his. "Quit it."

Her Majesty stopped next to my table. "Hola, chica."

I flipped my phone to be screen down. "Hello, Highness. Isabel, you made it. Excellent."

"I've never been in a place like this," she said.

"Way to start her at the bottom, pickle." Grimacing, Arkady wadded up the soggy napkins into a ball. "Well, darling, your worldview can only improve from here."

Isabel shook her head. "I love it. Did you know the term 'dive bar' originated in the 1880s because these places were typically located in cellars or basements where people could dive into and not be seen?"

Priya pushed Arkady down a seat. "I'm Priya. You're a super nerd and my new best friend."

"Suzy Jones is going to be so disappointed," I said.

Pri patted the chair. "Sit beside me."

The Queen raked a shrewd glance over my bestie and I stiffened, reaching for my magic.

Oh. Right. I sighed.

Her Majesty smiled warmly at Priya. "Isabel will be lucky to have a new friend such as yourself."

Isabel scowled at her mother. "I'm not five."

"That is too bad," the Queen of Hearts said, "because I had hoped to prepare goody bags."

I shivered. That could go so, so many ways and I was both intrigued and really afraid to find out what they would look like.

"Is your entire party not here yet?" Moran said, counting heads.

"We're here," I snapped.

"I believe this belongs to you." The Queen pressed the

gold token into my hands. "Levi told me what happened. You and I will talk soon. Nothing has changed between us."

Would hugging her land me in the Garden of People? Best not to test it. "I appreciate that."

"Great. Go now," Isabel said pointedly. "You too," she added to Moran.

"I'll sit by the bar," he said. "You won't even know I'm here."

Arkady barked a laugh. "Not likely."

"Ark," Miles warned.

Isabel pointed at Arkady. "What he said."

Miles sighed, directing his words to the Queen and Moran. "I'm betting you know exactly who each of us are and what we can do. Isabel will be fine. I promise."

"I'll hold you to that, Mr. Berenbaum," the Queen said. She pressed a kiss to the side of Isabel's head. "Have fun. And no drinking."

Isabel rolled her eyes and sat down next to Priya.

"Yes, yes. I am not wanted. Come along, Moran."

Moran made an "I'm watching you" gesture from himself to me.

As soon as he and the Queen left, Jodie came over to take our drink orders.

"Coke," I said.

Jodie's eyebrows shot into her hairline. "And rum?"

"No. Just Coke." Better stay sober on Isabel's first night out. Also, there was a one hundred percent less chance that I wouldn't drunk dial Levi before I had the chance to reflect on the ramifications of our next meeting with a clear and sober head.

"I'll have the same pale ale as Priya and…" Isabel glanced at the chalk menu over the bar.

"Fries," we all choroused.

"Oh. Okay."

Jodie fiddled with her silver earring that was shaped like a snake while the guys gave their orders.

Isabel leaned across the table. "Is she even listening?" she whispered.

"Somewhat?"

"Thunderation!" Jodie held the back of her earring. "Nobody move." Stiffly, she bent down to find the jewelry on the floor. She pushed our legs aside, making her way methodically around the table with no success.

After having her calf groped, Isabel asked directions to the washroom and fled.

Jodie gave up the hunt with an annoyed sigh.

"Are the earrings special to you?" Priya said.

"Yeah. My ex gave them to me. I was going to scratch his car with them. Now I only have one to throw back afterwards in his smug, cheating face." Her voice was rising.

A glint caught my eye. "Hang on." I reached under the table leg and extracted the silver snake from where it had lodged. "It's right here."

She took the earring and poked the sharp tip. "This cheap piece of shit will wreck his Mustang."

"Jesus, seriously?" I said. "Your ex is a jerk who didn't deserve you. He's not worth a vandalism charge."

She blinked at me. "You're right."

Arkady frowned. "She is?" Priya elbowed him. "I mean, yeah, she is, but does this change of heart not feel abrupt?"

Actually, it did. People usually got mad at me once I'd solved their problem, let alone when I tried to keep them from making a worse mistake.

Fucking fuck balls. This was three times now. My suspicion was right.

"Jodie," I said urgently, "if you want to key that bastard's car, then you go for it. Carve your name over every inch of his special edition paint job. In fact, I insist."

"Naw. I needed some sense talked into me. I'll be okay." Jodie threw her arms around me.

I sat there, wide-eyed.

"I'll get your drinks and fries for the entire table." Jodie dinosaur-sauntered off.

"What is even happening right now?" Priya said.

I shredded my napkin with my knife. "I have Charmer magic." I told them about Isaac and Nurse Sarah.

"You got to know her?" Priya clapped her hands.

"You're worse than the puppy with something shiny," I said.

"You have magic again? Fucking hell." Miles sat back.

"I knew you couldn't be Mundane," Rafael said. "You were tapped out. That's why you couldn't produce your armor."

"Yes, but the amulet told me to make a choice," I said testily, "and I made it, so I don't appreciate suddenly ending up with my father's magic, of all things."

"The amulet speaks to you?" Arkady glanced over at Kenneth, our karaoke host, who'd taken the stage to announce the first song, before grimacing at Rafael and me. "It is locked up, right?"

"As you don't have goddess-bestowed powers," Rafael said, "you're safe. Ash, tell me specifically what the choice was."

"Destroy Isaac's magic and lose my Jezebel power or keep my magic and the fight goes on. With the helpful reminder that immortal didn't mean unkillable."

"Aha!" Rafael jabbed a finger at me. "That. Your Jezebel magic. The amulet never said you'd lose it entirely, but if you think rationally about it, once the job was done, what would you need Jezebel abilities for? Unless you were planning to wander around ripping out people's powers?"

"That doesn't explain how I got Charmer magic."

"It's not Charmer magic, Holmes," Priya said. "If it was, Jodie would have changed her mind when you flat-out ordered her to key the car. You help them choose. You're not imposing a decision on them."

"What an excellent way of describing it," Rafael said to her.

Priya dipped her head. "You're so sweet."

"Back to me…" I said.

"You give them clarity," Arkady said.

"Clarity magic?" I tossed that idea around and nodded. "I can live with that, but it doesn't explain how I got it."

"I suspect Asherah isn't done with you," Rafael said. "You still serve her, just in a different capacity. You were chosen as a Jezebel for your Seeker abilities, and she's chosen to bestow clarity magic on you. She saw how much Jezebel magic allowed you to help people see things more clearly, so she gave you powers that would focus on that, without the blood magic part that took such a toll on you."

"Like how the maiden grows up to be the wise old crone in all the myths," Arkady said.

I threw a soggy napkin at him.

"It does fit thematically and is a logical progression with being a Seeker. You've sought, and now that you've found answers you can help share them with others," Priya said. "And it still ties in to your P.I dreams, because in solving cases you help people achieve clarity."

I glanced over at Jodie heading our way with the drinks, an ill-fitting smile on her face for me, and tried to hide behind Arkady. "Does this mean there is going to be more hugging?"

"So. Much. Hugging!" Priya said.

"Do you plan to be Rogue, *again*," Miles said, "or do you have some other explanation to put on record that I'm also going to hate?"

Arkady pulled a stress ball out of his jacket pocket and handed it over to his boyfriend without comment, who gave it such a workout the stiches were straining.

"The latter," I said cheerfully. "A recessive gene turned on after the trauma of Pastor Nephus trying to kill me."

"Well?" Arkady said.

"I'm thinking." Miles drained half his beer. "There's documentation on the event and we could categorize your magic with other Empath powers."

"Really?" I said.

Miles shrugged. "Since my boyfriend would nag me to death if I did otherwise, yeah."

"Boyfriend," Arkady said smugly.

I could legitimately be verified by House Pacifica. No more hiding. My P.I. dreams could finally and unconditionally come true.

I couldn't have done it without all my friends. I threw my arms around Miles. He shoved me off him so I raced around the table to hug Rafael, who gave me more of his awkward pats before squirming out of the embrace.

"I'm happy for you," he said.

He meant it, even if he sounded subdued. Rafael's life had been bound to this quest. I had my P.I. business, what would Rafael do now?

I tapped my finger against my lip. "How would you feel about making the business Cohen and Behar Investigations? I don't need an Attendant, but I would like a partner."

Rafael blinked at me a few times, then a slow smile spread across his face. "I'd like that very much indeed."

I held out my hand and we shook.

Isabel returned to the table. "What'd I miss?"

"The fact that it's time for celebratory singing," Arkady said. Miles groaned and Arkady elbowed him sharply. "Start us off, Mimi."

"No way," Pri said. "You're singing?"

"Whatever." Miles jerked a finger at Rafael. "If I have to do this, so do you. And you too," he said to Isabel.

Arkady pressed his hands together. "All the virgins. It's a

karaoke gangbang." He screwed up his face. "But not rapey and totally consensual." He brightened. "Plus, singing!"

I nodded sagely. "Good save."

"Must I?" Rafael looked vaguely ill until Priya whispered something in his ear. "I'm in," he said.

"What are you singing, Mimi?" I said sweetly.

A muscle ticked in his jaw. "Gimme! Gimme! Gimme!"

Isabel lit up. "You mean 'Gimme! Gimme! Gimme! (A Man after Midnight),' recorded by ABBA at Polar Music Studios in Stockholm, August, 1979?"

Miles crossed his arms, his mouth pressed into a thin line. "That would be the one."

Arkady barely contained his laughter.

"I love you," Priya said to Isabel.

"Hey. You still haven't said it back to me," I said.

"Don't be needy," Pri said. She blew me a kiss.

Isabel laughed. "I love you, too? Miles, that's a great song. I don't know what to sing."

Arkady made a shooing motion at the three of them. "Consult the book. You'll find something."

After one last scathing look at Arkady, Miles stalked off, while Rafael accompanied Isabel up to the front.

"Do I want to know how you got him to sing?" Priya said.

"Do I?" Arkady countered. They grinned at each other while I reconsidered my no drinking rule. He kicked my leg. "Commence your odes to my glory in battle."

I blew him a raspberry.

"Be nice. That asshole did chip me." He smacked his abs. "The bruising took forever to go down."

"Oh, whatever, Mr. Badass with the stone fists," Priya said. "I got us in and provided excellent cuffing service."

"About that." I planted my hands on my hips. "What part of 'stay away' was hard to understand? Change the security clearances and reprogram the chips on the keycard that Levi got hold of. That was it."

Priya tossed her hair. "And miss all the fun? Bitch, please."

The rest of the night marked a shift in my life. I had a solid friend group, with Isabel fitting in perfectly. Miles sang the most curmudgeonly cover of ABBA ever, Isabel bopped on stage with "Girls Just Want to Have Fun," and Rafael shocked the crap out of me with a rousing version of Blur's "Song 2" that had the whole joint rocking. He even lost his glasses during the performance.

There was no danger hanging over my head, no bad guys to stop, and with the return of magic, my professional future looked rosy.

I was a modern woman who had it all and I was complete on my own.

I downed my third Coke, eyeing my phone, then, before I could second guess myself, I typed a single-word text.

Yes.

Chapter 29

Levi greeted me at the front door in a loose gray T-shirt and jeans, his feet bare. He pushed his glasses up his nose with a boyishly awkward gesture. "Come in."

I sniffed the air hopefully, but he hadn't made biscotti.

"We broke Olivia's code," he said.

"Mazel tov." I slipped off my shoes.

The two of us headed into his study.

I waggled my fingers in front of the glass and a skinny little neon tetra swam over to investigate.

Levi reached into a banker box next to his laptop and pulled out a stack of ledgers. "Voilà." He motioned me over, flipping the top book open to the first page.

"Share the deets."

Levi tapped the page. "Olivia got suspicious when Jackson wanted Allegra to support the youth shelter because their other charities were far more high-profile. When she learned that the shelter had amended its mandate to take in Nefesh kids, those suspicions went into high alert."

"Fueled by Jackson's anti-Nefesh stance."

Nodding, Levi placed the ledger on his desk. "She began

documenting every conversation and detail even slightly connected to the shelter."

"Was it because she didn't like Jackson?"

"That and Richard had fallen ill. Olivia had a good thing going with his money laundering plan, because she was getting a cut."

"Olivia admitted that in the ledger?"

"No. The Queen didn't want us going public about Hedon's existence, not wanting the attention or the thrill-seekers, so she gave us permission to speak to Luca. He told us." Levi rubbed the back of his neck. "Moran stood over me with that damned sword for the entire meeting."

I laughed. "Been there. Okay, so Olivia saw the writing on the wall and created her insurance policy."

"Richard hid the money laundering from Jackson, but Olivia knew that with his death, Jackson would find out. As she put it, if he tried to take her down, she'd bury him, too."

"Gotta love a woman with a sense of vengeance. What was the blurry part I saw? Was it just smudged ink?"

"No." Levi reached into the banker box again and held up a key. "This was taped to the page over one section of code."

"Ah. Isabel's magic shows printed material and the key obscured the data. What's it for, a treasure chest?"

"Pretty much. It's Olivia's gym locker key. She had Jackson trailed by a private investigator and stashed photographic and audio recordings of meetings about funneling those Nefesh teens to Chariot."

"With all that, it has to be enough, right?"

"If it wasn't before, we absolutely nailed the bastard now." Levi smiled. "Talia, of all people, threatened to throw every other skeleton out of Jackson's closet if the party proceeded with the legislation. Not just his, the party's."

I crashed down into his chair. "You're kidding."

"Nope. Your mother is terrifying." Levi's voice was filled with admiration. "She wanted his head on a platter, but we talked her down, and now the current deal is Jackson resigning to spend more time with his family."

I snorted and made air quotes.

Levi smirked. "The legislation is being withdrawn. Should anyone in that party attempt to resurrect it, we take everything to the media."

"Then it's finally over," I said.

"There are still some things to be determined." He walked out of the room.

"Where are you going?" I jogged after him.

Levi led me into the living room where a brown wooden mantel clock sat on the coffee table next to a hammer.

"This looks like a wholesome evening activity." I sat down on the sofa and read the inscription.

You must not make idols for yourselves or set up a carved image or sacred pillar, or place a sculpted stone in your land to bow down to it, For I am the LORD your God. Isaac's clock.

Levi turned the hammer over in his hand. "I've been staring at it for two days. It was supposed to be a no-brainer."

"Here's the thing. Asherah took away my Jezebel magic, but she left me with clarity magic because apparently I'm not done serving her yet." I made woo-woo motions at him. "Be clear, Levi."

He stared at me, unimpressed.

I frowned. "Nothing? That should have worked. I thought I had this whole thing figured out."

"Oh no, it worked. You just need to practice your performance."

"What's your decision, Leviticus?"

"To end this." He swung the hammer into the heart of the clock.

The small round glass face cracked, the wood splintered.

I climbed over the back of the couch, hiding, while Levi methodically smashed the clock into smithereens.

There was a clatter of the hammer being tossed on the table and I peeked up over the top of the couch. "Feel better?"

"Yeah."

"Great." I scooped up my things, hands sweaty. It had been a good run, Ash.

Levi wanted to end this. That was his choice and I had to respect that. He'd gotten the closure he needed, and just because things felt unfinished for me didn't mean that his choice was wrong.

It was just that, his choice.

Clarity. I exhaled, and headed for the foyer. Well, clarity could be a real bitch sometimes.

"Hey," Levi said, "Where are you going?"

I stopped. "You ended it. Message received."

"I symbolically ended the hold my father has had over me my entire life." He spun the bent minute and hour hands on the shattered clock face, weighing things out. "I just wasn't sure if the best way was to go scorched earth with the clock or if that meant he'd won because he'd gotten under my skin, but actually, that was very freeing."

"Glad I could help."

He beckoned me closer. "Come to any epiphanies in the wake of being shot?"

The many, carefully worded variations of how I'd like to take things slowly because we'd been through so much, we'd hurt each other so much, and we needed time, crowded my throat.

While I'd swear I wasn't moving, somehow I drew closer to him. I tried to pull up short, terrified that if we touched, I'd spark, my emotions exploding like lightning.

"Say something." His quiet words were a plea.

My heart threatened to punch out my ribcage. I never planned on saying it first. Second maybe, somewhere far in the future, when it was a safe, sure bet. Except safe and sure were empty words in the face of this feeling filling me up and the clarity I no longer wanted to hide.

I took a deep breath and ripped the Band-Aid off. "I love you." I counted off twelve heartbeats before I punched him. "Say something."

The joy in his smile was so palpable that if I reached out, I could catch hold of it, like a firefly. "I love you, too," he said.

I swear the ground rocked like gentle waves as I leaned into him. My boat had found its safe harbor, nestled in the scent of oaky amber scotch and chocolate and my name written in his heart.

I pulled out my phone.

Levi tried to grab the cell but I shielded it with my body. "I declare my love and you're googling something?" he said.

"Yes."

"You baffle me."

"Like this is news." When I found the result of my search, my smile threatened to split my face in half. I showed Levi the screen.

He shrugged. "It's traffic cam footage."

"Of..." I prompted.

"House Pacifica. Why?"

I gave a little hop of excitement. "Because it's gold. Deep pure gold. That building is a giant mood ring of you. You really do love me."

He did this manly, frowning gruff thing. "I said I did."

"Yeah, but this is proof."

"Hmm. Good point." He took my hand. "Where's my proof? I mean, I'm a pretty amazing man who's dazzled you for fifteen years."

"Dazzled seems a bit excessive. I thought fondly of you for about a month."

Levi moved his thumb up my wrist, finding some magic point that shot wild heat through my body. "Dazzled. How can I be certain these feelings are real and not a byproduct of your incredible awe being in my presence?"

I punched his shoulder. "You've wrecked me totally and absolutely for any other guy, asshole, and I'm completely and utterly in love with you."

"Ah, insults." His blue eyes glittered between thick lashes. "Okay, now I buy it."

"Is it going to be enough though? After everything?"

"Well, you didn't kill my father, but I almost did after the ambulance took you away."

"You did?"

"Yeah. Ask Rafael about that." He flexed his hand. "It'll be enough because after everything we've both suffered all these years, we'll choose to make it enough."

"Every single day," I agreed. "Wanna kiss and make it official?"

"Fuck yeah." His mouth found mine, hot and hungry and demanding.

I rose onto tiptoe, my teeth scraping across his bottom lips, and my hands tangled in his hair.

Levi wedged his thigh between my legs and I whimpered, jerking him closer to me, and arcing my hips against him. He exhaled, then dragged his thumb over my lips.

I sucked it inside, and Levi shuddered.

He removed his glasses, setting them carefully down. "I love you so much." His words were a promise, anchoring me.

Light-headed, I clasped my hand around the back of his neck and drew his mouth down to mine. Every nerve in my body flared at the overwhelming rightness of it all.

Levi ran his hand achingly slow up my side, dragging my shirt along with it to pull it over my head. My bra followed, pitched into a corner. He bent his head to rasp his teeth along my nipple before sucking it into his mouth.

I tightened my fingers in his hair, letting the strands fall through my fingers.

Levi growled and dragged me over to the sofa, falling back to catch me in his arms. We lay there, tangled up together, kissing and exploring each other's bodies with a leisurely wonder. He tilted my head back to expose a spot under my ear, kissing it and making me shiver in delight.

Clothes were tossed off and we moved to his bedroom.

"New sheets?" I said lightly.

He curled me to him. "I couldn't sleep on the other ones. They reminded me of you too much."

"In that case, we should break these in." I crawled onto his mattress, cocking a finger at him.

He lay down on his side. "Touch me," he said, guiding my hand down.

My nipples hardened, feeling his hard cock, and I moaned into the hollow of his neck.

"That sound. It undoes me." He slid a finger inside me, rubbing my clit with his thumb.

We gazed into each other's eyes, a delicious spiral winding tighter and brighter inside me, as Levi played with my sensitive flesh.

He grew even harder in my hand.

"Fuuuuck." He rolled on top of me and I luxuriated in the press of his warm skin.

I sucked in a breath, dizzy with need.

Levi laughed, low and dangerous, and reached for a condom.

I stopped him. "I'm clean. I've been tested and there hasn't been anyone since you. You?" My pulse fluttered in the base of my throat. I wanted nothing between us.

"Same." He caught my lips for one more breath-stealing kiss, before thrusting inside me.

A quiver shot through me and I gripped his shoulders to draw him to me more tightly.

Our lovemaking was lazy, filled with messy kisses and soft endearments that danced like clouds around our heads. The moon beamed down a benediction of our love while the waves outside the window graced us with a gentle melody.

The spark between us grew hotter, until it erupted in a glorious flame of desire.

"Faster," I whispered.

Levi stood up at the edge of the mattress, sliding me across the bed until my ass bumped into his thighs.

I laughed. "Suave."

"Give me a second, woman. Geez, already busting my balls." He pulled my legs up so my feet rested on his shoulders.

"*Still* busting—oh. Yes. That."

He grinned at me, his teeth flashing white in the velvety darkness of the room, and placed my hand on my clit.

I touched myself as he thrust into me again and that was it. I shattered, crying out Levi's name.

He came right after me, clasping my head in his hands and kissing me sweetly, before rolling off.

Deliciously limp, I brushed his hair out of his eyes. "We both acquired new scars these past couple of months."

Levi traced the new one on my thigh. "A very smart woman once told me that scars aren't weakness, they're strength. They prove we survived."

"Wow. That does sound like an incredibly wise person," I said. He tickled me and I laughed, swatting at his hands. "I hope you kept her around."

"It was kind of touch and go. First, I masterminded the most pathetic break-up in the history of mankind." He drew lazily on my skin, and I pressed closer to him.

"Was this a 'reverse psychology, absence makes the heart grow fonder' kind of deal?" I said.

"It was more a 'too stupid to realize what I was throwing away' scenario. But the joke was on me."

My heart swelled at his admission of how he'd messed up. "How so?"

"I missed her." Levi pressed his forehead to mine. "I couldn't go a single night without seeking you out. You know how many times I drove past my parents' place hoping to see you parked there?" He paused. "You can admit to the same thing, seeing as this is a safe space where we've declared our love."

I shrugged. "I could, but I was there casing the joint." My voice rose in a shriek as Levi raspberried my stomach. "Ack. Fine. Yes. It was the same for me."

Levi propped his bent arm under his head. "Good thing we both smartened up. You do stay the night now, right?"

"Yeah, love." I sat up.

"I'm getting mixed messages here."

I kissed him again because he was there and he was mine. "I'm going to clean up and get water. I'll be right back."

I stood in my boyfriend's kitchen, letting the water run cold and marveling at how far I'd come. I was no longer the Girl Who Lived, I was the woman who had everything to live for. My life was far richer than I could ever have imagined.

I was happy.

"Ash?"

I jerked from the sink, flicking Levi with droplets.

He laughed, brushing off his naked chest. "All good?" He wrapped his arms around me.

I leaned against him. "Never better." I had my drink and held out a hand. "Take me back to bed, Leviticus."

He scooped me up into his arms and into our future.

Once upon a time, there was a gangly boy with blue eyes and an angry girl with a cane. One hid his scars, the other flaunted them to the world. And when they grew up, they played in the darkness, monsters capable of great damage themselves.

The stories they were in began, changed, and ended over time, but the two of them still stood.

When they finally stepped into the light, what they saw

wasn't monstrous, it was fierce and beautiful, so they made a choice.

Each other.

The monster support group was no more. But the girl still got biscotti whenever she wanted them.

THANK YOU FOR READING REVENGE & RAPTURE.

In the mood for more funny, sexy urban fantasy? Check out <u>THE UNLIKEABLE DEMON HUNTER</u>.

The Brotherhood wants her gone. The demons want her dead. Not bad for her first day as a Chosen One.

When Nava Katz half-drunkenly interrupts her twin brother's induction ceremony into a secret supernatural society, she doesn't expect to accidentally torch his life-long dream and steal his destiny.

Horrified she's now expected to take his place, Nava is faced with the one thing she swore off forever: a purpose.

The all-male squad isn't cool with a woman in their ranks and assigns her to Rohan Mitra: former rock god and their most ruthless hunter. He may be the perfect bad boy fling with no strings attached, but what happens when he won't let her run—not even from herself?

That might prove as dangerous as defeating the vengeful demon out for her brother's blood.

Odds of her new teammates expecting her to fail? Best not to think about that.

Odds her succeeding out of spite? Dive into this complete series and find out.

"Don't buy it if your offended by bad language, immoral behavior, lose ethics, sassy attitude, hot guys ... cuz it does it all - and its GREAT!!!"

Now, have I got a treat for you!

THROWING SHADE (MAGIC AFTER MIDLIFE #1)

features all the same funny, sexy urban fantasy storytelling, but this time, with a heroine in her forties.

Middle-aged. Divorced. Hormonally imbalanced. Then she got magic.

Underestimate her. That'll be fun.

It's official. Miriam Feldman is killing it in the midlife crisis department. She's mastered boredom, aced invisibility, and graduated Summa Cum Laude in smiling and playing nice in her post-divorce life.

Then her best friend gets tangled up with some vamps and goes missing. If that's not scary enough, Miri snaps, and in a cold dark rage, unleashes a rare and powerful shadow magic.

Now, with only a mouthy golem and a grumpy-yet-sexy French wolf shifter to help her navigate this world of hidden magic, she's in a race against time to rescue her friend and keep her loved ones safe from the skeletons in her past.

Sure, she's caught in a spiderweb of supernatural power plays, but she's a librarian, she's over forty, and she's definitely done with being sidelined in her own life.

She's turning her invisibility into strength; they'll never see her coming.

Throwing Shade features a sassy, slow burn romance, a roller coaster ride of a mystery, and a magical midlife adventure.

Buy *Throwing Shade* now!

Every time a reader leaves a review, an author gets ... a glass of wine. (You thought I was going to say "wings," didn't you? We're authors, not angels, but *you'll* get heavenly karma for your good deed.) Please leave yours on your favorite book site. It makes a huge difference in discoverability to rate and review, especially the first book in a series.

Turn the page for an excerpt from *Throwing Shade* ...

Excerpt from Throwing Shade

A man kneeled next to Alex's body. He seemed a few years younger than me, probably in his late thirties, and was about six inches taller, putting the shifter at about six-foot-two. His hair was a riot of dark curls.

The man's jaw was firm, his lips full, but right now, they were set in a severe line. Moonlight kissed the olive skin of his broad shoulders and leanly muscled torso, a trail of hair leading down to—

Jeans. I gusted out a breath.

The man huffed softly. "You came back," he said dryly, with a slight accent I couldn't place. "You've got balls, I'll give you that."

I gave a weak laugh and he locked his brilliant emerald gaze onto mine. Thickly lashed, his eyes were what I would have called beautiful in his human form, but there was a hardness to them—like he'd seen too much and all innocence was long gone.

Eli had looked that way after his first year in homicide. Fuuuuck! This guy had to be a Lonestar. Okay, looking on the bright side, he could help me find Jude—if he didn't destroy me. I'd been so bent on getting answers from Alex that I'd thrown away every single safety procedure that I'd lived by and shown a stranger my magic. I could have left when the shifter took off with Alex but no, I had to play detective.

I reached behind me, clutching the railing because my legs felt rubbery.

The Ohrist reached into a duffel bag, revealing a nasty silver jagged scar that ran halfway up the left side of his back, and pulled on a faded blue T-shirt that said "Bite Me." This wasn't a gym rat with a six-pack for show; he was a warrior and his body was his well-honed weapon, in or out of wolf form.

Ohrist magic was based in light and life, while Banim Shovavim powers were rooted in death and darkness. Historically, they'd taken that as clear-cut signs of good and evil. They pitied Sapiens but had hunted my kind into near extinction.

There was even a skipping game sung by Ohrist kids: "Clap for the light, 'cause light is right. All other magic is a blight. How many shadow freaks will we smite?" At which point they'd jump as fast as they could while counting.

I eyed the wolf shifter with a sinking feeling that he'd probably counted pretty damn high.

Maybe he didn't remember the exact details of his time in his wolf form? Could I bluff my way out of here?

"Did you want something?" he said, impatiently.

My brain short-circuited. "I'm guessing that light magic allowed you to cut through his breastbone and rib cage only using your claws," I said, "but why isn't there blood all over the place?"

I could have smacked myself. This was not the time for curiosity or further questions like "How do you have more than one magic ability?" It was the time for well-crafted lies.

"The magic cauterized the blood vessels." The man rolled his "r's." He grabbed a box of table salt from the duffel bag.

"Regular sodium," I said thickly. "How bland. I prefer

Pink Himalayan to balance the delicate flavor of human flesh."

"I'm not eating him." He dumped the salt over the corpse. "It interferes with the scent so animals don't show up before Ohrists get here to retrieve the body."

"That's good, because cannibalism can make you sick. You get this brain disease called kuru and—"

"Like mad cow?" He tapped the last of the salt onto the body with a contemplative expression.

I blinked. People didn't generally come back with follow-up questions to my random facts. "Not quite. People can't get mad cow disease, but in rare cases they get a form called…" I shook my head because cows, mad or otherwise, were not the issue. "Was Alex human?"

Or was he some other species entirely and did that make a difference to the answer? He had looked human, even if what was inside of him wasn't.

My moral compass was having trouble finding true north.

"Not anymore," the wolfman said.

I knelt down beside Alex to close his lids because his life-less stare felt accusatory, but the man batted my arm away.

He lay a hand on the deceased's forehead and stared into his eyes as if committing him to memory. There was both a gravitas and a resignation in the shifter's expression, and I couldn't tell if he did this to honor the dead or torment himself with a parade of his kills. Maybe it was one and the same.

When he was done, I checked Alex's back pockets for his wallet.

"The man's body isn't even cold and you're robbing him?" Wolf Dude said.

"I'm looking for identification," I said through ground teeth. There was a cracked phone but no wallet. It must have fallen out at some point during the fight. A vise tightened around my chest and I shoved the Ohrist, banking on the fact that if he'd intended to hurt me, he'd have done it already. "You ruined my chance to get information about—"

"I saved you." The man stuffed his bare feet into motorcycle boots, which also came out of the duffel bag. "I don't know what interrogation skills you think you have, but I can assure you that dybbuk wouldn't have given up shit."

"Dybbuk?"

"Merde," he said in perfect French. Ah. "You went after him without knowing what you were dealing with?" His full lips twisted. "Fucking BS."

He remembered.

I took two wobbly steps back, Delilah by my side, but he didn't come after me.

He laced up his boots. Okay, he was a derisive son of a bitch, but he lacked the horror others of his ilk displayed upon meeting my kind, nor did he seem inclined to kill me.

I'd take the win.

"Alex had attacked me once already," I said, "and if he did something to my friend—"

The shifter pulled out a beaten-up brown leather jacket and shrugged into it, his shoulders bunching. "Then she's gone. Sorry for your loss."

My eyebrows shot up. Yes, this guy was an ass, but surely he was connected to an infrastructure that could help me find Jude. "Sorry for your loss? How about you help me find her? Aren't you a Lonestar?"

He laughed without an ounce of humor. "Hardly."

Then what was he? He'd already killed one person, and yes, that dybbuk thing seemed to justify Alex's death, but I was alone out here. If he was working on his own vigilante moral code, how safe was I?

I eyed the stairs. How many were there? Thirty? Then perhaps another fifty feet to lose myself in the crowds in Terence Poole Plaza? He'd be faster than me, even as a human. I bit my lip. If I screamed for help, would anyone come?

Screw that. I had magic and could cloak and get away at any point, but his rudeness was grating. I threw my hands up. "That's all you have to say?"

"No." The man raked a shrewd glance over me. "Should we ever have the misfortune to meet again, get out of my way."

"Or what? You'll huff and you'll puff and you'll blow my house down?"

He bared his lips, briefly shifting his canines to wolf form. *My, what big teeth you have.* A strangled laugh burbled out of me. My epistemological crisis involved a hell of a Freudian undertone.

"I'll do whatever the fuck is necessary," he said.

"Is that your action hero catchphrase or something? Because it's a little on the nose."

He zipped up the duffel bag. "My reputation doesn't precede me? Shocking." His voice was laced with bitterness.

"Wow. Someone is full of themselves. I've got no idea who you are."

He peered at me suspiciously. "Are you new in town?"

"No."

He shrugged. "Then you know who I am."

"Hate to disappoint you, but you're just some rando who crashed my party and ruined my plan—"

"To get answers from someone who wouldn't tell you anything you actually wanted to know. Brilliant strategy. You've the mind of a tactician. Even if you did get something out of him, did you think he'd let you walk away after?" His accent thickened when he got annoyed.

"I had my shadow."

"I wouldn't brag about that if I were you."

"For your information, I'm doing an admirable job. Before yesterday, the only monsters I had to worry about were of the human variety." I shot him a pointed look.

331

"There's no way you didn't know about dybbuks. You're too—" He snapped his mouth shut.

Delilah puffed up behind me. "Oh, no," I said. "Finish that sentence."

The man crossed his arms, rustling the leather. "Old," he said levelly.

My shadow bopped Wolfman in the nose with a swift jab. Ha!

The man pinched his nostrils together to staunch the bleeding, his emerald eyes glinting dangerously.

My amusement drained away, my magic swirling around my feet, ready to cloak me, but I'd hit the wall and I was out of fucks to give.

"Should we ever have the misfortune to meet again, get out of my way," I said.

"Vraiment? Why?"

"I'm a woman in my forties who's remembered how powerful she can be. Don't fuck with me, Huff 'n' Puff." Head held high, Delilah and I sailed past him into the night.

Buy *Throwing Shade* now!

Become a Wilde One

If you enjoyed this book and want to be first in the know about bonus content, reveals, and exclusive giveaways, become a Wilde One by joining my newsletter: http://www.deborahwilde.com/subscribe

You'll immediately receive short stories set in my different worlds and available only to my newsletter subscribers. There are mild spoilers so they're best enjoyed in the recommended reading order.

If you just want to know about my new releases, please follow me on BookBub: https://www.bookbub.com/authors/deborah-wilde

Acknowledgments

It was really hard doing justice to Ash's story and wrapping it in up a satisfying way, while still in the midst of the pandemic.

Had it not been for my incredible editor Alex Yuschik, whose inspiring notes kept me excited for each draft, my husband and daughter for putting up with me rambling plot ideas at them, and my writing taskmaster Elissa for being a great friend and always wiling to get me back on track, the end of this journey would have looked very different.

Above all, I thank all of you for all your outpouring of love and cheerleading. You inspire me to push myself with every book and live up to your expectations and for that you have my deep gratitude and love.

About the Author

A global wanderer, former screenwriter, and total cynic with a broken edit button, Deborah (pronounced deb-O-rah) writes funny urban fantasy and paranormal women's fiction.

Her stories feature sassy women who kick butt, strong female friendships, and swoony, sexy romance. She's all about the happily-ever-after, with a huge dose of hilarity along the way.

Deborah lives in Vancouver, along with her husband, daughter, and asshole cat, Abra.

"Magic, sparks, and snark! Go Wilde."

www.deborahwilde.com

facebook.com/DeborahWildeAuthor
instagram.com/wildeauthor

CPSIA information can be obtained
at www.ICGtesting.com
Printed in the USA
BVHW082259020622
638534BV00007B/136